THE REEL OF RHYSIA
BOOK TWO

THE UNFAMILIAR

LILLA GLASS

CITY OWL
PRESS

THE UNFAMILIAR
The Reel of Rhysia, Book 2

CITY OWL PRESS
www.cityowlpress.com

Cover Design by MiblArt. All stock photos licensed appropriately.

Edited by Tee Tate.

For information on subsidiary rights, please contact the publisher at info@cityowlpress.com.

Hardback Edition ISBN: 978-1-64898-463-1

Paperback Edition ISBN: 978-1-64898-462-4

Digital Edition ISBN: 978-1-64898-461-7

Printed in the United States of America

To anyone who feels lost,
few wonders have ever been found
by clinging to well-trodden paths.

AUTHOR'S NOTE

The legends speak of faerie reels—intricate blends of song and dance so entrancing that any mortal who overhears one will be enchanted until the end of their days, perhaps longer. I cannot claim this tale is nearly so captivating (though that is every author's secret hope; we are tricksters, all), but I must warn you that, like most music, it could not have been composed without striking a few minor chords. Please consult the following list before the performance begins.

The Unfamiliar contains depictions of: violence, death, grief, childhood abuse and neglect, strong language and sexual references, alcohol and substance use, infidelity, and domestic assault.

THE UNFAMILIAR

"Though faerie reels flow rhythmically, they're challenging to learn,
Just when you think you've caught the beat, the tempo takes a turn."

PROLOGUE

he darkness reeked of blood and fetid flesh. Kaster inhaled it like rosemary perfume, desperate to remind himself he was not yet among the rotting. He no longer trusted the grit of the bars or the cruel laughter that keened beyond them. He doubted the drum of his pulse and the weight of his limbs.

Death was the one true reminder of life. It could not mock what it had already claimed.

Judging from his hollow stomach and the splintered remains of his fingernails, he'd been steeping in shadows for no less than three days, lulled to a stupor by the revels of his captors and the soft scrape of the vines that writhed around his cage. Enough rainwater had trickled through the tendrils to keep him breathing, but not enough to soothe his sandpaper tongue. The fruit the monsters left him had moldered untouched.

Others had been fed to the living walls in that time. Kaster had flinched at their screams, grieved at their prayers, commiserated with their curses. It had been a while since he'd heard so much as a cough, but they were surely still out there, tongues pinched between their teeth as they strained their ears for the cries of imprisoned loved ones.

Creator knows what Kaster would have given to hear Nella's voice again, no matter the context. Sorrow was selfish in that respect.

Not for the first time, he considered shoving an arm through the bars and rooting around until a thorn found an artery. A terse slice in the right direction would bring his misery to an end. Before he could muster the will, a vine shifted, allowing a sliver of light into the darkness. Though sickly green and faint as an afterthought, it served as a vague reminder of the world beyond the wall. Echoes of summer strolls and moonlit dances lent him strength enough to swear. If there existed a concept crueler than hope, he'd yet to make its acquaintance.

Kaster braced for the vines to swallow the glow as they had countless times before. To his astonishment, the sliver grew to a gash, spilling sallow light and laughter. A legion of spidery hands stretched forward, grasped the bars, and jarred his cage from the shadows.

Incandescent lichens spattered the bramble hallway, limning the caprine horns and tapered ears of his captors with a ghastly pall. They were not the fair and noble fae-folk of Rhysien lore, but a feral mockery of the myths, nearly human from the waist up with coarse fur covering them from haunches to hooves. Scarlet sigils painted their bare skin—some glistening wet, others dry and flaking—and bits of bone, still flecked with flesh, had been braided into their hair.

More disturbing than the hunters were their trophies. The captives that hadn't been caged now dangled from the walls like cattle carcasses, pierced through by sickle-sharp thorns. Some had been picked nearly to the bone; others, stripped of clothing and in many cases skin. A few still twitched and trembled, lips gaping around silent screams.

Bile burned Kaster's throat as he scanned the bodies for a swatch of floral linen, a lock of sandy brown hair. A few familiar faces numbered among the broken, but Nella's wasn't one of them. Not that it mattered. If the creatures hadn't yet killed her, it meant only that she was buried in a wall somewhere, waiting for her captors to return and...and...

Just what did they have planned for them, anyway?

Kaster probed the gloom as the monsters jostled him through the halls of their writhing fortress, finding only stray bones and heaps of offal. The corridor wound on for some time before a golden glow drowned the green, and the creatures hefted him into a massive hollow churning with their horrid kin. The throng parted to let them through, and several onlookers jabbed wooden pikes through the bars, cackling madly when Kaster danced to dodge them. The rest followed him with unsettling oval eyes.

A wide patch of earth had been left open at the crowd's center, its russet clay marbled with a red far deeper, more damning. After dropping the cage unceremoniously to the mire, three pairs of hooves trotted off to join their peers. One creature lingered behind, its fingers and teeth stained crimson. "You should feel honored," it said, sliding a key into the cage door. "Not many are afforded this opportunity."

Kaster would take any opportunity offered him. The moment the lock clicked, he rammed the bars with his shoulder, knocking the bastard off balance. Rage propelled him from his confines, but days of disuse stiffened his limbs. He landed only a few strikes before several monsters rushed to intervene. In subduing Kaster, they nearly tore his arms from their sockets.

"Now, now. None of that."

The voice was neither rich nor commanding, but it brought the brutes to heel. They shoved Kaster behind them and melted into the press, ears twitching toward a throne of thorns on the far side of the hollow. Upon it lounged another beast, elbow perched on a bramble armrest and a sharp cheekbone resting between their thumb and forefinger. The creature was neither male nor female, but a bizarrely beautiful blend of both, with burnished bronze horns that curled outward in chaotic spirals and a collar of autumn leaves draped over their torso. A long ebony spear rested across their lap, topped with a horned skull that matched their face for size and shape.

Kaster could only assume this was the beasts' ruler. The fae monarchs of folklore were twice as regal if not half as entrancing, but thrones and scepters—however sylvan—spoke with a certain auspicious tone. Strange how a legend could prove so false and so true in the same stroke.

"It's poor manners to damage a prop before the play begins." The ruler clucked their tongue. "There are toys aplenty for you to break, and our trove grows greater with every moonrise. Let us not act as scavengers when the hunt has never been more blessed. And as for you..." Their keen ochre eyes flicked to Kaster, and a smile strained their rot-black lips. "Right idea. Wrong target."

The crowd's attention shifted as a second copper cage was carried into the hollow. Shadows rendered the captive a huddled silhouette until a monster jarred the door open and flung them into the clearing. Firelight spilled over sandy tresses, glinting off strands of copper and gold. Kaster's heart plunged to his stomach.

Her cornflower dress was torn and tattered, the skin beneath it mottled plum, but when her sapphire eyes met his, all other hues faded. The same spark that had consumed him when they'd first locked eyes from across a Beltane bonfire sent Kaster sprinting forward, heels slipping on the mire. Nella met him halfway and twined her arms around his waist, burying her face in the crook of his shoulder. He breathed in what little rosemary still clung to her skin, and for one second—one blissful, ignorant second—he was overcome with joy.

Then he heard the laughter.

It started as snickers, soft and serpentine, then spread through the hollow, swelling to a storm. Kaster went cold. Nella stumbled back. A pair of blackwood short-spears landed in the clay between them.

"Life is a resource reserved for only the strongest of a species." The ruler's voice carried over the clamor. "It is hoarded by violent hands, bought with the blood of the weak, short on supply, and ever in demand." They leaned forward, fingers steepled beneath a wisp of a beard. "You both want it, and I am willing to offer it. To whichever of you proves most worthy."

A stone formed in Kaster's empty gut as he and Nella glanced down at the spears. Nella hesitated. Kaster did not.

The moment his fingers wrapped around blackwood, he barreled toward the crowd. He stood no chance of fighting his way to safety, but he could drag a few fae bastards to the grave with him.

The monsters scrambled back from his strikes before pressing in, sneering and shouting. A set of square teeth found his wrist. The spear tore free. Horns rammed his torso, sending him sprawling. Pain branched through his ribcage like lightning, and the landing stole what remained of his breath.

Each cough tasted of copper. Each gasp felt like shattered glass.

"Kaster!" A pair of trembling hands clasped one of his own. When he opened his eyes, Nella's face danced above him in triplicate. "Can you sit up?"

It hurt like hell, but he managed it. The moment her faces melted back into one, he cupped it with his palm, forcing the bitter truth to his lips.

"The fae can't lie, right?" Each syllable sparked pain in his side. "If we play by their rules, then one of us...one of us can..."

Nella squared her shoulders. Her eyes were bloodshot from weeping, but there were no tears in them now. Tender though she could be, no one had ever mistaken her for weak. "They want a show," she whispered. "Don't you dare go easy on me."

She tore away without another word. By the time Kaster rose and reclaimed his spear, she was armed and standing at the ready. She could easily have struck while he was down, but it wasn't in her nature. This would be a fair fight. They owed each other that much.

Seconds ticked past in silence as Kaster bolstered his resolve, attempting to reimagine his closest friend as a foe. Nella's trembling jaw set, a sure sign she was doing the same. Their reticence was met with impatient murmurs. Several monsters hurled taunts and curses into the makeshift arena. A few lobbed actual stones. If the horde didn't get a spectacle, and soon, they would claim both combatants' hearts as consolation.

Kaster gave a curt nod. Nella returned it, and they both rushed forward.

Their spears clashed like swords, sending tremors to Kaster's elbows. He twisted his weapon but failed to disarm her. Her strike missed his neck by a hair's breadth. Their every move was cautious and halting—a little too slow, a little too soft—and the result was more a dance than a battle, like the one they'd shared at their wedding feast. Nervous and giddy, they'd both tried to follow the other's lead only to wind up tumbling to the grass. What a vision she'd been, all giggles and lace and white satin ribbons.

Kaster clung to that memory as his spear sliced across her shoulder. Blood wept from the wound, staining her sleeve an unforgiving crimson. The ache that blossomed in his chest was brighter than that of his broken rib. Nella's startled cry set the rabble to cheering. She recovered quickly, flipped her spear, and rammed the butt into Kaster's side. His vision burst with violent sparks that guttered into shadow.

The impact of his head against the ground startled him lucid as Nella crawled atop him, pinning him in place with her knee. For a disoriented moment, he thought she meant to kiss him. How many times had they tangled like this, clothed only in candlelight?

The crowd's cruel heckles jarred him back to the present. He'd lost his weapon in the fall, but Nella's was still clutched close to her chest. The victory was hers, if she'd only take it.

"I...I can't," she whispered, tears streaming down her cheeks. The pink swell beneath her lashes made her eyes shine that much brighter.

"It's alright, love." Kaster forced a feeble smile even as terror spread through his veins. "I've had two years more than you already, and you've made these last four the best they could be. Just make it quick. Please."

Nella drew a shaky breath, whispering an apology as she raised her spear overhead. Kaster closed his eyes, picturing the life they might have built in a kinder world, the life they'd been planning over their morning porridge for years. Children, gardens, a little stucco cottage by the seaside. Resigning it all to dream, he let himself go lax.

He didn't feel himself prying the stone from the clay. Didn't fight its weight as his arm struck forward. But he felt her skull cave. Heard it crack like porcelain.

How heavy he became, as her weight rolled away. How empty. He should have been crying, cursing, condemning himself as another in a world of demons, but he lacked the strength for sorrow and the clarity for contrition. Cluttered as his mind was, it held room for only one coherent thought...

I won.

Promises of fresh air and sunlight drew him to his feet. He was careful not to look Nella's way as he wiped her blood from his fingers, lest a twitch ruin the moment. He needed to believe it had been quick and painless. That she'd died believing he loved her more than himself.

The roar of the throng was distant, dull. An ashen pall had fallen over the hollow, but with every blink, a color returned. Warmth oozed from flickering torches. Clay squelched beneath his soles. Soon, he was lucid enough to catch the musings of the monsters.

"A spear to the gut would do the trick!"

"I say we stick him on the wall and watch him wriggle!"

"How many bones do you suppose we can snap before the screams stop?"

Panic hit Kaster like a flash flood, scouring away what remained of his daze. He turned pleading eyes to the bramble throne, where the ruler welcomed suggestions with enthusiastic waves. "B-but...but you have to let me go!" he shouted, rousing fire in his ribcage. "Your kind can't lie! Y-you said I could live if...if I—"

"I *never* lie." The ruler jabbed a finger his direction. "You're breathing aren't you? Blinking like a halfwit? I know for a fact your heart's still pumping; I can hear its pathetic stutter from here. Just what do you believe you are owed, mortal?" They cocked their head, a smug grin slithering across their face. "I said I'd let you live. I never said how long."

One by one, the creatures turned to face him, hunger gleaming in their oval eyes. At the snap of their ruler's fingers, they rushed forward.

"The dark is unfamiliar, and the light is just as strange,
It isn't fear of death that holds us back, it's fear of change."

CHAPTER I

THE SMOTHERING SHADOWS

ELWYN

hree months and twenty-two days since the worlds ended.

Elwyn scrawled the words into a leather-bound log illuminated by the flickering light of a campfire. They were, perhaps, a touch dramatic, but they weren't altogether untrue. When the fae and mortal realms collided in the cataclysm now known as the Confluence, the worlds *had* ended, in a way.

Elwyn's world most certainly had.

The soil crackled beneath feather-light steps as someone approached the edge of the glade, where Chieftain Amatha Hearthblade stood surveying her troop. Despite her genial disposition, the Sidhe warrior was an intimidating sight—a mountain of onyx muscle rolling beneath a coat of coppery plate and patches of sharp, shimmering crystal. After over two months of serving at her command, Elwyn still struggled to hold her gaze. Partly because doing so required her to crane her neck to an uncomfortable degree.

"Nothing to report, Chieftain." The soldier's pleasant, honey-smooth timbre marked him as Maithe even before filigree armor glinted in Elwyn's periphery. "No survivors. No corpses. No hazards of any ilk. If it's all the same, I'd like to request a new assignment. Something with a touch more...anything."

Leave it to the light-fae to confuse peace for boredom.

Amatha shifted her weight, seeming to consider her subordinate's request. Firelight glittered off the amethyst shards that encrusted her scalp and shoulders, turning them from plum to clouded mauve. "We will discuss this matter after the reprieve," she said, pointing her obsidian spear toward a well-worn trail in the undergrowth. "For now, survey the northern shoreline once more. I want a full report by sunrise."

"But—"

Amatha's bejeweled eyebrow quirked, and the soldier's objection died on his tongue. As he vanished into the woodland shadows, Elwyn forced her attention back to the rations she'd been tasked with counting. Lately, inventory was about the most important duty a Myriad Guard soldier could merit. She would not risk losing it over simple distractibility.

As she sifted through a crate of dried fruit, tossing aside that which had begun to molder and tallying what remained, she eavesdropped on her troopmates' conversations. For a while, the Maithe brigadiers chittered about the latest fashions while the Sidhe compared the quality of their hand-hewn weapons, but the discussions inevitably melded into a flurry of complaints about bland rations and sliver-thin bedrolls. Nothing quite blurred lines of class and culture like communal discontentment.

Having lived in far worse conditions, Elwyn found the accommodations more than comfortable. She kept that opinion to herself, largely because her troopmates wouldn't have acknowledged it. Their derision was probably for the best. Though a small, lonely piece of Elwyn longed to connect with those nearest her, she knew well the damage such ties wrought when they inevitably snapped.

It was difficult, in those moments of self-enforced solitude, not to think back on the night she'd gone up against Yana and her Shadow Goblins. Elwyn hardly remembered the sting of the creatures' claws or the bone-deep bite of their fangs, but she would never forget the heavy chill that filled her chest when the Ghost Witch raised her dagger over Lydia's heart. The hopelessness that consumed her when the blade fell and a blinding glow spilled from the altar. The sorrow that crushed her when that light finally faded to reveal the fiends had vanished, leaving behind the twisted ruins of two worlds and a tiny, ashen corpse.

So she focused on fruit leather. On oat cakes and sunflower seeds. On the crackling warmth of the fire at her back and the rustic tang of the pines that ringed the glade. Anything tangible, tastable, *present* was preferable to the past.

She was contemplating whether a mildly musty satchel of berries was salvageable when the foliage rustled to her right. The Maithe scout had returned, his chest heaving and his eyes saucer-wide. His bronze complexion had paled from either shock or exertion.

"A ship has run aground not a mile off." A hint of a smile tugged on his lips. "A mid-sized vessel, in decent repair."

"Survivors?" the chieftain asked.

"If we hurry. From the sound of things, the sea-wolves have already found them."

Amatha beckoned several soldiers by name, Elwyn among them. The chosen fae rushed away from the campfire but lingered at the edge of its glow. Until recently, they had never known night, and the darkness still filled them with palpable dread.

Elwyn harbored no such fear, but she dragged her heels all the same. Her inclusion in the mission—and the Myriad Guard, for that matter—was owed not to her talents but to the whims of a headstrong friend who had begged the chieftain to watch over her. Not that he could be bothered to check in on her himself.

"I will signal a formation after assessing the scene," Amatha said. "Until then, stay quiet, stay alert, and stay close." Her indigo eyes swept those gathered, landing on Elwyn. "You especially."

Elwyn bristled, though the edict was well warranted. As the only mortal in the muddled troop of twenty, she made a convenient target for feral fangs and talons.

"Stick close to someone stronger, and your enemies will yield,
Life shapes some into weapons and others into shields."

That's what Luatha would have said. Or something like it, anyway. But Luatha was gone, so Elwyn would have to make do with her own shoddy little rhymes.

Luatha's gone...

Elwyn shoved the thought aside, mindful of its claws. For the moment, there were more literal monsters to deal with.

Amatha brought her fist to her breastplate. "May the sun rise swiftly."

"And may it light the path forward," the troop chanted, returning the salute.

Elwyn clung to the chieftain's shadow as they tore through tangled flora that had only recently begun to harmonize. Fae vines brimming with brilliant blossoms scaled the trunks of common oaks and hickories. Rhysien mosses dangled in curtains from Talunasan boughs laden with crystalline fruit. Here and there, a heap of rubble or a tarnished spire parted the undergrowth, grim reminders of all the Confluence had stolen. Elwyn tried not to think of the bodies buried beneath the wreckage, but it was hard to ignore the necrotic note that played on the autumn-crisp wind.

Soon the soldiers spilled out onto an alabaster beach turned silver by the light of a low-slung moon. An ill-fated frigate had sliced into the shore at a tilt, its white-and-blue sails marking it as a Pondrellen merchant craft. A chorus of chilling howls cut through the air as several serpentine silhouettes clawed up the vessel's sides. Judging from the screams that rang out from beyond the taffrail, at least one beast had already climbed aboard.

The chieftain raised her spear skyward. The brigadiers brandished gilded rapiers. The warriors hefted massive weapons hewn from all manner of metal and stone. Sorrow panged in Elwyn's chest as she drew the cold corpse of her dagger, *Gelah*. The runes that ran along the crescent blade no longer seared with magic at the taste of her blood, but the weapon was still deadly. Especially in her hands.

As Amatha's spear swept forward, she morphed it into a broadsword to signal a swarm formation. The Sidhe stormed down the shore in a perfect arrow with the chieftain at its point. Most were stonemelders like their leader, but a pair of emberweavers brought up the rear, their platinum growths setting them apart from their crystal-encrusted peers. Rays of thermal magic seethed from their clenched fists, glowing amber.

Several sea-wolves emerged from the shallows, needle-fangs bared. They were roughly the size of wolfhounds, with the long, curved claws of osprey and the soulless eyes of eels. Dusk-dark scales shimmered with their every sinuous step, and ridges of coarse fur spiked from their spines. They were not the most fearsome creatures Elwyn had ever encountered, but they were far from docile, and their numbers were vast.

As the chieftain neared the shipwreck, a pair of sea-wolves pounced. Amatha swept her blade in a wide arc, turning it into an axe mid-swing and cleaving them down their centers. The other stonemelders followed her example, weapons shifting at their whims as they pressed through the encroaching pack. Sparks rained from the palms of the emberweavers, startling several creatures back to the water.

On Amatha's signal, the brigadiers sprinted forward and formed tidy lines to either side of the Sidhe. A blink, and their numbers doubled, each producing an illusory twin with its rapier raised at the ready. The seawolves snapped and snarled, lurching forward only to skitter back at the thrust of a golden blade.

Elwyn's fingers flexed around *Gelah's* hilt. She had never been fond of violence, despite its constant presence in her life, but fighting one's way forward was far preferable to standing still. Idle hands made for restless minds, restless minds made for listless thoughts, and listless thoughts wandered down terribly dark paths.

The chieftain's warning echoed in her ears—*you are to serve as backup, and only that.* The decision had been made the moment Elwyn joined the Guard, and she'd been permitted only a few cautious swipes since. Surely her role would change in time. The Sidhe were built like cudgels and the Maithe like filigree foils, but Elwyn was a knife, honed for slipping silently between plates and leaving her foes bewildered by the blood pooling at their feet. She may not have been stronger or swifter than the fae, but she was sharper. Sooner or later, the troop would have need of her skillset.

In the meantime, they put on a decent show.

Protected by their Maithe colleagues, the Sidhe huddled near the shipwreck and pressed their palms to the shore. The sands between them shifted and shimmered, stretching toward the taffrail in a delicate arch. Silvery streams poured free, forsaking the commands of ancient magic for the familiar embrace of gravity. The emberweavers brought an end to the defiance with a coordinated pulse of heat, transforming the sands to a bridge of twisted glass.

The structure was too fragile to support even a single Sidhe, but the Maithe were more than light enough to scale it. Amatha ordered a trio to do just that before diving back into battle, the sands at her feet turning darker with every strike.

Elwyn watched with envy as the brigadiers vanished aboard the frigate. *So much for serving as backup.* Just how was she supposed to aid her troopmates if she couldn't tell how they were faring?

Then again, they'd never settled on a signal for a situation like this, had they? Perhaps the chieftain had meant to call her forward but had forgotten in all the chaos. Though a bit presumptive, the reasoning would hold up to a stern lecture, provided Elwyn lived to hear one.

She slipped toward the shipwreck, swift and silent as a shadow. Only a single sea-wolf noticed her passing, its teeth flashing silver. She dodged its attack with practiced ease, landing one of her own. The creature whimpered, snapping a second time, but Elwyn's next blow silenced it. She needed to aim more carefully now that *Gelah* had lost its supernatural sting.

Seconds later, she'd scaled the sand-glass bridge and vaulted over the taffrail. Her soles *thudded* on the deck, rousing a sea-salt billow. Not a single eye—friendly or fiendish—flicked her way. Some six feet off, the brigadiers stood haloed in the glow of a looming dawn, their shoulders brushing as they leveled their rapiers at the pair of beasts encircling them. One blade found a sunken socket; another, the tender dip of a clavicle. Both emerged scarlet as the sea-wolves fell limp to weathered planks.

The remaining soldier scowled at his spotless sword, grieving his lost chance at glory, only to notice another sea-wolf stalking toward a trio of mortals cowering near the stern. The beast was at least a foot longer than the others, with a far burlier build. Its tapered ears folded flat against its gills as it crouched low, preparing to pounce.

The brigadier rushed forward in a bout of careless courage, having failed to notice a second creature skulking behind the nearest mast. His rapier pierced his target's hide right as the hidden sea-wolf leapt from the shadows. Elwyn's feet raced faster than her thoughts. She shoved her troopmate to safety right as the beast landed, and it threw her to the deck so hard the planks splintered. Her dagger embedded in its belly, but not before its jaws clasped her shoulder. Fangs pierced her leather pauldron, finding flesh.

A startled scream tore from Elwyn's throat. Adrenaline flooded her wounds, muting the ache. She twisted her blade and ripped it to the right, freeing a putrid rush of blood and bowels. The sea-wolf collapsed, grinding *Gelah's* hilt against her sternum and forcing the breath from her lungs.

"Out of the skillet and into the flames,
Trade daydreams for daggers, you're bound to get...to get..."
Shamed? Lamed? Maimed? *Creator*, Luatha had been so much better at

the whole rhyming thing. In any case, the couplet was destined to end on a sour note.

As Elwyn struggled out from beneath her fallen foe, dawn broke, setting the sky aflame. The clamor of combat faded to a whisper as the remaining sea-wolves returned to the depths, repelled by daylight. Elwyn's thrill ebbed in time with the battle-din, leaving her with leaden arms and a somber spirit.

The fight had ended. The sun had risen. The shadows had retreated.

Now the *real* darkness would find her.

BRANNON

Somewhere beyond the gossamer tent, a flock of songbirds tittered musically. Brannon could not allow them to become a distraction. No matter how badly he wanted to snap their chipper little necks.

"Inhale." Ferea's voice was clear as a mountain spring, soothing as the incense that flooded Brannon's lungs with each breath. Notes of citrus wove through the sage, keeping him lucid through the lull. He trapped an aromatic cloud in his chest and counted his heartbeats as the darkness behind his eyelids deepened.

One-thump.

Two-thump.

Three-thump.

"Exhale."

Brannon breathed out, mindful of how his ribs contracted. Apparently, they needed to fold like a fucking parasol—and slowly, at that—or the whole routine would be for naught.

"Where are you?" Ferea asked.

A stupid question. Brannon had been trapped in the same place for months now, and he wasn't particularly fond of it.

"I'm in a tent in the Sylph encampment," he answered. "In a land that is both Rhysia and Talunasa."

Wind-chime laughter lilted past. "Try again."

Brannon's jaw tensed, but he exhaled his bitterness. The knot between his shoulders loosened ever-so-slightly. He focused on the void behind his eyelids, blocking out the birdsong and the whisper of rustling fabric until the darkness consumed him.

"I am nowhere," he said.

"And *who* are you?"

"I'm Bl—" Brannon cut himself off. He was no longer Black, the Greyscale's most esteemed assassin. That name had died with his loyalty to the Father. For the moment, he wasn't supposed to be Brannon either. Easy enough. He had no fucking clue who that was yet.

"I am...no one."

"Very good." If Ferea caught his belligerent tone, she gave no sign. "Now, picture yourself untethering from gravity. Imagine the chains that bind you to the world dissolving. Let the emptiness enfold you as you pour yourself into it."

Brannon hated this part. No matter how many times he meditated, it never grew easier. With significant effort, he conjured chains solely to snap them, channeled his focus far from the present, willed himself away, away, away...

Several seconds passed before his pulse softened, and several more before his form began to fade. Eventually, he'd lost track of time entirely.

Perhaps that was the point.

"Do you remember where we left off?" Ferea's voice was hazy, hollow—more thought than sound.

Unfortunately, Brannon did remember. That memory made his heart stutter, sending sparks through distant veins. He could practically feel the chains rematerializing, tugging him toward the waking world.

"You mustn't feel rage here."

Brannon bit back a laugh, his anger abating. "Well, in that case, I'll just stop feeling it."

They'd had the same conversation a mere day before the worlds merged, when Ferea had first suggested mentoring him. At the time, he couldn't have fathomed taking up the offer.

Oh, how fucking far he'd fallen.

Resigned to the path he'd stupidly chosen, he cast his regrets aside and concentrated on the void. Eventually, the shadows shattered, hurling him straight into the heart of Saint Aldrich's Sanctuary.

The building hadn't changed one bit since he'd last lain lucid eyes upon it. Except that it had caught fire. Sparks leapt between the vaulted rafters and devoured the silken tapestries. Billows of smoke, flecked with snowy ash, filled the halls. Ceramic vases cracked in the heat, and molten gold bubbled from statues and sconces, dripping from the edges of oaken tables to snake between the flagstones.

None of it mattered to Brannon. He had no skin to sear, no blood to boil, no bones to burn. The flames could only harm him if he let them.

"Who set the fire?"

Ferea had asked the question countless times, though Brannon had made it clear he didn't care about to know answer. If the fire was real—and it most certainly wasn't—dousing it would have been the more pressing concern. Then again, there was a chance his mentor would move him to the next step of his training if he solved her silly riddle. He could only hope it would involve less thinking and more doing.

"Let's figure it out, shall we?" he replied, unsure whether she could hear him. He always forgot to ask about it upon waking.

Brannon whisked through the halls, unhindered by the smoke and soot. He knew this sanctuary like the hilts of his daggers. Above him loomed the mountainous steeples where he'd first proven his worth to the Father. Below him snaked the tangled catacombs where he'd fought for the rights to eat and breathe and age. Beyond the walls lay the sleepy city where he'd honed his skills to a wicked edge, slice by crimson slice.

But Brannon hadn't returned to reminisce about the good times.

The flames had yet to reach the inner sanctum. Moonbeams filtered through stained-glass windows, painting the empty velvet pews with mosaic light. A shadow idled in the alcove at the end of the crimson aisle. In one hand, it clasped a gilded shepherd's crook; in the other, a half-empty bottle.

"My child," he rasped in two voices—the first, a throaty, gin-slurred drawl and the second, a sickly sweet tenor. "It has been too long since you last graced me with your presence. I was beginning to fear you'd wandered astray." He drifted closer, robes spilling down the alcove steps like ink. "But then, you always return to us, don't you, Black?"

Brannon growled, torn between bowing and brandishing a blade. Not that he could do either. A resonance tremored through him, reminding him that he'd been here before—more than once—and that he'd fled like a coward to the safety of his skin.

He would not be bested by a figment of his own twisted imagination. Not again.

Fire sparked to life behind him as he floated forward, filling the sanctum with flickering light. The figure's face came into sharp focus, half its features belonging to the first man Brannon had ever killed, and half belonged to the man who'd bid him kill countless others.

A world away, Brannon's pulse spiked. Flames surged through his veins, fiercer than those that danced around him.

"You mustn't feel rage here," Ferea warned.

Easier lectured than done.

The figure's laughter smelled of spirits both bottled and damned. "Aren't you curious why you're here again?" he asked, death-pale eyes glinting. "You could picture yourself anywhere, at any time, for any reason, yet you always come back to *us*."

Another question Brannon had heard too often, one he'd forgotten until that very moment. He loathed it even more than Ferea's, though they often fell in quick succession. Perhaps the two riddles were linked.

"I'm here because..." How had the Sylph put it? "Because you started the fire."

The words were wisps, and they landed like lies.

He'd spoken them before, hadn't he?

The figure grinned, exposing far too many tar-brown teeth. "Do you know what time it is?" he asked, raising his staff.

Somewhere in the distance, a broken pocket watch began to tick.

It was always the same time. Always.

"Time to toughen up."

As the staff swung forward, Brannon attacked, arms materializing even as he outstretched them. Tendons webbed across milk-white bones. Skin stretched over straining muscles. His fingers formed just in time to wrap around the figure's neck.

The sanctuary erupted in a cloud of ash and ember, hurling Brannon back to the void. He blinked the darkness away to find himself staring into startled periwinkle eyes.

Sparks danced across his fingertips as they pressed into Ferea's slender throat. Though her form was not quite solid, it offered enough resistance to challenge his strength. Her static aura pooled in his palms and skittered to his elbows, healing him even as he harmed her. No matter how he squeezed, he found no solace.

It was Ferea's fault. She should have been writhing beneath his weight, prying at his fingers, pleading for her life. Hell, if her powers were at their peak, she could have willed herself ethereal and wafted right through him. Instead, she simply lay there, not a hint of fear or anger on her face.

She was giving him a choice.

The illusion of power shattered. Brannon's fingers went lax, and he rolled off the Sylph, collapsing onto summer-sweet grass slick with dew. There he remained, breathing in the fading incense, until his pulse softened and the fire in his veins dwindled to an ashen film. A calmness seeped through his skeleton. This was how he preferred his malice—cold, heavy, malleable. So long as he could channel it, anger numbered among his allies, where the rage he'd felt in his vision wanted nothing more than to devour him whole.

A sensible person would have fled while he composed himself, but the Sylphs possessed more heart than brains. When he finally forced himself upright, his mentor idled mere feet away, looking every bit like a frosted-glass figurine painted in pastels. A few cherry blossoms had fallen from her silvery updo, and her petal-pink robe had wrinkled about the belt and belled sleeves, but the welts on her neck had already begun to fade. With her stoic smile and statuesque poise, it was impossible to tell he'd just attacked her.

"I'm...sorry." The words pricked Brannon's tongue like ground glass.

"No, you are not," Ferea replied, her voice light and airy. "But you recognize that you *should* be sorry, and that is progress."

It sure as hell didn't feel like it.

"Should I try again?" Brannon asked, though he would rather have chugged sulfur than endure another meditation. "I almost had him that time."

Ferea's smile faded, and feathered wings sprouted from her shoulders, already aflutter. "You have spent enough time in the past for one day." Her bare toes lifted from the ground. "Let us look, for a moment, to the future."

Brannon followed the Sylph out into the stinging light of a watercolor dawn. Sunlight glinted off the distant Talunasan spires, sparking a path to the massive oak at their center. Spite-dark woodlands cloaked the distant hilltops. Much closer, pallid tents sprouted like toadstools from the sea of unseasonable wildflowers that spread out in every direction. Sylphs flitted about the encampment in silence, toting tubs of tincture and baskets of brilliant blossoms. Their silken robes trailed through the air behind them, soft and gauzy as their skin, and their daisy-white hair wafted like tendrils of mist, whether bound in high tails or left to stream freely.

A softer soul would have found it all so very charming.

Brannon stared past the pastel paradise to where a line of soldiers had already begun to form beside the central hospice. Not for the first time, he wondered whether he'd have been better off among the wounded. If the Myriad Guard had made room for a petty thief like Elwyn, they'd have surely found use for a seasoned assassin.

Ferea shoved something into his hands, chasing the *what-ifs* away. The empty wicker basket had been woven from river-reeds, and mauve stains splotched the inside.

"What the fuck am I supposed to do with this?"

Where other still Sylphs flinched at his language, Ferea had built up an immunity. "Why, collect charmblossoms, of course." She gestured toward a sprawling patch of shimmering pink posies with silvery centers. "Their nectar makes for a splendid salve, and their petals are perfect for poultices. Once the basket is full to the brim, meet me at the hospice for your next assignment."

Brannon's palms had never itched so fiercely for his *icons*, a pair of twin dirks he'd named *Aras Tosc*, the Serpent Fangs. He'd entrusted the daggers to Ferea as a condition of his tutelage, along with his clothing, his pocket watch, and—he was learning—his dignity.

"But I apologized." His fingers clenched around the basket's handle. "Surely that merits a less torturous punishment."

"Not punishment. *Discipline*." Ferea placed a hand on Brannon's shoulder. He loathed how her touch tingled, though that same spark had once helped to revive his withered arm. "Your hands have long reveled in harm; it is time they learned to heal."

"So long as you can smile, you'll have a place to hide,
Few care to know if pretty things are shattering inside."

CHAPTER 2
SKIN DEEP
ELOANA

loana had always been patient, not that she'd had another choice. She'd been patient as a child, passing up play to practice her scales. She'd been patient in her youth, trading her countryside home for a palace and a prince. She'd been patient every minute of every hour of every day since arriving at Samhria—smiling when she was expected to smile, dancing when she was expected to dance, singing when she was expected to sing, and waiting when she was expected to wait.

And wait.

And wait, and wait, and—

Then, all at once, the world inverted. The ups were down, the lights were dark, the sun had sunk, and the stars had risen. Every constant in Eloana's inflexible life had become suddenly, radically mercurial...yet her routine hadn't changed in the slightest.

At long last, she was running out of patience.

For the third consecutive morning, she sat alone in a pinstripe parlor at a table arranged with her finest porcelain tea set. The high-back chair across from her own was a perfect match, only its padding was plusher and its fabric brighter. Unsurprising, given how rarely it was occupied.

The doorknob turned, and Eloana's hopes flared. They guttered on the downbeat when her handmaiden, Loenelle, entered with a platter of spriteberry scones.

"Your tea has gone cold, m'lady." Loenelle set the treats on the table. "Shall I refresh it for you?"

Eloana nodded. Loenelle filled a second teacup and stirred in the requisite two lumps of sugar before swapping out the tepid one. The sunlight streaming through the open window brought out the bewildering blue of the handmaiden's pupils and the ashy undertones in her tightly bound hair.

Glimpsing such imperfections further spoiled Eloana's already-sour mood. Clearly, one of the servant girl's ancestors had debased themselves with a leprechaun, or worse. Pity she should have to pay for their crimes, but she would not have been born into such sacrilege had the Creator deemed her worthy of better.

"I don't suppose you've any news on Aedyn's whereabouts..." She held her teacup beneath her nose, letting the steam waft over her face. "Creator knows you lowborn love your gossip."

Loenelle dipped her head. "Not a whisper, m'lady."

Eloana took a sip to hide her scowl. A little conjecture would have been nice. It may not have been a servant's place to remark upon noble concerns, but it *was* their place to anticipate the needs of their betters. And Eloana needed validation.

"Sit, Loenelle," she demanded. "Someone must."

Judging by the handmaiden's expression, she feared the chair might swallow her whole. She perched on the edge of the cushion, wisely fearing Eloana more.

"W-with all respect, m'lady." Her sheepish gaze found the tablecloth. "If I do not attend the laundry soon, your sheets will wrinkle."

"It is the laundry's turn to wait." Eloana took another sip of tea. It was a bit bitter, but then, so was she. "You are not my first choice of company, but you are here, whereas Aedyn is not. I suppose I shouldn't fault him for it. Given the chaos we've endured since the Confluence, it's hardly a wonder he should miss an appointment or two."

Loenelle wrung her hands like a washrag. They probably felt empty without one. "I'm sure you're right, m'lady," she said, though her tone contested the claim.

"My betrothed is heir to the Summer Throne," Eloana snapped. "That honor comes with responsibilities you could never understand."

"O-of course, m'lady."

"Yes, of course." Eloana set her teacup aside and scraped a polished nail around the rim, coaxing a crystalline note from the porcelain. "Aedyn and I have been betrothed for over a century, yet we hardly know each other. Some days, I feel like a piece of jewelry, tucked safely away until he decides his arm looks bare." Surprised by her own pensive tone, she straightened her spine and lifted her chin. "I mean only to say that it is *irresponsible*. If, light forbid, the worst should ever befall our honorable king, the prince and I would be wed straightaway. All of Talunasa would benefit from our good rapport. Provided we manage to build any."

The handmaiden bit her lower lip, still staring at her restless hands. Decades spent basking in the auras of the elite, and she'd learned nothing of conversation.

"Have you truly nothing to add?" Eloana rapped her nails on the tablecloth, loathing how the lace muted the rhythm. "I demand your opinion on the matter."

"It's as you say, m'lady."

Eloana trapped an indecorous sigh in her chest. "I'd rather have parrots than servants," she huffed. "If something means to echo me, it should at least look pretty."

Loenelle winced, somehow shrinking further.

Perhaps there is a reason I'm starved for company. Eloana pursed her lips, listening to the birdsong that warbled over the windowsill. After a few soothing measures, she tried again, more gently. "We fae cannot lie, but it is rare we speak truth." She folded her hands atop the table. "If you cannot be honest with me, Loenelle, whoever will be?"

The handmaiden looked up to search Eloana's eyes. For what, who could say?

"I don't want to speak out of turn."

"I have stated plainly that it is your turn to speak."

Loenelle took a deep, shaky breath. "Perhaps it would be best not to speculate on how the prince spends his time," she said, "or..."

"Or?"

"Or with whom."

The temperature in the parlor plunged a full fifty degrees. Screaming was beneath Eloana, and swearing was crass, so she answered with a simple flick of her wrist. Her teacup shattered against the wall, spattering sepia onto the pinstripe paper and the ivory rug beneath it.

"How clumsy of you." She glared at Loenelle, rising from her chair. "Not to worry, I shall see the costs taken from your monthly stipend. For now, you are to clean up this mess and spend the remainder of the morning taming your tongue, assuming you wish to keep it."

Eloana left her handmaiden scrambling to obey her orders, hoping the shards were sharp enough to slice the girl's fingers. It would have been one thing to confirm that Aedyn was careless; it was quite another to infer he was a scoundrel.

As her feet carried her through Samhria's halls, she thought back on her very first handmaiden, Rathelie. In her naivete, Eloana had mistaken the girl for a friend. It was all giggles and nursery rhymes until Rathelie claimed Aedyn had shown her interest beyond cordial conversation. Hopefully, the subsequent flogging had taught her not to misinterpret the benevolence of royals.

Sadly, the gossip had persisted even after the girl was tossed from the palace. Aedyn's peerless pedigree made him the constant target of petty rumors, all of them baseless. Eloana was unrivaled in beauty, in bearing, and in bloodline, yet he seldom spared her even the most chaste of kisses. Clearly, he was above the roguish appetites of the lowborn.

But then, there were the sidelong glances, the subtle smirks, the lengthy, unexplained absences...

A floral breeze swept the clutter from Eloana's mind as she stepped out into the Gilt Grove. The private garden had been beautiful back when King Aryn first presented it as her betrothal gift, but she'd since transformed it into a wonder. Ornate hedges and magnificent topiaries now stood sentry over its many paths, each sculpted with the utmost skill and care. Most were tributes to Talunasa's eternal king and queen—an effigy apiece for each of their legendary lives—but other heroes of lore loitered among them: brave brigadiers, celebrated scholars, even the lauded lightsingers she hoped to someday surpass.

Eloana followed a trail of amber stepping stones to her first and favorite creation, the floral likeness of her great grandmother, Enwa the Golden Voiced. In cultivating the very first sprigs of oraithvine—the gleaming plant-metal hybrid now woven liberally throughout their kingdom—Enwa had revolutionized Talunasan society and brought her family unprecedented renown. Though she'd passed into the cycle long ago and had yet to re-emerge, there were few Maithe whom Eloana admired more.

Autumn had been unkind to Enwa, bleaching her primrose eyes and wilting her once-florid gown. Soon, winter would render her a skeleton. The very notion of the wretched season made Eloana shiver. The sun had long endowed her people with the powers of lightsinging and illusion. Its absence would leave them defenseless.

Disheartened by the past and future both, Eloana slipped off her sandals and fixed her mind on the present. The grass tickled her toes as she drifted through her garden, breathing in the heady aroma of freesia petals and listening...listening...listening...

There it was! The music! It swirled gently on the wind, carried in bits of birdsong, in rustling leaves and the stiff crackle of Talune's bark. The Confluence had muted and distorted it, tearing its manifold strands asunder, but it cried out for a conductor to restore it.

Eloana sifted through the din, plucking only the choicest notes—a chirrup here, a skitter there—and stringing them together. She twisted and twined them, braiding a new melody that sprouted swiftly in her core, sweeping and swelling until it burst from her lips like laughter.

Within measures, the Gilt Grove caught the rhythm. Leaves shivered, branches swayed, and oraithvine chimed its shrill, metallic timbre. When Eloana next opened her eyes, she'd rent Enwa from crown to root, leaving stripped branches to writhe against the wind.

Eloana buried her toes in the soil, grounding herself in creation's deepest chords as she traded her destructive dirge for a soothing, legato ballad. Branches reknit at her command. Newborn leaves burst into being. Strands of gilt oraithvine slithered around the nebulous tangles, binding them into rigid shape. Buds parted and flowers bloomed. Berries burst and pollen plumed. Everything bleak and brittle and broken was buried beneath a coat of color twice as lush and vivid as the last.

The last note rang out like the pleasing peal of a silver bell. The resurrected Enwa smiled at the sound of it, her fern-frond lips furling upward. She looked twice as regal and stately as before, which was no simple feat.

Pride welled in Eloana's chest, potent enough to drown the morning's worries. Aedyn was an important man with an entire realm to fret over. Surely he'd been distracted by a matter of utmost importance.

AEDYN

Aedyn stumbled from the dream-den feeling as though an entire swarm of rot-fae had roosted in his skull, and every Shadow-damned one of them was trying to claw its way out. It made absolutely no sense! Mortals were creatures of comparably delicate constitution. Why in light's name were their potions so strong?

Perhaps the blame lay not on a single substance but a careless combination. He could recall nothing of the night before, save sneaking away from Samhria with a full satchel of coins jingling beneath his jacket. That very same satchel now hung empty at his hip.

He propped himself against a crumbling brick wall, squinting out at an obnoxious sunrise as he rummaged through his pockets. If he'd planned ahead, he would have packed some essence of ice-sprite before taking to the streets. As usual, he hadn't planned ahead.

"Never," he breathed, "again."

He meant the words with all his heart. Just as he'd meant them the previous morning. And the morning before that.

Once he'd collected a sufficient portion of his scattered wits, he started down the rubble-strewn street, scanning the wreckage for a clue to his whereabouts. No matter how far he'd wandered from the palace, the return trek promised to be dreadful. With each step, the swarm in his skull grew more restless, and the guilty pit in his stomach yawned a little wider. Whatever he'd partaken of—and whatever he'd subsequently taken part in—hadn't solved his problems. The worlds were still broken, their pieces were still scattered, and it was still his fault, at least in part.

Though he hadn't been the one to meld the realms, he'd failed to prevent it. Worse, it might never have happened at all had he simply stayed put for once. Of all the charms he'd fallen thrall to, adventure had always proven most alluring. Hence, the constant need to climb out his window solely to vex the guards who patrolled the palace halls and the king who'd tasked them with watching over him.

Judging from the disrepair, he'd somehow found his way to the eastern border of Rhysien-Talunasa. The restoration crews had focused their efforts on rebuilding the Maithe manors nearest the palace and had done little for the mortals on the outskirts, beyond stripping their homes of iron. That measure, though practical, had done nothing to foster trust between the Seelie and their new neighbors.

The few denizens who ambled about eyed Aedyn warily. Even the carriages gave him a wide berth, stallions veering at the whip of the drivers' reigns. It might have been kind to alter his appearance for the mortals' comfort, but he'd squandered much of his magic on the previous night's mystery antics and needed to save what remained for sneaking back into Samhria. Only once Talune's autumn-kissed canopy rose into view did he duck into an alleyway to don a disguise.

When he next emerged, he was two heads taller than before and thrice as thick. He'd traded his mussy bronze locks for amethyst shards, his copper complexion for dusky brown, and his rumpled raspberry suit for a coat of brassy dobhriste. As his oldest and closest friend, Amatha wouldn't mind his borrowing her face for a bit. It merited far less suspicion than his own, and a great deal more respect.

Relief flooded him when he spotted Samhria's gates winking out from among Talune's roots. The palace might well have been a prison, but deep within those suffocating halls, a heather-stuffed mattress, swaddled in silk and misted with sandalwood, sang to him like a Selkie. If he resisted its call much longer, he was liable to collapse in the street.

He slowed as he approached the palace, mimicking Amatha's heavy steps. The lightsinger sentries would not notice his *glamour*, as another illusionist might, but most anyone could see through shoddy acting.

"Good morning, Chieftain!" The guards saluted, fists ringing against their breastplates.

Aedyn could easily have grunted a greeting and been on his way, but an opportunity for mischief had presented itself, and restraint had never been his strong suit. "It *was* a good morning," he imitated Amatha's guttural tone, "until you addressed me improperly."

The guards exchanged bewildered glances. "Our apologies, Chieftain," said the leftmost of the pair. "Pray, inform us of our error, that we might correct it."

Aedyn barely stifled a smile. It was a wonder he wasted so much coin when the best entertainments were absolutely free. "You have not been made aware of the change to our salute?" he asked. "Not to worry. I will show you."

He demonstrated a lewd gesture he'd learned from Brannon, the crassest of his mortal friends. The sentries mirrored it with perfect innocence.

"Very good," he said, biting back laughter. "Pass this knowledge along to the next patrol and see that they do the same. I will perform a test before the day is out."

The sentries dipped their heads, stepping away from the entrance and slipping into their customary duet—a tangle of lilting tenor and rumbling bass. Oraithvine knots unraveled in time with their song, allowing the gates to open inward. Aedyn gave the guards a parting "salute" as he marched into the palace.

The climb through Samhria's winding stories took nearly as long as the trek through town. Countless illusionists wandered past in that time, but Amatha visited so frequently that none spared him a second glance. By the time he arrived at his private wing, his glamour was fraying to match his mood, and not a soul had noticed.

Seconds after he rang the visitor's bell, the door cracked open, and his attendant peered out from behind it. "Good afternoon *Amatha*," Learo said, visibly fighting an eye roll. "Shall I inform Prince Aedyn of your arrival?"

"That won't be necessary." Aedyn no longer bothered to mask his voice, but the rasp lingered. "Please, just let me in."

Learo clucked his tongue. "As the heir's attendant, I cannot receive guests without his express—"

Aedyn wriggled past and fell to the floor in an agonized tangle, his glamour shattering around him like glass. The door clicked shut, and a lethargic sigh drifted overhead.

"Another late night, sir?" Learo asked, looming over him. "I trust your little excursion was worth the pains I took in covering for it. Without a request on your part, I might add."

Aedyn rolled onto his back, groaning. Last he checked, the mural on his ceiling wasn't rigged to spin. "Everything is horrible," he whined.

"Oh, come now," Learo said. "It's not all that bad."

"Name one pleasant thing in this whole light-forsaken world."

"I've drawn you a warm bath."

"Learo, you're a saint!"

"Of course, that was hours ago, when you were first due to wake."

"Learo, you're a bastard."

"Indeed, sir." Learo proffered a palm. "That's why I'm the attendant, and you're the prince."

"I'm sure there were a few other variables involved." Aedyn grabbed Learo's hand, and the world tilted. It did not cease tilting once he found his feet. "Could I implore you to fetch me some essence of ice-sprite? Second drawer down in the cabinet nearest the chaise."

Learo crossed his arms. "I abhor that drawer."

Aedyn made his lower lip quiver.

Another lazy sigh trailed after Learo as he drifted to the cabinet in question and gave the handle a terse tug. "Let's see..." he said, sifting through the contents. "Lightleaf, spark-oil, two vials of fire-sprite, a year's supply of shadowroot, an...honestly, I don't know what *that* is, and I don't care to learn. Ah, here we are!" He plucked a tiny vial swirling with silvery blue from the drawer. "Essence of ice-sprite."

Aedyn swiped the vial from Learo's fingers, popped it open, and downed it in a single gulp. A blizzard rushed through him, freezing him to the marrow. Icy fractals clouded his vision, and his breath came out in terse, white wisps. In a matter of heartbeats, the chill melted away, taking his hangover with it.

"Thank the Creator," Aedyn gasped, blinking the last of the frost from his eyes.

"Ahem."

"Oh, and Learo. Thank you, Learo."

"My pleasure, sir," Learo replied, voice flat. "Speaking of pleasure, if anyone else ever finds that little contraband cache of yours—"

"I'll endure a little lecture, perhaps even a slap on the wrist." Aedyn slid his jacket off and tossed it over the nearest chair. "You needn't worry about me, flattering as it is."

"It is *my job* to worry about you."

"Then I'm giving you the day off. In fact, you can have all the days off with no consequence to your coffers. Aren't I a benevolent employer?"

"You don't employ me, sir, but speaking of my employer, and of worries, and of lectures..." Learo reached into a letter basket, extracting a ribbon-bound scroll sealed with a blot of golden wax. "This arrived for you an hour ago."

"A royal summons." Aedyn reluctantly accepted it. "How very official."

He cracked the seal down the center, and the parchment unfurled to reveal a familiar flourished script, inked in bitter black. "To Aedyn," he read aloud. "Oh, good, he remembers my name. But I digress." He cleared his throat dramatically. "You are hereby summoned—See? Very official—to my private balcony at three today. See that you are sober and presentable. Regards, *King Aryn*."

Aedyn grimaced. "It must have emptied his purse to have that message carted a whole two stories, but at least it was short and sweet." He tossed the scroll over his shoulder. "Well, it was short anyway. My father is a man of few words."

"Oh, I wouldn't be so certain," Learo said, a smirk tugging at his lips. "I imagine he's saving a great many for you."

"A tiny touch of honey might obscure a tincture's taste,
But it takes a bit of pressure to shove bones back into place."

CHAPTER 3
HEALING HURTS
ELWYN

he march to Samhria gave Elwyn time to think, and her thoughts grew heavier with every step. If she couldn't find a way to shake them, they would crush her long before she reached her room.

She'd been the first of several Guard members to relinquish her seat in the troop caravan to a shaken sailor who more sorely needed it, but the act of charity had only helped to delay the inevitable. Not a single soldier had ever wriggled out of leisure time, but as the woods beyond the borders melted into the dusty streets of Rhysien-Talunasa, Elwyn couldn't resist trying.

"Do you happen to know who's rotating in for us?" she asked, strolling up alongside the chieftain. Though a thin coat of dust stole the sheen from the Sidhe's armor and crystal shards, her strides were strong as ever.

"Chieftain Tanzan." Amatha eyed Elwyn warily. She'd yet to unleash a lecture about interfering with the mission, but her expression did the job well enough. "Why?"

"Oh, *of course* it's Chieftain Tanzan!" Elwyn smiled as though she recognized the name. "I've heard tell their troop is in desperate need of spare soldiers."

Amatha's bejeweled eyebrow quirked.

"Someone to prepare their meals, then?"

"*Elwyn.*"

"To shine their armor? Tend their campfires? Read them bedtime stories?"

"If any of that were true, it still would not matter." The chieftain jarred to a stop, fixing Elwyn with a glare. "This is not about what *they* need. It is about what *you* need."

"Well, it so happens I don't need rest." Elwyn crossed her arms, rousing the bite wound on her shoulder.

Amatha most definitely noticed her telltale wince.

"Conflict is a whetstone." The chieftain marched on at a slower pace, silently commanding Elwyn to keep up. "In measure, it may sharpen you, but too much will grind you to dust."

"Stonemelders don't even use whetstones," Elwyn muttered. The comment earned a chuckle, which she took as her final answer. Amatha's will was as strong as her strikes, and her wits sharper than her shoulder shards. Elwyn would just have to weather the four-day break as best she could. With luck, she'd sleep straight through it and wake up with her dagger in hand.

A brisk gale cut between buildings, carrying a flurry of fallen leaves. Amatha's gaze followed them to Talune, and a visible shudder swept through her. Elwyn doubted the chill was to blame. Not months before, the First Tree had boasted the most verdant coat she'd ever laid eyes upon. Now the gilt halls of Samhria winked out between brittle tufts of amber that would vanish entirely, soon enough.

"Some things are not meant to change," the chieftain mused aloud. Like most Seelie fae—and like Talune itself—she'd never known autumn.

After losing Lydia and Luatha on the same terrible night, Elwyn was in no rush to make new friends. Still, she couldn't help regarding Amatha as *friendly*. Enough so that the chieftain's burdens spilled onto her shoulders.

"Change can be a good thing," she said, desperate to lighten the load. Her sorrows were heavy enough on their own. "Talune was a seed once, wasn't it?"

"I...cannot recall." Amatha's pupils drifted from hovel to hovel as though the answer hid among them. "Even my most recent life is a blur, though it happened mere centuries ago. Perhaps King Aryn would have your answer. He remembers the Beginning with more clarity than most."

It had been a while since Elwyn last heard mention of the cycle. Most fae lived multiple lives, with each death ushering them into brighter light or deeper darkness, depending on their deeds. Some had been around since the worlds were first made. Apparently, Amatha was among them.

"Pretend I was talking about an ordinary tree..."

Amatha hummed softly, running her fingers over her scalp shards. "There is no growth without change," she said with a grin of approval. "You are wise, for a mortal. I am glad Aedyn convinced me to recruit you."

Elwyn grimaced at the mention of their mutual friend. In the weeks before she'd joined the Guard, she and Aedyn had been nearly inseparable. He'd even snuck out to meet her a few times since, ferreting citrinebread and amusing anecdotes to share over simple card games. Those visits had stopped abruptly about a month back, which bothered her more than she cared to admit. She'd always known he would eventually grow bored of their friendship, but she hadn't expected the novelty to wear off so soon.

Eventually, the road split around the market square—a colorful collective of wagons and booths brimming with fresh fruit, hand-dyed clothing, and all manner of common trinkets. Bins that had recently boasted citrus and summer linens now proudly displayed marbled apples and heavy winter furs. Elwyn resisted the urge to palm a fresh plum as she continued south, toward Samhria. She made it all of three steps before Amatha blocked her path, hands perched on her armor-plated hips.

"The Sylph encampment is that way." The chieftain pointed to the northern road. "In case you have forgotten."

For the first time since the skirmish, Elwyn spared her stinging shoulder a glance. Her leather pauldron had been shredded to ribbons, and the skin beneath it hadn't fared much better. "Nothing a splash of spirits and a stretch of gauze won't solve," she argued. "I have a little of each in my quarters."

"Ah, but the Sylphs have a surplus of both." Amatha grabbed Elwyn's good shoulder, steering her toward the aforementioned encampment. "I was planning to visit their Speaker-elect sometime this week. What better time than now, hm?"

"How convenient." Elwyn ducked free of Amatha's grasp, but the chieftain continued to march alongside her, unaffected. She probably suspected Elwyn would sneak off at the first opportunity. Which, to be fair, she would have.

The sun rose steadily higher as they walked, rousing the piecemeal kingdom from slumber. Mortals rushed from the marketplace with overstuffed baskets, eager to return to their dwellings before the fae crowded the streets. Drowsy-eyed Maithe peered out from their manor windows, welcoming the sun with grateful smiles. A few of Elwyn's Sidhe troopmates had already gathered beside a tavern, raring for a raucous start to break, and a single, green-skinned Undine sat hunched on a filigree bench, head propped between webbed hands, looking just as lost and listless as he surely felt.

The sight of that forlorn fae made Elwyn's chest tighten. She'd lost her closest friend in Chorial's collapse, and scarcely a minute had passed since when she hadn't mourned the piskie's absence. The few Undine who had been visiting Talunasa during the Confluence had lost everything and everyone they'd ever known—their kingdom, their culture, their history and future. Was it even possible to heal from so deep a wound?

Before Elwyn knew it, she and Amatha were winding between the gossamer tents of the Sylph encampment. A lengthy queue of wounded had already formed beside the central hospice, most of them soldiers from other troops. Though the Guard had yet to face the Unseelie threats it had been created to oppose, the uncharted woodlands boasted perils aplenty.

Dense though the crowd was, Amatha's reputation paved an easy path to the entrance. Guilt gnawed at Elwyn as they slipped past a brigadier with a dislocated arm and a bloodstained tunic, but she wasn't about to object aloud. The sooner a Sylph saw her, the sooner the chieftain would leave her be.

A cloud of floral spirits stung her eyes as she stepped into the hospice. By the time she blinked them clear, a Sylph man in flowing sage robes had pulled Amatha aside for a conversation made largely of nods and hand gestures. This went on for a several minutes before the chieftain returned to Elwyn's side.

"My presence is needed elsewhere," Amatha explained, a warning clipping the words. "I will be gone for fifteen minutes, perhaps twenty. When I return, I expect to find you here, either fully healed or well on the way."

Elwyn offered a half-hearted salute. "Your word is law."

"Yes." The chieftain sighed. "But you have been known to break those."

With those parting words, Amatha and the Sylph departed, vanishing with a flourish of shimmering gossamer. Elwyn was tempted to follow and investigate the mystery matter herself. It would surely prove more interesting than sitting around a hospice, waiting to be coddled like some child who'd never stitched her own wounds. Sylph healing was a luxury she would not always be privy to, and she knew better than to lean on fragile supports.

"Although rebellion often brings a swift spark of delight,
In this case, you'd do better to obey without a fight."

Elwyn's worst couplet yet—in content, if not in cadence. The real Luatha would never have argued in favor of compliance. But Elwyn had never possessed a surplus of luck, and she'd pressed her meager stores enough for one day. If she wanted to remain in the Guard, she needed to follow the occasional order.

The hospice had been partitioned off into tidy stations, each walled in lattice and furnished with plush pillows. Pollen and wind sprites flitted through the air above them, casting glimmers of pink and blue light onto the laboring Sylphs. The healers went about their work quietly, performing miracles with unfathomable ease. Bruises vanished with a brush of their fingers. Cuts closed with a splash of their salves. Ribs reset at the press of their palms, drawing winces of pain followed by sighs of relief.

Elwyn wandered the grassy aisles between stations, absently tracing the scar on her left cheekbone. That grisly crescent had been carved into her a decade before, and she'd hidden beneath a half-veil of her hair ever since. Perhaps, if she'd grown up in the company of Sylphs, she'd have no such flaws to bury.

No wonder the fae were so vain.

It was no simple task, capturing a healer's attention. Elwyn hovered by station after station as they cleared, but the Sylphs looked straight past her to the next person in line, and she wasn't keen to speak up about it. She was no longer *remarkably* unremarkable, as she'd been with Luatha fluttering by her side, but she was still unremarkable in the plainest sense of the word. It wasn't as though removing the magical shroud—or however the piskie's powers worked—had suddenly transformed her into a socialite.

She had just about given up when a boastful voice caught her ear. A few stations away, the Maithe man she'd saved from a sea-wolf that morning sprawled across a pillow heap, chest bared for a slender Sylph with cherry blossoms woven throughout her silver-white braid.

"...as I rushed to their rescue, a second beast attacked from behind," he said, puffing further. "His eyes blazed with hunger and slaver foamed about his fangs, but for all his rage, a simple slice did him in."

Elwyn bristled, snapping a glare the soldier's way. A simple slice had done the sea-wolf in alright, but he hadn't been the one to dole it.

She was headed over to untwist her troopmate's tale when a familiar figure trudged into view, toting a basket of shimmering blossoms. He hardly looked like himself, clad in a silk robe and bereft of blades, but his signature scowl hadn't changed in the slightest.

"Brannon?"

The former assassin paused mid-step. "Why, if it isn't history's most obnoxious thief." His scowl melted into a smile when he noticed her wounded shoulder. "Inept as ever, I see."

"Someone must take the blows for the more fragile fighters." Elwyn tipped her head toward the brigadier. "Had I been a second later in rescuing this one, you'd be shoving his guts back into his belly right now."

"Easier to rip them out altogether," Brannon said with a shrug. "A bit of advice: next time one of your troopmates tempts fate, try giving them some alone time with it. For now, it appears you have a wound that needs tending." He propped a bare foot on the Maithe man's back and kicked him from the pillows. "It just so happens Ferea has an opening."

Spiteful over the attempted glory-theft, Elwyn usurped her troopmate's seat. A trail of whispered curses spilled from the soldier's lips as he stomped away. The healer, by contrast, appeared surprisingly unfazed.

"You look familiar." She cocked her head, and a rumpled cherry blossom fell from her hair. "A friend of Brannon's, yes?"

Elwyn nodded, though *friend* probably wasn't the correct word. He hadn't tried to kill her in a while, which was a pleasant change of pace.

"Sorry to trouble you over something so trivial," she said, angling her injured shoulder toward the Sylph. "Chieftain's orders."

"Hmm..." Ferea peeled away what remained of the pauldron and prodded the skin below it. Magic sparked beneath her fingertip, dulling the ache. "This is shallow enough that even a mortal medic could treat it with the proper salves. It will be perfect for my pupil to practice on."

"For *who* to what?" Elwyn gaped at Brannon, who gaped right back. "Surely you intend to keep a watchful eye over the process..."

"Brannon is a competent mortal." Ferea plucked the basket from her surly student's fingers. "It will only take a few minutes to distribute these blossoms. I will assess his work upon returning."

Before Elwyn could object, the Sylph sprouted wings and fluttered away. Brannon slid into the space where she'd been, a sadistic smile slicing across his face.

"Isn't this an exciting turn of events?" His fingers danced across a tray of medical tools that could easily double as weapons. "Now, don't look so glum. If you stay very, very still, this won't hurt too terribly."

"I somehow suspect it shouldn't hurt at all."

"What is learning if not a series of trials and errors?" He plucked up a vial of lavender tincture and gave it a flick. The resulting bubbles somehow looked ominous. "Now, you probably think you need simple sutures, but to be safe, we should opt for a full amputation."

Elwyn glared, setting her hand atop *Gelah's* hilt.

"I see your sense of humor hasn't improved any." Brannon popped the vial open, tipping it onto a rag. "Rest assured, if I wanted to kill you, you'd be dead already."

"I seem to recall a few attempts," Elwyn said, patting her dagger. "Your intentions weren't the issue."

Brannon seized her shoulder and smothered it with the rag. The tincture burned like a bonfire, each bubble a tiny, searing spark. Though Elwyn managed to bite back a yelp, a hiss escaped her clenched teeth.

"What do you know?' Brannon chuckled. "Medicine *is* fun."

Elwyn shrugged him away, snatching up a roll of gauze. Already, a fresh sheet of slick skin had formed over the wound, tugging with every small movement. It wasn't healed, by any means, but it would fend off infection well enough.

She was in the process of wrapping her shoulder for good measure—all the while informing Brannon where he could shove the remaining surgical tools, one by one—when a massive shadow fell over her. She nearly leapt upright, having failed to notice anyone approaching. Such carelessness would be unacceptable once she set out on her own again.

"So, you *are* capable of following orders." Chieftain Hearthblade loomed beside the station, grinning at Elwyn's bandaged shoulder. "I will keep that in mind when you next ignore them. In the meantime, I have need of mortal eyes."

"I can help with that," Brannon said, plucking up a scalpel.

Elwyn stood, kicking his shin in the process. If Amatha weren't present, she'd have aimed higher. "How can I help?"

"I will explain along the way," Amatha said, appraising Brannon like a weapon in a sales bin. "You are the assassin, yes? The one trained by the Greyscale?"

Brannon grimaced at the mention of the syndicate that had ruthlessly discarded him. "I trained myself," he muttered, crossing his arms. "They happened to benefit."

"Then you will join us." Amatha started toward the exit, waving for the mortals to follow. "Bring the scalpel."

Elwyn had only ever entered Samhria through its gates, so she was startled when a trio of sentries bid Talune's roots to part, revealing a hidden tunnel that plunged deep below the First Tree. One of many such passages, according to the chieftain. Apparently, the Maithe were too proper to plague their palace with dungeons and holding cells, but they were not too proper to make use of them.

Amatha strode confidently into the gloom beyond the bark, but Elwyn waited for Brannon to follow before joining. There was little that unnerved her more than hearing someone slinking through the shadows behind her. Especially when that someone had pressed a knife to her spine on multiple occasions.

Where the palace proper was a labyrinth of painted halls and florid solariums, this passage was tiled entirely in slabs of taupe sandstone that somehow still managed to smell strongly of mulch and tarnished gold. Captive sprites fluttered inside the little glass orbs that graced the walls like sconces, their collective glow painting the path a dull rose. Elwyn didn't know whether sprites were sapient, but she pitied them all the same. Having spent half her life pinned beneath the thumb of a charlatan, she knew well how it felt to be caged.

"There were seventeen survivors aboard the shipwreck," Amatha explained once she'd summarized the morning's rescue for Brannon. "Not one of them will speak to us. At first, I thought it was my appearance that bothered them—I know how skittish you mortals can be—but they cowered back from even the scrawniest of Maithe."

"Sounds like a routine interrogation is in order." Brannon's predatory smile was nearly audible. "Do they have a leader?"

"I believe so." Amatha paused, nodding toward a smooth stone door toward the end of the hall. "He isn't dressed much different than the others, but with as often as their eyes darted his way, I assume he holds some sway."

Elwyn's curiosity eclipsed her caution, tugging her toward a window hardly larger than an arrow slit. The room beyond was much too warm and well-furnished to be a prison cell, but the man seated in the corner armchair was most certainly a captive. Sprigs of oraithvine bound his wrists and ankles, gleaming rose gold in the sprite-light, and his hands were balled in anticipation of a fight he sorely wished for.

"The others are being fed a warm meal as we speak," the chieftain explained, perhaps sensing Elwyn's unease. "The Creator tasked us long ago with watching over mortals, and we have not forgotten His instructions in light of their sudden...proximity. This man would be with his colleagues now, had he not taken a swing at every soldier who approached him."

Brannon scoffed aloud. "Even I would think twice about attacking my rescuers. Three times, if they were built like you."

"They're probably frightened." Elwyn slipped closer to her colleagues, lest the captive overhear their conversation. Best not to offend him before introductions were made. "Crossing uncharted seas is a desperate measure. We can only assume staying ashore carried the greater risk."

"That, I do not doubt." Amatha's voice darkened by several shades. "Talunasa and Réimsdarg both melded with mortal nations, so it is probable the Unseelie territories did the same. If these sailors encountered a herd of Augusky or legion of Dullahan, they have good reason to mistrust the fae."

Elwyn's stomach did a somersault. The Seelie could be callous on occasion, but if the folk tales held truth, the Unseelie were literal monsters. She had not considered how lucky Rhysia was to have melded with Talunasa, of all the possible fae lands. Or how lucky she was to have been standing there at the time.

"So, it's not just our eyes you need." Brannon admired his scalpel by sprite-light. "You want us to get him to talk. By any means necessary."

"By *most* any means." The chieftain's words set a boundary, though her tone implied it was made of twigs. "I cannot craft plans around guesswork and gut feelings, so any information we can gather about the Unseelie will play to our advantage. We cannot afford to let a single detail slip through our fingers."

"Then we need to retrieve it *gently*," Elwyn said, more for Brannon's benefit than Amatha's. "If this encounter reinforces that man's opinion of the fae, his fear will spread through the mortal districts like ragweed. Trust between our peoples is thin enough. There's no need to stretch it further."

Amatha grunted in agreement. "Gentle is preferable."

Still not a strong enough boundary.

When the door slammed shut behind Elwyn and Brannon, the captive's steely gray eyes slid their way. Up close, he somehow looked both more haggard and proud than he had from a distance. His ragged suit boasted a variety of fabrics and hues, with four silver lines slicing across the sleeve of his dusty blue jacket. The placement mimicked that of the badges Pondrellen nobles often foisted upon their private guards, only Elwyn had memorized every highborn crest in her homeland, and this was not one of them.

"I assume you had a reason for attacking my troopmates," Elwyn said, nearly wincing at her own clumsy preface. Conversation had never been her strong suit. She'd never needed it to be. "The sooner you spill the particulars, the sooner we can all leave this place. I imagine you'd like to stretch your legs."

The man snorted, pointedly turning his face away. Irritating as the dismissal was, Elwyn couldn't blame him for harboring suspicions. Some Maithe donned mortal masks for sport, and they were not the only fae who could bend light to their will.

She took a deep breath and tried again. "We're human, if that's what you're wondering. That I can say as much is evidence in its own right. Fae tongues cannot abide the taste of lies."

The captive's nose wrinkled. "If you're working with those monsters, you're no more human than they are."

The insult rolled off Elwyn's shoulders, but the mere mention of monsters lent credence to the chieftain's Unseelie theory. It wasn't the strongest thread, but it was something to tug on.

"The fae of this land are nothing like those you've crossed paths with," she explained. "If anything, they're opposites."

A muscle flexed beneath the man's salt-and-pepper stubble, but his lips remained sealed. Most Pondrellens disregarded Rhysien folklore as children's stories. Odd, how that habit held even after the legends proved themselves true.

"You're wasting your breath, Elwyn." Brannon paced the floor behind her like a caged wildcat, every muscle tensed to strike. "And mine by association. If you truly want someone to open up, the swiftest and surest way to go about it is, well..." he twirled his scalpel, "to open them up."

Elwyn refused to dignify the suggestion, even with a glance. Brannon's methods had suited the Greyscale just fine, but she had to believe the Myriad Guard was above them. She had not fled the Father's cruel clutches only to spread his sickness to other institutions.

"There may be value in the mindset you have long dismissed,
Where carrots fail to get results, perhaps consult the stick."

Imaginary Luatha had a point. The chieftain had invited Brannon along for a reason—probably to act as Elwyn's counterweight. Except a stick in the assassin's hands might as well have been a cudgel. For the sake of both the captive and her conscience, she would need to scrounge up a switch of her own.

"You haven't asked about your crew," she noted, scanning the man's face for any hint of emotion. His scowl deepened by a twitch. Good enough. "You do think of them as your crew, don't you? They clearly consider *you* their captain. A waste of faith if you ask me." She sighed, shaking her head. "When we came to their rescue this morning, you were nowhere to be seen. Probably cowering below deck, waiting for the screams to die down." She leaned forward to meet his glare, matching it for chill. "I would leverage information about their wellbeing, but we both know you're too craven to care."

The sailor's cold disregard jolted to rage, and he lurched upright, shoulder leveled as a ram. Elwyn sidestepped the attack with ease. The oraithvine bindings snagged his ankles, sending him stumbling forward. He would have hit the ground nose-first had Brannon not rushed forward and slammed him back into the chair, pressing the scalpel to his jugular.

Judging from the assassin's wildcat grin, the months with the Sylphs hadn't reformed him much.

"Off the top of my head, there are twenty-two places I could lodge this without impeding your speech," Brannon said, practically salivating as he placed pressure on the blade. "You'd be surprised how much agony a soul can endure before fleeing the body."

The captive tipped his chin back in invitation. It wasn't a challenge so much as a plea.

Elwyn knew well that broken, bitter resignation. It fell on her whenever she glimpsed a pale-haired child in the crowd or conjured an ill-metered couplet.

Brannon could not threaten a man with nothing left to lose, but that did not mean the cause was likewise lost. If the sailor's sorrow was truly a match for Elwyn's own, there was still one reward worth dangling, however impossible it seemed.

"Justice," she whispered, a cold resolve seeping through her. "We can't mend whatever bones your foes have broken, and we can't erase the scars they've left behind, but we can see their deeds repaid—blow for blow, slice for slice."

"Justice?" the man repeated like he was tasting the word for poison. "You really think those creatures you've cozied up to would turn on their own for our sake?"

Elwyn could guarantee no such thing. While Amatha would take pity on the Pondrellens' plight, hers was not the final word on the matter.

"Not *their own*." She shrugged her doubts aside to parse through later. "As I tried to explain before, the Seelie and Unseelie are opposites. But yes, I believe our allies would relish a chance to confront their foes, if only as a show of authority. Don't trust their goodwill? Fine. Trust their sense of self-preservation. That note rings the same in any chamber."

Her words seemed to reach Brannon first, and he lowered his scalpel with eerie calm. The sailor slumped in his chair, exhaling the last of his defiance.

"What do you need to know?" he asked.

Elwyn pulled the logbook from her satchel, flipping to a blank page. "Start from the beginning."

He laughed, cold and curt. "You're gonna' need a bigger ledger..."

"Each action begs a consequence, so take them all in stride,
A fall from grace won't kill you, though it might well bruise your pride."

CHAPTER 4
A LOFTY VIEW
AEDYN

 he staircase to the royal balcony seemed to stretch for miles. Aedyn took his precious time in climbing it, pausing every few steps to straighten his stag-spike circlet or smooth his silk jacket. He had no idea what manner of lecture awaited him at the end of the trek, and the unknown had never felt so intimidating.

Desperate to cobble his defense in advance, he ran through a mental checklist of recent misdeeds. There were dozens of options, really—the trysts, the gambling, the potions, the...well, there was that one time he'd hopped worlds and inadvertently brought about the greatest disaster in recorded history. He'd been waiting for *that* hammer to fall for months now, but it seemed content to hover there, gleaming darkly just above his skull.

Too soon, the staircase spilled out onto a glittering sandstone balcony overlooking the patchwork kingdom. King Aryn stood at the railing, his armor and antlered crown set ablaze by the midday sun. Were it not for the soft rustle of his emerald cape, Aedyn might have mistaken him for one of Samhria's gilded statues, so sharp were his features and so sturdy his stance.

"You're late," the king said, eyes fixed on the horizon. "Again."

Aedyn swallowed a useless apology, drifting forward to join his father. "You asked that I be both sober and presentable. Punctuality was out of the question."

"It's a miracle you bothered to show at all. To hear Eloana tell it, you're still struggling to keep appointments."

Aedyn stifled a sigh. Ever since the Confluence, his father had been inordinately concerned about the state of his... Could it be called a relationship? Aedyn hadn't spent a single unenforced second with his betrothed, and his fancies were famous for fluttering about wildly. The one time they'd threatened to land, it had been far from Eloana.

"It's complicated." He buried thoughts of an endearing, raven-haired thief before they could bury him. "You wouldn't understand."

"Oh?" The king arched an eyebrow. "You speak as though I was never young."

"You weren't. Not really."

Where Aedyn was freshborn—a new soul, as yet untested by the cycle —his father had been crowned at the creation of the worlds. He'd lived dozens of auspicious lives since, each lauded in legend. Those memories had surely spurred him past any rebellious bouts he might otherwise have humored.

"Our pasts filter in as we ripen," the king explained, eons dancing in his golden eyes. "As a child, I remembered only my childhoods. As a youth, I remembered my youths. Now a man, I can call upon guidance from countless trials and triumphs, blessings and blights, pleasures and pains, and I know well what each will ask of me. Unfortunately for the both of us, I've no past fatherhoods to lean on." Something strange flickered across his face. It might even have been an emotion. "Perhaps that is why I've failed you."

The sentiment startled Aedyn. There was only one failure in the royal bloodline, and it was certainly not the king. "You haven't failed me," he said, fighting the strangest impulse to pat his father's shoulder. "You've never failed at anything. That's my point."

"Oh, but I have." The king's fingers flexed around the marble railing. "I have been far too patient with your antics. What I had figured for phases have settled into traits, all of them empty. Clearly my lenience has stunted your growth."

"Lenience?" Aedyn spat, rage blazing through him. "You've shown me anything but. From my birth on, you've chosen my studies, my trainings, my duties, even my *bride*! I've stolen every freedom I've ever tasted; of course a few were poisoned!" He waved toward the realm's ruined outskirts and the feral wilds beyond. The uncharted regions had been begging to meet him, and their call was growing unbearable. "If you hadn't barred me from joining the Guard, I could be out there right now, helping to—"

"Enough!"

The shout ricocheted off Samhria's ramparts and struck Aedyn like an arrow. He stumbled back, defenses shattered to splinters.

King Aryn closed his eyes, exhaling slowly through his nose. It was the closest he'd ever come to sighing aloud. "Do you think I haven't noticed where your *help* has gotten us?" he asked. "Rant about redemption all you'd like. I will not give you a chance to make matters worse than you already have."

The unpleasant truth rubbed Aedyn's skin raw. If he hadn't meddled in the affairs of mortals, Blithely would have captured Lydia before her sacrifice could bring about the Confluence, and nothing would have changed for the worlds or their inhabitants. But then Lydia wouldn't have lived out her final days among friends, Brannon would still be serving a sadistic priest, and Elwyn...

Aedyn couldn't bring himself to regret his decisions. Were the choices presented anew, he'd have made the exact same ones.

"This is not how I wanted this conversation to go," the king continued, his voice uncharacteristically soft. "The desire to defend one's realm is noble, and you if you must fixate upon something, you've chosen well. While you are not yet ready for the battlefield, the tactical table is another matter."

Aedyn blinked, bewildered by the shift in tone. "What are you saying?"

"I am saying your wit might one day prove useful, if properly applied. As luck would have it, I just received a message from Chieftain Hearthblade requesting a Seelie Council. Pending the approval of my peers, we will meet tomorrow at noon. Your presence is expected."

Amatha loathed bureaucracy nearly as much as Aedyn did. She wouldn't have requested a Council without good reason.

"You can count on me," he said, interest piqued.

His father dismissed him with the flick of a wrist. "Wouldn't that be refreshing?"

TAWNY

A watched pot never boils. That's what Yana always said. Tawny stared the cauldron down, refusing to heed her once-mother's warning. That woman was not to be trusted. Not anymore.

Steam wafted from the placid brew, adding to the already sweltering humidity of Chieftain Hearthblade's workshop. The Red Realm—Réimsdarg, as the Daoine Sidhe called it—was equally stifling and intriguing, with its molten rivers and zealous crimson sun. Amatha's clay cliffside building wasn't much cooler than the wilderness that sprawled around it. And to think, the temperature had supposedly dropped since the Confluence, when the kingdom melded with a barren desert in the mortal land of Selea. At least, the cacti and wild game were Selean, according to mortal field guides. It had not yet been determined whether the realms had merged according to location, climate, or some mysterious factor no one had thought to consider.

Réimsdarg probably wasn't the best subject for a study. Its inexplicable link to Talunasa had survived the Confluence, making even cartography impossible. In descending the stone staircase that swept down from the Capitol Colosseum, one would soon find themselves climbing Talune's roots. Wander too far in any direction—in either realm—and Rhysia's alabaster beaches would sweep into view.

It was a puzzle. One Tawny would have quite enjoyed solving, had she space in her schedule. Alas, as the Myriad Guard's foremost (and only) spellcrafter, her time was not hers to waste. The chieftain had requested another travel potion, so Tawny would not rest until the order was filled. It was the least she could do, with how Amatha had taken her in—no questions, no aspersions, no eying her like the Shadow-damned specter of a girl she'd only met in passing.

Tawny sprinkled a dash of rot-fae flakes and a pinch of Pondrellen petal blend tea into the cauldron, praying to the Shadows that she'd guessed the correct components. She'd been lucky to get the Rhysien-Talunasan travel potion right on her third try. The first attempt had her tasting sounds for an hour, and she'd turned a lovely shade of teal for a day after testing the second. In the end, it had taken an ingredient apiece exclusive to the realms in question—oraithvine from Talunasa and Rhysien russet potatoes —to craft an effective tincture. Hopefully, that pattern held for the supposed Pondrellen-Shifting Wilds.

Impatient as ever, Tawny paced around the workshop, perusing a plethora of militant wares she'd never have need of. The Sidhe were renowned for their metalcraft, and Amatha's creations were especially stunning. If someone were to display them within the gilded halls of Samhria, the Maithe murals would weep with envy.

An ornate silver axe stood proudly atop a sculpted marble plinth, its shaft braided from gold and platinum. Filigree swords and burnished spears sprouted from overstuffed bins, so sleek they seemed to glow in the lamplight. Gemstone-studded boots and gauntlets overcrowded the shelves, and full suits of dobhriste stood sentry in the corners, each plate etched with dancing flames, fearsome beasts, or sprawling deciduous trees.

Tawny grew a touch more restless with every marvel glimpsed. Amatha was a brilliant smith, a fearsome fighter, and an inspiring leader, whereas *she* still struggled with simple spellcraft. She envied the fae their do-overs. How convenient it must have been to have tried it all before—to begin the trek with an idea of which paths led to dead-ends, which would prove too steep, and which were formed to suit one's feet. To know, deep down, that if you failed to find your purpose, you could simply try again the next time around.

She jarred to a stop, catching her reflection in a polished buckler. Nothing about her body seemed to match her spirit. Her frame was too soft and spindly, curved in all the wrong places. Her eyes were too young and bright for the dark deeds they'd witnessed. The long, yellow hair her once-mother had lauded was tangled and unruly, and it weighed on her like grief.

Perhaps her features fit wrong because they belonged to another. Technically, Lydia had been *Tawny's* changeling, but the opposite might as well have been true. Everyone who'd known the girl saw Tawny as an echo —hollow, redundant, and fated to fade away. That, or they suspected Yana had sent her to spy on the Seelie Court, as many whispered when her back was turned. Those rumors couldn't have been further from the truth.

"Well, you won't prove them wrong by glaring at yourself all day," she muttered to the makeshift mirror. The gargle of a bubbling brew caught her ear, and she whirled to glare at the rebellious cauldron. *Yana's still a liar in every way that counts!*

Tawny ladled a serving into a tiny tin tumbler, allowing it to cool before downing it in a single gulp. In her roughly seventeen years, she'd subjected herself to many a foul flavor—syrups thickened with toad slime, medicines mixed with muddled molds, spirits distilled from the putrid pollen of the grave flower—but this potion made the worst of them seem sweet. Her surroundings melted to an eddy as the drink stabbed its way through her, and the earthy smears spun a little more swiftly with each pang. Gravity tugged her in all directions, suspending her in the haze for a disorienting moment before spitting her out onto a crisp carpet of autumn leaves.

Eyes clenched tight, she lost herself in a comforting chorus of *crackles* and *snaps*. Soon, the taste of bile abated, and a pleasant nutmeg breeze coaxed her upright.

The world still churned, but it was not the potion's doing. Branches swayed in defiance to the wind, their watercolor leaves flickering like fire. Serpentine roots writhed through chocolate-dark dirt patched with all manner of creeping mosses. Marshmallow fog billowed between trunks, cloaking sliver-thin trails and shifting streams. In the span of a sip, Tawny had leapt from a rigid realm of tedious order to a mercurial haven, devoid of absolutes. It felt like curling up hearthside after hours spent diving for river snails.

Laughter bubbled from Tawny's lips, unbidden. The Wilds did not shift as swiftly as before, their colors had muted, and their scents had dulled, but they still danced to a music of their own making. Her heart leapt at the thought of racing through the undergrowth, of scaling the knotted trunks of ancient oaks, of rifling through rot-rich soil in search of acorn caps and pink, wriggling nightcrawlers.

"There will be time for exploring later." She had to say the words aloud, or they wouldn't have convinced her.

She went about her business slowly, savoring every sight, sound, and smell she hadn't realized she'd missed. Too soon, she spotted a circle of standing stones perched atop a red clay mound—a fixed point in the otherwise labyrinthine landscape and a perfect tether for future travels. It took only a minute to mark the stones, half that to gather soil from their center. It took a full five to pull a shimmering green potion from her satchel and uncork it. The Rhysien-Talunasan potion tasted far better than most, but she dreaded drinking it all the same.

"I'll be back soon," she promised, sparing the Shifting Wilds a final, bittersweet glance before raising the bottle to her lips.

*"Your conscience and your consciousness may clash from time to time,
The more virtues you adhere to, the less often they align."*

CHAPTER 5

HOLLOW OATHS

AEDYN

alune's Heart was silent, save for the hushed conversation of the rulers gathered at its center. Aedyn had never been fond of the place—suffocating despite its spaciousness and cold despite the prolific sunlight—but it was doubly dull with politics at play. He would not be welcomed at the table until the guest of honor arrived, so he waited beside the throne room doors, trying and failing to read the High Judges' lips.

They were an impressive sight, for a trio of bureaucrats—seated in places of honor and dressed in full ceremonial regalia. Creagor, High Chieftain of the Daoine Sidhe, leaned forward in his sturdy bronze chair, sunbeams glinting off the jagged angles of his battle-worn obsidian shards. The silhouettes of flames flickered across his armor, and rubies studded the seams of his ceremonial cuirass. Soen, the Sylph Speaker-elect, perched primly in her silver chair, threading her fingers through silvery locks. She'd donned a gray gown as gauzy as her frosted glass complexion, and bluebells twined around her neck and wrists, several shades darker than her ice-water eyes. Aedyn's father stood behind his golden chair, hands folded atop the filigree backrest. He wore the same emerald cape and oraithvine armor as always, a tribute to his steadfast nature.

A fourth chair, crafted of cobalt and sea glass, sat empty.

As much as Aedyn hated to admit it, the Court looked incomplete without Mearalas, the insufferable Queen of the Undine. Though many believed Chorial had shattered, killing her and most of her subjects, he preferred to think they were simply lost in uncharted waters. He had never cared for Mearalas, but he cared very much for Elwyn, who had left her piskie in Chorial on the night of the Confluence. Piskies were loathsome parasites—Luatha more than most—but he far preferred her presence to Elwyn's sorrow.

Just thinking of Elwyn steeped Aedyn in guilt. It had been too long since he'd last visited her. Hopefully, she'd forgive his absence when he finally worked up the courage to end it. All he needed was a decent reason. Until then, he'd pass the time as he always had: by distracting himself with whatever was nearest and most shiny.

Bored with the judges and their mumbled musings—since when could Creagor whisper, anyway?—Aedyn shifted his attention to the dais beyond them, atop of which sat two gleaming thrones. The king's was crafted of golden antlers to match his majestic crown; the queen's was all frillroses and filigree, reminiscent of the slender floral circlet that rested upon its emerald cushion. It had been sitting there for as long as Aedyn could remember, awaiting a rebirth that would not occur until his father, too, passed into the cycle.

For perhaps the thousandth time, Aedyn imagined his mother smiling down at him from that throne. He knew from the portraits that he'd inherited her brazen eyes and slender frame. Legend held he'd also inherited her temperament. Capricious and clever, she'd long played the playful counterpart to her pious husband. If the War of Light and Shadow hadn't stolen her away, Aedyn might have known what it was to find favor in the eyes of a parent.

Metal bootsteps rang against marble as Amatha entered the room, clad in full dobhriste plate. If the High Judges noticed her entrance, they gave no sign.

"Chieftain Hearthblade." Aedyn bowed at the waist, playing at propriety. "I was beginning to fear you'd never show."

"I was delayed at the palace gates." Amatha feigned a glare. "Someone taught the sentries a rather peculiar salute, and they are convinced it was a direct order from me. You wouldn't know anything about that, hm?" Before Aedyn could answer, she pulled him into a crushing embrace. "I have missed you, friend, antics and all!"

Aedyn would have laughed had he the breath for it. "Careful...with the...suit." He wriggled from her arms and smoothed his jacket with his palms. "The last thing I need is another lecture on appropriate presentation."

"One benefit of armor." Amatha struck a statue-worthy pose. "No wrinkles."

"You wear it well," Aedyn said, genuinely impressed. Like most Sidhe, Amatha often attended events in uniform, but she'd never before looked quite so *leaderly*. Gemstone badges cluttered her crimson bandolier, each denoting a lofty accomplishment, and the violet cape clasped to her shoulders perfectly complemented her crystal shards. "You can't have put this effort in for the Judges' sake. I assume you're meeting up with someone pretty after the council..."

"I am not so lucky." Amatha chuckled, running her hand over her scalp shards. "It is possible the ladies find my armor intimidating."

"That settles it, then; I'll be reserving my armor for battle. Assuming I ever see it."

"Battle is not all the stories make it out to be." She leaned against the wall beside him, nodding toward the Judges. "Any idea what they are speaking of?"

"Us, probably." Aedyn shrugged. "Or rather, *me*."

"Do you not enjoy being the subject of talk?"

"Not this one, I don't think." He tipped his head toward his father. "I imagine he's apologizing in advance for my behavior, knowing it could never rise to his lofty standard. Do you know why he's still standing though everyone else is seated?"

"I am certain you will tell me."

"My father must be very careful in sitting," Aedyn smirked, "lest the stick up his ass poke straight through his skull."

Amatha burst into laughter, and it caught swiftly to Aedyn. The outburst drew a glare from the king and quizzical expressions from his more genial peers. Aedyn composed himself in record time, a mere chuckle behind his friend.

"Are you quite finished?" King Aryn asked as he and Creagor pulled a stool apiece from beneath the table.

The guests took it as their cue to approach. Amatha naturally nabbed the stool nearest her father, dooming Aedyn to beside his own. Envy flickered through him when Creagor patted his daughter on the back, the very picture of paternal pride, but he snuffed it out before it could flare. In cobbling together and leading the Myriad Guard, Amatha had earned every bit of praise tossed her way. Aedyn's most impressive accomplishment to date was going a full week without causing any chaos, and he'd been unconscious for most of it.

Once everyone had settled, the Sylph Speaker-elect raised her right hand. She waited for the others to follow suit before launching into the ceremonial oaths.

"For Honor," said Aryn.

"For Justice," said Creagor.

"For Love," said Soen.

The rhythm hitched, and eyes slid to the empty cobalt chair. If the silence was any thicker, it would have been visible.

"For Law," the rulers said, nearly in unison.

The words did not echo as they ought.

King Aryn finally took his seat, and to Aedyn's surprise and begrudging relief, no stick burst through his skull. "According to your missive, you've received distressing new information about the Unseelie," he said to Amatha, skipping over what remained of the traditional fanfare. "I trust you would not sound the alarm in vain. For the next thirty minutes, our time is yours. Use it wisely."

"As you are aware, the Guard has made great strides in recent months..." Amatha began by listing her many accomplishments as a chieftain, wisely reminding her audience of the value her opinions held. Having heard it all before, Aedyn struggled to pay attention. That is, until Amatha began to speak about a shipwreck her troop had stumbled upon the previous morning.

"Even after we rescued the sailors, they regarded us with an alarming level of distrust," she explained, sliding a leatherbound journal to the center of the table. "As it turns out, the Pondrellens have good reason to revile fae-folk. This record details the travesties they have suffered at the hooves of the Augusky. Murders, maulings, all manner of vile deed. You are welcome to read the specifics, though I suspect you will lose sleep to them."

Aedyn had never encountered an Augusky, though he knew them by their horrid reputation. The High Judges—all of whom had faced their hordes in one cycle or another—betrayed no fear at the mention of the beasts, but their apparent indifference meant little. That lot swallowed feelings more often than food. Which was saying something, given the sheer number of ritual feasts they organized and oversaw.

"I believe I understand what you are asking of us." King Aryn folded his hands on the table, attempting a sympathetic smile. "While I am certain your heart is in the right place, I'm afraid I must now appeal to your mind. Even if we could find the Shifting Wilds by testimony alone, the Treaty of Dusk forbids us from setting foot on Unseelie soil. This new world is unstable enough without provoking our foes. We must honor our alliances now, more than ever."

"What alliances?" Soen fluttered her lashes. "If I am not mistaken, the Treaty of Dusk was established along borders that no longer exist, and I am not convinced the Unseelie will recognize the spirit of the law, once the letter proves faulty. The sun has been rising and setting for months now. Let us not pretend the world stands still."

"Chaos exists to disrupt order," Creagor agreed, his heavy accent weighing on the words. "Mailair will attack soon enough, guaranteed. Is no telling whether Fuara will join them."

Aryn bristled at the mention of the Korrid queen. "She will honor the spirit of the law as she always has," he said, each syllable a razor. "Fuara has as much to lose as we do, should war break loose between our realms. Do not forget that it was she who penned the Treaty of Dusk in the first place." He inhaled deeply, smoothing the hard lines from his face. "Mailair is enough a threat in their own right. Should they discern our location, the Augusky will strike when the nights are long, and we are at our weakest. We should focus on shoring our defenses, not meddling in the matters of mortals beyond our reach."

"What, then, separates the Seelie from the Unseelie?" Aedyn's interjection earned a glare from his father, not that it made a difference. His tongue had slipped from its bridles, and there would be no wrangling it now. "Did the Creator not task us with shepherding mortals as proof of our penance? I know I've yet to pass through the cycle, but it seems this verdict would move us all a step backward, ascension-wise."

"We are shepherding those He has placed in our care," his father replied, jaw taught. "With winter on the way, we cannot afford to leave our shores unguarded."

"Nothing would be left unguarded," Aedyn argued. "A scouting mission would require only a small reconnaissance troop. Five, perhaps six of us—"

"Us?"

"—would do the trick, and to avoid detection, we—"

"We?"

"—would require only a touch of glamour. I've been practicing, and I—"

"*I*?" Aryn lurched upright, slamming his palms on the table. "If you think for one second that I would allow you to take part in this lunacy—"

Soen cleared her throat, and it somehow brought an end to the king's rant. "Clearly, this is a sensitive matter," she said, her placid tone contradicting the claim. "One we must discuss at length once our emotions have had time to settle. I move we reconvene in a week to cast our votes with clarity."

Soft though her voice was, Aedyn flinched at the suggestion. "But—"

"I second Soen's movement," Amatha interrupted, locking eyes with him. For once, he could not read the sentiment behind them. "I am grateful my concerns were heard, and I look forward to revisiting them."

"That settles it, then," Aryn said, returning to his gilt chair. "I cannot imagine my opinion will change, but these are strange days. Who knows what might happen in seven of them?" A hint of genuine concern— perceptible as a wisp of smoke—crossed his face when he next looked toward Amatha. "In the meantime, you must promise not to act without our express permission."

"Yes," Soen agreed, almost too swiftly. "It is important we don't act in haste, even for the most valiant cause. You must vow not to depart from these shores until we've rendered our verdict."

"More, you must promise not to send others in your stead," Aryn added, ever on the lookout for loopholes. Oath passed through fae lips served as sturdy chains, and he would not allow for weak links. "I would not spare a single soldier for this fools' errand."

"You have my word," Amatha said, bowing from the shoulders up. "I will not depart from these shores, nor will I allow another to do so."

Aryn arched an eyebrow at his son. "And you?"

Aedyn's nails bit his palms. He shot Amatha one final, pleading glance, but she returned it with a resolute nod. This was her meeting, her mission, and her decision. He should never have usurped the conversation to begin with. So he repeated the vow, syllable for syllable. It left a sour taste in his mouth.

Apparently satisfied, the High Judges dismissed the meeting with a second round of hollow oaths.

Aedyn lay listless on his heather mattress, staring past the puzzle cube he'd been fiddling with for hours. Embroidered leaves had once branched across a cloudless blue canopy above, but he'd recently traded them for a silver starscape on navy. Some of his very best moments had been lived beneath a midnight sky; the sun had witnessed the worst of them.

The potions hidden in his parlor promised decadence and distraction, but he resisted their call, knowing they wouldn't solve a Shadow-damned thing. What he truly wanted was to crawl out his window and descend several stories to knock on Elwyn's, though she'd likely shove him straight to Talune's roots. Creator knows he deserved it.

The door creaked open without so much as a cursory knock.

"I'm terribly busy, Learo." Aedyn twisted the puzzle cube at random. "Whatever it is, can we reschedule?"

Learo sighed "And to think, I've already prepared her favorite tea."

Aedyn sniffed, catching a whiff of mushrooms beneath the usual honey and charmblossom perfumes that permeated his private wing. He knew only one person who took her tea with moss flakes. He'd figured she'd give him a wide berth through the night, given how he'd stormed from Talune's Heart.

"Is everything alright?" he asked, sitting up.

"I cannot possibly know the state of everything, sir." Learo shrugged, rattling the porcelain atop his tea tray. "Amatha looks to be in good spirits, though she claimed her business was urgent. If you truly wish for me to turn her out—"

"Unnecessary." Aedyn hopped to his feet, tossing his puzzle cube aside. "As it happens, my schedule just cleared."

"I thought it might."

Aedyn followed Learo to the dining hall—a room he'd been avoiding for months. Simply glimpsing his banquet table summoned phantoms of overturned dishes and food spatter, and of Elwyn crouching at its center with a butterbread loaf raised like a rapier. That mock battle had been the single beam of sunlight on an otherwise stormy day, yet the memory made his chest ache. He could take meals in his parlor just fine without dredging up unwanted daydreams.

Thankfully, Amatha's presence at the table would help to ground him in the present. Her dobhriste plates and gemstone pauldrons gleamed in the light that rained from the crystal chandelier, but both paled to the grin with which she greeted him.

"Don't take this as a suggestion," Aedyn took the chair beside hers, "but shouldn't you be seething? Not three hours have passed since you presented the High Judges with news about our nemeses, and they brushed it aside like you'd suggested rescheduling the Midsummer Ball for late autumn. Surely that bothers you."

Amatha's smile somehow stretched wider. "They did not *all* brush it aside."

"Not directly, perhaps. Soen has always been the most compassionate of the lot, but she's also the cleverest and the most subtle by far. If she truly believed in your cause, she'd have twisted the meeting to your favor."

Amatha nodded, gesturing for him to carry the thought a step further.

Aedyn's cheeks warmed. He was often a fool, but it was rare he felt like one. "If Soen left a loophole large enough for us to jump through, I missed it," he admitted. "I noticed she'd put her guile to work diffusing the general tension, but I never suspected she'd subvert the will of her peers."

"Oh, for light's sake!" Learo thrust the tea tray onto the table, toppling a tower of salted biscuits. "At least wait until I leave the room before you start conspiring against the Court. I swear, you two strive to make my deniability implausible!"

Amatha chuckled as Learo marched away with his ears covered, a mumbled rant trailing after him. Aedyn's nostrils burned at the rich aromas of peat and puffball mushrooms wafting from the kettle as she poured herself a drink. Personally, he preferred sweet to savory, but he'd long made a habit of keeping Sidhe refreshments on hand for his friend.

"Did you not notice how swiftly Soen composed our oaths?" She dipped a biscuit into her tea and let it soak. "Where your father would have banned our travels altogether, she clarified that we are not to leave the shores. Specific, hm?"

Aedyn hadn't thought so at the time. Magical transportation was once commonplace, but that was before the Melding Caverns collapsed, the Seer's Mirror went missing, and the travel potions stopped working altogether. "You clearly know something I don't..."

"Many things, actually." Amatha devoured the biscuit in a single bite. "Though, in this instance, my spellcrafter's knowledge is more relevant. She discovered the recipe for a Rhysien-Talunasan potion a week ago. Upon learning the Shifting Wilds merged with the mortal nation of Pondrelle, she was able to craft another."

An impressive feat. The palace potionsmiths had been given the same task months before, but they'd yet to report any progress. "Soen knew about this?"

A mischievous gleam sparked in Amatha's eyes. "The Guard has been trading components with the Sylphs for months now. I made a point of dealing with the Speaker-elect directly, dropping little details here and there. I do not doubt she pieced them together before the meeting."

"And you're certain she hasn't told my father?"

"She will tell him when it suits her." Amatha drained her teacup. "With Mearalas gone, judgement tips to your father's favor, but his passive politics do not suit a world where knowledge translates to literal power. Our mission will provide Soen with valuable information, and she will not have to move her hand, much less show it. If that information happens to prove protecting Pondrelle is in the Court's best interest..." She shrugged. "Everyone wins."

Aedyn couldn't help smiling. For once, Soen's mind had not been the sharpest at the table. "I have to hand it to you, Amatha—you're becoming quite the trickster."

"*Tactician*," she corrected with a humble smirk. "If trickery slips into the occasional plan, it is only because I have learned from the best."

Aedyn chuckled. "If that's the case, I hope you've been crediting me in your award speeches."

"You make a decent point." Amatha looked down at her cluttered bandolier, carefully eying each of her badges. After a moment's consideration, she plucked a pale crystal from among the many. "This was presented to me for remaining calm in the midst of chaos," she said, pinning the brooch to Aedyn's collar. "Managing *your* chaos was decent practice. Besides, quartz is said to ward off sorrow and confusion. I suspect you need it more than I do."

"Are they that obvious?" Aedyn asked, resisting the urge to fold inward. "The sorrow and confusion?"

"Not at all. But I know you."

That she most certainly did. Aedyn had always been an illusionist, and not all his disguises were magical. Amatha could see through each of them. For some reason, she liked him anyway.

"It sounds like we have quite an adventure ahead of us." Just glancing at the gifted badge brightened his spirits. Perhaps the quartz was doing its job, though he suspected it was simply the company. "High stakes, vague goals, a hefty helping of danger. Dare I ask which lucky souls you plan to invite along?"

"Some sentiments are not content to fade into the past,
They cling to you despite the fact they weren't made to last."

CHAPTER 6

PHANTOM PAINS

ELWYN

lwyn startled awake, thrust from slumber by yet another nightmare. She drew her dagger on reflex, slicing through her pillow's slipcase and freeing a flurry of feathers. Rosy dusk-light filtered through her lattice windows, only a shade deeper than when she'd last glimpsed it. Hours spent sulking had bought her mere minutes of sleep.

It wasn't the echoes of battle that bothered her—she could handle the haunting howls, the snapping jaws, the scarlet spatter. Nor was it the sailor's stories, though his bloody account still churned her stomach. But the memories of timid giggles and cautious questions, of corpse-cold fingers clasping hers for comfort and lavender eyes shining up at her...

Sleep was overrated, anyway.

"Why do you think that you deserve a single night's reprieve?
You've done nothing to avenge the child, and even less for me."

"Not for lack of trying," Elwyn muttered to herself. The words rang hollow. She hadn't tried so much as begged, and feebly at that. The chieftain had no answers to her questions about the Shifting Wilds, and the Guard had more pressing matters to attend to. Hopefully, the

Pondrellens' sad tale would stoke interest in the lands beyond the sea, especially given the supposed proximity of Unseelie forces. People tended to care more about wildfires when a shift of wind could send the flames searing toward them.

A knock on the door spurred Elwyn to her feet, dagger raised, but she tucked *Gelah* beneath her ruined pillow a moment later. While most soldiers were housed near Talune's roots, her connections had afforded her a lavish chamber near the crown. If something sinister had climbed all that way to find her, it would not have bothered knocking.

The rapping continued, growing louder by the second.

"One moment!" She pulled a random tome from a bookcase she'd yet to peruse and splayed it, pages down, on her bedside table. If the chieftain had decided to check in on her—as she'd often threatened—she didn't want to look like she'd been moping for two days straight. Even if she had been.

The door opened on a slender Sylph woman. At least, it *looked* like a Sylph, with its clouded quartz complexion and daisy white hair. Elwyn had grown so accustomed to Aedyn's illusions she could practically see through them.

"Miss me?" he asked, pitching his voice an octave too high.

She slammed the door in his face.

"Oh, now don't be like that!" He pounded on the door, oblivious to the unlatched deadbolt on the other side. "If you don't let me in, how can I properly grovel?"

It wasn't the worst argument. That, and his ruckus was bound to draw unwanted attention. She counted to ten before opening the door and allowing him to stumble inside. He regained his poise in a matter of steps, dropping his disguise with a snap of his fingers. A blink, and his colors returned—a palette of rich, golden-brown hues not dissimilar from Talune's sun-soaked bark or autumn-touched leaves. His pressed emerald suit and golden circlet might have looked proud, were it not for his wilted shoulders and downcast gaze.

Just like that, Elwyn's resentment fled, displaced by inexplicable pity. It was infuriatingly difficult to remain angry at Aedyn long enough to make an impression.

"So, to what do I owe this honor?" She perched on a side table, worried her feet might wander his direction if granted access to the floor. He didn't need to know she'd forgiven him just yet. "Have you finally grown so tired of drunken carousing that a night of biscuits and board games sounds novel?"

"Tempting," he said, all but collapsing into the nearest chair. "Alas, I'm here on business, though I understand why you'd like another round of Stand-off. Given my recent victory spree, you must be desperate to repair your shattered honor."

Elwyn had won three of the last five games. "My honor is very much intact, thank you."

Aedyn arched an eyebrow. "I could help with that."

"Cad!" She plucked an apple from the basket beside her and lobbed it at him. He caught it with far too much ease, took a crisp bite, and tossed the rest in a waste bin. "And since when do you go anywhere *on business?*"

"Since the Unseelie overtook the mortal mainland," he replied, suddenly serious. "I had the supreme displeasure of attending a Seelie Council yesterday, when Amatha told the High Judges about the Pondrellen refugees. You played a part in their rescue, didn't you?"

The note of admiration in his voice made Elwyn uncomfortable. She ought to have felt a sense of accomplishment, but grief had claimed too much of her heart to allow for petty emotions like pride. "The chieftain vowed to bring the news to the Court," she said, tamping that grief down as best she could. "I didn't think they would hear her out so soon."

Aedyn huffed. "Hearing is all they're any good for."

"I take it they refused to look into things." Elwyn failed to filter the disappointment from her voice. She hadn't expected the rulers to care about mortals they'd never met, but she'd still *hoped*. A terrible habit, that.

"They weren't always like this, you know?" Aedyn half-sighed, sinking against the brocade backrest. "At least, that's what everyone claims. The High Judges are bound to their words, like any common fae, only they vow themselves to the same ideal over and over until there's nothing else left to them—no whimsy, no wonder, no *nuance*. Creagor and Soen aren't so bad, being sworn to Love and Justice, but Honor is a stringent virtue, unyielding by nature. Even if Amatha had swayed the others, she never stood a chance of changing my father's mind."

"So, that's the end of it..." Elwyn shook her head. A miserably short story, given the stakes.

"Don't despair." Aedyn smiled, and the shadows fled the room. "It's not as though I've never defied the judges before!"

That didn't make Elwyn feel better. She'd witnessed what happened to fae who rebelled against the Court, and it wasn't pleasant. Images of Elgard Springbristle's forced transformation had clung to her like field burrs. He'd shared a moment—perhaps even a genuine connection—with an enemy of the Seelie. For that, they stole his color, his light, and his soul, banishing him to a land of endless winter.

Elwyn couldn't help picturing Aedyn with sallow skin and milky eyes. Would he still be able to smile like that if they robbed him of his warmth?

"You can't simply ignore their wishes."

"Never underestimate my ignorance," he said, much too lightheartedly. "Besides, it's not as though I intend to go alone. Amatha's gathering a few others with plans to meet at the Feral Ferret. I was hoping we could head out early and catch up over drinks." He rubbed his neck, color kissing his cheekbones. "That is, assuming you're interested in any of this."

A trip to the Shifting Wilds could well place Elwyn within stabbing distance of Yana—the opportunity she'd been desperate for since that first tragic meeting. Getting out of the palace didn't sound terrible either. "I'm mildly interested."

"I thought as much." Aedyn's confidence returned all at once. "Creator knows you could use a break from the constant moping."

"I have not been moping!" Elwyn gestured toward the alibi on her nightstand, grateful she'd thought to secure one. "I've been reading."

"That so?" Before she could answer, Aedyn darted across the room and scooped up the book. "*A Visual Guide to Fertility Rites and Rituals*," he read aloud, examining the cover. "What exactly did I interrupt, Elwyn?"

Her cheeks caught fire. "What? No! I was just—"

Aedyn chuckled, turning the tome toward her. The title read *A Comprehensive Catalogue of Talunasan Songbirds*.

"—lying," she said, her shoulders sinking. "I was just lying."

"You're terrible at it." He tossed the book over his shoulder. It landed on her bed with a silk-muffled *thud*, stirring a feathery plume. "So, what do you say? Shall we have a little fun before we march off to our doom?"

Elwyn sighed, slipping to her feet. "You certainly know how to persuade a girl."

"Lots of practice."

"Cad!"

"So I keep hearing. Now, about preparations. Don't worry about supplies—Amatha's got those covered—but a decent ensemble..." Aedyn flung her wardrobe doors open and scowled at the monochrome contents. "*Creator*, Elwyn! Do you own nothing but uniforms?"

"Technically, those are on lend." She plucked her threadbare cloak from the back of a chair. "But this is mine."

Aedyn eyed the garment like it owed him money, shook his head, then resumed his rummaging. By the time Elwyn crossed the room to join him, he'd scrounged up a basic tunic, some suede tights, and a set of leather armor.

"I suppose I should give you some privacy," he said, thrusting the clothing into her arms. "Unless, of course, you'd like help undressing. I'm something of an expert."

"Out, Aedyn!"

BRANNON

Once more, Brannon drifted through darkness, freed from the weight of his bones, the confines of his skin. He clung tightly to memories from the last meditation, lest they abandon him to relive the same nightmare. If he had to confront his fathers again, he would do so with full knowledge of his past failings.

Any second now, the void would vanish, spewing him into Saint Aldrich's Sanctuary. Any second now, the oil in his veins would spark alight, catching to vaulted rafters and velvet pews. Any second now, he'd break the men who had broken his spirit one welt at a time.

Any second now...

The darkness dissolved all at once, retreating from a nascent inferno, and a sudden burst of color nearly blinded Brannon. Sunshine yellow paint bubbled on every surface. Golden flames gnawed their way up quaint floral curtains. Paper curled from the walls in brittle, blackened spirals, and ghost-gray smoke swirled against the ceiling slats. There were no stained-glass windows present to cast murals on the floor, but the mosaic remains of shattered dishes had a similar effect.

A world away, Brannon's pulse spiked.

"Who set the fire?" Ferea's voice rippled like a mirage.

Whoever it was, they'd done him a massive favor. He'd contemplated setting the farmhouse aflame when he'd abandoned it all those years ago, but cremation was too good for his pa. That bastard deserved to bloat, to fester, to serve as a banquet hall for maggots and darkling beetles until nothing but bones remained.

Dozens of buried memories unearthed themselves, guiding Brannon through the farmhouse even as they grasped at his ankles. He tried to keep his focus trained on the present as he slipped between the cluttered rooms, but each crocheted shawl and overstuffed flowerpot brought with it an echo. Most were stark and brutal, shadows of balled fists and broken bottles, but the softest somehow struck the hardest—slender hands guiding his to knead oatcake dough, willowy arms outstretched to shield him, a sorrow-thick voice reciting poems once the evening's danger had passed and he could safely drift to sleep.

The garden door swung ajar on rusty hinges. Brannon blew across the threshold into the pall of a shrouded moon, breathing deeply despite his troublesome lack of lungs. A wind-tousled pasture stretched ahead of him, and a lone figure sliced a gash through the tall grass. Her silver-streaked hair wafted in a gentle breeze as she marched toward a distant, autumn-gilt forest.

Brannon fell still. He did not need to see her face to know her. He did not need to hear her voice or smell the flour on her skin.

He remembered her best for walking away.

Anger seared through Brannon, brighter and more consuming than the flames that devoured the farmhouse at his back. He stalked forward on impulse, becoming more solid with every step. Rage thrummed through his veins even as they formed. Fresh teeth clenched so hard his jaw ached. A pair of trusty daggers appeared in his hands, his knuckles flushed red around the hilts.

Though his skin prickled with anticipation, he could not feel the moonlit breeze on his cheeks, couldn't smell the dry reeds or hear them crackle underfoot. Try though he may to ground himself in the meadow, incense burned his nostrils, and a gossamer tent rustled in his ears. He could practically feel Ferea's presence, buzzing with healing power and impractical faith. He slowed his steps, straining to catch a lecture that never came.

You mustn't feel rage here, Brannon told himself.

It didn't ring the same in his own voice.

Perhaps the Sylph had fluttered off, foolishly trusting him to his own devices. Test or not, he would treat it as an opportunity, perhaps even a gift. How fortunate he was to slip the shackles of time and space, to revisit his past as a fully formed monster, claws and fangs at the ready. Few wolves were given the chance to avenge the whelps they'd once been.

He hastened toward his target, fire springing from his footsteps. The woman somehow failed to notice the violent bursts of red and gold that swept through the field. Soon he was close enough to spy the little buttercups that dotted her linen dress, the violets embroidered on her belt, the sprig of larkspur tucked behind her ear.

She'd been fond of flowers of any ilk—asters, daisies, wild mountain honeysuckle. He used to pluck lilies and goat willow from the creek and bring them to her by the bundle. She'd cast roses from centerpieces to make room for them.

"Brannon."

Ferea's voice made Brannon trip over his newfound feet. Leave it to his mentor to interrupt at the least opportune time. He gritted his teeth, casting the Sylph's warning aside and clenching his daggers tight as he continued after his quarry. Just a few more steps, and vengeance would finally be—

"Brannon, wake up."

Static sparked around his upper arm, and the world around him wavered. He pried the invisible fingers free and broke into a sprint. He needed only to stay under a little longer, to press a little further, to reach a little—

"Brannon!"

Where Ferea's commands hardly registered, *this* voice was a thunderclap. It rippled outward through the tallgrass, growing deeper and denser and louder by the wave. Brannon buckled as the dreamscape shattered—the field, the woods, the woman dissolving to dust. He woke to shadows and lanternlight, coughing up a cloud of incense.

A pair of silhouettes loomed over him. One was a familiar, hazy wisp, the other a massive blotch. Brannon knew that blotch, with its broad shoulders and jagged edges. He'd known the voice from his vision, too. Connecting the traits to a name was another matter.

"The waking process is meant to be gradual." Ferea's words hovered near his ears, one flit away from landing. "His thoughts may lag for a few minutes, and his words will do the same. Please, Chieftain, forgive the wait."

"Cheefan?" Brannon's lips were too numb to connect correctly, which only served to further frustrate him. He vaguely recalled having spoken to a chieftain the day before and would have liked to be fully present for the follow-up conversation.

"What are these herbs?" chimed a voice bright enough to make his skull ache. It came not from either shape but from somewhere behind him. "I've read that Sylphs use charmblossom and shadowroot to enhance trances, but I don't recognize these petals or little yellow seeds. Are they from some kind of poppy?"

Brannon's stomach tossed when he spun, forcing acid to his tongue. With a bit of squinting, he recognized the gangly silhouette that knelt beside the censer—Tammy, or Tipsy, or...Well, it wasn't Lydia, he knew that much!

"Whutryoudoinhere?" He aimed the question at not-Lydia, but he would have accepted an answer from anyone.

"Sifting through incense," Not-Lydia replied innocently. "If I can subdue the hallucinogenic effects, these components might make a decent numbing agent. Only I'll need to know the origins of each, and whether—"

"Those matters must wait." The chieftain's voice sounded less thunderous in the waking world, but only just. "Soen kindly granted us permission to go about our business, but she was clear we are to do so swiftly and without causing a stir."

Brannon turned around, cautiously this time. After a few blinks, the blot took on shape, color. Violet crystals jutted from onyx shoulders. Gemstones studded her copper armor. Indigo eyes stared him down, sharp enough to pierce steel.

Hearthblade. That's what Elwyn had called the Sidhe woman. An imposing presence, but not a threat.

"I did not mean to interrupt." She studied his face in a way that made him wonder if the incense had made him drool. He absently rubbed his lip.

"Unfortunately, our business cannot wait. Do you recall yesterday's interrogation?"

"Bits and pieces." Brannon smiled at the sound of his consonants falling in line. If his speech was clearing, his thoughts would soon follow suit.

"Which bits?" The chieftain's eyes darted to the Sylph and back—the universal signal for *watch your words*. Apparently, Ferea was not in whatever loop he'd somehow fallen into. "Do you recall enough to accept an invitation to follow up on the information gathered?"

If it meant avoiding another pointless meditation, he would have accepted an invitation to wrestle a brown bear. Brannon nodded slowly, lest he come across as overeager. With how Ferea winced, one might've thought he'd stabbed her.

"I trust that you have thought this through," the Sylph said, her tone transparently untrusting, "and that you have fully weighed the consequences."

Brannon knew exactly what she was asking. Sylph mentorships were seldom offered, especially to outsiders. Once cast aside, they could not be taken up again.

That was probably for the best.

"I'll need my daggers back," he said, refusing to meet her gaze straight on.

Ferea turned to Hearthblade and bowed at the waist. "Please allow my pupil to accompany me in retrieving his possessions. It will take but a moment."

Not-Lydia chittered to the chieftain about herbs and other such nonsense as Brannon followed Ferea out into the gloaming. The crisp air cleared the remaining haze from his lungs almost instantly, and the previous day's interrogation came tumbling back to him. According to the sailor he'd helped to question, Pondrelle had combined with the Shifting Wilds, where Yana lived. Elwyn had all but assured him they'd be following up on the claim.

Brannon's fingers clenched, aching for his daggers. In slaying Lydia while she was under his protection, the Ghost Witch had bruised his pride. He would bruise her every rib in recompense.

Ferea remained perplexingly silent throughout the trek. Brannon had been expecting some manner of speech, perhaps an appeal to his better nature—assuming she still believed he possessed such a thing. This Sylph had wasted nearly three months trying to mold his emotions into something sightly, oblivious to how few he possessed and how shallow they truly were. Why not knead the misshapen clay one final time before the shape set?

Only once they reached Ferea's little pink tent—far smaller than the one she'd spared him, which said something of the Sylphs' perception of leadership—did she finally speak, and only then to instruct him to wait while she retrieved his worldly possessions.

Brannon did as told, but not without a profound sense of unease. The lack of a lecture felt...*anticlimactic*? No, that wasn't the right word. Disappointment was a dull emotion, too blunt to pierce skin and too soft to leave bruises. Whatever sentiment now plagued him had teeth like a scavenger hound, and it seemed intent on ripping his intestines free and devouring them in one sitting.

Guilt, perhaps?

He didn't care for it.

When Ferea next emerged, Brannon tore the burlap sack from her hands and ripped away the twine that bound it. He rifled through the trappings of his former life—smoke orbs, stockings, a broken pocket watch—and pulled one *Aras Tosc* free before dropping the sack at his feet. The hilt seemed to melt against the contours of his palm, familiar and firm.

"Oh, how I've missed you," he said, sliding the dagger from its supple leather sheath. The blade smiled back—a little too sleek, a little too silver. At the first opportunity, he would add a pleasing splash of scarlet.

"This is wrong." Soft though Ferea's voice was, it shattered the reunion. "I do not know the details of this mission, and it is not my place to question the Speaker-elect, but I know in my spirit this is wrong."

Brannon forced a laugh, carefully stowing his dagger. "I've done a lot of wrong things, and I've survived them all. Others were not so lucky."

"If you leave this path now, there will be no coming back to it," she replied, either missing or ignoring the joke. "Would you really risk all that you have learned? All that I have taught you?"

If that last meditation had proven anything, he'd learned fuck-all from Ferea's tutelage. But she didn't need to know that.

"My failures aren't yours." He hefted the sack over his shoulder, certain he'd have time to change after leaving the encampment. "You promised to teach me, and you kept your word. The learning part was my responsibility. Moving forward, I suggest you save your pity for more malleable pupils."

"It is not pity." Ferea donned what was likely her very first scowl. "I am not the sentimental fool you believe me to be, Brannon, and you are not... not as..." She stomped a dainty foot, balling her fists. "You are not as *fucking* broken as you think!"

Brannon had never heard a Sylph shout before, let alone swear. He blinked at Ferea for a few seconds before reclaiming control over his tongue. "You've been learning."

"As have you." She dipped her head, disappointment eclipsing her anger. "I hope, one day, you are wise enough to recognize it."

"There are few who offer solace where many would cast doubt,
Be mindful of the voices but learn when to tune them out."

CHAPTER 7

THE MEANING IN THE MADNESS

YANA

he screams might have shattered Yana's eardrums, were they coming from the outside.

Unfortunately, they were hers alone—echoes of the lives she might have lived, the paths she might have tread, the loves she might have... might have...might....

Shadows, they were loud!

And frenzied.

And shrill as claws on windowpanes.

Working despite the wails, Yana grabbed a fistful of thistle from her components shelf and chucked it into the cauldron. The brew bubbled its putrid thanks, steaming like a death-dank bog on a muggy afternoon.

One more ingredient, and she would finally buy herself some peace and quiet.

If only she could remember what it was.

With every sunrise—those happened in the Wilds now, thanks to her treacherous little bargain—it grew increasingly difficult to find meaning in the madness. If she let her thoughts wander, they seldom returned; if she grasped them too tightly, they crumbled like dried larkspur.

"Tawny!" she called out over the dread chorus. "Be a dear and hand me a cupful of...of..."

Tallow? Deathcap? Mint Leaf?

"...mint leaf. Yes, hand me the mint leaf."

Yana held out a palm and waited.

And waited.

And...

She whirled around, hands perched on her hips. "Tawny, I gave you an order!"

Her voice tolled like a funeral bell through the empty cabin.

Well, not *entirely* empty. Her spectral cat, Solstice, lay curled up beside the hearth, snoring softly atop a goat-skin rug. Dozens of vacant eyes blinked out from beneath the staircase, awaiting any orders she might shout on a whim. A cage of wingless rot-fae hung from a silver chain beside the door, chittering in their rhythmic, inscrutable fashion.

Tawny should have been there too, humming a skipping song as she went about the evening's chores or sitting hearthside with a spell scroll angled toward the firelight. She *would* have been there were it not for Yana's selfishness.

If only she hadn't...she hadn't...hadn't...

Oh, for Shadow's sake, would the screaming never cease?

Yana pored through her component bins, desperate for a salve. Blithely had warned her of this very plague on the selfsame night she'd bested him.

"You'd have been better off in my belly," he'd said, tearing their contract down the center. *"You've been marinating in your malice for far too long, lass. Simmer any longer, and you'll fall straight to pieces."*

Before the week was out, her mind began to fray. It hadn't stopped fraying since.

Thistledown and cinnamon spilled across the countertop. Shells, cloves, and rodent bones rattled on the floor. As Yana scoured her collection, a maelstrom of morbid memories drove her deeper into madness.

A dusk-dark dagger with a serpentine hilt.

A basalt altar etched with blasphemous prayers.

A pair of innocent emerald eyes darkened by betrayal.

The mint leaves were stashed on the bottom shelf between a shaker of rot-fae dust and a matchbox stuffed with spriggan tails. Yana couldn't remember placing them there.

"I wouldn't have gone through with it." The brew swallowed her offering, sparkling venom green. "She must have known it was all a trick. I could never have—"

The lie coiled around her chest and squeezed tight, cutting itself short. If the Shadows accepted substitutes, her dagger would have found Tawny's heart as surely as it had lodged itself in Lydia's.

"Missstresssss...Yaaana..." a Shadow Goblin croaked, skulking into the hearth light. "The sssun...ssseeetssss...sssoooooon."

Yana's gaze darted to the window. The faintest rose-red glow filtered through moth-eaten curtains stitched with jacquard, signaling a world she could safely walk through.

"I'd best be on my way," she said, more to herself than the goblin.

She stirred the brew one final time, then ladled it directly into her mouth, not caring when it singed her lips, her tongue, her throat. After a decade of detachment, pain was a welcome reminder of the woman she'd once been. Never a saint, ever a survivor.

The moment she swallowed the potion, the screams softened to whispers. A second swig, and they vanished altogether. Inebriating as the silence was, she had no time to savor it. The tincture's effects would fade within hours, and she had business to attend.

"I'm off to an important meeting." She wrapped a herringbone shawl over her shoulders on her way to the door. "Tawny, be a dear and douse the..."

Yana's sentence snagged, catching on the present.

The standing stones spoke without uttering a word. Prayers and wishes spilled across their wind-worn surfaces, etched in ages past and having long outlived the supplicants. The scent of death hung heavy in the air, drawing in a frenzied swarm of flies.

Yana idled beside a basalt altar, darker than the one that plagued her dreams, though crafted as its kin. A polished agate sat atop it, etched with runes of binding and bathed in the blood of the highest Unseelie. Wulver, Selkie, Korrid—three sinful souls sent spiraling toward the Shadows.

A fourth would sate its thirst.

The soil inside the circle neither churned nor shuddered, but the forest beyond stirred like the contents of a cauldron. For all its fervor, the Wilds danced slowly now—more a waltz than a reel. Yana blamed it on the iron intermingled with the mortal soil. Fae foliage, though tenacious as those who trod it, struggled to flourish in poisoned earth.

She probed the shadows for the gleam of oval eyes or the glint of a yellow smile. Her allies were not known for punctuality, but she had hoped they would try this once. If they tarried much longer, the opportunity she'd been waiting for would sweep right past, violent and untethered.

At last, the foliage rustled—not merely with the eternal ripple of the canopy, but with a halting clutter of *crackles* and *snaps* undercut by marl-muted hoofsteps. Two Augusky trotted into the circle, starlight slicking off their horns and the tips of their blackwood spears. Yana had not summoned them specifically, but she'd been expecting them all the same. The Prince-Often Princess-Sometimes Both-and-On at Least One Occasion-Neither rarely represented themself. Yana had grown accustomed to passing whispers through their whores.

The taller of the pair was Sasta, Mailair's beta. Fresh scarlet glyphs smeared across her skin, and a rotting pink ear dangled between her breasts, strung through a necklace of bones and broken teeth. Her comrade—Eigent, if memory served—was slighter and far mangier. Too emaciated to make for a decent guard, Sasta likely kept the whelp present to bear witness to her atrocities. Cruelty was the Augusky social currency, and violence unrecounted added nothing to one's coffers.

"How kind of you to finally show your faces," Yana said, adopting her most syrupy smile. "I trust you'll send your ruler my regards."

"That depends on the nature of the regards." Sasta's voice was coarser than the calico fur that cloaked her from the waist down. "There is much misery to be gleaned from this new world and its subjects. Mailair has no time for pointless plotting."

"Pointless?" Yana threw the word like a dagger. "From your testimony, our coalition has bought your kind ample entertainment, though I suppose all deals have their drawbacks." Her gaze traced Eigent's flaking blood sigils, settling on a deep gray gash that slashed across their belly. "Mortals can be fierce as they are fun, wouldn't you say?"

Eigent pulled their spear close in a futile attempt to hide the iron wound. "What good is pleasure without a little pain?" they asked, unconvincingly.

"Silence, Eigent!" Sasta stamped her hoof, causing her lesser to flinch.

"You are not incorrect, Ghost Witch, but we are grateful for the mortals' zeal. Their bodies break too easily; we relish the challenge presented by their spirits."

"And what of the challenge presented by their *strongholds*?" Yana lifted her chin. "Rumor has it, Ebensburg has been giving you some trouble, what with its iron gates and that pesky guard its citizens have cobbled together."

Sasta's nostril's flared. "Why should we care for Ebensburg?" she asked, a bit too brusquely. "The Wilds will devour their defenses in time. Until then, there are countless other settlements to plunder."

"Not countless." Yana had seen the damage herself—whole districts razed in a matter of nights. "You're blazing through them like chaff, aren't you? At this rate, the mortals will die out before the Procession of Autumn." She sighed, shaking her head. "Pity. I should think Mailair would want to celebrate in style. Your people have gone so long without a proper Procession, I'm sure it would be dreadful to settle for goblins and pookas once again..."

The Augusky pursed their withered lips, but their grimaces spoke volumes. Not that Yana needed confirmation. The Procession of Autumn was once the most revered of Unseelie rites—a time when the Shadows were at their darkest and the veil between worlds stretched thin. Before the Treaty of Dusk barred them from the Mortal Realm, the Augusky would celebrate by crossing over in droves to hunt their favored prey. The substitutes they'd settled for since didn't suffer quite as beautifully.

Before Yana could prod the wound a second time, a chorus of screeches rose from the woods behind her, thought-rendingly shrill. Sasta startled, ears flicking toward the clamor. Eigent shuffled back, visibly shuddering.

Right on schedule.

"The Wailing Wind." Yana folded her hands at her waist. "The Host, the Sluagh, the Spectral Horde—call them whatever you'd like, their reputation shrieks for them. They are but a step above the Shadows themselves—a legion of souls so wretched Hell spat them out, and I..." She offered her sweetest smile. "Well, you know the story, don't you?"

"You were meant to be one of them," Sasta hissed through square teeth. "Doomed to weave between worlds, sowing misfortune like salt as your twice-damned siblings gorged themselves on your agony."

"Only they could not capture me." She leaned over the altar and tapped a nail against the blood-bathed agate. "I, however, know precisely how to capture *them*."

The Augusky stared at her for a stretched second before Eigent burst into bleating laughter. Apparently, their amusement outweighed their terror. "Even if..." they wheezed, wrangling their breath, "even if that were possible, what would it merit us?"

"The Sluagh are not true fae," Sasta answered, the sharper beast by far. "They were mortals once, and now they are pure malice, unbound to any realm. They are stronger than the whole of us, yet they do not share our weaknesses."

"Hence, iron cannot harm them," Yana cast a glance back at the screeching woods, "but they could easily harm *it*. If Ebensburg's walls fall to the Wailing Wind, your hordes could storm the streets without fear. Of course, if left to their own volition, they far prefer flesh to iron."

The screams were closer now, louder. Soon, the Sluagh would descend on the stone circle like a storm, drowning Yana and both Augusky in anguish, feeding on their regrets, and ripping them to ribbons. Unless...

"How do you intend capture it?" Sasta asked, glare twitching toward the host stone. "Clearly, that rock plays a role."

Yana cocked her head. "I never give secrets for free, dear."

"This is ludicrous." Eigent's voice trembled to match their knobby knees. "Mailair wouldn't stand for this nonsense. We need to leave. Now."

"It's a ritual, isn't it?" Sasta said. "It's always a ritual with you."

"But of course," Yana replied, eyelashes aflutter. "I've already completed much of the spell, but you possess the final component. After such a fruitful alliance, it would be rude of me to take it by force."

"Out with it, Ghost Witch."

Yana's gaze slid to Eigent.

Sasta nodded, turning her spear on her lesser.

"Like pauses in the soft refrain of solemn, silver bells,
The silence between words oft says more than the words themselves."

CHAPTER 8

MISSING A BEAT

ELWYN

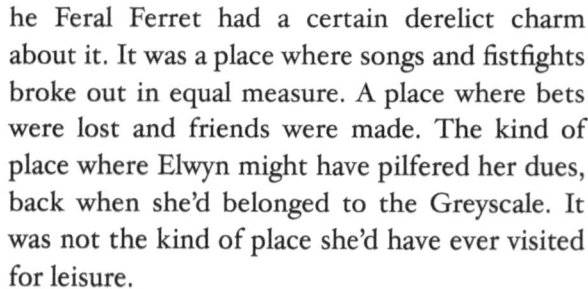he Feral Ferret had a certain derelict charm about it. It was a place where songs and fistfights broke out in equal measure. A place where bets were lost and friends were made. The kind of place where Elwyn might have pilfered her dues, back when she'd belonged to the Greyscale. It was not the kind of place she'd have ever visited for leisure.

Far too many bodies crowded between those four wooden walls—fighting, dancing, more-than-dancing. A band of bards rollicked upon a makeshift stage in one corner, weaving an up-tempo reel for a mob of writhing revelers. Along the opposite wall, a belabored barman scurried frantically to and fro, filling orders for the impatient press of patrons.

"Oh, rats." Elwyn stepped back from the doorway. "It appears they're far too busy to seat us. We'll just have to wait outside for the others."

"Don't be silly!" Aedyn tapped his lopsided circlet. "You forget who you're with."

His confidence was insufferable. Unfortunately for Elwyn, it was also justified. The throng parted at the sight of his crown—the fae, with tipsy bows; the mortals, with cautious scowls. Elwyn had never seen so many of each intermingling in the same place before. Hopefully, it was a sign that their peoples could learn to coexist. More likely, it was a testament to the strength of the house ale.

Old habits tugged on Elwyn's fingers as Aedyn urged her toward the bar, tempting them to dip into the pockets of every sot her shoulders brushed. That life was behind her, and she'd resolved to leave it there. So she busied herself by scanning the patrons for a lock of Silva's yellow hair, the charcoal checks of Rayen's favorite jacket, the hoary red of Mr. Elliot's beard. Despite the steady influx of survivors from around the isle, her Amblewick acquaintances were nowhere to be found. Perhaps the quiet, uneventful town had perished in the Confluence. A horrible thought, and one Elwyn refused to dwell on.

A pair of pretty Maithe women slid from their barstools to greet Aedyn with painted smiles and fluttering lashes. Both were dressed far too finely for such a venue, in elegant gowns and sparkling gems. Just one of their rings would have fetched a month's rent in the Pondrellen slums where Elwyn had grown up.

"My prince." The taller of the two dipped into a curtsy, her sleek bronze braids brushing the floor. "It has been far too long."

Aedyn looked at the girl like he'd never seen her before. Which Elwyn very much doubted. "Indeed," he said, recovering with a bow. "I trust you've been well, um..."

"Jaeda." She twined her fingers with those of her flaxen-haired friend. "And this is Merilla, in case you've forgotten her as well."

"We were about to have a dance." Merilla twirled a glossy curl around one finger. "You're more than welcome to join us."

Aedyn tipped his head Elwyn's way. "Another time, perhaps. I'm here with a friend."

"But of course you are." Jaeda's tone turned brittle. "You know where to find us when you grow bored of her."

Aedyn's gaze trailed after the girls as they sauntered toward the stage, sending an irrational spark of envy through Elwyn. She smothered it swiftly, claiming one of the abandoned barstools. Sitting with one's back to so large and rowdy a crowd was foolish, so she angled to face the press, hand resting on *Gelah's* hilt.

The barman rushed over the moment Aedyn sat, abandoning his washrag in a half-dried pint glass. Such was the call of the crown.

"Two honeyed whiskeys." Aedyn dropped too many coins on the counter. "And one for my friend."

"I'm not much of a drinker," Elwyn reminded him.

"Then don't drink much." He winked. "Worst case scenario, you don't finish it, and I carry the burden for you."

"Fair enough." Elwyn had no moral aversion to spirits, only she treasured her wits and preferred to keep them about her. "I'll try a sip, as the honeyed part sounds appealing."

"I thought it might."

Three tumblers slid down the counter in rapid succession, each brimming with amber drink. Aedyn pushed the first toward Elwyn, nudged the second aside, and lifted the third in a toast. "May the sun rise swiftly."

"And may it light the path forward."

Their glasses *clinked*, whiskey spattering over the rims. Aedyn emptied his in a single gulp, and his face flushed rose from the warmth. Elwyn's sip was far less elegant. The drink burned its way down her throat, provoking a muffled cough.

Aedyn grinned. "Not so terrible, is it?"

"The whiskey?" Now that the fire had dwindled, the honeyed notes lingered on Elwyn's tongue, smooth and sweet. Curse him for knowing her tastes so well. "I suppose not."

"That too, but I was referring to the socializing." He swapped his empty glass for the full one. "Don't get me wrong, a little wallowing is necessary now and again, but it is unhealthy to *only* wallow."

"Because it would be *so* much better to drown my grief beneath a sea of illicit potions and half-remembered trysts." Elwyn's second sip seared far less than the first. "Besides, I do not only wallow!"

"No, of course not. You also sulk, brood, and mope."

"So you *have* been spying on me through Amatha," Elwyn teased, elbowing him in the side. "And here I thought you'd forgotten me altogether."

Aedyn brushed the mussy bronze hair from his eyes only to let it fall right back. This time, his blush could not be blamed on the whiskey. "I know I've been distant for a while. It's only...I've just been..."

"Wallowing?"

His smile stuttered. "Aren't we a pathetic pair?"

Elwyn shrugged. Pathetic? Certainly. But a pair...

Her next sip turned to a swig, and before she knew it, she'd drained the glass. Warmth blossomed beneath her collarbone, spreading swiftly. It felt nearly like courage.

"You know what's interesting?" she asked, setting the empty tumbler aside. "I haven't sulked, brooded, or moped for a single second of the last hour. I can't imagine what's made the difference."

Aedyn's grin nearly blinded her. He hopped from his stool, sweeping into another of his ridiculous, grandiose bows. "Care for a dance?"

"Drinking *and* dancing?" She laughed, shaking her head. "Don't press your luck."

"Luck is meant to be pressed! Besides, we made a deal, remember?"

That they had. She'd promised to teach him temperance, and he'd promised to teach her spontaneity, but he'd also vowed not to gamble with their friendship. Offering a dance felt a lot like placing a bet.

"We're about to sneak off to realms unknown in direct defiance to the Judges," she whispered, mindful of possible eavesdroppers. "Is that truly not spontaneous enough?"

"Ah, but you're not afraid of death or damnation." Aedyn offered his hand. "You're afraid of *fun*."

He just had to go and make it a challenge, didn't he?

Elwyn placed her hand in his, and they were off—weaving through the raucous crowd, dodging the swings of rowdy drunkards, ducking between zealous dancers. The speed and whiskey combined their efforts, turning the tavern to a tumult. When Aedyn jarred to a stop in the middle of the dance floor, she tripped over his toes, tumbling right past him.

He caught her by the waist. "Careful," he said, whirling her into an effortless dance. "We can't have people thinking I'm trying to seduce some drunken innocent."

"Because your reputation is spotless, otherwise." Elwyn slipped from his grasp, finding her balance and rhythm both. "Besides, I'm not—"

"Innocent?" Aedyn quirked an eyebrow. "That's shocking, given how you blush at the mere mention of—"

Elwyn gave his arm a playful punch. "I'm not *drunk*!"

He chuckled. "If that's the case, match me with words, not fists."

"Now, I couldn't do that stone sober." Elwyn laughed, mirroring his steps. "Honestly, how is it you speak so quickly and cleverly all at once?"

"Wit and whimsy aren't opposites." Aedyn grabbed her hand, twirling her toward him. "The trick lies in getting the words out before your cowardice can dull them."

She pivoted away. "Well then, I pity the girls you kiss with a tongue so sharp."

He pulled her back in. "I pity the boys you scorn with one so blunt."

"Is this a duel?"

"That depends." He dipped her low, brushing his nose against hers. "Would you like it to be?"

Elwyn paused, torn between sarcasm and sincerity.

"See there." Aedyn tipped her back to her feet, holding her close in defiance to the music. "If you'd spoken freely just then, it might have been brilliant."

"It might have been foolish."

"It might have been both." He pressed his forehead to hers. "As I said, wit and whimsy aren't opposites."

Elwyn became suddenly, achingly aware that the slightest tilt of her chin would force their lips to touch. The thought dizzied her more than the drinking and dancing combined. Then, the song ended with a few staccato strums of a lute, and her senses snapped back into her skull.

Aedyn was her friend.

And he was a cad.

And he was *betrothed,* for Creator's sake!

Elwyn tore away, resolving to return to a whiskey-free existence. Clearly, strong drinks led her mind down peculiar paths.

DEINUA

Deinua's stomach keened like a wounded wolfhound. His sandpaper tongue scraped the roof of his mouth, and his throat burned with the relentless resolve of hellfire. His body would just have to suffer until it relearned how to savor the pastries and roasts his mother baked. His soul could not abide his father's diet.

Unsettled by the growing unrest in his belly, he turned his focus outward and resumed his hike around the toadstool ring that hedged the family cottage. He held his pike at the ready as he peered between luminescent stalks tall as trees, scanning the shivering woods for the slightest hint of danger. The darkness made the task difficult. Where his crimson eye could pierce the shadows like a lance, his hemlock green was roughly as sharp as a spoon. They worked together to rob him of depth-perception, but his mind was learning to compensate, translating size to distance, and distance to steps.

"Deinua!"

Lieri's voice carried through the garden, bright and unassuming. Deinua rushed to answer it, lest it lure something hungry or, worse, inquisitive.

"*Mother*," he hissed, rounding the corner of the cottage. "Unless it's urgent, you really ought to keep your voice low."

"Nonsense!" Flour wafted from Lieri's hand as she tried to wave his concerns away. "You and your father are paranoid, both. I'm sure it's coming from a good place, but I've survived in the Wilds just fine for decades. You weren't even a prayer when I first arrived."

"Things have changed," Deinua half-sighed, certain his point would flutter right past her. When the mortals first appeared in the Wilds, he'd hoped they'd shift the culture for the better. Alas, that branch of his family tree had proven just as rotten as the rest.

"Everything changes, dear." She tucked a wavy red lock behind his ear. "It's the one constant we can count on. Now, come inside; you'll catch your death in this chill, and I'll perish of boredom if left to pace the parlor much longer."

Deinua glanced back at the fungus fence. Anything or anyone could have been lurking in the dark beyond it, waiting for him to lower his guard. "With Father away, I should really keep watch..."

"I've made spriteberry scones and hot chocolate."

Again, his stomach grumbled. Chocolate wouldn't help much, but it was rich and smooth and heavy. With a sprinkle of river salt, he could pretend.

The sitting room was crisper than usual, with a hearth that boasted more soot than flame. Still, the dying embers cast light enough to give his eyes a rest. He set his pike aside and grabbed firewood from the stack. His mother might have been a survivor, but she'd die of self-neglect before she used a Shadow-damned resource for herself. It was reason enough to stick around. Twenty-one years were a few too many to share a roof with his parents, but he would humor her smothering for as long as it kept her warm and safe.

By the time Lieri returned from the kitchen, Deinua had coaxed the fire back to life and settled onto their battered old bench. She handed him a steaming mug and set another beside the platter of scones, nudging aside one of far too many floral arrangements that crowded the table. Deinua gripped his cup with both hands, savoring the warmth of the ceramic against his palms. He'd been cold for weeks, and it had little to do with the weather.

"Pleasant night." Lieri wrapped herself in a blanket she'd crocheted months before. "Crisp and clear, with a nice, full moon to see by. A perfect night for hunting, according to your father."

"I'm not interested," Deinua said for the hundredth time. "You promised to stop chiding me for it. Just because you can lie doesn't mean you *have* to."

"I'm not chiding!" She ruffled his hair, grazing over the stubby remains of the antlers he kept filed low. "I'm simply stating one option of many. We always knew there was a chance you would inherit his traits someday. Now that it's happening, there's a lot he could teach you."

Deinua tossed his head back, groaning. "The cruelest constellations couldn't map a more mortifying fate, and frankly, I doubt I could stomach the sight."

Lieri's smile darkened, and Deinua wished he could breathe his words back in. He'd often wondered how she kept her sanity while her husband was off wooing supper. Perhaps she acted aloof for her family's sake, just as they acted strong for hers.

"Besides," he said, steering the subject toward safer waters, "if he and I were both away at the same time, who would you bake for?"

"Fair enough." She sipped her drink and grimaced, thrusting the mug toward Deinua. "Seems I kept the wrong one."

He hadn't even noticed her bandaged palm, her trembling fingers. There were, it seemed, worse fates than hunting with his father. "You're too kind," he said, meaning it.

Lieri's smile was heartbreakingly sincere. "What are mothers for?"

Not this. Deinua swapped mugs and took a tentative sip. Before he knew it, he'd drained the cup, and his stomach felt settled for the first time in weeks. He hated the heat that oozed through him like molasses, the savory brine that clung to his tongue. He hated himself for not hating it nearly enough.

"Stay inside for at least a little longer." Lieri cracked a book open, angling it toward the firelight. "I could read to you."

"I'm not a child," Deinua said, resting his head on her shoulder in a distinctly childish manner. "Besides, I've memorized Kerri Longfellow's entire collection."

"Now, that can't possibly be true." Lieri clapped the book shut. "Prove it."

Deinua sighed.

"The wind ushers in silent change,
As summer's last breath fades away,
When everything bright falls asleep 'neath the amber,
The chaos lies dormant, our every excuse held at bay..."

"So, you can recite one stanza from a single piece. That hardly means you've memorized the whole collection."

Deinua cleared his throat.

"The tea leaves spelt an omen, and the ravens cawed in threes,
And while facts fit my fancy, they hold nothing on beliefs.
So, be it fate or folly, I—"

"Oh, fine then!" Lieri tossed her tome aside. "If you're going to be choosy, you'll bear the burden of choice. Pick a poem that suits you."

"How about a story instead?" Deinua had been honing his own verse and was cautious of external influence. "It's been ages since you last spoke of how you and Father met."

"I thought you were bored of repeats. If you've memorized all those poems, you've surely done the same for that tired tale."

"I know the general order of events, but it doesn't rhyme or alliterate, so..."

"If you absolutely insist, I'll indulge you." Already, a smile stretched her voice. It was Deinua's favorite part of the tale. "Like all of the brightest stories, this one weaves through bitter darkness, but you mustn't be discouraged..."

"For light means little, lacking contrast."

"I knew you'd memorized it." Lieri wrapped her arm around him. "Now, I was pretty in my youth, and precocious, and troublesome—"

"You're still pretty and precocious."

"And troublesome." She chuckled. "But I was more of each, back then. My parents were eager to marry me off before the troublesome could grow to eclipse the pretty, but I was less keen on the notion. I'd devoured full libraries of sonnets and stories ending in happily-ever-afters. The suitors they rallied wanted my dowry, not my hand, and with effort—though admittedly not much of it—I frightened off all of them.

"Then, one day, a man named Hendrick Bristol moved to town."

"The brigand!" Deinua interrupted. "Surely, someone could have predicted—"

"You're getting ahead of the tale, dear."

"Sorry."

Lieri shook her head, and a lock of her hair tickled his nose. "To my parents' profound relief, Hendrick hadn't heard of my more problematic traits, and he was interested enough to ask after me. I grudgingly obliged, only to be surprised by his charm and, I'll admit, a smidge smitten by his smile. Within weeks, we'd arranged to be wed.

"When the day finally arrived, I was giddy as a gillyflower. It was a huge celebration, bustling with neighbors and relatives who'd traveled from afar. If I'd been shrewder, I might have noticed my groom's lack of guests, and I might have wondered why. As it turned out, no one showed for Hendrick because no one cared for Hendrick, and no one cared for Hendrick because Hendrick cared for no one."

Lieri's voice grew heavy, as it always did at this point in the tale. *It weaves through darkness,* Deinua reminded himself, anxiously awaiting the next sunbeam.

"Hendrick treated me as kindly as ever through the vows, the dance, the dinner," his mother continued, "but the moment we arrived at the farmhouse, he transformed into a monster. He swore I'd brought it on myself, and I believed him. I'd never been a wife before. For all I knew, I was the worst who'd ever lived.

"In time, I grew numb. It was a blessing in some respects, a reprieve, but I had already tasted what it meant to be alive, and this wasn't it. I drifted through my days in half-slumber, clothed in sorrow thick as fog. Each night, I prayed for the Creator to take my soul. Each morning, I woke with a stone in my stomach, saddened by the weight of my skin."

Deinua grabbed her hand, squeezing. He wished she'd skip that part of the tale, as she had when he was younger, but she insisted he learn from her errors. *Dreamers too often find themselves in nightmares*, she claimed.

Lieri squeezed back, her bandages scratching his palm. "My first memories of your father are a blur," she said, voice warming. "I'd made a habit of gathering firewood after dark, when Hendrick passed out, sweating gin. I paid no heed to the rumors of monsters in the woods. There was a monster in my home, and I'd survived him for a decade.

"On one such evening, bittersweet music drifted through the trees. It stirred my spirit from slumber even as it lulled my mind to sleep. I abandoned my kindling, my doubts, and the path. Within minutes—at least, it felt like minutes—I stumbled upon a secluded glade carpeted in creeping violets.

"Your father claims he was playing his little glass flute, and that he drew me closer with a dance. Had I been more lucid, I'd have probably found him quite silly. As I remember it, I blinked a haze clear to see ruby eyes smoldering against the shadows. I should probably have been frightened, but I found them peculiarly pleasant."

"You were enchanted."

"And I am to this day." Lieri lifted her wrist toward the hearth fire, admiring the chain that wreathed it. The gold gleamed bright even in the shadows, a sure sign of its magical origins. "Though I suppose it is a very different spell. Now, where were we? Oh, yes, I remember...

"Your father was famished. He claims that, had his fangs found my neck, he'd have left me a withered husk. You get your dramatic bent from him, I swear it! I suppose it doesn't matter either way. Upon glimpsing my bruises, he was moved to mercy, and he dropped the spell without a second thought.

"He expected me to run, repulsed by his glowing eyes and gleaming antlers. You can probably imagine how shocked he was when I drifted closer instead. From my perspective, I'd been visited by an angel, and a beautiful one at that. That's not the sort of thing one runs away from."

No, it wasn't. Their situations were not similar, but Deinua had spent his whole life split between worlds only to realize neither would ever accept him. If anyone were to offer their hand, he would probably take it without a question, whether it led to a deep love, a pleasant friendship, or an unmitigated disaster.

"We spoke until sunrise," Lieri continued, oblivious to his ambling thoughts. "Koa told me all he could about Faerie. He spoke of the verdant Talunasan forests, the flowering Spring Isles fields, the crystalline waters of the Parting Seas, and the gemstone peaks of the Red Realm. His stories soaked into my spirit, thawing me from the inside out. I'd never felt more humbled than when he asked of my own adventures.

"My tales were far from wondrous, but he listened with rapt curiosity as I recounted childhood friends, both real and imagined, and festivals spent dancing in village squares. I told him of my favorite foods to make, of an ailing dove I once nurtured back to health, of the time I mistook pyrite for gold and dredged the family creek for weeks, certain I'd found my fortune.

"By the time dawn broke, we were *both* enchanted."

"That's lovely." Deinua stifled a yawn, his eyelids growing heavy.

"It is, isn't it?" Lieri sighed happily. "Alas, it had to end, lest Koa perish of thirst. He begged for me to leave with him, to travel the lands he'd spoken of with fingers laced. I'd never yearned for anything quite so strongly, but I had commitments, and their pull was stronger even than his."

Deinua stifled a grimace. He'd never understood her reasoning. Marriage was something to be honored, true, but Hendrick had betrayed their vows when he'd first raised a hand against her. Who could possibly have condemned her for walking away?

"My return trek was disorienting, like waking from a half-remembered dream. By the time I returned, I'd convinced myself I'd imagined it all. Unhappy souls can summon the most wondrous phantoms. Hendrick was none too thrilled to find I'd stayed out overnight, and he made his anger clear. I stayed indoors for a week after that, frightened and sorry and wracked with guilt. Dream or not, Koa was a sin, and I was a wretch for having humored him.

"But the nights were frigid, Hendrick loathed toil, and firewood doesn't gather itself. When I next returned to the woods, it was at his bidding.

"This time, when I heard the music, I followed it of my own volition. It led me to the same moonlit glade and ember-eyed angel as before. He'd brought gifts this time—salve for my bruises, a flower for my hair, a golden apple that smelled of cinnamon spice. Grateful though I was, I'd read much of the fae-folk and their tricks. 'You aren't trying to ensnare me, are you?' I asked, examining the apple. 'You mean I haven't already?' he replied. 'And here, I'd hoped it was mutual.'

"Just as before, we chatted through the night, and just as before, the sunrise called him home. He begged for me to join him, to share a life sweeter than any he'd known and fuller than I could imagine. Tempting as the offer was, there was much I couldn't leave behind."

A teardrop rolled down her cheek. This part of the tale had always been bleak—the dark before dawn, as she liked to say—but it seldom affected her so.

"Is everything alright?" Deinua asked, sitting upright.

Lieri wiped her eyes, a sad smile trembling on her lips. "Have I ever told you what Deinua means in Pondrellen?"

Deinua shook his head. He'd always assumed it a Glaistig name.

"It means second chance. Redemption."

"That's beautiful," he said, straining to find the connection. "But what does it have to do with the story?"

"Never you mind that." She squeezed his shoulder. "Now, to summarize a sad situation, Hendrick had taken note of my absence, and he responded according to his nature. Though he had no want of my affection, his pride would not suffer its wandering. He stocked the cabinets with gin and ale so he could keep me under a closer eye, and it stayed that way for some time before he inevitably heeded the tavern's call.

"I made my escape without pausing to think it over. By that point, I half-feared your father had given up on me, but I ought to have known better. You see, there is a rule most stories follow, mine included."

"The rule of threes," Deinua said.

"The rule of threes." Lieri confirmed. "Even without the music to guide me, my feet found their way to the glade. Koa was furled against an alder trunk, flute abandoned in the violets beside him. When I called his name, he sprang to his hooves. My guilt snapped like shackles, as I sprinted forward to embrace him, and—"

The door clattered open, and Deinua scrambled to take up his spear. He lowered it with a shake of his head when his father entered, face flushed from a recent feeding.

"And I begged you, one final time, to run away with me." Koa continued Lieri's tale. "I vowed to cherish and protect you, to whisk you away to a world of endless autumn and dance with you nightly beneath a blanket of stars."

Lieri drifted toward her husband like he'd enchanted her anew. "And I promised to share my life with you," she said. "To love and honor you, and to craft our own story, twice as wondrous as any we'd recited for each other."

"And the words were true," said Koa, clasping Lieri's hands. The vow-chains on their wrists shimmered and wound together.

"And the words were true," Lieri echoed.

Deinua pretended to retch. "I'll take this as my cue to leave."

"I thought you were a hopeless romantic," his father teased.

"Yes, but you're my parents," he said, starting up the stairs. "It's one thing to *hear* the tale; it's quite another to watch a reenactment."

If his parents heard him, they gave no sign. Already, they had stepped into their nightly waltz—a promise kept through the decades. Koa whistled a soothing melody, the *clack* of his hooves keeping perfect time. Lieri's bare feet whispered against the hardwood slats, the softest of lilting harmonies.

Deinua hummed a few measures as he crawled beneath his covers, dreaming up his own someone to dance with.

"Mirrors make the poorest portents for auguring one's fate,
They reflect the past and present both, but not what lies in wait."

CHAPTER 9
REFLECTIONS
ELWYN

usic and merriment spilled into the street, swelling whenever the pub door opened, only to dwindle a heartbeat later. Elwyn spent the muted moments calling her thoughts to heel. The most foolish among them had wandered off in a dangerous direction, and she was not about to chase them into unfamiliar territory.

"Fix your focus on the mission and the risk it's bound to bring,

You are not the kind of person who gets lost in silly dreams."

It was the first couplet she'd conjured since Aedyn had appeared at her door. That realization made her heartsick. She would not lose Luatha—not even the echo of her—to a foolhardy sentiment she'd never agreed to carry.

She'd been idling in the glow of a streetlamp for only minutes when Aedyn's shadow stretched beside hers, too distant and too close all at once. The silhouette's shoulders were stooped to such a degree she could practically read the sorrow on its face.

"Are you alright?" Aedyn asked, hardly audible over the tavern revels. "It isn't like you to run off without a word."

Yes, it was. She simply hadn't run from *him* before.

She wrapped her arms around herself, warding off a chill she hadn't felt until that moment. "You know how I feel about crowded spaces." The words came out sharper than she'd intended, more accusation than statement. "Besides, the others will arrive soon enough. It will be easier for them to spot us away from the throng."

"Fair point." Aedyn's shadow reached for hers. His fingers hovered just shy of her shoulder for a conflicted moment before drifting back to his side. "You know you can talk to me about anything, right?" The gilt toe of his boot scuffed the cobbles. "I can be obtuse at times, but I neither plan nor wish it. If I've said or done anything to—"

The sentence ended with a yelp as a dark blur enveloped his shadow, tearing it from view. Elwyn whirled, dagger drawn, to see a silver blade glinting at Aedyn's throat. Darkness cloaked his assailant, save for the gloved hand that held the knife.

"If you want the prince to live," the brigand rasped, "you'll lower your dagger, and..."

Elwyn's fingers flexed around *Gelab's* hilt. She had nothing to offer but her blade, and he wouldn't appreciate the method of delivery.

"...cluck like a chicken."

She lowered her dagger—not with a cluck, but a sigh. "Very funny, Brannon."

"Brannon?" Disregarding the very real, very sharp knife at his throat, Aedyn whirled and threw his arms around the assassin. "I hadn't expected the Sylphs to release you so soon! You must tell me everything about your stay with them—the food, the rituals, the culture, and of course, the women. Surely, that whole 'static aura' thing has a few uses beyond—"

"I may have been joking before," Brannon broke free with a shove, "but I swear I'm not above stabbing you."

"Promises, promises." Aedyn smoothed the assassin's cape for him. "While I'll admit I've missed that scowl of yours, I don't suppose anyone's ever told you that you'd catch more flies with honey?"

"I'd catch even more flies with your corpse."

"And what are your plans for all these flies, hm?" The lamplight caught on Amatha's smile before the rest of her lumbered into view. Her scuffed dobhriste armor and pack of obsidian spears made Elwyn feel underprepared, though her own threadbare cloak had seen many a skirmish.

She froze mid-salute as a lanky youth ambled from the alley to stand beside the chieftain, buttercup curls pulled back in a braid. Tawny was taller than Lydia and several years older, but with that round face, that button nose, and those curious eyes, she was the ghost of the girl Elwyn had sworn to protect. The girl she had failed.

Elwyn flung an accusatory glare at Aedyn. His wince told her that he hadn't known, he hadn't asked, and he'd seen the same specter she had.

If the chieftain noticed the exchange, she didn't acknowledge it. She appraised the group swiftly before turning on her heel, motioning for them to follow her lead. Four unlit alleys and a crumbling brick staircase later, they spilled into the vacant cellar of an abandoned outbuilding. Half-molten tapers cast feeble light over the spiderwebbed concrete, catching on the roots and vines that clawed their way through the cracks. Chalk sigils had been scrawled on an unbroken patch of mortar near the center. Perhaps it was owed to the candlelight, but the markings gave off the faintest of powder-blue glows.

Once the group had settled in a clumsy half-crescent, careful not to smudge the sigils, Amatha handed them a satchel apiece. Elwyn couldn't help but marvel at the sleek oiled leather and the watertight flap that opened at the push of a copper tab. Inside were two changes of common clothing, some basic toiletries, and a few pressed oat cakes—roughly enough for a five-day journey, and far more than ought to have fit in so small a space. Fae magic was often wielded frivolously, but they occasionally put it to good use.

"So, we *are* leaving straightaway," Elwyn said, flinging the strap over her shoulder. "Will we be stealing a vessel from the docks, or—"

"Patience," Amatha chided, pulling a fifth satchel from her pack. "We will travel by potion, which takes only a moment. The Unseelie abhor daylight, so a dawn arrival will allow for the safest scouting. Until then..." she turned the sack over, and dozens of wax-paper bundles spilled out onto the concrete, "let us savor what might well be our final feast."

The others dove in, tearing the wrappings from a banquet-worth of delicacies—citrinebread slathered with buttercream frosting, braised peppers wrapped in honey-cured bacon, flaky pastries filled with ground meat and tomato gravy. Between bites, they competed to control the conversation. Amatha reiterated the mission goals a dozen times, pressing the need to scout Unseelie strongholds and investigate their plans. Tawny was more interested in locating mortal survivors and teaching them tricks for protecting their dwellings. Aedyn further plied Brannon for lurid details about the Sylphs, and Brannon replied with the occasional colorful word.

Elwyn picked absently at a cheese tart, her focus flitting in and out of the discussion. Her thoughts wandered continually to the goal no one dared mention—a spectral fiend with violet eyes, snow white locks, and a withered heart. Be it personal or professional, everyone present had reason to see the Ghost Witch slain. Elwyn didn't truly care who thrust the blade, so long as it found its way between Yana's ribs.

"Still in there?" Aedyn waved a hand in her face, concern etched on his own.

Elwyn blinked herself back to the present, forcing a chuckle. "I was just thinking."

"Dangerous hobby."

"Indeed. Since you're so fond of danger, you ought to try it sometime."

"And risk wrinkling this perfect brow?" Aedyn winked. "Light forbid."

Elwyn smiled at their clockwork conversation, the ease and rhythm of it. This was how their friendship was meant to be—warm and simple and, most importantly, *enough*. She was glad their dance-floor gamble hadn't been the death of it, doubly so when he snuck the last of the citrinebread into her satchel, a finger pressed to his lips. A mix of nerves and excitement had turned her stomach to a tumult, but she would have regretted passing up her favorite treat after several days of eating only seed mix.

Some hours later, dawn's first ray filtered through a crack in the ceiling. Amatha drew a glass bottle from her pack, bidding the others to do the same. Elwyn held hers toward the light and gave it a little shake. Bits of orange and indigo danced through murky brown. Unappealing as the potion appeared, it looked leagues better than the Chorialan recipe she'd once been forced to ingest. Simply thinking about that briny brew made her gag, a phantom polyp wriggling down her throat.

A chorus of corks *popped* free, and Amatha raised her bottle high. "May the sun rise swiftly!" she cheered.

"And may it light the path forward."

The potion oozed past Elwyn's lips, burning and bitter as a cough draught. As the last drop hit her tongue, the walls began to spin. What started as a charcoal blur melted into an eddy of amber and umber, jostling her in all directions at once before hurling her to a bed of fallen leaves. There she lay with one eye cracked as she waited for the world to stop spinning. Several seconds ticked past before she realized that wasn't going to happen.

She was the second to find her feet, right behind Tawny. Judging from the leaves still flitting through the air around the others, they'd just landed. Crude stone columns stood sentry around them, forming a massive ring. It was not unlike the structure in which Yana had slaughtered Lydia, only no altar stood at its center. If it had, Elwyn would have toppled it as swiftly and violently as the last one.

The world beyond the stones was a spectacle. Branches swayed in defiance to the wind, their leaves flickering like flame. Vines and gnarled roots slithered through the soil, wrapped around lampposts, and devoured the splintered remains of cabins. The underbrush swelled and ebbed in shivering waves, dipping here and there to reveal an abandoned carriage wheel, a discarded rag doll, a...was that a human skull?

"This place is phenomenal!" Aedyn turned in a circle, wide eyed as a raven in a treasure trove. "The colors, the scents, the sounds, the—"

"Nausea?" Brannon asked, face flushing green. He attempted to find his footing but succeeded only in finding his knees. "Next time, we're taking a damned boat!"

As though his sea legs were any sturdier. Elwyn had been sent on a seafaring mission with him once—a combination burglary and assassination that required them to spend a week aboard an ambassador's carrack. Brannon had eventually managed to toss the target's body overboard, but not before tossing several meals.

"You believe we will live to see a next time?" Amatha grabbed him by the collar, hoisting him upright. "I did not take you for an optimist."

He stumbled away from her, bracing himself against a standing stone. "It's still moving," he groaned, gaping at the autumnal tumult. "Why the fuck is everything still moving?"

"It's called the Shifting Wilds for a reason," Tawny replied, a giddy grin plastered on her face. "Not to worry, you'll catch the rhythm soon enough. By the time we head back, you'll find stationary trees boring!"

"They *are* boring, aren't they?" Aedyn said, tapping his chin. "I hadn't realized it until this very moment."

"Enough dawdling." Amatha checked her side satchel and spear quiver, finding nothing amiss. "If we wish to find shelter by nightfall, a mortal settlement is our best hope. The sailor left from a port, yes?"

"That he did." Elwyn fought a shudder as the tale trickled back to her. He'd left his humble hamlet with a group of forty-five. Only twenty remained after the three-day trek to the docks, and three more had died to the sea-wolves. "He mentioned a naval port on the southern shore, not half a week from Ebensburg."

"South it is, then." Tawny tilted to her tiptoes, sniffing at the air like a deerling. She repeated the process in several directions before falling back to her heels. "We'll need to follow the cardamom breeze until it intersects with nutmeg." She pointed toward a sliver of a game trail. "From then on, the slope of the soil will guide us."

"I knew bringing you was a wise call," the chieftain replied, as though the girl's words had made any sense at all. "Lead the way."

The group filed behind Tawny as she scampered down the path, lithe and spry as a wild hare. She seemed uncharacteristically perky, though perhaps that was her normal state. It was hard to think of a person as lively when glimpsing them felt like cracking open a coffin.

The further the group marched into the Wilds, the more bewilderingly beautiful it became. Fiery leaves rippled against the overcast, falling free to sprout anew. Fiddlehead ferns stretched toward patches of dappled light, serving as perches for damselflies and pollen sprites. Fog wisped through the undergrowth, curling along in languid, gray tendrils. Even Aedyn—who could rarely be threatened into silence, much less fall into it naturally—glanced about in quiet awe. Jealous of his mercurial surroundings, he altered the color of his cape more than once—first to citrine yellow, then to sunset coral, and finally to a bramble-dark burgundy that melted to dusky brown along the hem.

Eventually, the forest parted, and the group stumbled out onto a stony bank hedging a silvery expanse. Foliage churned along the opposite shore, perhaps a half-mile out, and the waters stretched endlessly to the left and right, seeping into the cloudy gloom above. The ground beneath Elwyn's boots no longer shifted or shuddered, and the sudden stillness caused her to stumble.

"The Mirrormurk!" Tawny rushed to the water's edge. "I've read about it in detail, but I'd never hoped to chance upon it. I couldn't even tell from the accounts whether it was a solid or liquid." She touched a toe to the surface, sending prismatic ripples through the silver. "This is most certainly the latter."

"If it's liquid, we can swim across!" Aedyn said, much too giddily. "I haven't had a decent swim since I last visited the crystal springs with these three gorgeous..." He bit his lip, eyes flicking to Elwyn. "Actually, the circumstances aren't important. What matters is it's been a while, and it would be wonderfully refreshing after so long a hike."

Elwyn shuddered at the very notion. Treading water was one thing, but long-distance swims were quite another. She was a thief, not a pirate, for Creator's sake!

She crept forward to investigate and nearly brandished her blade at the sight of her own reflection. Her sallow skin and weary eyes pointed to a desperate need for rest, but at least she looked intimidating—all dark wool and leather, *Gelah* glinting at her hip and the tip of her scar curving out from behind a loose lock of onyx hair.

"If accounts of the Mirrormurk are vague, there's a reason for it." She tried and failed to see through the surface. "The scribes whose works you read were smart enough to observe from a distance, and their less cautious colleagues are probably still down there. Bits of them, anyway."

"I am sure we can find another way to cross," Amatha said. "If we follow the shoreline, we will eventually stumble upon a land bridge."

"Eventually?" Brannon scoffed. "I thought you wanted to find shelter by nightfall."

"Precisely! A swim would be faster and far more refreshing." Aedyn's reflection popped up beside Elwyn's. His armor had already withdrawn into golden bands on his wrists and boot cuffs, and he was in the process of wriggling from his tunic.

Elwyn averted her eyes from a flash of bronze skin. Lives of leisure and unwarranted flattery often had ill effects on the physiques of nobles. Aedyn had suffered none of them.

It was not the sort of thing she usually noticed.

"Why...why not use magic?" she managed, shifting her focus to Amatha. She wasn't sure how Sidhe powers functioned, but she'd seen them work wonders with stone and sand. "Would it be possible to craft a bridge?"

The chieftain stomped on the bank, and the ground before her spiked into a stalagmite only to crumble a heartbeat later. "I am not familiar with this composition," she said, running a hand over her scalp shards. "A bridge is a lofty task for a single stonemelder, but perhaps I could conjure enough steppingstones to—"

"Too late!" Aedyn shouted, and the conversation ended with a splash.

*"Who knows what sacrifices the adventure will demand,
When testing foreign waters, best keep one foot on dry land."*

CHAPTER 10

DECEPTIVE DEPTHS

ELWYN

lwyn waded out to her shoulders, watching helplessly as the others sank beneath the silver. Amatha did so in full dobhriste plate—a testimony to her impossible strength—and Tawny and Brannon followed close on her heels. Aedyn had convinced them to follow his lead after scouting far and deep enough to declare the Mirrormurk safe. Elwyn believed *he* believed his assessment, but that didn't make it true.

She slogged forward one cautious step at a time, shuddering whenever a riverweed brushed her leg. Any number of monsters might have been lurking beneath the glassy surface, their fanged maws stretched wide, barbed tentacles grasping for anything foolish enough to wander past.

"You're falling behind!" Aedyn shouted, bobbing up several feet ahead of her. "What in light's name are you waiting for?"

"Oh, you know; the screaming, the thrashing, the blood..."

Aedyn shook his head, flinging metallic droplets from his tangled hair. "Your imagination is nearly as vivid as my own, albeit wildly less salacious. If you don't hurry up, I'll have no choice but to drag you under."

"You wouldn't dare!" Elwyn said, knowing well that phrase had never applied to him.

He flashed a lopsided grin and dipped below the surface.

Before Elwyn could react, his hand wrapped around her ankle and tugged. She closed her eyes as she crashed into the surface, keeping them clenched as he dragged her deeper. When he released her, she settled to the silt, and her eyes popped open to a world so vivid it made the richest Rhysien forest look like a wasteland.

The waters below the surface were somehow crystalline. Brilliant red eels and jade diving beetles shimmied through gardens of peridot rivergrass. Schools of cerulean minnows wove around branches of ivory coral and feathery fuchsia fronds. Time-polished rocks, veined with strands of quartz or amber, glinted out from the golden sands, and spiral snail shells rose from the silt, striped with every conceivable color.

Aedyn floated above it all, wearing his arrogant *I-told-you-so* smirk. The surface ripples cast iridescent fractals on his skin and painted his wafting hair an ethereal, ashen hue. He might have looked angelic were it not for the devilish glint in his eyes.

He crooked a finger, daring Elwyn to retaliate, but she couldn't even move forward without flailing wildly against the currents. A giggle bubbled from Aedyn's lips before the silt stirred up around her, filling her vision with hazy gold. When the sands settled, Elwyn was floating forward, her hand wrapped tightly in his. Normally, she'd have pulled away, unnerved by his warmth. The water must have muted her sense of touch.

The scene below grew even more wondrous as they drifted through the deep. Fish with fins like painted fans fluttered between patches of pale lichen. A turtle the size of an ox slumbered in a kelp garden, its turquoise shell embellished by marine moss and anemones. Tiny, twinkling lights winked out from the pores of sponges and the fissures between stones, forming chaotic constellations that shifted with the shadows. Were it not for the few, jarring instances they went up for air, Elwyn would have dismissed it as a dream.

In time, the foliage thinned to scraggly tufts of color amidst a field of dull, gray gravel, and the shore rose up to meet them. When their toes touched down, Aedyn released Elwyn's hand, and she felt a little colder for it. She struggled upright against the pull of her waterlogged clothing, and a brisk wind sliced to her marrow. Soon, she would amble ashore and wring herself warm, but first...

She waited for Aedyn to shake his hair dry, then slapped the surface, drenching him in prismatic spray. "That's for dragging me under, you cad!"

He chuckled, blinking away the droplets that clung to his lashes, then returned the attack twice over. The spat swiftly devolved into an all-out battle, ending only when Amatha trudged between them with crossed arms and raised brows.

"I must be a terrible chieftain," she said, eyes shifting between them. "It seems I have mistakenly recruited children."

Elwyn and Aedyn exchanged conspiratorial glances, then struck the water in unison, burying Amatha in a shimmering swell. She laughed heartily, raising her arm to retaliate, but was interrupted when Tawny shouted from the shoreline. "Behind you!"

The trio turned in unison to find the surface roiling only feet away, its surface alight with flickering patterns. A heap of jagged rubble breached the silver, churning with bits of bone and broken seashells. Though amorphous, its movements reminded Elwyn of a prowling panther or a wolf at hunt.

"Another charming trick of the shifting landscape?" Aedyn asked.

The mass replied with an ear-piercing shriek, pelting them with a wave of spoiled-seafood breath. Rows of sea glass fangs glinted from its maw, dripping algae, and segments of several spines and skulls gleamed in its dark depths.

Elwyn's first instinct was to flee. Aedyn's was quite the opposite. He lunged forward, drawing his sword and plunging it hilt-deep into the detritus. Bits of rubble broke from the whole to skitter over the guardrail. They bit into his fingers, spilling red into the silver. He stumbled back, shaking them loose, and the rubble swallowed his rapier.

Emboldened, the creature reared. Amatha grabbed Aedyn and Elwyn by their shoulders, tearing them from the monster's shadow right as it crashed forward. The resulting wave parted them and forced them toward the bank. Elwyn lost her breath to the landing, pain bursting between her bones. She struggled upright, blinking the stars from her vision in time to watch a second creature haul itself ashore. Barnacles scaled its stony skin, and a tangle of kelp and mussels trailed behind it, clattering with its every clumsy lurch.

Brannon rushed the beast, daggers flashing at his side. His strikes were swift and sure, spraying debris in all directions, but his efforts were in vain.

The moment a bit of rubble hit the ground, it skittered straight back to its source and melted into the roil. The creature fought back, shifting sharply. Its kelp tendril twined around Brannon's ankle, dragging him to the bank. The assassin howled, seashells biting through his leather armor and into his skin as the creature reeled him closer.

Before Elwyn could draw her dagger, Aedyn flashed forward, filigree armor unfurling and illusory doubles spawning to his left and right. Neither his armor or magic would merit him much without a plan, or—more importantly—a weapon. Thankfully, Amatha moved more swiftly than her friend. She brought her boot down on the bank, sending a wave of stalactites spiking toward the creature. The largest burst through its belly, showering the shoreline with gravel and salt. It was not a death blow, but it stunned the monster long enough for the chieftain to charge, a spear in each hand. She transformed them into axes mid-strike, severing the kelp chord down the center. Brannon snapped free, and Aedyn helped him to his feet. The monster shrilled, retreating to the water's edge.

If the creatures could not die, they could at least feel pain.

Always a convenient trait in a foe.

Tawny shouted from the trees, but her words were lost to the clamor of churning rubbish as a massive shadow swallowed Elwyn's. A saltwater droplet shivered down her spine. She whirled to see a wave of shells and sea glass cresting overhead.

Years of struggles swept by in an instant, but a few blissful moments lingered, wrapping Elwyn in long-forgotten warmth.

A mother's trembling hands placing pieces on a game board.

A violet piskie in a gravestone garden offering protection at a price.

A little girl with ghost-white locks nuzzling against her shoulder as she slept.

A beautiful boy in an icing-smeared suit trading a bit of her burden for a moment of his mirth.

The wave crashed forward. The shadow consumed her. She closed her eyes, bracing for impact. It came, not in a storm of bone-crushing debris, but in the press of palms against her shoulder, the jolt of an armored hip against her own. She tumbled sideways across the shore, rolling to a stop right as a gilt figure vanished beneath a rubble rain.

A blink, and she was on her feet, racing toward the creature with her dagger in hand. She had no means for slaying the beast, no hope of repaying Aedyn's rescue, only a breathless prayer that thrummed in her chest, growing louder and fiercer and more desperate by the heartbeat...

Take anything else.

She attacked with blind fury, using *Gelah* as a spade more than a weapon. If she could only dig deep and fast enough, she might spot a glint of gold amidst the gray. Bits of the creature flew away only to scurry straight back. Other pieces found their way beneath her bracers, biting to the bone. She ground her teeth and tightened her grip on the bloody hilt. Finally, an oraithvine glimmer winked out from the tumult. She thrust her free hand into the roil, wrapping her fingers around Aedyn's. They didn't squeeze back. Though tears and blood loss blurred her vision, Elwyn braced against the bank and pulled with all her might.

The creature pulled back, bucking and heaving, pelting her with drowned-corpse reek and stinging, salted shrapnel. Soon, it had swallowed her up to the elbow, consuming her nearest leg to the hip. Ache turned to fire, fire to embers, embers to soul-numbing frost. Silver folded in like fog as the ice spread through her veins.

Shapeless shouts rose above the rattle. Blue-green silhouettes blurred past, half-hidden by the haze. The sharp scents of metal and weapon-oil blended with those of rot and brine. Those details meant nothing until a lilting voice pierced the din, bright and beautiful and achingly familiar. Elwyn could have plucked it from the chords of any choir, the clamor of any crowd, the chaos of any storm. This time, she was not simply imagining it.

"I have been searching far and wide, through leagues of open sea,
I've finally made it to your side; don't dare abandon me!"

Weak though it was, Elwyn's heart leapt.

Luatha was alive.

And so was *Gelah*.

The dagger's runes burst alight, brought to life by blood and rhyme. Their violet glow effused the mists and lent strength to Elwyn's limbs. Clinging tight to Aedyn's hand, she drove the crescent blade deep into the rubble. Hundreds of tiny terrors screeched and withered, clattering against the bank. A second strike drove the rot deeper. Inky tendrils spread from the third, melting stone and seashell alike and causing the mass to crumble inward.

Aedyn fell free, pulling Elwyn to the ground alongside him. She rolled over and flung an arm across his chest. Though crimson snaked through the gaps in his filigree armor, his ribs rose and fell in a steady rhythm. Relief flooded Elwyn, bursting free in a single, shaky laugh.

With that laugh came a light, searing violet. With that light came a peace, softly building. With that peace came a wish. With that wish came a dream.

With that dream came the darkness.

"Live wholly in the moments or regret them when they're through,
Time is a petty lender, and it always takes its due."

CHAPTER II
ONE PRECIOUS THING MORE
ARYN

he stood, tall and fierce, in the middle of the battlefield, crimson snaking through her gilded armor, dripping from her blade. A single teardrop trickled down her cheek, twinkling like an ember where the salt caught the sunrise.

Only Tearan could cry fire.

Aryn shuffled numbly toward her, stumbling over the corpses of enemies and allies both. He wasn't certain who all he'd slain throughout the tumult, but it didn't really matter. The blood had found its way beneath his armor, soaked into his skin, and stained his spirit an unforgiving red. In the end, death was death—warranted or not—and blood was blood, and war was war, and he had seen too much of each.

Tearan was the one beacon of hope on that whole, light-forsaken battlefield, and she wasn't supposed to be there. If the other Maithe discovered that their queen had slipped into the skirmish, the consequences would be dire, and not for Tearan alone. A wiser man might have sent her away when she'd crept into his tent weeks before, but she'd batted her pretty lashes and flashed her stunning smile, and he'd given her a sword and a suit of armor.

If she noticed him approaching, she gave no sign. She'd fixed her gaze on the rising sun as though it held an answer. Perhaps it did, but not a pleasant one. A dark *penumbra clung to the horizon, obscuring half of the healing light as it spread like ink through the cerulean sky. The Unseelie had brought their world with them. Much like their army, it was winning.*

Aryn stood with his hand a twitch away from Tearan's, fighting the urge to twine his fingers with hers. His fellow soldiers were busy scrounging spoils, tending the wounded, and heaping bodies onto pyres, but they were not too busy to seek out fresh gossip. Entertainment was a scarce commodity of late, and scandals traded through camp faster than lightleaf.

"We can't fight them." Tearan's voice was distant, devoid of its usual flair. "We won't win."

Aryn placed a hand on her shoulder, hoping the gesture would pass for comradery. "We can, and we will."

"They are stronger than us," she argued, turning to face him "and wilier, and more ruthless. Already, they outnumber us ten to one, and their ranks grow nightly while ours dwindle."

"But we are right.*" Aryn inched closer, and his daze began to melt away. All Maithe exuded warmth, but her spark smoldered so much deeper. "As long as there is even a glimmer of light on the horizon, there is hope."*

Tearan's smile was an unexpected break in a rainstorm, and her kiss, a sudden, blinding burst of sunlight. For a moment, Aryn was back at Sambria, holding her tight after a tedious day at court. For a moment, he knew what it was to be at peace.

Then he remembered where he was. Where they *were.*

He tore away, scouring their surroundings for witnesses. Tearan's giggle dissolved his worries all at once. So far as his weaknesses were concerned, iron had nothing on her.

"You mistake my meaning, dearest." Her lips tilted into the mischievous smirk that had won his heart a hundred times over. "I'm not worried we will lose to the Unseelie; I'm simply saying that we cannot win through *combat."*

Before Aryn could inquire further, she started toward camp—a patch of colorful tents perched on the nearest hilltop. He rushed to catch up, unsettled by the irreverent skip in her step, the distant, dreamy look in her eyes.

"What are you thinking?" he asked with a prescient cringe.

"If I told you, you'd try to stop me."

"You don't know that for certain."

"In all our lives, you've served a steady anchor." A trace of contempt clipped her words. "You are the gravity that keeps me grounded, the roots that anchor me to soil,

the staff that binds my notes in place. There are times when you are right to rein me in. I assure you, this is not one of them."

Aryn swallowed his remaining worries. Better they churn in his stomach than cause contention. Having been placed in power at the dawn of time, he'd long tired of others snapping their spines to cater to his will. He would never expect the same of Tearan. Terrifying though it could be, her passion was the source of her brilliance. He would let it consume him before he ever dreamt of smothering it.

The sun rose beyond the shrouding shadow, spilling light across the carnage. Skulls helmed in either gold or onyx rolled about the soil. Severed hands clutched gilt rapiers, obsidian axes, and ever-ice staves. Corpses crusted in crystal or fur lay piled over one another, allegiances forgotten. It no longer mattered who'd been a friend, who'd been a foe. If the bodies weren't burned by nightfall, they'd be added to the Unseelie ranks.

Perhaps Tearan was wise to seek another path to victory.

An agonized wail tore Aryn from his musings as his wife sank to her knees, arms clenched around her waist. Panic seized him by the throat as he knelt beside her, but he managed a few gruff shouts. Thankfully, Kyllean's ears were attuned to his cries, however strained. Within seconds, Aryn's closest friend came barreling down the hill, a second brigadier sprinting alongside him.

"I-I don't know w-what happened," Aryn stammered. "There was no sign she'd been wounded. I don't see any blood. She...she was fine a moment ago!"

Kyllean sent his colleague to fetch a Sylph before helping Aryn remove Tearan's amor, starting with the helm. His eyebrow quirked upon glimpsing her face, but he wisely kept his comments caged. Aryn no longer feared discovery anyway. Tearan's safety meant more than his reputation, more than pointless traditions, more than the Summer Throne itself.

Freed of her heavy plate, she curled against him, embers spilling from her eyes. Aryn kissed away as many as he could, promising she'd be alright and praying it wasn't his very first lie.

Aryn lurched awake at the peal of a visitor's bell, cold sweat beading on his brow. His bedchamber was dark, save for the flicker of a few hallway sconces. His brocade curtains rustled around a stretch of star-spackled sky.

It was only a dream.

A dream, and a memory.

The bell chimed a second time, and he wiped his forehead, coaxing his heartbeat calm. He'd dismissed his retainer lifetimes before and never hired another, loathing the delegation of menial tasks. Ruling his people honorably meant drawing his baths, sweeping his floors, and steeping his tea the same as they did. It also meant answering his own Shadow-damned door in the middle of the light-forsaken night.

He draped a velvet robe over his nightshirt, wishing he had sufficient time to don proper attire. If the sentries had allowed someone into his royal wing at this hour, there was good reason for it. That reason probably weighed more than his pride.

He opened the door, and his son's attendant dipped into a rushed bow.

Aryn arched an eyebrow, studying Learo closely. Glamour shimmered softly against the attendant's face and hands, perhaps a shade brighter than usual, but nothing else appeared out of the ordinary. "What has he done this time?"

Usually, that question was met with a sigh and a sardonic summary of Aedyn's latest mischief. This time, Learo drew a deep breath, clasping his hands behind his back. "You might want to take a seat, sire."

Aryn's heart lurched, but he was careful to keep his expression calm. It was his job to serve as a steady pillar for his people. If they could see him cracking, they would fear for the realm's stability. He lit a few sitting room lanterns before settling into his favorite armchair, waving Learo toward the nearest bench. The attendant perched lightly on the cushion, as though prepared to flee at the slightest provocation. It wasn't like him.

"He's left again, hasn't he?" Aryn asked, hoping that was the whole of it. His son often absconded in the middle of the night, but—so long as he came back by morning—it was no cause for alarm.

Judging from Learo's furrowed brow, this was no simple trip to town. "I'm afraid so, sire."

"Do you have any idea where he's gone?"

"His letter said you would know."

Aryn leaned forward, gripping his armrests. "He left a letter?"

"Yes," Learo said, wincing. "Only..."

"Only it wasn't addressed to me." The realization was an arrow to Aryn's heart, but he wasn't the type to shy away from harsh truths. Not anymore.

He held out an expectant hand. Learo sighed, pulling something small and shiny from his vest pocket. A paper frog, folded from filigree stationary.

Aryn trapped a breath as he accepted and unmade it.

Dear Learo,

I'm genuinely sorry for any trouble I'm about to cause. With luck, this won't be the last time you clean up one of my messes. My father will be furious when you tell him I've left, but I promise he won't take it out on you. He'll know exactly where I've gone and why. I hope that, by the time I return, I'll have done something to make you both proud. If not, I am prepared to face the consequences in full.

Your favorite headache,

Aedyn

Aryn tried to read the note a second time, but the script began to blur. His attempt at refolding the letter was a miserable failure. He had no idea when or where Aedyn had learned to make paper frogs, but it hadn't been from him.

Perhaps it should have been.

Learo's fingers trembled as he took the letter back, but his fear was entirely unmerited. As the letter predicted, Aryn's anger was not directed at the attendant. For once, it wasn't directed at Aedyn, either.

"Over a century," he mused aloud, steepling his fingers beneath his chin.

"Excuse me, sire?"

"Before you came along, my son managed to scare off no less than two attendants weekly. I believe eight was his record. You've lasted over a century."

"Your son is spirited," Learo replied, the slightest smile finding his lips. "It just so happens that I am too."

Aryn chuckled brusquely. "I do not question your spirit, Learo. Through the decades, you have proven resilient, wise, and incomparably loyal...though I often wonder where that loyalty lies."

The attendant's smile vanished, and he sat a little straighter. He'd probably waxed pale beneath his glamour veneer. Having long counted Learo among Samhria's least vain residents, Aryn had often wondered about the illusion, but not enough to inquire. The citizens of Talunasa were known for picking at flaws like crows with a carcass. It was wise to keep one's imperfections buried.

"It is not treachery I am accusing you of, but brilliance," Aryn clarified. "I doubt Aedyn would have ever confided in you if he suspected you held my interests above his own. You remind me a bit of Soen, actually—always weaving your will into the plans of others, and ever for their betterment. Hence, my numerous offers to promote you." Aryn cocked his head, scanning the attendant from polished toe to glamour-dyed locks. "Tell me, why have you rejected them all?"

Learo folded Aedyn's letter into a perfect paper frog before tucking it away. "I'm exactly where I'm supposed to be."

"I see." The words came out colder than Aryn intended. A strong ruler could not humor the presence of a usurper, and Learo had stolen something far dearer than a throne. "Thank you for the report. You are dismissed."

The attendant rose and bowed in a single motion. He was halfway to the door when one last question burst from Aryn's lips.

"Have I been a good father?"

The footsteps fell silent.

"I am not the warmest person," Aryn confessed. "Ironic, given the realm I've been placed over, but that is the truth of it. I have done my very best to lead my son, though I now fear I should have been *guiding* him instead. I had not realized, until this very conversation, that those are not the same thing." Sorrow climbed his throat, but he choked it down before it found his face. "Speak honestly, Learo. I will not treat your thoughts as daggers."

Learo's chest heaved. "I think you've done everything in your power to keep Aedyn safe," he said, "and I think that is the very last thing he needed."

Aryn dismissed the attendant anew, this time with only a flick of the wrist.

When the door clicked shut, he drifted numbly back to his bedchamber. He passed his mattress by in favor of the open window, folding his arms atop the sill and peering out at the crescent moon. For the first time in nearly two centuries, he allowed his thoughts to drift freely to the War of Light and Shadow, picking up precisely where his dream had ended.

He remembered it well—the madness he'd felt pacing outside the hospice, his wife wailing just beyond the canvas. At one point, he'd attempted to slice his way inside, only for Kyllean to confiscate his sword and drag him away from the tent.

"The Sylph do not require your oversight," he'd said, gripping Aryn by the shoulders. *"They will fetch you the moment it is safe to do so. In the meantime, trust in the Creator's plan. He has blessed their hands for healing, where ours were built for blades."*

Even in their most foolish lifetime, Aryn's friend was the wisest being he'd ever met. He should have known they'd eventually be reborn to serve alongside him as a High Judge.

Less than twenty minutes passed before Aryn was granted entrance to the hospice, but it might as well have been hours. He shoved his way into the tent, heart pounding in his desert-dry throat, only to be greeted by the most unexpected surprise.

The bundle in Tearan's arms was all dark hair and brazen eyes. A little fire, much like his mother. He even wore a sliver of her mischievous smirk. The babe cooed as Tearan passed him over—a tiny trill caught between a laugh and a sob—and a touch of worry fled Aryn's cluttered heart, making room for one precious thing more.

Try though it might, time could not unravel that moment's miracle. His son's safety was out of his hands, but the boy's light had not yet guttered out. Aryn could only pray the Creator would hold him gently.

AEDYN

Aedyn dreamt of fresh beginnings—of days spent traipsing through enchanted groves as reward for his kindness, of nights spent slogging through snow-steeped wastes as payment for his sins—but he woke to the rustle of tarpaulin and the caustic scents of smoke and seawater. Voices melted together beyond the tent, muddled by the crisp crackle of flames and the whisper of wakes on stone.

His attempt to furl upright roused a hundred tiny aches, sending him back to the wadded cape that had served as his pillow. The battle trickled back to him in blinks. A silver seascape shattering. A rubble monstrosity rising from the depths. Shells and sea glass scraping against his armor, finding the gaps, and slicing to the bone.

The tale would have ended there but for the violet light that pierced the darkness. Deep in the tumult, a hand had clasped hold of his—strong and slight and slick with blood...

Suddenly, standing wasn't an issue. Aedyn burst out into a stinging sea salt spray only to skid to a stop, bewildered by the transformation the shoreline had undergone while he was sleeping. A driftwood bonfire blazed down the bank, casting a feverish glow over a campsite brimming with hundreds of Undine.

Sea green soldiers clad in cobalt marched dutifully across the gravel, hefting supplies and weapons between tents. Civilians clad in tattered robes and gowns huddled near the bonfire, chatting glibly between sips of stew. A row of sentries hedged the Mirrormurk, spears glinting in the light of a crescent moon.

The remnants of a civilization many had dismissed for dead abounded all around Aedyn—battered and bedraggled, but very much alive. He should have felt relieved. *Would* have, were his thoughts less scattered.

"Aedyn!" Amatha's shout came a second before her embrace crushed him against her cuirass, waking his wounds anew. "It is good to see you up and about. I was worried you might sleep through the week." She released him but kept an arm wrapped around his shoulders. "Come along. There is much to discuss."

Aedyn allowed her to guide his steps, his focus torn in too many directions, but there was only one discussion worth having. "Where's Elwyn?" he asked, scanning the shoreline for a tattered gray cloak, a veil of raven hair. "Tell me she isn't...I need to know if..."

"She is alive." Amatha squeezed his shoulder, gently this time. "You survived the shellicoat attack, and she is far tougher."

Aedyn forced a chuckle—mostly air. "I can't argue with that."

"You should know better than to argue with me at all," she replied, urging him toward the bonfire. "Speaking of, Queen Mearalas was among our rescuers. She and a fraction of her subjects escaped Chorial before the collapse, but that is her tale to tell. I promised I would send you her way once you were back on your feet.."

Aedyn dug his heels into the gravel, slipping from his friend's grasp. She was right to assume he'd argue about that, and for more than one reason.

"Tomorrow," he promised. "I'm sure Mearalas is eager to berate me for one matter or another, and I'll bear her lecture with a smile, but it can wait a little longer. Tell me where Elwyn is, please."

Amatha pursed her lips, indigo eyes searching his. "Tawny is tending her wounds, as she tended yours." She gestured toward a little green tent just beyond the campfire's glow. "Make your visit swift, then get some rest. You will meet with Mearalas at dawn."

It wasn't a request.

Aedyn poked his head into the tent and was immediately accosted by the clashing scents of mint and dandelion leaves. Elwyn lay at the center of the space, wrapped in a woolen blanket as Tawny tended a series of deep gashes that carved their way up her right arm. The witchling was far too focused to notice the intrusion, but the dot of violet iridescence that zipped through the air above her was another story.

The piskie flitted up to block Aedyn's view, her ink-drop eyes narrowed.
"I've missed much of the world above—green grass and skies of blue,
I've missed my mortal, whom I love, but I have not missed you!"

"Likewise," Aedyn muttered, swatting the pest away. He vaguely recalled hearing the piskie's voice from inside the Shellicoat, but he'd dismissed it as delirium. Elwyn would be thrilled to learn the creature was alive, of course, but she had lost enough warmth without that little leech sinking her teeth in.

Concerns renewed, he crawled into the tent and settled cross-legged beside his unconscious friend. She looked even paler than usual, which was saying something. Deep gray circles shaded her eyes, and lavender tinged her lips.

"Why couldn't you have been selfish, just the once?" he whispered, taking her frigid hand in his. He'd known exactly what would happen when he shoved her to safety. He'd counted the cost, and he'd been willing to pay it. He should also have known she'd refuse to carry the debt.

Thankfully, Tawny continued working as though he wasn't there. When she swept a salve over a gash on Elwyn's wrist, the cut closed instantly, leaving a faint pink flush.

"Is that a Sylph recipe?" Aedyn asked, watching in wonder as another wound faded. "I wasn't aware their magic could be bottled."

"Most any magic can be," Tawny answered with a shrug. "The base is a standard Sylph tincture, but I added a few of their feathers—not easy to preserve, as I'm sure you can imagine—and I blended it with a recipe I learned from..." She flinched, dropping the sentence like it had somehow burned her tongue. "Doesn't matter where I learned it. What matters is it's effective, at least for a time. This tin would've expired soon, so we're lucky those shellicoats attacked when they did."

"Lucky," Aedyn echoed coldly, though he supposed it wasn't wholly untrue. At the very least, they were lucky Tawny had agreed to join the mission. Even if she served as a breathing reminder of his greatest failure.

Luatha was unimpressed by the girl's talents.

A witch's cure is bound to curse as quick as it can heal,
What is that tincture's special base? It smells a lot like eel!"

"Fermented butterbreeze, actually," Tawny replied with a smirk. "Though you shouldn't dismiss eels so readily. They make an effective burn cream and a decent pie."

Unconvinced, the piskie turned her wrath on Aedyn.

"I'll hold you both accountable, should my mortal's life end,
What fool would trust a witch-ward with someone they call a friend?"

"And what treatment should we apply, in your expert medical opinion?" Aedyn asked. "Wait, don't tell me. Bloodletting?"

If looks could kill, Luatha's glare would have...given him a papercut, probably?

She was very small.

After healing one last wound, Tawny passed the tin to Aedyn. "There's a little left, and it won't keep through the night now that the seal's been broken. Might as well use the last of it on that arm before it scars."

Aedyn hadn't considered his own health once since waking, though he'd felt a vague pressure in his chest and the slightest sting in his right wrist, now that he thought about it. He glanced down to see several crimson lines weaving up his right arm, far thinner and shallower than those Elwyn had suffered. Still, they would stick with him forever if he didn't tend to them soon.

But then, Elwyn hadn't been fully healed either. A plum-dark bruise peeked out from her camisole to drip down one shoulder, and raw skin reddened her collarbone and cheeks.

"Her remaining wounds are superficial." Tawny cocked her head, studying him like a spell-scroll. "Of course, they say the same of you."

Aedyn winced. The collective *they* had always been busybodies, but they weren't entirely wrong. Or they hadn't been, historically.

"I could probably do with a few scars." He scraped the remaining salve from the tin, shuddering at the chill of it, then brushed it over Elwyn's bruise. The pressure in his chest eased a little as he watched the colors fade. "I've heard ladies love them."

"Well, for your sake, let's hope the rumors are correct for once." Tawny stuffed a few supplies into her satchel and hiked the strap over her shoulder. "I should probably go check on Brannon's ankle before he claws the gauze away again. Can I trust you to keep an eye on her?"

Aedyn nodded. Keeping his eyes *off* Elwyn had been the bigger challenge lately.

But Tawny didn't need to know that.

"You can have that, if you'd like." Tawny nodded toward a little wooden bowl that sat to her left. "It's the last of the stew Amatha made, but working with salves always robs me of hunger. Something about the scent."

Aedyn's stomach keened at the mere mention of food. As he scooped up the bowl, the rich aromas of rosemary and black pepper cut through the medicinal bouquet that staled the air, coaxing his tongue to water. The stew must not have been sitting for very long, given the steam that rose from it.

Too full of worry to choke down a singly drop, he cradled it in his lap to preserve its warmth as Tawny slipped from the tent, an autumn gale bustling in behind her. After nearly a minute of solemn silence, he brushed the hair from Elwyn's cheek and traced her crescent scar with his thumb. If he wore his own scars half as well, he'd do just fine.

"You've really done a number on me, haven't you?" he mused aloud.

The piskie flitted closer on wings of shadow, nipping at his fingers.

"Do you really think she needs you, now that I am home?
I doubt you're truly falling, but I hope you break some bones!"

"Now, that's just rude." Aedyn pulled his hand back, scowling. "If you think you'll hoard her attention once she wakes, I suggest you reevaluate. I know your tricks, parasite."

Luatha answered with only a smug grin. She'd not been back a full day, and already her curse was taking hold. Like all the best enchantments, it was subtle—the softest smudging of lines, the slightest muting of hues. Soon, Elwyn would be all but invisible. A face that could blend into any crowd. A form that could melt into any shadow. A memory that fades the very moment it's made.

It wouldn't work on Aedyn. He'd seen Elwyn—really *seen* her—no piskie, no magic, no pretense whatsoever. He'd memorized the tune of her laughter, the curve of her smile, the way she tucked her hair when she was nervous. There wasn't a curse in existence strong enough to make him forget a single detail.

Elwyn coughed, startling Aedyn from his musings. Luatha landed on her collarbone and wiped a stray strand from her face, cooing brightly.

"Many have abandoned you, although you might have died,
But I, the one who loves you most, have waited by your side."

"It's not a competition," Aedyn mumbled.

Elwyn's eyes fluttered open, brightening when they landed on the piskie. Any resentment Aedyn held toward Luatha faded for a moment. If it *was* a competition, there were no losers. Not when Elwyn smiled like that.

"You're back." she rasped, propping herself up with her elbows. "I feared it was another dream, but you're really, truly, back!"

Luatha nuzzled her cheek, purring.

"The nights were dark. The waters, cold. The journey, far too long,"
But I was never gone for good, and neither was our bond."

Elwyn's laughter made Aedyn's heart ache in the most pleasant way possible. His own contented chuckle drew her attention, and her smile grew even wider. He hadn't thought it possible.

"Care to catch me up on what's happened?" She glanced down at the scratchy blanket the Undine had lent her, turning her arm over to examine the freshly healed cuts. "I feel like I've lost time. Or maybe just blood."

"I'm sure it will come back to you soon enough," Aedyn said, though he hoped the worst bits stayed buried. He could still feel the bitter sting of sea glass, smell the rot of the creature's belly, taste the brine of his own blood—and *he'd* been wearing armor.

He offered her the bowl, its contents still steaming. "You must be famished."

Elwyn eyed the stew like it was the most beautiful thing she'd ever seen. Until that moment, Aedyn hadn't realized it was possible to be jealous of soup.

"I can hear your stomach growling, you know." She tucked her hair behind her ear, a comforting dab of color finding her cheeks. "You're a fool to think I would sup while you starve."

"You needn't worry about me," he said, placing the bowl in her hands. "I want for nothing."

He'd never been able to speak those words before.

"Proffered palms are oft much more dangerous than swinging fists,
One shake is all it takes to clasp a shackle 'round your wrist."

CHAPTER 12

AN UNSTABLE ALLIANCE

ELWYN

 thick morning fog rolled off the Mirrormurk, blanketing the bank and obscuring the woods beyond. Elwyn's memories weren't much clearer, though that was likely for the best. She'd scrounged up fragments enough from the previous day to know she didn't want to remember more. Besides, the future took precedence over the past, and it looked a whole lot brighter in Luatha's violet glow.

"I don't know who you're looking for, but I say leave them be,
There's no one present on this shore more interesting than me!"

Simply hearing that sing-song lilt brought a smile to Elwyn's lips. Whenever she'd tried to conjure it herself, the pitch had been a little too low, the cadence a little too clipped. The real thing was far sweeter than any imitation. If the piskie had opted to swear at Elwyn for hours, she'd have listened with rapt attention.

Fortunately, Luatha was perfectly content to recount her journey, verse for verse. If Elwyn understood the couplets correctly, the Undine had pulled the piskie from their collapsing kingdom only to wind up wandering the seas for months. They'd surfaced several times, finding only confusion and danger until Luatha sensed Elwyn's struggle from afar and led the sea fae to her rescue. Of course, she also claimed to have slain several of the rubble creatures on her own, so her version of events was likely stilted.

"You know I'm thrilled to have you back," Elwyn said, following the piskie's giddy loops through the air. "But if we hide away chatting the whole morning through, how am I supposed to secure your breakfast?"

The piskie perched on her shoulder, clicking her little purple claws together. This close, her carapace had a near-metallic scrape to it—another sound Elwyn hadn't realized she'd missed.

"I suppose such an endeavor might be worth our precious time,
I'm glad that, after all these months, your brain still works just fine."

Elwyn forewent an eyeroll in favor of a chuckle. Months of apparent hardship hadn't changed Luatha one bit. In an unfamiliar world teeming with unfamiliar risks, it was pleasant to have one constant to fall back on, however cheeky.

A trail of pungent smoke led her to the dying remains of a campfire. Brannon sat beside it, stirring what remained of the poppy-orange embers while nibbling absently on roasted cashews. Elwyn called for his attention several times to no avail, then settled for swiping the wooden bowl from his knee. She and Luatha made it through half the remaining treats before he realized they were missing.

"What the—" Brannon burst upright, hands leaping to his *icons*. He scanned his surroundings twice before noticing Elwyn. "Oh, it's you." He glared, tucking his daggers away. "I attempted to find you a few minutes back, but you're so damned—"

"Unremarkable?"

"I was going to say *obnoxious*, but sure."

Elwyn nodded numbly. More than one Undine soldier had nearly collided with her that morning, and she suspected the phenomenon was not owed wholly to the haze. As thrilled as she was about Luatha's return, she wasn't sure she wanted to be remarkably unremarkable again. It was one thing for random strangers—or even Brannon—to overlook her, but...

Her cheeks warmed, remembering the brush of Aedyn's fingers. Even in the dark of slumber, she'd felt him hovering beside her, heard the honeyed timbre of his voice.

"You've really done a number on me, haven't you?"

Elwyn shrugged the echo away, certain she'd dreamt it. When someone said something like that to her, it was usually because she'd stabbed them.

"Well, if you stopped glaring now and again, your vision might improve." She handed Brannon's breakfast back, and he dumped what remained into the fire like she'd spoiled it. "Why were you seeking me out, anyway?" she teased, fluttering her lashes. "Were you worried about my well-being?"

Brannon's nose wrinkled. "The Sea Bitch called on the others about fifteen minutes back," he explained, crossing his arms. "No mortals allowed, apparently."

Elwyn fought a shudder at the mention of Mearalas, whom she'd met once before under less-than-ideal circumstances. The Undine Queen would probably have skewered them for the crime of having been born, had the other High Judges permitted it. "Let me guess: you'd like to eavesdrop?"

"The chieftain needs at least one Pondrellen native for this mission," he said with a shrug. "They probably won't execute us both."

The reasoning was far from flawless, but Elwyn's curiosity bolstered it. She followed Brannon through the misty tarpaulin labyrinth until a massive tent rose above the fog, its cerulean hue and beaded trim reeking of impractical pomp. Sentries formed a crescent around the entrance, barnacles scabbing their armor and sea salt crusting their matted, midnight curls. They'd left the rear portion of the tent—which dipped ever-so-slightly into the Wilds—unguarded. Either they were frightened of the churning woodlands, or they expected everyone else to be.

Luckily, Elwyn had faced far worse foes than rattling leaves, so she slipped wordlessly into the foliage with Brannon trailing after her. Remembering their old routine, Luatha crawled into her hood to conceal her glow. The Wilds shifted and shivered around them in its usual chaotic fashion, but they padded carefully between the writhing roots, timing their steps to the chorus of *crackles* and *snaps*. Soon enough, they'd settled in the wriggling undergrowth beside the tent. Elwyn carefully lifted the fabric, ducking low to peer beneath it.

Four pairs of shoes shuffled beyond the blue. Amatha's dobhriste sabatons and Aedyn's gold-trimmed boots were easy to recognize. The ragged teal slippers likely belonged to Mearalas, and the cobalt sollerets to one of her soldiers.

"...brash as ever, aren't you, Heir of Aryn?" Disdain dripped like ice water from Mearalas' words. "I'm surprised to see you survived your encounter with Yana. I'm less surprised to learn that you've decided to keep your *pets*."

"Elwyn's fought more for our realms this month than you have in your entire reign," Aedyn snapped, "and Brannon...Well, I'm sure the Sylphs taught him something useful."

"And what of the waif?" Mearalas asked. "If this mission is truly as delicate as you claim, why in light's name would you entrust even a portion of it to the Ghost Witch's ward?"

"There is no cause for concern," Amatha insisted. "I assure you, Tawny—"

"Oh! I wasn't expecting to find you here!" Tawny called through the trees, as though summoned to the forest by the mere mention of her name. "I don't suppose you've stumbled across any fringeberries? This bank is a treasure trove of components, but I've yet to find anything with refractive qualities."

Elwyn winced, releasing the tent's side right as it wrenched upward. A familiar sea-green face peered down from beneath the brim of an oversized cobalt helm. Lapa had once been charged with supervising Elwyn and Brannon through a trial and a trip to Chorial, and they'd made her job suitably difficult. From her mildly amused expression, she wasn't surprised to see them again.

Mearalas was another story.

The Undine Queen was paler than her subjects, with far sharper features and a permanent scowl, but there was beauty in her severity. Her tattered blue gown and kelp-tangled hair didn't detract from her decorum one bit.

Upon spotting the eavesdroppers, she crossed her slender, seafoam arms. She leveled a frigid glare their way before returning her attention to Amatha. "Tell me again how trustworthy your mortals are..."

"They ought to have been invited to begin with." Amatha lifted Brannon and Elwyn by the hoods and dragged them into the tent, nodding for Tawny to follow. "They joined us of their own volition, and they have as much to lose as we do."

More, actually, Elwyn mused. When she died, there would be no renewal, no rebirth, no reformation. The same went for Brannon and Tawny.

"They joined because you *invited* them, Hearthblade." Mearalas spat the chieftain's name like a swear. "If you insist upon calling yourself a leader, at least take responsibility for your mistakes."

"For her *insight*," Aedyn corrected. His eyes flicked to Elwyn, and the briefest of smiles softened his otherwise-fraught face.

He could still see her, which was a relief. He was happy to see her, which was...

Not important at the moment.

"You place far too much faith in these creatures, Heir," Mearalas hissed, her glare narrowing further. "Don't be surprised to find knives in your back before the week is out. That is, provided your strays know how to wield them."

Elwyn was tempted to prove just how well she could wield her knife, but fileting the Undine Queen wouldn't have helped their case any. Surprisingly, Brannon also managed to keep his *icons* sheathed. That Sylph training must have made an impact after all.

"How kind of you to worry about our spines," Aedyn said with a smirk, "but shouldn't you be focused on growing one of your own? You can't possibly be content with cowering in your mother's shadow for all eternity."

"Better a shriveled spine than an empty skull," the Undine Queen snapped, her rage taking on the timbre of personal offense. "Have you even stopped to consider the—"

"Stop this now!" Amatha stomped between the feuding royals, palms raised. She inhaled deeply through her nostrils before continuing more calmly. "I assume you called this meeting for a reason, Mearalas. Now that we are all present, it is time to make that reason known."

The corner of Mearalas' mouth twitched upward in a mockery of a smile. "I called you here to explain just how foolish this mission of yours is," she said, webbed fingers tapping on her forearms. "You've already presented my peers with a firsthand testimony of Augusky cruelty, and yet, they were unmoved. Do you truly believe your efforts will unearth something damning enough to change their minds?"

"We have to try," Elwyn said, too softly.

Mearalas would not have acknowledged her answer, even if she'd heard it. She did not deem mortal voices worthy of her royal ears.

"You underestimate the hold of the ideals." The Undine Queen pulled a kelp ribbon from her hair and flicked it to the gravel. "Love abhors violence, Justice is retributive, and Honor is focused ever inward. Only the Law justifies preemptive action where the situation merits it. Why, if King Aryn hadn't barred my forces from investigating when we first heard whispers of Yana's power, this whole disaster might well have been averted."

Aedyn's lips went lax. "What..." He recovered with a few gold-brown blinks and perhaps a touch of glamour. "What are you suggesting?"

"I am not *suggesting* anything." Mearalas snapped her webbed fingers, and Lapa seized Tawny's satchel with an apologetic grimace. "I am confiscating your remaining travel potions and placing you under arrest for conspiring against the Court."

"You have no right!" Amatha barked.

"Do not lecture me about rights." The queen accepted the satchel from Lapa, flipping it open with the press of a tab. "I have memorized the Light Realms' every statute, every amendment, every loophole. Whenever I do or say anything, you can rest assured it is well within my rights."

Elwyn scowled, thinking back on countless underhanded deals the Greyscale had brokered with bureaucrats. Those who made the law their identity often did so with every intention of exploiting it. Mearalas may have been bound to her ideal, but that didn't make her motives any less suspect. "You want something from us."

Aedyn echoed her words, and the corner of Mearalas' mouth twitched a little higher.

Amatha sighed. "Name your price."

"Oh, it's nothing much." The queen rummaged through Tawny's satchel, pulling a grass-green potion free. She dropped the sack without bothering to close it, spilling acorns and river rocks. "Just Mailair's head."

Several seconds of silence oozed past before Aedyn asked the question everyone was thinking. "Why?"

"Because you're here." Mearalas held her pilfered bottle at eye level, watching flecks of gold drift through the green. "And because it might make an *actual* difference. I've been traversing the Shadow-damned depths for months now, and I've felt the temperature dropping by the day. Come winter, the Unseelie might well be able to march straight across the ocean, as they did in the War of Light and Shadow. Even if it doesn't freeze over, their spell-crafters can't be far behind our own." She tucked the potion into her ragged bodice. "Fortunately, chaos is only a threat when it's organized."

"Of course!" Tawny beamed like she'd just heard the most brilliant plan in history. "The ruler of the Shifting Wilds isn't chosen by bloodline or ballot, but by battle. It's a lot like the Sidhe Throne Tournament, only anyone can compete, there's no set timeframe, and the price of losing is death."

Amatha scratched her scalp shards. "So...not like the Throne Tournament at all?"

"The prize is the same, more or less." Tawny shrugged. "If a Wilds denizen kills Mailair, they win the throne by right, but if *we* kill them..."

"They'll be too busy slitting each other's throats to go for ours." Brannon's grin was almost approving, though Elwyn suspected he just wanted to behead something.

"It is not a permanent solution," Mearalas said, eyes darting between Aedyn and Amatha as though the input had come from them. "The Wilds will eventually recover, and it will hardly affect the Winter Wastes. Still, we will have bought ourselves time, perhaps a full season of it." She jutted her shoulders, as though she hadn't looked haughty enough before. "Next to knowledge, there is no resource more precious."

Luatha peeked out from Elwyn's hood, brushing her hair aside like a curtain.

"It's rare assassinations help to quell impending war,
Even if this was bound to work, there's still one worry more..."

There were several worries more, actually, but one stood a few heads taller than the rest.

"How are we supposed to find Mailair, let alone slay them?" Elwyn asked. "Do they even live in a fixed location, or do they drift about at the whims of their realm?"

"Fómhar, correct?" Aedyn looked to Tawny for confirmation. "I don't remember much of my history lessons, but I believe the bramble palace is the beating heart of the Shifting Wilds."

"It is, and its location is fixed." Tawny ground her toe against the bank. "Only I have no clue how to find it. Thankfully, that won't really matter with the Procession of Autumn approaching."

Amatha's bejeweled eyebrow quirked. "The Procession of Autumn?"

"An Unseelie rite that takes place on the darkest night of the mortal year." Tawny knelt beside her satchel and began to gather the spilled contents. "Many call it the Samhain, some, the Wild Hunt, but it's equally dreadful by any name. M—*Yana* always locked me indoors until it passed, but one time, the horde came near enough that I watched them from the window. They were hundreds strong, and each carried a torch, a weapon, or a trophy. Most of their victims were goblins and pookas, but there was this one little girl, the ward of a local swamp hag..." She paused her scrounging, staring at the gravel, and Lapa stooped to clean up what remained. "We used to forage for toadstools together."

For an irrational second, Elwyn was tempted to pat Tawny's shoulder. She'd been young, too, the first time she'd glimpsed a familiar corpse—six, maybe seven years old. The neighbor lady had asked to be woken each dawn in exchange for toffees and licorice sweets. One morning, she wouldn't stir, no matter how Elwyn shouted or shook her. Elwyn had seen that same glassy look on her mother's face countless times, smelled the same rotten-poppy reek on her clothes. So she stole some candies from the bedside bowl and left, certain the woman would wake when the dream-smoke wore off.

"As chaos incarnate, the ruler of the Wilds doesn't typically adhere to traditions." Tawny shrugged her bad memories away, prompting Elwyn to do the same. "The Procession of Autumn is the one exception."

"It should give us ample opportunity to complete this task," Amatha said, hesitant. "Do we know when this Procession is set to occur? Time once flowed differently in the Light, Shadow, and Mortal Realms. Now that they are one, our calendars are flawed."

"Our seers have been mapping the paths of the stars." Mearalas' midnight eyes flicked to her guard. "Lapa, have you been keeping up with their charts?"

"Yes, Your Majesty." The soldier bowed at the shoulders, helm slipping over her eyes. "If the pattern holds, the darkest night of the year should occur in..." she ticked her webbed fingers against her thumb, "roughly six days, though I suggest we factor in a small margin of error and time to recuperate."

"Ten days it is." Mearalas leveled the order squarely at Amatha, as though it affected no one else. "Bring me Mailair's head within that time, and I will officially approve of this mission, tip Court opinion to your favor, and absolve you of your crimes."

"And if we fail?" Elwyn asked.

If Mearalas heard the question, she ignored it.

ELOANA

Eloana lay fuming at the center of the Gilt Grove, hair spilling around her like chrysanthemum petals as she glared up at the sky. The granite clouds that marred it were poor substitutes for the fragrant mists that had nourished the realm in times past. If Aedyn had been capable of simply sticking to his station, she would never have glimpsed the hideous things. Too bad he wandered off whenever the fancy struck him.

Apparently, the fancy had struck again.

She might never have learned of his departure were it not for Loenelle's report. A wiser handmaiden would have passed the news through the lips of another, thus saving herself a sound thrashing. Honestly, how long would it take to knock some sense into that girl's skull?

Eloana forced herself upright, stretching her spine straight and squaring her shoulders. Skirts balled in her fists, she marched past row after row of her creations, reading boredom on their carefully sculpted faces. How tedious it must have been, idling about for all these years, tasked with nothing but posing for passing tourists.

Enwa's likeness stood tall at the end of the steppingstone lane, proud and prim as ever. Her fern frond lips held a haughty tilt, as though she had any right to cast judgments upon the living.

"This is all your fault!" Eloana glared into her great-grandmother's primrose eyes. "If you hadn't been so ambitious, our family wouldn't have drawn attention, my parents wouldn't have brought me to this light-forsaken palace, and I wouldn't have been auctioned off to that...to that..."

She growled, stomping her foot. After all Aedyn had put her through, she *still* could not coax her tongue to curse him. To do so would mean he didn't deserve his crown, which would mean the Creator hadn't intended for him to wear it, which would mean...

Eloana shook the heresy from her head before it could settle. Her fate had been mapped before she was born, and it would play out as planned no matter what obstacles she faced along the way. She deserved it all—the station, the servants, that delicate floral tiara sitting abandoned in the throne room—and she would have it.

All she had to do was stand there, look pretty, and wait.

The garden began to blur. Eloana kicked her slippers loose and stormed out onto the grass, blinking her eyes clear to better survey the sculptures she'd spent half her life crafting. She committed the details to memory— every dip, every curve, every sweeping strand of oraithvine—savoring each note of their summer-green scent, each rasp of their rustling leaves.

Then she closed her eyes...filled her lungs...

And screamed.

A hundred harmonies unbraided at once, and the garden followed suit. Hedges shook and shivered. Leaves shot past like shrapnel. Branches broke, saplings snapped, roots tore free from crumbling soil.

If it were up to Eloana, she'd have torn Talune to splinters, but her lungs were nowhere near as strong as her wrath. Her shrill excuse for a song faded in time with her breath, dwindling to a hiss that could not have cowed a dandelion, much less the first and most majestic of trees.

Exhausted and breathless, she paused to survey the carnage she'd wrought. Topiaries had toppled like towers. Birches had broken like bones. Petals pooled throughout the threadbare lawn, the same foreboding hue as clotted blood. The weight of her actions settled on her, forcing her to her knees. She buried her face in her hands, shoulders shaking.

She'd stolen the song from her sanctuary, the one place she'd ever truly belonged, all because it hadn't been enough, because her life was not enough, because *she* was not enough.

"You poor, beleaguered child, what madness grieves you so?

Why do you now revile the things that you once helped to grow?"

Though soft as swaying grass, the voice startled Eloana's spine straight. She glanced around the ruined garden, finding only scattered twigs and wilted blossoms. "H-hello?" she managed, composing herself as best she could. "Is somebody out there?"

"You have a useful talent; that much is plain to see,

Whyever would you waste it on such meaningless things?"

They couplet rang from somewhere within Enwa's fallen likeness. For a moment, Eloana nearly let herself believe her great-grandmother was reaching through the Veil to offer comfort. A rubbish notion if she'd ever had one. Had Enwa played witness to such a tantrum, she'd have surely turned up her spectral nose.

"This isn't funny," Eloana rasped, suspecting a bored servant was having a laugh at her expense. "Reveal yourself this instant, or I'll see you thrown from the palace!"

A giggle rose from Enwa's floral ribcage, and a tiny golden glimmer burst from the leaves. Every color imaginable glittered in the air around the mote as it drifted closer, growing brighter and bolder by the blink. Soon enough, Eloana spied a silhouette within the glow—that of a slender woman with limbs like a cricket. Metallic wings sprouted behind her shoulder blades, woven like lace and bedecked with twinkling gemstones.

Eloana had seen piskies before, bobbing amidst the sprite constellations that gathered above festivals and fetes. But it was one thing to spot a fawn bounding through the forest, and quite another to feed one from your hand.

Very carefully, she offered her palm. The piskie perched atop it, folding her filigree wings as she dropped into a curtsy.

"I am the augur of the light, the harbinger of day.
The counterbalance to the night, but please, call me Anye."

Eloana dipped her head, uncertain of how else to respond. Despite her size, the piskie had a remarkably regal air about her. "Eloana, the Golden-Voiced," she said. "You must forgive the state of my garden; you've caught me at a rather inconvenient moment."

The piskie nodded solemnly.

"I've seen this fate too many times—rare blossoms hung to dry,
Now, is the man you've pined for truly worth the tears you've cried?"

"You're mistaken." Eloana wiped the tear-drenched curls from her cheeks. "I'm no dried blossom, and he's no ordinary man. My betrothed is Heir to the Summer Throne, and I am destined to someday rule by his side." The ghost of a smile touched her lips. "If there is anything worth crying over, surely it's a crown."

A little smirk found Anye's face.

"More than one auspicious realm has thrived without a king,
Whoever said to claim a crown, you first must claim a ring?"

Eloana nearly flung the creature away in shock. "Either you're speaking of treason, or you're clueless about the Maithe line of succession," she said, sincerely hoping it was the latter. "When the Eternal Monarchs pass into the cycle, a regent is placed in power until they return, and that regent is always their closest living relative or advisor. As their first-ever child, Aedyn was literally born to reign in their stead. I have no claim to power, except through him." The truth made her stomach clench, but she could not deny it any more than she could change it. "Now that you're clear on the particulars, is there a reason you approached me, or do you simply revel in causing confusion?"

Anye took flight, the faintest of melodies trailing behind her. It blossomed with every beat of her wings, fracturing into dozens of flawless harmonies.

At first, Eloana feared she'd offended the creature into casting some manner of curse. Then she recognized her own destructive dirge lilting from her wings, only woven backward and transposed to a major key. Sprigs of oraithvine crept out from the wreckage, lured by the piskie's song. They twisted and turned at her bidding, braiding into an elegant band. By the time the performance ended, she'd crafted a dainty floral circlet, pretty as Tearan's own.

The piskie plucked the crown up and set it atop Eloana's head. A perfect fit.

"Your powers have their limits, and sadly, so do mine,
But if we combined our talents, imagine how they'd shine."

Eloana traced the circlet with her finger, weighing the creature's words. Piskie bonds were rare, and rarer still for fae. The only thing scholars agreed on was that piskie blessings came at a price, oftentimes a steep one. Aedyn called them leeches, and her mother likened them to lichens. But this was not Aedyn's decision to make, nor was it her mother's, or even the Creator's. It was Eloana's choice, and hers alone.

She hadn't realized how badly she'd needed that.

"I want to reach my fullest potential." She rose, smoothing her skirts with her palms. "Help me to achieve that goal, and I'll grant whatever you ask of me."

The piskie grinned, flashing needle teeth.

"Until this very moment, we have beamed and built in part,
Now that your light is bound to mine, the world will know our art."

"When learning from experience, the whole world is our class,
But every truth we chance upon is viewed through tinted glass."

CHAPTER 13

LESSONS LEARNED

ARYN

ryn stormed through the camp, ignoring the stares and salutes of the soldiers who scrambled from his path. His and Tearan's dwelling was nestled against a canyon wall, far from the dangers of clashing swords and fast-flung curses. When she'd refused to return to Sambria with their newborn babe, he'd taken her side in the matter, and their combined wills had won out against more reasonable voices.

Never in his twenty-three lives had he made such a terrible decision.

He tore into the tent, hurling his helm to the floor. Tearan glanced up, only to hold a finger to her lips, head tipping toward the cradle in the corner. Several scrolls peeked out from the satchel she'd been packing, each boasting Aryn's unbroken seal. No wonder the reinforcements he'd sent for had never arrived.

"How could you?" The question barely reached his lips. "You've kept your little secrets in every lifetime, but this?"

"And which of your little sycophants spilled it, I wonder?" she asked, tucking some rolled stockings into the sack. "Lo'en? Byrean? Misha? It can't have been Talyn; he was one of mine."

"One of..." Was the Court truly so divided? Aryn had been so focused on protecting his people, he hadn't noticed schisms forming between them. "It doesn't

matter who told me, and I'm not interested in hearing a list of your accomplices. What I really need is a reason. You owe me that much."

"There is no reason I could give that would make you understand." Tearan cinched the satchel tight and stood, proud and poised as ever. "It's in your nature to follow the rules, no matter how ridiculous those rules are. You declare your every move a month before making it, allowing time for your foes to repent, retreat, or— more realistically—run us through with their spears. These are among your most heartwarming traits. And they are why you keep losing."

Aryn shook his head. Tearan often spoke of life as a gameboard and of people as pawns, but he could not picture things so simply. Especially when the stakes were so high. "There are no winners in war, my love. We are all losing."

"For now." Her laugh was a winter wind, devoid of her usual mirth. "I have already told you, we cannot hope to win through combat, but there are other methods at our disposal. You may be willing to wager your realm on your Honor, but you forget that it is my realm, too. I will not allow my people to perish over something so foolish."

"I agree that the situation is dire." Aryn forced his voice soft, desperate to reason with her. "But this is not a solution; it's a trap. The Korrids you've been conspiring with do not possess our scruples. When they betray you—and they will betray you— you will have damned your soul along with our realm."

"Damned?" Tearan tossed a glossy lock over her shoulder. "If the Korrids are truly our shadows, their virtues must surely mirror our own. What is Chaos without the Law to define it? Has Love ever flourished without Desire? Justice and Vengeance are but a double-edged blade, and Honor..." Her smile was a brittle mask. "Does Honor truly lack for Ambition?"

Honor might well have been ambitious, but Ambition was seldom honorable. That was the thing about shadows—they could not exist without the light, yet they strove only to devour it. A world left to their mercy would be empty indeed.

"You speak of Honor as though you understand it." Aryn drifted forward slowly, carefully. "Life after life, you've cast that ideal aside like an empty cask, but never so soon, and never like this. Have you drunk your fill so swiftly, darling?" He took her hand and placed it on his breastplate, hoping she could feel his heart breaking beneath it. Hoping she would care. "Will this ever be enough for you?"

Tearan scowled, but she did not rip her hand away. "I have always acted with Honor, dearest. Have you ever considered we might define the word differently?"

"Nothing good has ever sprouted from poisoned soil." He cupped her cheek, searching her eyes for even the smallest spark. "I know you have to hurt me. Not a

lifetime has passed in which you haven't shattered my heart, but I always choose that suffering for the joy that precedes it, for the chance to know and love you all over again." He kissed her forehead, lingering. "Please, Tearan; if you must destroy me, find another way."

"It's too late." She looked up at him with something just shy of affection. "I've been careful to be careless. Soon, the other High Judges will catch wind of my dealings. Once I am sentenced, I will be branded a traitor, and you will be branded a fool. Every ounce of trust and loyalty we've earned through the ages will vanish in the span of a single trial. Unless..."

"You don't know what you're asking." Aryn stumbled back. "Descension would wring every last spark from your spirit, dooming you to dwell in eternal darkness. Whatever you think of your new allies, you cannot truly wish to become one of them."

Tearan smirked, her gaze unwavering. Her silence coiled around him, slithering across his chest and throat, squeezing tighter and tighter and tighter until...

He understood.

"This is madness," he breathed. "The light has always guided us to safety, and it will do so again if we only stay the course."

"It is bold," she argued. "When the high road is no longer safe to travel by, you must chance the canyons, no matter how deep."

"It is foolish!" he growled. "If the Unseelie truly have every advantage, why would Queen Neachta ever agree to a truce?"

"It is clever," she countered. "You will not be negotiating with Neachta, but with her usurper."

"It is treason!"

The shout echoed through the space, rousing a cry from Aedyn's cradle. Tearan crossed the space in a blink, scooping the infant into her arms.

The sight of his wife cradling their son stoked an ember of hope in Aryn. In twenty-three lifetimes, he had never been enough for Tearan, but surely this boy—the only child they'd ever been blessed with—could thaw her frozen heart.

Then he saw the knife.

It was a Korrid design, hewn from glistening ever-ice, its hilt and handguard forged from frosted pewter and set with blood-red garnets. She held it almost reverently, flashing Aryn a bitter smile as she pressed the blade to Aedyn's belly.

"Render your verdict."

A trumpet sounded, mercifully pulling Aryn back to the present. He straightened against his throne, tearing his gaze from Tearan's abandoned circlet to better focus on...whatever was happening.

The throne room doors had already been cast open, allowing a small band of brigadiers to march forward. The woman who led them wore the marigold robes and copper coronet of a lightsinger priestess. She stopped before the dais and touched a knee to the emerald runner. The soldiers behind her followed suit, oraithvine armor shifting soundlessly as their capes spilled in veridian pools around them.

This level of spectacle was reserved for the most auspicious of announcements. Aryn tempered his hopes as best he could. If he let himself believe Aedyn had returned only to receive an invitation to another pointless ceremony, his disappointment would swiftly translate to outrage.

He bid the priestess rise and introduce herself.

"My name is Leneae Pollenbright, and I have numbered among Talune's Tenders for the better part of a century." The woman paused as though her service warranted admiration, which perhaps it did. Aryn had never spared much thought to his kingdom's various religious sects. He remembered the Creator's voice, and he'd yet to meet a single Maithe who spoke with it. "I was helping to cast the daily frost ward on Talune's roots when I noticed something shimmering like a heat mirage atop a nearby knoll and took it upon myself to investigate. I think you will be quite interested in what I found—or rather, *who*."

"Someone traveled here by potion?" Aryn knew the shimmer the priestess spoke of. He'd been puzzling over how Amatha and Aedyn had defied the oaths he'd made them recite, though he wasn't shocked when it happened. If those children were half as cautious as they were clever, he'd spend far less hours with his heart in his throat. Leneae beamed at his obvious interest. "Not just anyone, Your Highness. Our esteemed guest is none other than—"

"I can announce myself, thank you kindly." The ice-water voice flooded Talune's Heart, dousing what little hope Aryn had humored. "Step aside and still your tongue. You've wasted more than enough time already."

The priestess and her escorts scrambled to flank the aisle, and a slender, seafoam figure strode through their midst. Though salt stiffened her tattered gown and matted her midnight hair, she carried herself with the same decorum she'd have flaunted in seamless silk and a coral crown.

"Mearalas." Aryn's heart plunged even as he rose to greet her. The Undine Queen's return called for enthusiasm he could not muster. Not while his son still skulked about Unseelie lands, one misstep away from tumbling into darkness. "I am relieved to see you alive and well."

"Yes, your excitement is palpable." Mearalas waved a webbed hand, and the onlookers scrambled from the throne room. "While a heartfelt reunion is doubtless in order, I suggest we save it for the first true Seelie Council to convene since the...*Confluence*." She spat the word like venom, probably because she hadn't contributed to choosing it. "If your messengers are worth their salt, Creagor and Soen should arrive by nightfall."

"You've sent missives already?" Aryn blinked, wondering just how long the priestess had prepared her announcement. "I assumed you'd just arrived."

"The climb from Talune's roots takes roughly twenty minutes, and I'm perfectly capable of dictating a letter while walking. On that note, I suppose I must apologize for my appearance." She sneered down at her ruined garment, kicking the tattered hem. "Your subjects insisted I make myself presentable before greeting you, but such matters are trivial at best. A queen must put the needs of her people before even the simplest luxuries."

"Your people?" Aryn freed a captive breath. It wasn't the news he'd been hoping for, but it was still a notable blessing. "Rumors of Chorial's collapse have spread like poisonmoss, and the few Undine seers who dwell among us have all but confirmed it. How did you manage to escape?"

Mearalas' smile fled, taking her pride with it. "I will explain everything at the Council. In the meantime, I must call upon your aid. Roughly two hundred others escaped from Chorial and will require food and lodging upon arrival. You'll have roughly a week to prepare for them, assuming that Hearthblade girl's directions can be trusted."

Aryn's head felt suddenly light despite his crown. "You saw Amatha? Was she well? Was she...was she alone?"

"I swear, the way you parents fret over your spawn." Mearalas rolled her midnight eyes. "To answer your *actual* question: yes, your son was with her. You lack Soen's tact, friend. Next time, speak plainly and save your mind the strain."

An unprompted laugh burst from Aryn's lips, genuine and bright. His little fire had not yet been extinguished. Now to see him safely home.

"Clearly, you're going to stand there slack-jawed for a while, so I'd best tend to this horrid hair while I have a chance." Mearalas tossed her tangled curls as she whirled toward the exit. "I suggest you wrangle your wits before the meeting. You're going to need them."

DEINUA

Petie's Pub was located at the end of an unlit alley, stuffed between abandoned breweries like the rancid filling of a month-old meat pie. The pink noses of rats twitched out from behind the empty barrels stacked to either side of the entrance. Mosses and molds spattered rain-weathered walls, and little black mushrooms sprouted from the gaps between bricks. The entryway rug was worn and bedraggled, smeared liberally with what Deinua sincerely hoped was mud.

He'd heard the best poets could find beauty in the bleakest of circumstances, so he decided to give it a try.

I've never seen the value in tarnish, rust, or grime,
Though beyond these boarded windows, there winks a glint of light.
There's yet a chance that this won't be a waste of precious time;
I'll not find proper company but might well grab a bite.

Not perfect, but far better than his last ballad. It might even have been funny if the subject was less grim.

He cursed the hollow stomach he'd tried desperately to fill with salted meats and potato rolls, and it cursed him right back. If he could quell its grumblings for even a short time, perhaps he could find a more lasting solution—preferably one that didn't include his mother bleeding herself dry. The justification helped to quiet his conscience, and he preened his copper forelock one final time, ensuring it cloaked his crimson eye before pressing into the tavern.

The building was far more pleasant on the inside, despite the sour-hop stench and the din of clattering dice and ale-slurred curses. Tapers flickered three to a tabletop, dripping wax beads onto rustic clay coasters, and a few modest embers seethed in the hearth, casting a soft glow on the floor. Wreaths of dried hyacinth and elderberry had been hung from the walls in a misguided attempt to ward off fae folk. Their humble charm only drew Deinua closer.

Business was good but not bustling. Two women flanked the fireplace, flutes perched between their fingers like finches. Judging from the ease of their conversation, they were nigh inseparable, and Deinua was nowhere near ready to ensnare a pair. A cluster of tables along the wall hosted a rowdy group of self-proclaimed hunters in mismatched blue jackets, iron swords and crossbows slung over their backs. According to the guard at the city gate—who'd sported similar garb—the crew called themselves the Iron Claws, and they'd tasked themselves with slaying any fae folk who dared breach mortal borders.

Where a pair would prove troublesome, a pack would spell disaster. Still, Deinua scanned their ranks, testing for a weak link among the many. Since they were so intent on slaying his kind, he would feel less conflicted if he accidentally killed one of theirs.

His gaze flitted over half of those seated before snagging on a man in a striking blue tailcoat, his coiled hair bound back with a matching ribbon. Candlelight caught in oaken eyes just a shade or two lighter than his skin, and a trio of silver slashes cut across his sleeve. The bow on his back looked more decorative than dangerous, though his half-stocked quiver implied it had seen recent use. To his left lay a case of colored chalk sticks; to his right, an untouched glass of dark wine. The striped quill of his pen bobbed furiously behind the open journal he'd propped against the table.

Somehow sensing Deinua's attention, the man glanced up from his project and flashed a dimpled smile. Deinua looked away, blushing as brightly as his scant warmth allowed. That was not the sort of connection he'd come there to make.

By either fate or fortune, Deinua's gaze landed on the perfect quarry. The young woman sat alone at the bar, staring at her tankard as though the pewter reflected her future. She was pretty but not inordinately so, and her dress was of a fitted, practical make. Sidling up to her would draw neither envy nor reproach.

He took the stool next to hers, sliding the barman a copper pia and ordering whatever was cheapest. Either unobservant or uninterested, the woman kept her gaze fixed on her drink, tapping calloused fingers on the counter. She smelled of thyme, soot, and rich, red blood. If he'd have inherited his father's talents, he'd have been able to scent her sins as well.

According to the legends, the Glaistigs had been created to cull evildoers from the mortal world—murderers, bandits, and anyone else who gorged themselves on the suffering of others. It would have been nice to know whether this woman deserved such a fate, and better still to possess the talent required for luring her into solitude from beyond the city walls. How horrid, to be burdened with the hungers of a beast and denied its natural gifts.

"Excuse me, miss." He nudged her elbow with his. "I couldn't help but notice you're in dire need of cheering."

She breathed a bitter laugh, wiping her eyes with a ragged sleeve. "I've had quite enough cheering from your type, thanks."

Deinua sincerely doubted it.

"I won't try to cheer you then." He caught the glass of port that the barman slid his way. "If I have any inkling what you're going through, and I suspect I might, an open ear will serve you better than a silver tongue."

She peered at him from the corner of her eye, visibly weighing his intentions against her sorrow. "You're just gonna' mock me for it," she said, swiveling to face him. "You Ebensburg lot are all the same."

"Ebensburg?" Deinua knew the name. The wealthy district sat at the center of several overlapping slums, made separate by a daunting wrought-iron wall. Rumor held that nothing from the Wilds had breached its borders, save swarms of winged rot-fae. Even blackthorn brambles withered trying to climb the bars. "You're mistaken. I've never been to Ebensburg."

"Is that right?" Her eyes raked over his veridian ensemble, not wholly disapproving. "That suit don't look like it was pulled from a rubbish heap."

For once, Deinua wished he could have donned something drab. Vibrant dyes were a sign of wealth among the mortals, but his garish green garb was a matter of necessity. Blues itched something fierce, no matter the fabric. Yellows made him nauseous. Reds and purples gave him hives. He didn't even like to think about browns.

Hopefully, the mortals never caught onto that little quirk.

"I'm no noble, miss." He sipped his cheap ale as evidence. Though it singed his thirst-dry throat, he managed to avoid wincing. "My mother tried her hand at tailoring, and it happened to prove deft. You can hardly fault me for showing off her handiwork."

"Well, I ain't from Ebensburg neither." She waved down the length her piecemeal dress. "He said he loved me anyway, enough to leave his name and wealth behind. Claimed he'd marry me, no matter...no matter..." A sob tried to escape her lips, but she drowned it with a wash of ale. "I was a fool to believe a word of it, and I'd be twice as foolish to believe whatever lies you're about to spout." She wiped the foam from her lips. "Better to die than live this over again."

Well, when you put it that way...

Deinua shook the notion from his head. He may have been a monster, but that didn't mean he had to think like one.

"I have no intention of wooing you," he placed his hand atop hers, "and I certainly don't intend to wed you. What I'm offering is a reprieve from your sorrows in hopes you'll sate my thirst. No promises. No commitments. No words whatsoever, should mine displease you."

The woman's gaze softened, dropping briefly to their overlapped hands. Now that Deinua had captured her attention, he needed only to cage it. He tucked his forelock behind his ear, certain the shadows would hide his crimson eye from all but her. Her pupils swelled like ink drops, leaving only a sliver of sage along the rims, and the worried creases fled her forehead. Deinua could practically feel her will binding to his. The ease of it churned his stomach.

This is a good sign, he reminded himself. His thirst was not as strong as his father's; he needed only a sip or two to quench it. If he wove a strong enough enchantment, this woman would forget his face, and there would be no harm in allowing her to live. He could only hope he was up to the task.

"Let's go on a little walk." He stood, twining his fingers with hers. "You look like you could use some fresh air."

The woman's nod was slow, rigid—a motion forced by unseen hands. Deinua tugged her to her feet and started across the room. She matched him step for step, breath for breath, not a movement made of her own volition. The sight brought the ale back to Deinua's throat, which was going to make dining difficult.

They were nearly at the door when a riotous din erupted behind them. Deinua glanced back to see a hunter scooping a heap of coins into his lap. His comrades were in an uproar, either slapping his back or cursing his name. The man in the tailcoat shook his head, not bothering to look up from his journal.

The distraction lasted but a blink. Apparently, that was too long.

The woman tore her hand free, then slapped Deinua so hard his vision spun. By the time he shook the blur away, she was gone. He hovered beside the door for a moment, allowing her an opportunity to melt into the evening crowds. By the time he crossed the threshold, he'd convinced himself the outcome was for the best. An enchantment that snapped so easily would never have held though a feeding, and a little discomfort weighed far less than a life.

Surely, better souls had suffered for less.

"Justice may be valiant, but vengeance is her twin,
Even perfectly weighted scales tip at a feather's whim."

CHAPTER 14
EQUAL OPPOSITES
BRANNON

he sun rose high behind the clouds, slowly burning a hole through the gray. Brannon resented it with every bitter fiber of his being. He'd started the day with an optimistic outlook —at least, optimistic by *his* standards—but his patience was wearing thinner than the stockings that had failed to protect his heels from blisters.

"Trees and roots and trees and roots and trees and roots..." Aedyn droned on, as he'd been doing for the past twenty minutes of the five-hour hike that had yet to bring them to a single fucking settlement. "I wonder what awaits us beyond the bend. A circus, perhaps? A gambling house? A mildly interesting rock formation?" He sprinted ahead to peer around a curve in the trail. "Oh, joy. More trees. More roots. You know, I had expected the Shifting Wilds to be a touch wilder."

"I'm just grateful we haven't run into anything feral," Not-Lydia...er, *Tawny* said, skirting around the prince to resume her role as navigator. "The Unseelie rarely stir before dusk, but there are plenty of Solitaries around here who would view us as an opportunity to either fight or feast."

"Don't you dare get my hopes up," Brannon muttered, hands perched on the hilts of his *Aras Tosc*. "Those rubbish bastards—"

"Shellicoats," Tawny corrected.

"—didn't even bleed." A phantom pain twinged in his ankle, grating against the bones. The wound may have fully healed, but the memory was still sharp as sea glass. "I stabbed the damned thing multiple times. It could have at least had the courtesy to whimper."

"Cheer up, Grumbles." Aedyn patted Brannon's shoulder as he squeezed back into formation beside Elwyn. "I'm sure we'll stumble upon something worth stabbing soon enough."

"Are you volunteering?"

"Do *not* stab each other," Amatha said, exasperated from repeating herself. "If at all possible, do not stab *anything*."

"What's the point of this mission, then?" Brannon kicked a pebble from the path, and it rolled against the tilt of the slope. Apparently, that meant they were headed southwest.

He really hated this place.

"If there's a chance something hungry might spot us, shouldn't we be disguised?" Elwyn asked, having long preferred skulking to slicing. "Surely, it wouldn't hurt to be cautious."

An enchanted dagger was wasted on that one.

"I know I look like a god, but even I have limits," Aedyn replied, chuckling. "That stubborn overcast is making it difficult to draw fresh sunlight, so I'd rather save my stores for direr straights. Or darker ones, at the very least."

"You could always preserve your magic by scouting down the trails,
We'd learn which routes we'd best avoid by listening for your wails."

A begrudging smile found Brannon's lips. He hadn't necessarily missed Elwyn's little pest, but she had a better sense of humor than the others. At least, Brannon *thought* she was jesting. If not, even better.

After roughly another hour of wandering and complaining, the group crested a heavily wooded hill to find a sad excuse for a city waiting on the other side. The cluster of shanties and crumbling workhouses was wreathed in a wall of sharpened logs. A watchtower rose to the right of the gates with a single sentry posted inside.

It would have taken only a minute to scale the tower, slit the man's throat, and crank the gates open. While efficient, Brannon's allies would not have approved.

According to Tawny, who'd been tracking the movement and meter of the Wilds, the trail would remain more or less in place for roughly an hour. She sprinkled some salt sigils on the earth to ensure it, and Amatha opted to stay behind while the others scouted the settlement, volunteering Aedyn to wait alongside her. The prince sputtered numerous objections, having apparently forgotten about preserving his magic, but the chieftain's will won out. It was nice to know *someone* could get the insufferable fop to follow instructions now and again.

Brannon took the lead, knowing introductions would fall to him. He wasn't exactly a people person, but he possessed far more presence than Elwyn, and Tawny seldom acted like a person at all, what with all her sniffing and scampering about.

As the trio drew nearer to the fence, the city's stance on their new neighbors became obvious. Bundles of dried herbs dangled from the gates, and iron wires wove around the walls. He doubted such precautions would fend off the foliage for long, let alone the fae.

The severed heads, however, seemed a decent deterrent.

There were ten in total, mounted atop wooden pikes and propped into two tidy rows to form an entryway path. Most had rotted beyond recognition, just bits of blackened flesh clinging to bone. A few were fresh enough to draw flies. A raven was perched atop the pronged antlers of a redheaded woman and was trying its damnedest to pluck a crimson eye from her socket.

"Who goes there?" the guard demanded, aiming a crossbow at Brannon's chest. "State your business or join our little welcome party."

With stabbing off the table, Brannon shouted a few random names up to the sentry and claimed their party had been ambushed while traversing the Wilds. He ripped details of the account from that of the interrogee back at Samhria, so it rang with a touch more truth than a wholly imagined tale.

"That answers one question." The guard snorted like the hog he vaguely resembled. "Now, onto the bit about your business…"

"Your handiwork is impressive." Brannon flicked the nearest skull between the eye sockets. "I wouldn't mind making a few of these myself."

The guard broke into a gap-toothed grin. "Well then, the Iron Claws might just have use for you!" He rested his crossbow against the railing and placed a hand on an iron crank. "I'm inclined to let you through, provided you pass the test. Simply step closer and repeat after me." He cleared his throat. "I am a mortal human."

A clever test, actually, given that the fae could not lie. It would also make it impossible to sneak Aedyn and Amatha into the city, no matter how they disguised themselves. That is, unless Brannon fell back on his throat-slitting plan.

Shoving the thought aside for the moment, he approached the tower with the others and recited the simple pledge. Satisfied, the guard began turning the crank. What a strange world, where any man could be trusted so long as literal monsters prowled the shadows. It would have made business so very easy.

Brannon idled at the base of the tower even after the gates groaned open. "Who are these Iron Claws you mentioned?" he asked, hoping they might have information on the neighboring Augusky, perhaps even the Procession itself.

"Why, we're the ones responsible for them trophies you was admiring." The guard's chest puffed as he threw a thumb toward the severed heads. "Protectors of five slums in total, and one prissy district at their center—though that's by chance more than choice. If you're really interested in fighting, we could use the help. We were over two-hundred strong at the offset, but months of nightly raids cut our ranks in half."

"The Unseelie attack *nightly?*" Elwyn asked.

The sentry jumped like he hadn't noticed her—which he likely hadn't—but his surprise swiftly morphed into confusion. "Un*what*sy?" He scratched his beard. "If that's a funny name for them goat-folk, then yes. Though, now that I think of it, these past couple nights are the exception. I've been meaning to ask Kade and his boys if they know why, but you might just beat me to it. They frequent Petie's Pub at this hour." He pointed to the widest of several shit-strewn streets. "Follow the main road around three curves and you'll come to a pair of twin breweries. You'll find Petie's at the end of the alley what runs between them. I'd say you can't miss it, but Ma didn't raise no liar." He angled his left shoulder forward, flashing a trio of silver stripes on his sleeve. "You'll know us by our claws."

Brannon and Elwyn exchanged a knowing glance. Their interrogee had worn the exact same emblem in the exact same location, and he'd mentioned fighting alongside others. Elwyn had been too soft to pry for further details—especially where fingernails and teeth were concerned—so they would have to use what little information they'd gathered to garnish more. Worst case scenario, Brannon could loosen a few tongues the old-fashioned way. Such tasks were made easier by pliers, but he was nothing if not resourceful.

Having wasted too much time already, the trio started down the street. Brannon tried to focus on his surroundings, but his colleagues' peculiar behaviors made it difficult. Tawny practically frolicked around puddles and piles of horseshit, gaping awkwardly at the townsfolk and their crumbling cottages. Elwyn shrank into her cloak, giving passersby a wide berth. More than once, she vanished into shadow only to reappear a second later. If Brannon hadn't made a point of tracking her, he'd have probably forgotten her altogether. He'd long envied and loathed that convenient little trait, though he was beginning to think it had less to do with Elwyn's talents and more with the piskie hidden in her hood.

For a while, it was easy to dismiss the thief's actions as common cowardice, but as they pressed further into the city, the source of her apprehension became clear. There was a degree of familiarity to these particular brick stoops and shuttered windows, the dirt paths that meandered underfoot and the thatched eaves that cast shadows from above. A farm boy by birth and an assassin by trade, Brannon hadn't wasted much time in the slums, but he'd often passed through them often on his way back to...

Ebensburg.

There was no mistaking the jumble of towers and spires that rose above the rooftops the moment Brannon turned the next corner. Saint Aldrich's lay hidden behind a forest of manors and citadels, but he could practically feel it beating at the district's core, steadily pumping poison through its every blue-blooded vein. He'd hoped the sanctuary had fallen in the Confluence, but it was made of stronger stuff than the houses on the outskirts. If they were still intact, it most certainly was. Just picturing Father Beaus nestled safely in his study, meting orders to the captives he called his children, lit a vengeful fire beneath Brannon's skin.

He stomped ahead, making himself large and conspicuous. Elwyn could hide from the Greyscale all she liked, but he *wanted* an agent to spot him, capture him, drag him back to the syndicate to face his fate. Sure, he'd wind up shackled to an altar, intestines dripping from his open belly, but not before he set the inner sanctum aflame and watched the Father burn to the bone.

A tug on Brannon's sleeve jarred him back to the present. He elbowed Elwyn away, and she tipped her head toward the pair of breweries they'd nearly passed by. Embarrassment sped his steps as he corrected his course. In his haste, he nearly slammed into a redheaded stranger who was rushing the opposite direction.

"Watch it!" Brannon growled, drawing his daggers.

"I'm so sorry!" the man replied, smoothing his shamrock vest with his palms. "I was a touch distracted, and—"

Their eyes met—the same dusky hemlock hue—and the stranger staggered back, inhaling sharply through a narrow nose that matched Brannon's for size and shape. In fact, his every feature might have been a mirror reflection, save for his garish garb and cinnamon hair. Both men stammered for a moment, searching for words that suited the situation.

Brannon found them first.

"What the fuck?"

ARYN

"You demanded *what?*" Creagor lurched to his feet, slamming his fist on the table so hard it dented the oraithvine. Aryn felt like doing the same, though it would not have had as large an impact—literally or figuratively.

"It's not as though I asked them to present it on a platter." Mearalas straightened the silver crown she'd borrowed. The palace seamstress had also lent her a beaded gown and silk shawl on Aryn's orders—an act of charity he already regretted. "Mailair's head is the only logical choice. I doubt any of us could identify them by their hoof, and I imagine they could hobble along just fine without one."

"You have placed Amatha in danger!" Creagor barked, reaching for the axe slung across his back. "If someone must lose head..."

"She placed herself in danger." Mearalas sat perfectly still despite the obvious threat. "I simply made the risks worthwhile. Had anyone present objected to my orders, they had every right and opportunity to refuse them."

"And what alternative did you offer, I wonder?" Aryn motioned for Creagor to sit, though his blood was no less heated. If the Undine remnants weren't so scant, he might have attacked her himself. "Mark this order well, Mearalas. The moment your people arrive on these shores, you will send a portion back to retrieve our children, and you will do so without complaint."

Mearalas' scowl deepened. "Do you truly believe they've idled in place all afternoon?" She folded her webbed hands on the table. "With the fate of the outposts and lesser citadels unknown, it is possible only my small company of Undine remain. You are a fool if you think I would risk a single subject on such a pointless errand." Perhaps realizing how calloused she appeared, she softened both her expression and tone. "The witch-ward has potions to spare, and my presence is a testament to their efficacy. When the task is complete, your spawn will return of their own volition, at which point I expect an apology in addition to your heartfelt gratitude."

"Gratitude?" Aryn had already thanked her for intervening against the shellicoats, and that was far more thanks than she deserved. "For saving my son only to have him dig his own grave?"

"Do you truly have so little faith in him?" Mearalas' lips quirked into a smug grin. She wouldn't have cared if Aedyn came back in pieces, so long as her goals were met. "You're clearly letting your emotions cloud your reasoning. Rest assured, I weighed the options and made the logical call. True, we would best Mailair's hordes in battle, but not without suffering wounds. Do not doubt that Fuara would sweep in after them to deliver a killing blow. Usurpers are scavengers all."

Aryn had to grip his armrests to remain seated. "Speaking from experience?"

Mearalas narrowed her midnight eyes. "I am not a usurper, but a liberator," she replied. "My uncle was abusing a crown that was never his to wear. It was my duty, as daughter of the Eternal Queen Enkata—"

"*Queen* Enkata," Creagor corrected, raising a finger. "Not Eternal anymore."

"Precisely." The words hissed through Aryn's gritted teeth. "Your mother removed herself from the cycle, squandering eternity over reckless emotions, all because—"

"The Undine should be arriving soon, yes?" Soen chimed in for the first time that evening. "Should we not be preparing the—"

"—she grew bored and impatient." Aryn continued. He would not let Soen reroute the conversation this time. "From the dawn of time, your mother was a selfish, vain, short-sighted ruler, and you..." He met her glare, matching it for chill. "You have proven no better."

Mearalas rose, stretching as tall as her spine allowed. "My mother was not shortsighted; she was deceived, and I have done everything in my power to protect not only my people, but *all* of Seelie-kind from making the same mistake. I will not sit quietly and let myself be lectured by a man who can't control his own child, much less a kingdom." She whirled sharply, whistling a cue to the sentries beyond the doors. "Do not call on me again until you are prepared to address me as your peer."

A light-song slipped across the threshold, bidding the doors open. For a tense moment, the only sound in Talune's Heart was the whisper of borrowed slippers on the silk rug.

Once Mearalas vanished from view, Aryn folded forward, burying his fingers in his hair and releasing a sigh he'd been holding back for ages. His outburst had only worsened matters, but he could not yet bring himself to regret it.

"Is past time you rebuked her." Creagor patted Aryn between the shoulders. "Mearalas seldom minces words, and turnabout is always fair."

"Yes, but it is not always loving." Soen threaded her arms around herself, making her slight frame that much smaller. "True justice would see us spinning in circles forever. I, for one, would quite like to move forward, and I believe the circumstances demand it."

The circumstances had been demanding an awful lot. Soon, Aryn would have nothing left to offer them.

"You can leave." He waved his peers off with a flick of his wrist. It wasn't a demand, and he didn't truly want them to obey it, but he couldn't well ask them to hover nearby while he sulked away the evening. "I promise to send word if Amatha and the others appear."

"*When* they appear." Creagor rose, rolling his neck and heaving his shoulders like he was about to enter an arena. "Is appreciated. In meantime, I must crush things. Is better those things belong to me."

Soen hovered a moment longer. Even as peripheral blurs, her ice-water eyes pierced straight through him. "Are you going to be alright?" she asked.

Her concern felt genuine, not that it redeemed her. If she thought he hadn't figured out how she'd aided in Amatha's rebellion, she wasn't half as insightful as he'd long believed her to be. He'd have called her out on the matter, but it would have meant confessing his own mistakes. He wasn't ready for that. At least, not aloud.

For as often as he cited the Treaty of Dusk, he'd only ever been trying to protect Aedyn from his darker nature. In doing so, he'd shoved the boy down the very path his mother had blazed centuries before, and his kingdom was no safer for it.

Soen had made the right call, dangerous though it was. Perhaps, once the matter was settled, they would discuss it plainly.

"I need to be alone for now," he said. "I have much to think about."

"I understand," Soen offered a solemn bow, ethereal wings sprouting from her shoulders. "Should your thoughts grow too heavy, you know where to find me."

She passed up the throne room doors in favor of an open window, trailing snowy feathers as she flitted out into the night.

Aryn sat in silence for a minute more before waving a hand over the damaged oraithvine, humming a simple tune. He hadn't used either of his gifts in decades, preferring an austerity to illusion and honest labor to lightsinging, yet the filigree danced to his bidding, curling back into shape one elegant whorl at a time.

It was good to know he still had the power to fix things.

*"Worlds get a little smaller when they're forced to overlap,
But you will still find monsters at the edges of the map."*

CHAPTER 15

WHEN WORLDS COLLIDE

BRANNON

or once, Aedyn's offhanded prediction had proven correct—Brannon had indeed stumbled upon something worth stabbing. Only he couldn't justify stabbing his double. Not before he found some answers about their uncanny similarities.

After introducing himself as Deinua, the man had offered to lead the group to his cottage, hoping his parents could provide insight into the situation. He hadn't stopped talking in the twenty minutes since. In fact, if he spouted one more flowery sentence about how the fucking sunset filtered through the fucking canopy for the fucking pleasure of alighting on Aedyn's smile, Brannon's *Aras Tosc* were liable to find his spine of their own fucking accord!

"Careful, viper." Elwyn eyed his trembling fists. "Save your venom for a worthy target."

"He stole my face," Brannon hissed, "and he's *composing sonnets* with it."

Judging from Elwyn's grin, she found his frustration thoroughly amusing. "Now, have you considered that you might have stolen *his* face?" she teased. "You're clearly the evil twin in this scenario."

Brannon missed the days when she'd feared him too deeply to taunt him. Finding her attempts at levity supremely unhelpful, he waved her off with his middle finger and fixed his focus on the object of his unease. The stranger traipsed along at the head of the formation, having swiftly recovered from the initial shock of their meeting. Apparently, more peculiar things happened in the Wilds on a daily basis. Tawny had been pacing around him for most of the trek, studying him like a museum exhibit. She'd even poked him a couple times, as though checking for the illusions Aedyn had already assured her weren't there.

"You're certain you're not a changeling?" she asked for perhaps the dozenth time. "Most are clueless about their nature until the spellwork begins to unravel."

"I'm not a changeling," Deinua replied, chuckling. "I'm pretty sure my parents would have mentioned something about it."

Tawny wilted from the shoulders up. "You'd be surprised."

With how he wove through the tumult without a care, it was tempting to believe he *was* a changeling, and that Brannon would've inherited the same blissful ignorance had the swap never occurred. Deinua had claimed to be half-fae, after all. Maybe that meant he could half-lie about his origins.

"If you don't believe me, you can ask my parents yourself." Deinua hopped over a log as it rolled across the trail of its own volition. "I'm sure they'll have just as many questions for you. My father spent several lifetimes among the Seelie. He'll be curious to learn how the Light Realms have fared since the Wedding."

"Since the *what*?" Amatha scratched her scalp shards.

"The Wedding of the Worlds." Deinua turned to face her, walking backwards as though the path was not rerouting behind him. Somehow, he managed not to stumble, even when a bramble vine reached menacingly for his ankles. "What else would you call the night the realms merged into one?"

"We've been calling it the Confluence," Aedyn answered, tapping his chin. "Though, come to think of it, the whole ordeal was dramatic and unnecessary, and all involved are worse off for having endured it. I suppose 'Wedding' fits well enough."

"Getting cold feet before the date's even been set?" Elwyn's blithe tone didn't quite mask her bitterness. "I'm sure Eloana would love to hear it."

"Aedyn has eternally cold feet." Amatha elbowed the prince's side. "His blood is busy elsewhere."

The pointless prattle carried on for a few minutes more before jarring to a stop with Deinua. He turned sharply, sniffing the air to the side of the trail. "The cottage should be just beyond this maple grove," he said, vanishing into a billow of yellow leaves. "Try to keep up!"

Despite having fallen to the rear of the group, Brannon followed first. He took great care to walk in his double's precise footsteps, lest a lurking trap catch him unawares. Behind him, crystals scraped, branches snapped, and curses flowed liberally, but not a single snare or steel claw sprang. The group burst from the trees one after the other, gasping in unison at the massive ring of mushrooms that encircled a bluegrass clearing, their caps glowing yellow-green against the gloaming.

The tallest of the toadstools rivaled the nearest sycamores; the shortest rose a bit higher than Brannon's shoulders. Naturally, Aedyn sprinted straight up to a stalk and poked it, sending a shower of phosphorescent spores raining down around him. Tawny rushed forward with an empty potion bottle and tried to catch the glimmers as they fell.

It was a miracle those two hadn't gotten themselves killed yet.

"I've never seen mushrooms like these before!" The girl shook her bottle, and the captured spores flared briefly back to life. "Are they edible?"

"I've never tried to eat them," Deinua answered with a shrug. "I doubt my father would appreciate it, given he's been tending them since before I was born. They require far less upkeep than a standard sigil ring or stone circle, and their secondary property is incredibly convenient."

Amatha stepped closer, craning her neck. "Which is...?"

Rather than answer, Deinua winked over his shoulder, slipped between two toadstools, and...vanished.

Brannon rubbed his eyes, squinting at the gap between stalks. Only wind-tousled grass moved in the field beyond. Unwilling to be bested by his lesser imitation, he drew a sharp breath and sharper daggers, then stepped into the ring.

A quaint cottage appeared at the center of the glade, painted in hues of mint, mauve, and marigold. Giant squashes and ripe red tomatoes spilled around one side of it, while foxglove sprigs and butterfly brush bordered the rest. A wisteria tree hung over the whole, its lavender boughs forming curtains around the entryway door, and morning glories climbed the gray brick chimney.

Not a single flower in the garden should have been in bloom this time of year. It bothered Brannon that he knew as much.

"Mother!" Deinua shouted as he opened the door, a hand cupped over his mouth. "I hope it's alright I've brought guests!"

"That depends!" A muffled voice shouted back. "Do you intend to have them over for dinner, or over *for* dinner?"

The reply drew a forehead slap and groan from Deinua, but it gave Brannon pause. Just what kind of half-fae was this man, anyway?

Apparently unbothered, the rest of the group piled into the house. Brannon followed with his knives at the ready. The sitting parlor was a small space, made that much smaller by a plethora of mismatched chairs, benches, and tables. Planters and overstuffed vases crowded every possible surface, and floral vines climbed the windows and doorframes, guided by little bronze hooks. Amatha claimed a relatively clear corner by the staircase, where she stood still as a statue to avoid breaking anything, and the others swiftly found seats to their liking. Brannon's feet ached as much as anyone's, but he opted to linger by the entrance, *icons* in hand.

Upon noticing the weapons, Deinua moved a step closer to the wooden pike leaning against wall beside the hearth. "My father should return any minute now," he said, a forced smile flaunting wicked fangs. "In the meantime, I'm sure my mother will happily answer what she can, though she'll probably demand to feed you first."

"You know me well, dear!" She nudged a cracked door open with her elbow, then entered carrying a tray of butterscotch scones. "It's lucky that I was already trying out a new recipe. I wasn't expecting to host any—"

The moment she saw Brannon, she dropped her platter. He nearly lost his daggers to the same spark of surprise. Time had spun far more silver into her hair and carved a permanent smile at the corners of her lips, but the shape of her face, the freckles that bridged her nose, even the daisy-dotted dress she wore were ripped right from Brannon's memories.

Countless vulgar phrases flooded his skull, but only the foulest found his lips.

"Ma?"

Brannon's daggers carved a splintered path through the trees. The branches fought back, grasping at his cape, his collar, even his bootlaces. It didn't matter that his armor would be torn to leather strips before he reached a game trail. If the Wilds didn't devour him by sunrise, some ancient horror would take up the task, and either fate was preferable to spending one more second in that fucking cottage!

He was charging through a birch thicket when a root finally snared him, sending him sprawling to a tangle of ferns and leaf rot. He lost one blade to the tangled undergrowth; the other twisted in his grasp, biting the skin between his thumb and forefinger.

"Shit!" He dropped the dagger, clenching his fist. Blood welled from the gash in his glove, but the sting told him the cut wasn't too deep.

Several lectures snaked through his mind as he retrieved his *icons* from the foliage, not one of them ringing in his own voice. A broken pocket watch ticked a reminder for him to toughen up. Amatha chided him for breaking from the group in direct defiance to her orders. Father Beaus demanded he return to the cottage and add an artful crimson accent to the parlor. Ferea implored him to close his eyes, inhale deeply, and picture a parasol folding.

He was already on the ground, elbows tucked at his sides, so he decided to give the Sylph's advice a try.

After only three breaths, the cinnamon air soothed something feral inside him, allowing the darkness behind his eyelids to deepen. The clamor of the churning forest made it impossible to untether entirely, but it also served as a decent distraction—a savage breed of lullaby composed of swaying branches, croaking frogs, and chirping crickets.

Had he been less attuned to the surrounding din, he might have mistaken the approaching *skitter* for roots writhing through brackens, or the rattling *hisssss* for a breeze tousling the canopy. The wildlife fell quiet, and the soil beneath his knees began to writhe as countless nightcrawlers squirmed to the surface. A chill ticked down Brannon's vertebrae as the foliage *crackled* and *crashed* behind him, begging a careful glance back.

Were it not for the faint gleam of its carapace, the creature might have blended with the shadows. No less than eight feet of it wound through the underbrush before vanishing behind the trunk of an elm. Far too many legs unfolded from its underbelly as it stretched skyward, spittle webbing between its mandibles. The milky residue dripped to the ferns below with a sizzle, reducing them to wilted, mucous lumps.

Brannon could not so much as think of a centipede without his inner ear itching. The Greyscale enforcers had used them to teach perfect stillness, as thrashing about or trying to pry them free would damage an agent's hearing and, subsequently, their value. As this monstrous version spread its pinchers, its throat convulsing like a hearth bellow, Brannon realized perfect stillness wasn't going to help him. He rolled aside right as a stream of venom arched through the air, spattering a birch trunk. Bark flayed away like flesh, bleeding black pitch.

Brannon had never found his feet so swiftly. They carried him through the dark, winding around ghost-pale trees, bounding over fallen logs, forging recklessly through tangles of prickly briarbrush. The forest took the creature's side, bowing beneath its serpentine form. Brambles and branches grabbed hold of Brannon, slowing him as best they could. Soon, acrid spittle gusted his boots, gnawing through leather and linen to sting his skin.

Desperate, he dove between the roots of a partially unearthed oak. Pinchers clasped around his heel, but he struck back, sending a twitching antenna to the soil. The monster shrieked, freeing him, and he attacked before it could recover. His daggers glanced off carapace twice before a blade found a beady eye. Vibrant blue blood gushed from the wound. The centipede spasmed before falling limp, head lolling to the side.

A shaky laugh burst from Brannon's lips as he pulled the dagger free. He hadn't felt so satisfied in months. He crawled out from beneath the tree and took a moment to gloat over his quarry, placing a boot atop its back and spitting in one of its five remaining eyes. If only his own saliva could melt through flesh.

The carapace shifted underfoot, and a second rattling *hissssss* found Brannon's ears. Breath caged beneath his collarbone, he turned to see the monster's tail curling forward like that of a scorpion. Six more beady eyes stared down at him as a second pair of mandibles stretched wide.

"Well, fuck."

The monster lunged, pinning Brannon to the ground beside its own lifeless head. Several legs pierced his cape and hood. One lanced through the leather on his upper arm, taking a strip of skin with it. Cloudy droplets rained from its maw, gnawing though leaves and twigs and locks of dark hair. One hit the tip of Brannon's ear and sizzled straight through it. He trapped a scream behind clenched teeth as pain dimmed his vision.

A spear caught the creature beneath the chin, lodging deep, and the monster toppled sideways. Next thing Brannon knew, his mystery rescuer was hauling him to his feet. The sight of a single crimson eye burning in the night sent him scrambling for his fallen daggers.

"I've always wanted a brother." The voice was anything but menacing. "Now that I finally have one, it seems he's determined to get himself killed."

"Brother?" Brannon squinted, rising with weapons in hand. The forelock that had hid Deinua's glowing eye before was now tucked neatly behind his ear. Between that mismatched stare and his sinister smile, any traits the two of them shared seemed suddenly trivial. "We are *not* brothers!"

Deinua wrenched his spear from the fallen centipede. He grimaced upon seeing that the blood had stained it blue. "Well, we share a mother, so..."

"*That woman* is no mother!" Brannon sheathed his *icons* after a moment's hesitation. Deinua had saved his life. He could keep his own a little longer. "If you must spout nonsense, I think I preferred the poetry. And that's saying something."

"I didn't mean to strike a nerve." Deinua kicked the ground, rousing a flurry of leaves. "If it's any consolation, I'm not sure how to feel about this either."

"I take it she never mentioned me."

Deinua bit his lip, a single fang poking free.

Figures. She hadn't glanced back the night she walked away. Why would she have glanced back in the years since?

"If we must have this conversation, I suggest we finish it back home." Deinua tipped his spear toward the slain monster. "Ollphéists are a tad cannibalistic, and they release a pheromone upon dying that calls to their kin like nectar to pollen sprites. I'd rather not stick around for the funeral."

Brannon crossed his arms. "You can't possibly think I'm going back to that shithole."

"Well, that Procession you're waiting for is nearly a week off." Deinua shrugged, starting through the woods without him. "If you'd like to rendezvous with a few more monsters in that time, you're welcome to it."

Brannon looked over at the slaughtered centipede and the milky slaver slowly eating through the foliage around it. After carefully weighing his dismal options, he decided to follow Deinua back to the glade. He was there on orders, after all. He wasn't the type to abandon those easily.

"I'll be sleeping downstairs, so you and your friends can share my loft," Deinua said as the toadstool ring rose into view. "I imagine you need time and space to process, and you'll have plenty of both. Mother has already vowed to announce herself before ascending a single stair, and she'll have passed the edict on to my father by now."

Brannon froze mid-step. It wasn't the first time Deinua had referenced his father, and logically, *something* had to have sired him, but the word now carried new implications. "How old are you, exactly?" he asked.

"A month shy of twenty-two." Deinua paused between toadstool stalks, half-hidden behind the illusion of rippling bluegrass. "Why?"

"I just turned twenty last week."

Deinua chuckled, vanishing into the glade only to reappear a blink later when Brannon followed him beyond the barrier. "She always told me time moves slowly in the Mortal Realm," he said with a bemused head shake. "I'd never have guessed the extent of it. I suppose this makes me your big-little brother. Or is it little-big brother?"

"We're not brothers," Brannon growled, pressing past him and into the cottage.

The air in the parlor was warm and dry, though the hearth-fire had already been doused. Candlelight and whispers spilled out from behind a cracked door along the far wall.

"...not even two weeks, love." The women's voice set Brannon's teeth on edge. "I owe him that much."

"People change, Lieri." The reply was a guttural growl, almost beastly. "The boy you knew before might not be the man we're harboring now."

So, not everyone in the cottage was an utter fool. Brannon would have to watch himself around that one—assuming he had to be around that one at all. With any luck, the group would be moving on soon, not a conversation suffered.

He followed the sound of his colleagues' chatter and the pale gleam of lanternlight up a narrow staircase to a surprisingly uncluttered loft. A single vase of lilies sat atop one of two side tables, and a bookcase had been shoved into a corner, the tomes stacked sideways so more fit on the shelves. Aedyn had already claimed the bed and was half-jokingly suggesting Elwyn share it with him, and Amatha and Tawny were sorting components nearby while the latter rattled on about the metaphysical properties of each.

Both conversations died when a floorboard creaked beneath Brannon's heel.

"I have no need of your pity," he said, gesturing vaguely to the gash on his arm. The sting had already faded to a dull throb, but the last thing he needed was an infection to fret over. "Salves, on the other hand…"

"On it!" Tawny rifled through her satchel and arranged several supplies on the floor beside her. "I'm out of the good stuff, but I've still got all the basics."

Basic was Brannon's preference. He'd spent so much time among the Sylphs, he'd begun to miss the twisted pride that came with a well-earned wound. He shooed Tawny away as he settled on the rug, insisting on tending to his own injuries. She scurried off to join the others as they resumed their conversation, this time focusing on more pertinent matters.

"Koa may prove a valuable resource," Amatha said as though everyone knew the name. Probably the second voice from the kitchen. "He has never participated in the Procession, but he has offered to guide us to an acquaintance with strong ties to the Augusky. If we know the route in advance, we can better prepare an ambush."

Brannon poured a cleansing spirit directly onto his wound. The burn was strong enough to make his teeth ache—a welcome reprieve from the conversation.

"Do you think his acquaintance could point us toward the bramble palace itself?" Aedyn asked, swinging his legs over the side of the bed. "If this Procession is half as pompous as a Seelie fete, the crowd is bound to be dense. Wouldn't it be safer to, you know…" he slid a finger across his throat, "without every monster in the Wilds present to see it?"

"The crowd will be an asset, actually," Tawny chimed in. "In order to create the panic Mearalas wants, we'll need at least a few Augusky present to witness Mailair's assassination. Otherwise, how will they know the throne is up for grabs?"

"I don't particularly care what Mearalas wants," Elwyn said, leaning against the bookcase. "She stated her terms, but we never agreed to them. Why not gather information from the locals and head back, as we'd originally planned? We were on our way to question a troop of hunters when," she shot Brannon another sympathetic glance, "things took a turn."

Brannon pointedly ignored her, scooping poultice from a tin with his bare fingers and slathering it over the gash. A nauseating chill drowned the sting in an instant.

"I fear Mearalas might be correct for once," Amatha said with a sigh. "While I still hope to sway the Judges, it is probable their minds are set. In slaying Mailair, we will buy time not only for ourselves, but for the local mortals." She rubbed the crystalline grit that served as her hair. "For now, we should plan for both possibilities. Tomorrow—"

"Is anyone hungry?" The voice chimed from the parlor below, sickly soft as cobwebs. "I made another batch of scones."

Most everyone responded with childish enthusiasm, Brannon being the exception. He wrapped his arm as swiftly as possible and shoved Aedyn from the bed before collapsing atop it, fully clothed. Eyes clenched tight, he rolled to face the window, cocooning himself in an obnoxiously soft quilt. If he had to watch that woman climb the stairs, there was a decent chance he'd shove her right back down them.

The syrupy scents of berries and butter ascended the steps first, followed closely by the whisper of bare feet. Brannon cursed his tongue for watering.

"The scones are for everyone," the woman said, "but the raspberry tarts are for... Oh, he's fallen asleep already?"

"It's been a trying day for all of us," Elwyn answered. Finally, a practical use for all that pity. "I'll watch over them, in case he wakes soon."

"They won't be wasted, either way," Aedyn added.

Ceramic and silverware *clinked* around the loft, and small talk was made of the weather and pastry recipes. Apparently, a storm would be rolling in soon, and almond pulp could replace butter in a pinch. Within fifteen minutes, the group was unraveling their bedrolls, half-heartedly complaining of stuffed stomachs and heavy eyelids. Through all of it, Brannon kept perfectly still, pretending a centipede had curled up in his ear. He maintained the ruse even when a second blanket fanned overtop him and a mournful goodnight found his ears.

The gesture might have been heartwarming had Brannon a heart left to warm.

*"Even the boldest wanderers have somewhere they can hide,
It isn't where we lay our heads, but where our dreams reside."*

CHAPTER 16

WHERE THE HEART IS

ELWYN

lwyn found a peculiar joy in dicing carrots. The same went for celery, zucchini, and potatoes, all of which were now thinly sliced and piled neatly throughout the kitchen. It wasn't a particularly large contribution, but it was the least she could do to repay Deinua's family for their hospitality, and it reminded her of the brief time she'd spent in the quiet, uneventful town of Amblewick.

Alas, the time for menial chores was coming to an end. Beyond the shuttered windows, the downpour that had halted the mission for two days was finally fading to a drizzle. They were now free to tackle the objectives Amatha had assigned them throughout the wait. Brannon and Tawny had already left with Deinua's father to collect information on the Augusky palace. The assassin hadn't looked particularly thrilled about the arrangement, but a stern word from Amatha had sent him trudging out the door. Hopefully, all three would return intact.

"Oh, goodness!" Lieri stumbled back, having nearly bumped into Elwyn for the fourth time that morning. "You're so quiet, I forgot you were here. I was even beginning to feel lonely." She scanned the countertop, appraising the heaps of diced produce. "This is excellent work, and efficient. Have you cooked professionally?"

Elwyn was practiced in slicing things, but food seldom entered the equation. "I worked at an inn for a short time," she said, opting for the safest possible answer. "It was a surprisingly pleasant experience."

"You'll have to tell me all about it someday." Lieri scooped some potatoes into a kettle of tepid water. "I have a weakness for stories, and that sounds like one I'd enjoy."

"There isn't much to tell." Elwyn plucked a carrot from a basket and set to work on it. "I can say with absolute confidence those were the least adventurous days of my life."

"Not all stories need be adventurous, and certainly not all chapters," Lieri said, hanging the kettle in the as yet unlit brick oven. "I prefer odes to epics for that very reason. What good is a life spent slaying monsters and toppling tyrants if you never take time to listen to birdsong and gather daisies? Surely, constant exposure to enchantments and curses would steal the magic from mornings spent sipping tea beneath the sunrise and nights spent curled up hearthside with a good book. It's a pity those moments are seldom memorialized in legend. What were all those valiant knights fighting for, if not home?"

Elwyn had encountered a decidedly unfair share of monsters and curses, but survival had been her only motivation for overcoming them. "Not everybody has a home, and not everybody needs one." She slid a perfectly sliced carrot aside to start on the next. "Places are places, and only that. Any affection we feel for them is one-sided."

Lieri smiled warmly at the gold chain on her wrist. "Now, whoever claimed home was a place?"

Before Elwyn could ask about the bracelet, the paring knife—which had been rhythmically slicing through the carrot—swept suddenly through open air, nearly nicking her thumb. Luatha cackled maniacally from atop the pilfered produce.

"I knew you'd return to your antics eventually." Elwyn half-glared at the piskie. "You know I appreciate the occasional jest, but I'd prefer you not maim me before the mission is out."

Luatha smirked, rubbing her purple palms together.

"Will it truly be a plague when one or two spare fingers fall?
You'll wield your weapon well enough if you don't lose them all."

"Someone's grumpy when she's hungry," Lieri cooed, setting a raspberry tart before the piskie. Luatha pounced on the treat, spraying the counter with crumbs and jelly flecks.

"She's literally surrounded by food." Elwyn waved the knife haphazardly between the produce piles. "You're going to spoil her."

Lieri tossed a second tart, which Elwyn caught and devoured at once. It wasn't citrinebread, but the blend of clashing flavors were nearly as delicious.

Perhaps a little spoiling wasn't horrible, so long as the rot was equally distributed.

"Are you ready to head out?" Deinua entered the kitchen with a flourish, a forest green cloak trimmed in ivy satin draped over his veridian suit. He'd offered to guide Elwyn back to Wiltshire so she could question the Iron Claws. Apparently, it was a formal occasion. "Dress warm. There's no telling how long this lull will last now that your people brought your fickle skies with you."

"Yes, we had so much say in the matter," Elwyn said, wiping her hands on a washrag. She threw on her ratty gray cloak before following her chipper guide out the door, Luatha fluttering beside her. Before the trio could breach the toadstool hedge, Aedyn rushed out from the woodshed, calling after her.

"I'm glad I caught you," he said, nearly slipping on the damp grass. "I needed... Well, it's just that...I was wondering..." He looked around like he'd lost something—his mind, perhaps—then glanced skyward, turning his palm toward the drizzle. "This weather could worsen at any moment. Are you certain that cloak is warm enough?"

"Um...yes?" Elwyn's garment had seen better days, but it was far more practical than the frilly blouse and pressed slacks Aedyn had been stacking wood in. "It's survived far worse than a little rain, as have I."

"What about your dagger?" he asked. "And the piskie? We've already learned the hard way that one isn't too helpful without the other."

Judging from Luatha's tiny huff, he'd offended her. Elwyn might have been offended, too, were she less bewildered. Since when did he question her survival instincts?

"I'm not a fool, Aedyn." She patted *Gelah's* hilt, scanning his face for signs of fever. He was looking a bit flushed, come to think of it. "Are you feeling well?"

"I just don't think two people are enough for this job," he said, fidgeting with his sleeves. "I know I can't enter the city without drawing suspicion, but I could at least accompany you through the Wilds. Brannon encountered something dreadful out there, and I'm sure there are more monsters—"

"Aedyn!" Amatha emerged from the woodshed with her obsidian axe hefted over one shoulder. "We agreed to help our hosts with firewood. *We* being the key word."

"Your concern is heartwarming." Deinua shooed Aedyn off. "Wiltshire cannot have wandered far in only two days, and our errand won't take long once we arrive. If we're not back by supper, feel free to shine your armor, tame a mount, and charge the gates."

Before further conversation could be had, he grabbed Elwyn by the hood of her cloak and tugged her past the toadstools. Aedyn watched them leaving until the illusory barrier hid him, possibly longer.

"That was difficult to watch," Deinua teased, pressing into a pine grove that had been a maple grove days before. "And utterly adorable."

"I have no idea what you're talking about," Elwyn said.

"Oh, don't play daft with me!" He gave her shoulder a playful push. "Surely you've noticed how his eyes follow your every move, how his laughter echoes yours, how he strives to make you smile and practically melts upon success." He sighed deeply, hands folded over his heart. "Why, if I wasn't so invested in your mutual bliss, I'd envy every longing glance he casts your way."

Elwyn shook her head. *Of course* she'd noticed Aedyn staring at her. She'd stolen several glances right back, though hers were far more surreptitious.

He'd always been pretty, in an objective way—elegant and bright, like a sunset or a wildflower glade—but that beauty had taken on a new hue of late, one that made her pulse flutter whenever he drew close. As far as she could tell, his features hadn't changed any, not that any feature had ever captured her attention. It was more like something on the inside had found its way out. Or perhaps she'd found her way *in*.

"His eyes wander so often it's a miracle he hasn't lost them," she said, more to herself than Deinua. "They'll move along the moment something pretty prances past."

"Something pretty has pranced past." He flipped his coppery hair. "Several times, and not a single stare."

Elwyn laughed. "It's a miracle you fae can fit in the same rooms as your egos."

"Ah, but I'm only *half* fae. Thus, my ego needs only half a room to flourish."

"I've been meaning to ask about that, actually." She scanned him from the corner of her eye. With his lips pressed shut and that crimson eye covered, he was basically a fancier, redheaded version of Brannon. That human appearance—coupled with technical half-truth of his heritage—explained how he made it past Wiltshire's city guards so easily. "I've spent quite a bit of time around the fae lately, but I've never met a half-fae before."

"Didn't you mention meeting the Undine Queen?"

Elwyn stopped in her tracks, knee deep in shivering brackens. "Mearalas is half-mortal?"

"On her father's side. Haven't you heard *The Ballad of the Sea Queen?*"

Elwyn had, and the memory was a knife to the heart. In the days before the Confluence, Lydia had often begged Aedyn to sing her to sleep. That ballad had been her favorite.

"Her mother was one of the Eternal Rulers of Spring." Deinua stepped onto a game trail, holding an evergreen bough aside. "She was supposed to live the same life over and over—wearing the same form, marrying the same man, ruling the same people—and she did, until about four centuries ago. According to the song, she spurned her Creator-appointed husband for a mortal man who later betrayed her. The tale ended with her removing herself from the cycle and throwing her entire kingdom into chaos." He released the bough once Elwyn stepped safely out onto the clay. "The era that followed is known as the Chorialan Cold Years, and it was worse than it sounds. It ended only when Mearalas wrenched the crown from her tyrant uncle and took her rightful place upon the Coral Throne."

That certainly helped to explain her treatment of mortals, but it didn't excuse it. "You're certain she's an improvement?"

"From your accounts, she's sterner than I'd hoped." Deinua sniffed the air, then continued the hike. "If I'm honest, I can't really blame her for being bitter. There aren't many of us, and we've never been held in high regard. No half-fae has ever been reborn through the cycle, so the fae dismiss us as soulless abominations, and the humans..." He sighed, shoulders slumping. "I'd hoped, when the worlds first wed, that I might find comradery among them, perhaps even acceptance. But, well, you've seen those heads by the gate, haven't you? Seems all I've found is a natural foe."

Or a natural feast. Elwyn had heard much about Glaistigs. The stories claimed they were powerful Solitary Fae—beholden to neither Court—and that they'd been blessed with beguiling magic and cursed with a thirst for human blood. In ages past, the Rhysiens would call on them to enact vengeance against their foes, sometimes offering their own lives in payment. Then again, the stories also claimed all Glaistigs were beautiful women, so it was probable they'd been scribed by lonely men with peculiar tastes.

"People, fae and mortal alike, find the silliest things to judge others for," Elwyn said, having often been looked down upon for her own parentage. "They think it will make them feel better about their own flaws, though it's seldom effective. For what it's worth, I suspect you have an overabundance of soul."

Deinua smiled so brightly his fangs no longer seemed fearsome. "I knew there was something sweet lurking beneath those sour scowls you so love sporting," he said. "Now, if only you would show *Aedyn* a little of that sweetness..."

Elwyn shot him her most acrid scowl as Luatha zipped protectively forward.

"We fae-folk do not share well, and this mortal is mine,
Stop shoving foolish sentiments into her crowded mind!"

A challenge sparked in Deinua's hemlock eye. He popped his collar and cleared his throat.

"Oh, silly little worker bee who's crowned herself a queen—
You think that you're the only one to wield verse like a sword?
Despite your plum complexion, you've been looking a tad green.
Your jealousy is childish and, frankly, untoward."

Luatha jarred to a stop mid-air, her ink-drop eyes flexing wide. After a moment of stunned hovering, she flitted forward with an angry whir.

"Raw angst will not make up for the inherent skills you lack,
You think yourself a lyricist, but really, you're a hack!"

If anything, the slight emboldened Deinua. He puffed his chest, examining his nails in mock indifference.

"With a touch more talent, that barb might have stabbed deeper,

A poet is made more by threads of eloquence than rhyme,
It seems that you have only crafted couplets in your time,
Now, would it somehow kill you to attempt a change of meter?"

Luatha sputtered furiously for half a minute before quipping back, and the battle raged on for the remainder of the trek.

Petie's Pub wasn't the rancid latrine Deinua had described it to be. At least, it wasn't any worse than most other back-alley taverns Elwyn had visited through the years. Sure, the smells were questionable, and the air was somehow arid and humid all at once, but the rats and roaches hid themselves well, and the patrons weren't too numerous or rowdy.

The Iron Claws were the exception to the rule. Five burly men dressed for dock work, a twig of a girl who could swear with the foulest of them, and an unexpectedly refined young nobleman had gathered around a cluster of tables to drink, laugh, and swap tall tales. Their blue jackets were of different hues and makes, with identical silver slashes embroidered on the left sleeves.

"Again, I cannot reasonably count it toward our tally," the nobleman said, scribbling something in his journal. "The average Augusky is six feet tall with biceps the size of gourds, and they typically wield weapons in addition to their horns. That whelp is worth a quarter-mark at most. Slay three more, and you might have cause for boasting."

"Don't underestimate the lil' ones!" the burliest of the bunch barked, kicking over the canvas sack at his feet. A fox the size of a sheepdog tumbled out of it, black as coal and limp as a ragdoll. "She ambushed me out of nowhere and got a few good swipes in before switching forms, but them teeth of hers..." He propped a boot on the table's edge and rolled up his trouser cuff, flaunting a grisly bite mark. "Smarts more'n a goat bite, that's for damn sure!"

"Pookas aren't even aggressive." Deinua huffed, crossing his arms. "They're just bad luck to the bad-hearted. Unless, of course, they feel threatened." He examined the iron weapons that hung from the hunters' backs and belts. "Anything might lash out when it feels threatened."

The hunters blinked in surprise, having failed to notice anyone approaching. The nobleman offered Deinua a dimpled smile. If Elwyn wasn't mistaken, that glint in his oaken eyes was recognition. "You wouldn't happen to be interested in becoming our new lorekeeper?" He set his journal aside, marking the page with a striped quill pen. "We've had an opening for a couple weeks now, and you clearly know a bit about the local beasts."

"I dunno' Kade." The twiggy girl tipped her flat cap back to better scan Deinua. "This one don't look like he'd last as long as Barte did. Which wasn't long to start with."

"We're not here about a job." Elwyn's interjection startled the hunters, who still hadn't seen her thanks to the piskie hidden in her hood. "We're looking for information on the Augusky. The gate guard said their attacks stopped a few days back. Any idea why?"

"I have my theories," the nobleman said, his smile shrinking. "Why, pray tell, should I share them with the likes of you?"

Having been remarkably unremarkable for much of her life, Elwyn was used to evoking surprise upon "appearing out of nowhere," but not...was that disappointment?

"Forgive my failed introduction." She placed a hand on Deinua's shoulder, testing a theory of her own. "My *cousin* and I have been living in the woods for much too long. We often forget the etiquette of polite society."

Just like that, the nobleman's grin returned in full. He rose, buttoning his tailcoat in the manner common to Pondrellen elites, and strode confidently up to Deinua. "Kadence Carroway," he said, offering his hand. "Captain of the Iron Claw's Wiltshire branch."

"Deinua Winrut." He eagerly accepted the captain's handshake. "Poet by choice, and hermit by fate. If you know the cure for either ailment, I'll happily jot it down alongside those theories of yours."

"Heaven forbid we ever find a cure for poetry." The captain's handshake lingered a touch longer than was customary, and he failed to offer one to Elwyn. "The hermit issue will vanish the moment you join our ranks, which I very much encourage. If you've truly survived in the woods all these months, you're far tougher than Mari assumes." He leaned closer and lowered his voice. "To be fair, she's dismissive of most newcomers. Like many a rat-hound, barking makes her feel bigger."

Elwyn glanced back over at the girl in the flat cap, who was far too busy to have overheard her captain's assessment. The whole troop seemed to be engaged in some kind of drinking game, and she was holding her own against her much larger peers.

"About that information..."

"Of course." Kadence scowled like Elwyn had interrupted something important. "Judging from the fact your organs are all in their rightful places, I can only assume you live in a low-conflict region. I've been trying to pinpoint those, so I'll happily trade intelligence. Wait here a moment while I retrieve my journal."

Deinua's stare followed Kadence back to the table, drifting slowly down the length of him. Had the troop of his been paying closer attention, his transparent interest would have earned an eyebrow raise, if nothing worse.

Equally concerned and amused, Elwyn leaned over to whisper in his ear. "Smile any wider, and you'll flash a fang."

He shrugged her away, cheeks flushing redder than his hair.

Kadence returned a blink later and opened his journal, flipping past page after page of colorful illustration rendered in exquisite detail. Swans taking flight over a crystalline lake. Damselflies perched on fiddlehead fronds. Dandelions forcing their way through cracks in cobbles. Each image was crafted with precise, delicate strokes, but vivid yellow highlights and stark shadows lent them a stylized air—somehow making them simultaneously less realistic and intrinsically more *real*.

"You're an artist," Deinua said with the reverence many reserved for royals.

"My eyes are drawn to beautiful things," Kadence replied, shrugging. "This world needs artists more than ever before, and dancers, and bards, and playwrights, and poets." He gave Deinua a pointed look. "Beauty is all the more valuable for its scarcity. We must capture it however we can."

His thumb caught on a surprisingly detailed map, which he angled toward them for ease of study. Elwyn's eyes found Wiltshire first—one of five slums which blossomed like petals around Ebensburg, near the book's seam. The Wilds themselves filled the bulk of the page, complete with color-coded streams, trails, and groves of all variety. There was no key, but the symbols were easy enough to decipher. The little black arrows noted the direction in which the foliage was moving, and the blue numbers beneath them tracked the estimated rate of that movement. Brown houses, scribbled over with tiny black skulls, were probably settlements that had fallen since the Confluence. Scarlet X's littered the parchment, heavily concentrated in the upper right corner with sparser spacing elsewhere.

"The attacks stopped precisely four nights ago." Kadence tapped his pen against the clustered districts. "Not just in Wiltshire, but in all the surrounding slums. Though I'm tempted to believe we've finally frightened the bastards off, I can't help suspecting something more nefarious is at play."

Deinua tilted his head to scan the symbols. "Why is that?"

"We've been scouting our surroundings since this whole upset first happened," Kadence explained. "It's important to have some idea of our whereabouts, however changeable, and if we happened to stumble upon the monsters' stronghold, we could finally launch an attack on our own terms." His expression darkened along with his voice. "For some time, our scouts came back battered and haunted, assuming they returned at all, but lately, the Augusky have been chasing them back to the border unscathed. It almost feels as though they're rounding us up for something."

"Like a buffet," Elwyn mused aloud. The Seelie celebrated their holidays with feasts; why would the Unseelie be any different, menu aside?

Kadence gave her an appraising once-over. "You're a sharp one, too, aren't you? Not lorekeeper-material, per se," he appraised Deinua in a far more favorable manner, "but I always have need of hunters and scouts. Speaking of, these symbols mark the very points at which our scouts are being driven back." He brushed his quill beneath a red X. "You'll notice there are a lot more markings to the northeast. It's safe to surmise an Augusky stronghold—if not *the* Augusky stronghold—is hidden somewhere in that region, not that we can sneak past them to investigate further." He offered the journal and pen to Deinua. "Now, a deal's a deal, and I'm a stickler for fairness. Mark your settlement so we can note the area as clear of fiends. Who knows, maybe I'll swing by sometime to ensure you're faring well."

Deinua rubbed his neck, blushing even more brightly than before. "It's not so much a settlement as a single cottage. As for the location—"

"It's over here." Elwyn swiped the pen away and marked the map at random, fearing Deinua's innate honesty might put his family at risk. "We don't know the layout as well as you, but that's the general area. Speaking of, we really ought to be heading back. My aunt is a terrible worrier. She'll pace a rut in the floorboards if we're gone much longer."

"Fair enough." Kadence clapped his journal shut and tucked it beneath his arm. "If you reconsider joining us, the troop gathers here around three each day. I'd be remiss not to add that I'm often here as early as noon, in case," he grabbed Deinua's shoulder and gave it a hearty squeeze, "just in case."

Worried that Deinua might stand there stammering for hours without her intervention, Elwyn hooked his arm and tugged him toward the alley. Thankfully, he collected his wits and finished the walk on his own, a giddy grin finding his lips as the door snicked shut behind them.

"That was painful to watch," Elwyn teased. "And utterly adorable."

"The rains carve caverns deep, and the winds gouge canyons wide,
The seasons come and go, but they leave scars to mark their time."

CHAPTER 17

A PASSING PHASE

AEDYN

 edyn missed Elwyn. She hadn't been gone a full hour, yet he couldn't help staring at the forest beyond the fungus fence, hoping she'd emerge with a triumphant smile on her lips and a silver gleam in her pretty gray eyes. He didn't need to touch or speak with her. He didn't even need her to acknowledge his existence. He needed only to know that she was safe, that she was happy, and that she was *near*.

It was not the first time he'd suffered this madness. In the months after the Confluence, he'd found her side as often as possible, even once she'd joined the Guard. He'd savored those moments like fine whiskey, but he hadn't anticipated the hangover they'd leave him with. One night, he'd snuck into her tent with a deck of cards and pilfered pastries, and they'd chatted until they were both bereft of words. He'd crept away from the camp just before dawn, and by the time the sun breached the horizon, he missed her so sorely, his chest ached.

That's when he'd resolved to keep his distance, hoping to spare them both the pain of parting. Unfortunately, the pain of being apart had proven equally burdensome.

Surely there was a third option he hadn't yet considered...

He dropped an armful of firewood beside the cottage door and clapped the dust from his hands. The pale scars that snaked out from his right sleeve were hideous by Maithe standards, but he couldn't help feeling proud of them. It wasn't anything like the shallow hubris he'd long conjured as a shield, but something much more intrinsic and well-deserved.

It had been terrifying, offering his life in Elwyn's stead. It had been agonizing, letting that shellicoat swallow him whole. It had been foolish and frightful and hopeless and desperate, but—more than anything else—it had been worth it.

Aedyn was beginning to believe there was nothing worth keeping that didn't come at a harrowing price.

Forcing his mind to more pressing concerns, he peered through the open window to check on Lieri, who shooed him off with a bemused flick of her wrist. Koa had tasked him with keeping watch over her throughout the day, but she wasn't half as helpless as the Glaistig feared. She claimed to have slain more goblins with her rolling pin than Aedyn's rapier would ever skewer, and something about her belligerent tone made him believe her.

Satisfied he'd kept his word to the best of his ability, he spared the toadstool ring one final, fleeting glance before trekking back through the garden. Upon rounding the shed, he found Amatha sitting atop the stump she'd been using to chop firewood, her obsidian axe cast aside. A lecture lurked behind her pursed lips, where it had been prowling since the shellicoat skirmish, perhaps longer.

"If you're exhausted, I'll happily take over," he offered, hoping he'd misinterpreted her expression. "I'm bound to make for a terrible woodsman, so you'll have entertainment while you rest."

His friend scooted over, patting the trunk beside her. A sit-down conversation, then. Those were never particularly pleasant.

Aedyn hung his head and trudged forward. There were simply some battles he couldn't win, and any which pitted his will against Amatha's made the list. When he drew near, she pulled him down beside her, wrapping an arm around his shoulders. Whether she meant to comfort or constrain him, he couldn't say.

"What I am about to say will anger you, but you must hear me out," she said, voice grave. "I cannot simply sit by while you put yourself in danger."

"You're the chieftain." He shrugged as much as her heavy forearm allowed. "Technically, *you're* putting me in danger."

Amatha merely sighed at his clumsy attempt at levity. "How long have we known each other, hm?"

"*Creator*, let me think..." It was difficult to recall a time before Amatha. She'd been inside his every inside-joke, party to his every plot, the warmest strand of many a fond memory and the sole sunbeam in several dark ones. "We were still learning our basic letters, if that's a clue."

"Ages and ages." Amatha nodded, a phantom smile tugging on one cheek. "Do you remember stealing our first sips of wine? We would have been allowed to drink it in a matter of months, but you were convinced permission would rob it of flavor."

"So I stole the key to the royal cellar, and we drained no less than a dozen bottles." The memory was hazy for that very reason, but it numbered among the good ones. The only flavor he'd truly been seeking was that of freedom, and it had proven even sweeter than he'd imagined. "I'd never been so sick before, but it was absolutely worth it! Do you remember the look on that maid's face when she found us passed out in the dirt? I thought she was going to faint."

"She had good reason." The warmth fled Amatha's voice. "When her superiors discovered her keys had been stolen, they blamed her for the whole situation and relegated her to the kitchens. She was lucky they did not expel her altogether."

Aedyn hadn't noticed. If he'd suspected someone else had paid for his folly, he'd have spoken up for them, but it wasn't the kind of thing he often considered, especially in his youth. "That was ages ago, as you pointed out," he said, smothering his guilt before it could grow. "What does it matter now?"

"What about the incident with the rot-fae? You released an entire swarm on a hallowed Sylph ceremony and wound up delaying the mortal springtime by a month. If Soen and your father were not so close, relations between your nations might have been damaged for decades, and that says nothing of the plight of the mortal farmers."

"It was only a prank." Aedyn crossed his arms, bristling. Amatha had always been more responsible than himself, but it wasn't like her to lord it over him. "If I recall correctly, you were in on it, too! Yes, we caused a momentary mess, but we've laughed about it several times since. I honestly don't understand why you're digging it up now."

"I am only reminding you that actions have consequences. I often wonder whether you have ever felt the weight of them, given how swiftly they roll off your shoulders."

"What's the harm, so long as they don't roll onto anyone else?"

Amatha's raised eyebrow contested the statement. "Do you remember Trinea Daleos? She was the daughter of an Undine diplomat who transferred to Samhria decades back. Short blue hair, big teal eyes, wore a lot of bright, beaded dresses..."

She sounded vaguely familiar, but then, there had been quite a few diplomats' daughters.

Amatha plucked the answer from Aedyn's silence. "You spent weeks chasing her affection only to cast it aside the next morning." Her grip on his shoulder tightened like she expected him to flee. "She wept until her family returned to Chorial, yet you never spared her another thought. Hers was not the first heart you broke; do not fool yourself into believing it was the last."

"I never promised her anything." Aedyn may not have remembered the girl, but he was certain of that much. His betrothal had been arranged at a woefully young age, and not a soul in the realm—past paramours included —was unaware of it. At least, that's what he'd always told himself. "If you're trying to make me feel like a villain, you've met your goal." He shrugged free of Amatha's grasp and found his feet. "Unfortunately, I can't return the favor. I've been too busy tracking your triumphs to tally your failures."

Her shoulders sank, casting violet fractals on the grass. "I am not trying to hurt you," she said, though she'd been doing an exemplary job of it. "And I am certainly not trying to throw a shadow over fond memories. I am only trying to protect you. Your whole life, you have suffered a curse: you are restless and hungry—always, always, *always* searching for something new to consume. When you find it, you believe it will sate you, and you worship it with all the fire in your spirit, but it never lasts. Wines become whiskeys, potions become poisons, kisses become trysts, and when they burn away, you are left with ashes on your tongue."

Aedyn knew what she was getting at—a part of him had known since the moment she sat him down—but for once, she'd read him all wrong.

Yes, the novelty of the situation had gone to his head, and yes, his senses were thoroughly scrambled, but even if this was not different—even if *she* was not different—he was.

He knew well the ashes his friend spoke of, and he loathed the taste of them.

"She's not a phase, Amatha."

"I am sorry to hear that." Pity darkened her eyes. "If she was a phase, she alone would be hurt, and while she does not deserve to suffer for your whimsy, she would recover soon enough. If she is not a phase, *you* will be hurt, and there will be no bouncing back. Need I remind you of your vow to Eloana?"

"You mean the vow my father wrote for me?" Aedyn raised his hand in mock oath. "I, Aedyn of the Daoine Maithe, Heir to the Summer Throne, hereby accept this betrothal to Eloana the Golden-Voiced. I vow to wed her on the day of my coronation, and to serve beside her as regent ruler of Talunasa for the duration of my reign." Those words had been buzzing about his skull for a lifetime, growing louder with every echo. "Would you like to hear my oaths of heirdom, too? Or do I need to recite both the Maithe and Sidhe alphabets before you deem my memory sufficient?"

Amatha winced. She did not deserve his ire, and they both knew it. "It is a binding oath, no different from the treaty you were nearly cursed for breaking. Do you truly believe you can escape that fate a second time?"

Aedyn's throat went dry. He'd only witnessed Descension and Exile once, on the very same day as his own trial. Doubtless, the High Judges had timed the verdict to serve as a warning. As he watched them rip the spark from that man's soul, he could practically feel the warmth draining from his veins, the color leeching from his skin, the hope bleeding from his heart. He'd never been so terrified.

Not until that shellicoat attacked Elwyn.

"You needn't fret over me," Aedyn said, belatedly noticing the bags beneath Amatha's eyes. She'd lost sleep to her worries; the least he could do was attempt to assuage them. "We have an assassination to plan and an Unseelie celebration to infiltrate. Surely those concerns deserve your focus more than I do. As you've made painfully clear, I move on swiftly."

Amatha looked entirely unconvinced. "I want you to be happy," she said, rising from the stump. "But I also want you to be safe. Must those two goals always be at odds?"

ELOANA

It should have taken Eloana months to restore the Gilt Grove to its former splendor. With Anye at her side, she repaired it in mere days. Improved it, even.

A herd of rosemary hinds bounded across the lawn where floral effigies of Aryn and Tearan once rose. Twin tributes to the Dobhar-chú—benevolent sea-wolves of the northern depths—frolicked through the flowerbeds, their spirea pelts blaring white against a sea of vivid violets. Peafowl with fern frond tails and azalea wings strutted along the rim of a crystal fountain, their feathers splayed like painted fans, and a legion of lightsinger acolytes lined the stepping stone paths where gilt brigadiers once stood sentry, their verdant heads bowed in obligatory reverence.

Eloana drifted past the sculptures, her heels *clacking* on amber steppingstones as she approached the platform where Enwa's likeness once stood. Rather than rebuild her great-grandmother's image, Eloana had replaced her with a self-portrait in a spectacular charmblossom gown, buttercups braided through her willow-bough tresses. She'd spent several hours perfecting the details, choosing the exact right summer green buds for her eyes and weaving oraithvine into intricate chains to match her favorite pieces of jewelry, but still, she wasn't satisfied with the results.

"Something's missing," she mused aloud, tapping a polished nail on her cheekbone. "But what?"

Anye flitted from her shoulder to inspect the topiary more closely. After a second of staring, she looped around the figure's head, prismatic glimmers trailing behind her.

"Yes, I think you're right."

Eloana no longer needed to serenade the plants to sculpt them. Simply *thinking* a tune was effective, so long as Anye was near. She composed an intricate melody, wrapping it in harmonies so close they almost touched, and those very notes lilted from the piskie's thrumming wings. Eloana herself could hardly hear the song—and then, only when she strained her ears—but the plants responded readily. Strands of oraithvine and ivy coiled in Anye's glittering wake, forming a floral crown so stunning it put Tearan's legendary circlet to shame.

The ease of the endeavor brought a smile to Eloana's lips. Had any lightsinger in history ever known such power?

"I'd say that's more than enough sculpting for the moment." She peered past her garden wall to the amber leaves that blocked the midday sun. "Now that we've remedied my little mishap, we can finally focus on something grander. Talune has been looking fragile of late, and the Tenders' wards have done nothing to help it. Do you know of a light-song that might coax it back to life?"

"It is fated that Talune's leaves should shrivel, bleach, and fall,
If that's all you'd like to change, you're dreaming much too small."

"Our home is the First Tree, Anye." Eloana started toward garden doors framed in lattice. "The Creator Himself sang it to life. Wielding the selfsame power as a god sounds like a sizable dream to me."

Anye fluttered beside her, humming brightly.

"I was suggesting something a little more advanced,
What makes you think your talent is limited to plants?"

Eloana pondered the couplet as she climbed the steps that led to the palace. All Maithe could manipulate sunlight in one way or another, but where illusionists sculpted raw refraction, lightsingers required a vessel. To her knowledge, only plants absorbed enough brilliance to serve that purpose. Oraithvine was a mild exception, being partly metal, but even it had been hybridized from a rare species of ivy.

Perhaps the piskie meant Eloana was destined to craft something even more spectacular than oraithvine. The very notion made her heart flutter. Having lived her whole life in her great-grandmother's shadow, the thought of outshining Enwa held undeniable appeal.

The palace door swung inward as she reached for the handle, and a brigadier stepped aside to let her pass, bowing deeply. He'd probably been patrolling the hall when he noticed her approaching. People had been doing that a lot lately—*noticing* her. Their eyes found her the moment she entered a room, and they followed her until the moment she left it. As the heir's betrothed, she was used to a certain level of customary deference, and even the occasional lustful gander, but this was something more akin to awe.

She didn't hate it.

Anye seemed to revel in the attention, though it wasn't quite directed at her. She glowed a little brighter whenever someone bowed to the passing princess, a happy thrum lilting from her wings. It was possible she was simply proud of the progress her pupil had shown in such a short time, but Eloana couldn't help suspecting there was more to it.

The softest hum found her ears as she slipped past the soldier. It reminded her of the music she guided when shaping plants, only it was brighter and a touch airier, and it seemed to resonate directly from his skin. She rushed away, certain her ears were suffering strain from working so tirelessly, but when she came upon a trio of maids a moment later, what she'd dismissed as an anomaly became a pattern.

The maids' music was nowhere near as pleasant as the soldier's, with each woman emitting a shrill note to match their frightened scowls. Their separate strands melted into a single dissonant chord as they huddled close, making room for Eloana to pass them by.

Eloana did just that, lifting her skirts to race up the nearest spiral staircase. She didn't breathe until she reached the next story, which was blessedly empty. After a measure spent wrangling her scattered thoughts, she turned wide eyes to Anye.

"Am I hearing what I think I'm hearing?"

The piskie's gilt grin was all the confirmation she needed.

Logically, Eloana had always known her people absorbed sunlight—otherwise, their powers would have been useless indoors—but she'd never dreamed those stores could be accessed, much less manipulated. "Something a little more advanced..." she muttered, equally thrilled and intimidated by the implications.

She was drawing close to Talune's upper branches when she next crossed paths with a member of the palace staff. Viridian robes hemmed in gold marked him as a private attendant for lesser nobility, and he carried a platter of honeyed crème puffs that smelled positively divine.

Like his peers, Eloana captured his attention the moment she stepped into view, and he skirted swiftly aside to let her pass. His light-song—that seemed a fitting enough name—had a pleasing, bell-like tone to it, but it was frantic as a hornet hive. Its timbre jumped up half and octave when Eloana approached him, scanning him from plaited hair to sandaled feet.

"You're in a dreadful hurry, aren't you?" she asked, tuning her thoughts to match the music. Anye smiled, her wings thrumming in the very same tone. "Surely you'll spare a moment to indulge my curiosity. For whom are these delectable pastries destined?"

The servant's eyes flicked to Anye and back. "L-lord Thornbranch, m'lady," he stammered, clearly startled by the piskie's presence. "He craves desserts at precisely three hours past the zenith, daily. As you have deftly discerned, I'm running low on time."

"Anticipating the needs of your betters." Eloana approved of his outlook, and yet, she sought to sway it. She raised the tone of her silent song by a quarter-step, then another, spooling it like a harpsichord wire. "You clearly know your place, and I have no doubt you're aware of my own. With as much regard as you show your employer, and rightly so, he is only a minor noble. Surely he is not so bright as to notice a few missing puffs."

"I-I'm afraid I can't oblige you, m'lady." He clutched the tray closer, both his voice and light-song wavering. "If you'd like, I could send for another batch, but I must stick to my schedule. I'm sure you understand."

Eloana didn't.

"It is you who needs to understand." She wound the string a little tighter, and a little tighter still. The higher the servant's light-song climbed, the warmer his expression became. "There's no reason I should wait for anything when I'm feeling peckish now."

His gaze flicked to the platter and back, growing softer. "I...suppose I could part with one or two..."

It was a step in the right direction, but Eloana was demanding a mile. "I will not be obeyed in part," she hissed, tugging sharply up the scales. "You will hand over that platter, or—"

The string snapped, and the servant stumbled back, flinching like he'd felt it.

"I'm...I'm going to be late!" He blinked free of his stupor and sprinted down the hall, pastries in hand. Anye doubled over mid-air, overcome by laughter.

Eloana grit her teeth. For the first time since the piskie introduced herself, she questioned the wisdom of their bond. "If I'd known you meant to make a fool of me, I would never have indulged this silly game," she muttered.

The piskie composed herself, flicking a tiny tear from the corner of her eye.

"I hadn't guessed your first attempt would face such strong defiance,
Might I suggest you practice on somebody more compliant?"

Someone more compliant than a lowly lord's attendant would be difficult to come by. Eloana's station, though lofty, was entirely ceremonial. The palace staff were not beholden to her, but to her future husband and his royal father.

There was but one paltry exception to the rule.

Loenelle had been dancing to Eloana's whims for decades. It was time to test the tensile strength of her tractability.

"There's only so much storage in the average human heart,
You can't gain something brilliant without losing something dark."

CHAPTER 18

GIVE AND TAKE

BRANNON

he only thing worse than accompanying Koa into the Wilds would have been brooding in that loft for another day. Since those had been Brannon's only two options, he was bearing the lesser evil as best he could.

He walked along with his eyes fixed on the trail, both to avoid the writhing vines and to better ignore his guide. Though the choice spared him glimpses of branching antlers and gleaming red eyes, the hoofmarks Koa left in the marl were equally unsettling. How that woman could have been lured away by such a beast was beyond Brannon. Then again, she had an established taste for monsters.

"Not much further now," Koa said, sniffing at the air. "The Blight Bogs have shifted a lot closer in recent weeks. I should warn you Muna can be a bit off-putting at a glance, but I'm confident she can help you complete your mission."

Brannon certainly hoped so. With the week he'd been having, decapitating a tyrant sounded downright cathartic. In the meantime, it would have been nice of something small to scurry from the undergrowth and allow him to snap its spine, but that wasn't going to happen with

Tawny trundling along behind him, rifling through the brackens like a truffle hog.

They were passing through a cluster of elm trees when a squeal cut through the air. Brannon pivoted with hands on his hilts only to find that Tawny was not in danger. Quite the opposite, actually.

"Peridot pears!" The youth bounced on her toes, pointing up at the branches of an unseasonably green tree. She slipped her satchel from her shoulder and tossed it at Brannon's feet. "Watch that for a moment, please and thanks!"

"Do I look like your fucking handmaiden?" Brannon growled, but Tawny had already shimmied halfway up the trunk. Damn, if she wasn't a nimble little imp.

"Eccentric isn't she?" Koa's hulking shadow stretched out beside Brannon's, muddled by the cast of the canopy. "Deinua was never one for catching crickets or climbing trees. It was always flowers and nursery rhymes with that one, not that I minded. The occasional wilted bouquet is easier to clean up than the mud trails I plagued my parents with."

Brannon glanced pointedly away, clenching his fingers to keep them from his daggers. It wasn't the first time Koa had attempted small talk. Sooner or later, he'd take a hint.

"I don't suppose you have any interests worth sharing?" Koa pried. "You don't seem like you'd care much for posies and poems, but I've yet to see you scale an oak. You must have developed a hobby or two through the years..."

Brannon took a deep, centering breath. As badly as he wanted to demonstrate his hobbies, he needed to cast his grudge aside. It was nice to have a mission again, and he wasn't about to put it at risk. So he turned his back on the beast, desperate to keep his rage wrangled.

"Listen here, you thankless cur!" Koa gripped his shoulder and whirled him back around, bringing his face uncomfortably close. "The moment you set foot in my home, I could smell the spite on you. Creator knows you have reason to be bitter, but you also have reason to be grateful. You've already accepted my wife's hospitality; when she's prepared to render her apology, you will accept it just as readily."

"Let me go," Brannon hissed, glaring a warning.

"Do not mistake my patience for pity." Koa snarled, flashing sinister fangs. His breath smelled of salt and copper. "I am humoring you for her sake, but my mercy is a limited resource. If you so much as think of harming my family, I swear to the Creator I will drain your veins and hang your head above my mantle."

"Let. Me. Go."

"I will let you go when you agree to my terms. So long as you are staying under our roof, you will treat us with civility. I have enough cause for fretting with mortal hunters on the prowl and an Unseelie festival around the bend. The last thing I need is some feral creature poking about my cottage."

"Funny." Brannon forced a cold smile. "The last thing I needed was some feral creature poking about my Ma, but—"

The butt of Koa's spear met Brannon's gut, turning the quip into a groan. Brannon recovered swiftly, catching the monster's jaw with an uppercut. Koa cast his weapon aside and punched Brannon square in the spleen. Fists flew for a few frenzied seconds before they caught each other by the shoulders and locked, their strengths and wills equally matched.

"I...hate...you," Brannon huffed, lungs burning.

"The...feeling's...mutual," Koa growled, teeth gritted.

"You're...a...monster," Brannon hissed.

"You're...an...ingrate," Koa seethed.

"You...had...no...right!"

"I...had...no...clue!"

The revelation rang through the forest, startling a flock of quails from the trailside brush. The men released their grips in unison, stumbling backward with trembling limbs and heaving lungs. Brannon hadn't been surprised that woman had hidden his existence from her coddled whelp, but he'd figured her husband was in the know.

Moral superiority was a strange and thrilling sensation. Brannon doubted he would ever feel its like again.

"Look out below!"

A storm of pears followed Tawny's shout, pelting both the assassin and the beast. The girl slid down the trunk a second later, looking proud of her venture and somehow oblivious to the row that had broken out beneath her.

"What the Shadows happened to you two?" she asked, eyes flitting between Brannon and Koa as she knelt to collect the fallen fruit. "I heard shouting."

Koa rubbed his jaw, which had already begun to bruise. "We've wandered into badger territory," he said.

It seemed a strange excuse, but Tawny accepted it without question. "They get pretty big near the Blight Bogs, don't they?" She tucked a final pear into her satchel. "Next time, we should stuff our pockets with peppers to ward them off. I'm surprised one managed to get the drop on you, given how they rattle the trees."

The conversation ended with a chuckle as Koa resumed his role as guide. Tawny scampered on his hooves, chatting glibly about the warding properties of pome fruits. Brannon kept a few paces back, hands perched on his daggers' hilts as he scanned the roiling woodlands for giant badgers.

Brannon smelled the Blight Bogs long before he saw them, and both sensations were incredibly unpleasant. It seemed the Unseelie had taken a literal approach to naming their territories. With what he'd seen of the Shifting Wilds, the Mirrormurk, and now this, he could only imagine the Winter Wastes were suitably barren.

Hardly any light filtered through the ashen cypress boughs that dangled like cobwebs over olive waters reeking strongly of algal bloom. Pond lilies clustered near the banks, their ghostly petals tipped in crimson and leaves spotted by disease. Dragonflies and pallid green sprites darted through the cattails and spike rushes, and swamp sparrows flitted through the pungent gray mists, little more than flurries of smoke and birdsong. The constant, discordant thrum of midges underscored the squall of bullfrogs and herons hidden by the haze.

As Brannon searched the fog for a bridge or barge to travel by, a face popped up amidst the riverweeds, the same sickly hue as the swamp. Bulbous eyes peered out from a stringy curtain of sopping hair as the creature beckoned him closer. Her lips parted, and Brannon's thoughts grew murkier than his surroundings.

Next thing he knew, he was being hauled backward by the hood of his half-cape. He wrenched himself free with a belligerent scowl, belatedly noticing that his trousers were soaked to the knees. Mud leaked from his boots and squelched in his stockings, sending prickling shivers across his skin.

"Never stare at a Selkie." Koa rubbed the space between his furrowed eyebrows. "They take any attention whatsoever as permission to perform. While I don't personally care whether you join the captive audience they've wrapped up in the weeds below, Lieri would likely skewer me for allowing it."

As much as Brannon wanted to curse the man, his ire lay with the Selkie. He glared in her direction, determined to prove how little sway she held, only to find she'd already vanished. A sleek brown otter frolicked through the weeds where she'd been lurking. Brannon flipped it off, hoping it would pass the message along. Perhaps the fumes were getting to him, but he could swear the little fucker winked at him.

"Just how are we supposed to find this hag hut, anyway?" he asked, already eager to leave the Blight Bogs behind. "There are no viable paths, and only a fool would build their house upon this mire to begin with."

"You don't visit hag huts, silly." Tawny giggled. "They visit you."

"With a little prompting," Koa added, pulling a little glass flute from his belt. The instrument was delicate and slender, wreathed in frosted vines, and the music it made was equally ethereal. Brannon managed to keep his thoughts wrangled, though each crystalline note threatened to unravel them.

While he'd long been indifferent to music, he was beginning to sincerely hate it.

As Koa's melody rang out over the swamp, a hulking shape appeared in the fog. It looked, from a distance, like a massive tortoise. That resemblance only increased as it lumbered closer on four thick, scaly legs. Its shell was marbled black and gold, domed like an elaborate citadel. Amber light seethed from the hollow where a head ought to have been hiding.

"You're certain this 'friend' is trustworthy?" Brannon asked as the hut drew nearer.

"She's never once threatened my family, though she knows they're of mortal blood." Koa grinned, eyes gleaming in the gloom. "Of course, if you're frightened, you can always wait here. I'm sure that Selkie you spotted would love to perform an encore."

"I'm not frightened," Brannon muttered, watching with something more than unease—*definitely not fright*, he told himself—as the hut lowered itself into the bog, folding one vast leg at a time. Wooden planks stuck out from the ridge of the shell, forming a precarious wraparound pathway. Koa stepped confidently onto it, bidding the others to follow, as a robed figure shuffled out to greet them, face shrouded by a hood.

"What brings you-hoo here?" she shrilled, cocking her head. "Best be important this time!"

"It's lovely to see you too, Muna," Koa replied with a bemused chuckle. "If it's all the same, I'd rather discuss our business indoors."

"I have no doors," she answered, though she led them into the shell anyway.

As disturbing as the hag hut looked from the outside, the inside was even eerier. A spine formed a seam across the ceiling, each vertebra an ivory stalactite. Rows of shelves curved around the walls, cluttered with animal skulls, jarred organs, and other curiosities. The marble gaze of a stuffed raven followed Brannon toward the central firepit, where a copper cauldron simmered atop smoldering coals. Any curiosity he felt about the potion's purpose vanished when he peered into the pot. Rodent bones and wads of fur floated throughout the murk, which somehow managed to smell worse than it looked.

Once the visitors were as settled as they could possibly be, Muna lowered her hood. Ember light caught in eyes the size of saucers, shrinking her pupils to pinpricks. A squat beak hooked over her lower lip in lieu of a nose, and feathers spiked from her scalp instead of hair. Her other features looked nearly human, but not enough to put Brannon at ease.

"Who-hoo are these mortals?" Her curious voice contrasted comically with her dwelling. It would probably have irked Brannon, were he less desperate for levity. "And what do-hoo they want?"

"They are Lieri's guests," Koa answered with a dismissive wave, "and they're on the hunt for information. You've hoarded more of that than anyone else in the Wilds, and I've known you to be generous with it."

"When it su-hoots me." Muna smiled as much as her beak allowed. She plucked a ladle from the nearest shelf and began stirring her brew. "What manner of information are they after?"

"Anything you know about the Procession of Autumn," Brannon said before Koa could answer. He loathed being spoken of as though he wasn't there. "Better yet, anything you know of the bramble palace, Fómhar."

Muna's pupils blossomed, nearly consuming her massive eyes. "You-hoo should not go to Fómhar," she warned, staring at—or perhaps through—

Brannon. "Mailair's guest will be arriving to-hoo-morrow night. The Ghost Witch never fails to-hoo stir up mischief."

"She and Mailair barely tolerate each other." Tawny remarked, her voice strangled by one pesky emotion or another. "Why would she visit their palace?"

"The why is less important than the *where*." Brannon's fingers tensed, aching to pry open Yana's ribcage and rip out her still-pulsing heart. "Tell us how to find her, and we'll ensure she never stirs up anything again."

Muna clucked a thick gray tongue against her beak. She pulled a jar of slugs from her shelf and shook it out over the pot. They melted swiftly into the brew, producing a cloud of pungent steam. The hag inhaled it deeply.

"I could tell you-hoo," she said after a beat, feathers bristling, "but the knowledge will cost you-hoo dearly."

"Name your price." Brannon was fully prepared to slit his wrist over the cauldron. Hell, he'd chug its contents if that's what it took to avenge his battered pride.

"That is not what I meant." Muna's avian features were hard to read, but the slope of her shoulders hinted at sorrow. "Very well. If I cannot dissuade you-hoo, I will offer my assistance. Allies of the Augusky are barred from speaking of Fómhar's location, but there is no rule against *showing* it." She rasped a sigh, tapping her spoon on the copper rim. "My offer is this: a memory for a memory. I beg you-hoo not to take it."

"A memory for a memory?" Tawny's question rang with sincere curiosity, opposed to Brannon's utter bewilderment. "What does that even mean?"

Muna gave an awkward shrug. "I require a token from your past. Something with a special meaning. Something you-hoo treasure."

Tawny fiddled with her unkempt braid, her gaze finding the floor. When Brannon and the others first found her, she had nothing to her name but the tattered dress she wore, and she hadn't hoarded anything but berries and beetle shells since. There was no way she could meet the hag's demands.

Brannon was another matter. He wasn't about to give up his *icons*, though they certainly fit Muna's criteria, but a lesser token sprang to mind. Before he could second-guess himself, he rifled through his satchel for his pocket watch. If he hadn't plucked the broken timepiece from his Pa's fresh corpse, it would have been utterly worthless. He assumed that would make it all the more valuable to Muna.

The hag's eyes widened as he pulled the bauble free, a sure sign he'd assumed right. "A perfect choice," she said, extending her upturned palm. Her nails, though thin and pale, curved like talons. "You-hoo'll feel lighter without it."

Given the watch's scant weight, Brannon highly doubted it. He felt nothing at all when he handed it over, though he cringed when she tossed it into the pot and gritted his teeth while she crushed it with her ladle, each metallic *crunch* sending a shudder through him. Before he could ask what the fuck she was doing, fog welled over the cauldron's rim, filling the hut with a noxious green haze.

Brannon covered his nose with his cape, but the reek was still thick enough to taste. It nipped at his eyes and coated his tongue, turning his stomach to a tempest. Strange sensations filtered through him—the abstract spectacle of a star-smattered twilight, the bone-deep bite of a frigid breeze, the faintest whiffs of spearmint and vanilla—displacing something dark and dire.

When the air finally cleared, he was standing in the mire beside Tawny and Koa, staring out over the bog. Muna and her hut were nowhere to be seen.

"That watch must have been something special," Tawny said, rubbing a glassy film from her eyes. "She would never have accepted it, otherwise. Do you think you'll miss it?"

Brannon thought he might, though he couldn't quite remember why. What he did remember, bizarrely, was how to get to Fómhar.

"Disguises aren't exclusive to the fearful and disgraced,
Sometime a mask one chooses fits far better than their face."

CHAPTER 19

A CHRYSALIS CRACKS

ELWYN

ana was headed to Fómhar. According to the hag's prediction, the Ghost Witch had curried favor with the Augusky ruler and would be visiting that very night. Elwyn couldn't bring herself to care about whatever atrocities the fiends were planning together, though those details would matter greatly if the assassination failed. For now, all she could focus on was how convenient it would be to slay two villains in a single stroke.

"Do *not* attack without a direct order," the chieftain said, as though she was privy to Elwyn's thoughts. She paced beneath the Winruts' wisteria tree, crystals shimmering in the dappled midday sunlight as she ran through the mission yet again. "If all goes well, we will complete our quest tonight, but we cannot move unless the situation merits it. You must not allow your emotions to impede your judgment, and you must not allow your judgment to eclipse mine."

Elwyn tore a patch of grass from the lawn beside her and released the loose blades to the breeze. They flurried right past Tawny and Brannon, brushing beneath Aedyn's nose and eliciting a dainty sneeze. Elwyn's chuckle drew an accusatory smirk as he ripped his own ammunition from the ground, fully prepared to retaliate. A stern look from Amatha wrangled his attention.

"We must make a few more preparations before heading out." The chieftain came to a stop, hands folded behind her back. "Tawny, it is your turn to speak."

The girl scrambled upright, pulling a tangle of cord necklaces from her satchel and handing one to each member of the group. Elwyn held hers toward the light, examining the hole-riddled river rock that served as its pendant. It was tacky to the touch and smelled vaguely of...apples, maybe?

"Hag stones offer protection from divination spells," Tawny explained, slipping her necklace on and pulling her ratty braid through the cord. "Yana's paranoid enough that she always has one active. So long as she's paying close attention, she can pluck unwarded threats from any crowd." She lifted her medallion to her nose and sniffed at it. "The peridot pear varnish is for fooling the Augusky themselves. Unlike most High Fae, they don't possess elemental magic, but they can sense physical weaknesses with uncanny ease. The most powerful among them can even sense emotional ones, which would be telling, to say the least. That tincture should shield your innermost thoughts."

"My turn!" Aedyn hopped to his feet, rubbing his palms together as he looked Amatha over. "With your dimensions, you'll never pass for an Augusky, but Solitaries often visit the palace, according to Koa. How do you feel about Trows?"

"I have only met a few," Amatha answered. "They were amiable enough."

Aedyn snapped his fingers, and a wave of glamour washed over the chieftain, coating her in dull, gray rock and turning her amethyst pauldrons to spikes of jagged granite. Petrified roots snaked up her left leg and across her torso, and stalagmite fangs jutted from her smile.

"Excellent work." Dust plumed from the joints of her elbow and fingers as she raised her hand to examine the illusion. "Your talents have grown to an impressive degree."

"Haven't they, though?" Aedyn's chest swelled to match his ego. "Unfortunately, the rest of us will need to be a bit more understated if we hope to blend with the rabble. The illustrations I've seen should serve as a decent base for the design." His golden-brown gaze swept to Tawny. "Think you can help me hone the smaller details?"

The girl offered an eager salute and a bevy of advice, and Aedyn went about his work. In mere heartbeats, three peculiar fae had replaced Elwyn's companions, each boasting the hooves, horns, and unsettling oval eyes of goats. Coarse fur covered them from waists to ankles, but they were otherwise unclothed.

Luatha fluttered in a loop around Elwyn, clucking her tiny tongue.

"Leave it to the scoundrel prince to make these disguises lewd,
Why am I not surprised he chose to render your form nude?"

Startled, Elwyn glanced down and was relieved to find that long, illusory locks covered the bits that needed covering. The strip of pale skin stretching from neck to navel should have embarrassed her, but it hardly felt like her own, for lack of scars.

Tawny inspected her artfully censored figure with a disappointed pout. Upon noticing the reaction, Aedyn deflated.

"I've gotten them all wrong, haven't I?" he asked, inspecting his hands. Having blanched his skin from bronze to bright beige, his transformation was easily the most jarring among them, Amatha's notwithstanding. "In my defense, I've never seen an Augusky in person, and the backwards knees are tricky. Glamour can't erase so much as alter or add, so I was hoping the wooly pelts might negate the issue."

"Your work is impressive." Tawny kicked at the grass with an illusory hoof, looking momentarily more sheepish than goat-like. "It's only...well, I've pictured myself as an Augusky quite often. My best friend was one of them—not a member of Mailair's horrid harem, mind you—and there was much I'd always envied about his kind. It's just... I was really hoping... Is there any way..." A faint flush bled through her glamour mask. "Could you make me a neither?"

Aedyn looked puzzled for half a second. The moment her meaning settled, he smiled and waved his hand. Tawny's every feminine slope stretched to a neutral angle, and her face lengthened to match. With nothing left to cover, her wild tresses wound back to match her actual braid. "Better?" he asked.

Tawny exhaled a long sigh of relief. "You have no idea."

From that point on, there was a notable levity to Tawny's voice and movements. At her instruction, Aedyn lengthened his colleagues' ears, swapped their metallic weapons for wood, and threaded teeth and bits of bone into their hair. As a finishing touch, he gave them each a blood sigil that would set them apart from the Augusky hordes. He painted a blazing sun across his chest and swept a crescent moon over Elwyn's facial scar. Tawny asked for a swirling forehead rune that symbolized transformation, and Brannon was satisfied with simple scarlet bands on his forearms. Apparently, Amatha needed no such adornment, as the placement of her petrified roots worked just as well.

The remainder of the afternoon was spent preparing for the mission. Tawny trained them in Augusky mannerisms, demonstrating with eerie prowess how to walk, talk, and even sneer like a true denizen of the Wilds. Aedyn followed up with a lecture on the nature of glamour, detailing how he could feel the general presence of his illusions and teaching them how to remove their disguises if needed. He also insisted, several times, that there would be no reason to remove them at all, and that doing so would be an egregious waste of glamour.

Elwyn couldn't help marveling at how light and warm the magic felt against her skin, like a sunbeam trapped in spider silk. If she didn't think about it, she would forget its presence altogether. "What if it drops away on its own?" she asked.

"That would probably mean I'm unconscious," Aedyn explained with a grimace. "Or worse."

Elwyn decided against prying further.

Once they were as prepared as they could possibly be, they broke for a meal of Lieri's barley soup and butterbread, then started off toward the bramble palace. At least, they were fairly certain that's where they were headed. The "directions" Brannon had received from Koa's friend were useless before sunset, given the first landmark was a constellation, but the travelers were not helpless in the meantime. The Iron Claws' map had detailed abundant Augusky activity to Wiltshire's northeast. By heading that direction, they'd be getting a decent start.

The group was about to breach the fungus fence when Deinua came skipping through it, whistling a cheerful tune. Elwyn had been so preoccupied with thoughts of slaying or being slain that she hadn't even noticed he was gone. Upon spotting their disguises, the half-fae skidded to a stop, drawing the wooden pike from his back. Tawny raised her palms, explaining the situation, and Deinua chuckled, wiping cold sweat from his brow.

"You look to be in an exceptionally good mood." Elwyn paused beside him while the others pressed on. "Dare I ask what you've been up to?"

"I was simply visiting town again." Deinua poked at Elwyn's illusory bicep, snickering when his finger pressed through the glamour to her leather vambrace. "Those locals might be in terrible danger if your plans go awry. I figured it couldn't hurt to keep communications open."

"Just in case?" Elwyn squeezed his shoulder, mimicking Kadence's bold farewell.

Deinua blushed, swatting her away. "Just in case."

The march through the Wilds was quiet, save for the constant rattle of the roiling foliage. Even Luatha had curled up peacefully beneath Elwyn's hair. The chieftain hadn't barred the group from talking, but she'd cautioned discretion, as an Augusky herd traipsing about before dusk could easily draw scrutiny, especially with a Trow mingling amongst them.

Amatha's contemplative silence was not alarming, nor was Brannon's soundless sulking, but Aedyn's distant, dark demeanor was cause for concern. Either his glamour had done something to mute his lively, inquisitive attitude, or the gravity of the situation had begun to weigh him down. Elwyn strongly suspected the latter. It was one thing to cook up schemes of revenge and quite another to serve it.

For the sake of both her companions and the Light Realms in general, she needed to focus on slaying Mailair, but Yana's head was the more compelling prize, albeit the more difficult to claim. Monsters or not, the Augusky were mere flesh and blood, subject to all the same weaknesses as mortals, maybe more. Yana was called the Ghost Witch for a reason. If Elwyn came close enough to land a strike, would that wretched woman even flinch at *Gelah's* bite?

Only one member of the party stood a chance of knowing the answer. Despite the others' apprehension, Tawny had maintained a chipper mien. She reveled in the role of guide, trotting through the undergrowth with oval eyes aglitter. Perhaps the glamour was to blame, but Elwyn was beginning to forget why she'd ever confused the girl with Lydia. For all their shared features, they had about as much in common as Brannon and Deinua. Tawny was precocious where Lydia had been meek, stubborn where Lydia had been soft, and curious where Lydia had been cautious. She could never replace the girl Elwyn had failed, but she did not deserve to be treated as a shadow.

As much as Elwyn hated to spoil Tawny's mood with talk of the mother who'd abandoned her, the conversation could be put off no longer. She strolled to the front of the formation and tapped her shoulder, nearly startling the poor thing from her fur.

"Shadows, Elwyn," Tawny whispered, pressing a hand to her chest. "You're quieter than a spiderling."

"It's a condition, I'm afraid," Elwyn replied, neglecting to mention its metaphysical nature. "I'm sorry to have frightened you, and sorrier still for the subject I'm about to broach."

"You want to know about Yana." Predictably, Tawny's mirth evaporated. "If you truly intend to kill her, don't make the mistake of aiming for the heart. You're sure to find a hollow."

The sheer potency of her resentment took Elwyn aback, understandable though it was. Love gone sour was so much fouler than hate. "Are you being literal, or...?"

Tawny chuckled, a touch of tension fleeing her shoulders. "She's assembled from all the usual bits—skin to slice, bones to break, blood to spill, and so on. The trouble is those bits aren't always as solid as our own. I can't know whether things have changed for her since the Confluence. Before, there were times when she was entirely spirit and times when she was entirely flesh, but she was often caught somewhere in between, a little like the Sylphs."

Elwyn hadn't spent much time among the Sylphs, but she knew they could waft through walls with some effort. "Can anything harm her while she's in between?"

"Perhaps not normal weapons, but magic should do the trick." Tawny flicked a finger toward *Gelah*. "Of course, those glowing runes would draw attention, so it might be best to wait until she's solid and strike with simple steel. It's worked before. One time, she fell into a trap my friend set for me and wound up spraining her ankle. It mended the moment she went ethereal, but she was furious until then, as was I." She shook her head, shoulders wilting. "If I'd known how things would turn out, I'd have begged him to break every bone in her body. I'm sure he'd have relished the opportunity."

"You must be talking about your Augusky friend." It sounded like a very Unseelie attitude to have about bone-breaking. Or a Brannon one.

"Daulle." She flinched like the name singed her tongue. "Mailair killed his father when he was very young. Upon fleeing Fómhar, his family settled in a thicket beside Yana's cabin—and it was just a cabin at the time, no winding wings or towers, just three simple rooms, a cozy hearth, and a waterwheel." Her wistful smile didn't quite suit her gaunt disguise. "Daulle and I grew close quickly, and we stayed close even when his thicket shifted elsewhere. It was his dream to one day kill Mailair, just as he'd hoped to someday steal the throne from his father. How strange that burden should now fall to us."

"He'd planned to assassinate his own father?" Elwyn's childhood wasn't exactly riddled with kittens and rainbows, but that sounded dark even to her. "Was the previous ruler as cruel as Mailair?"

"Not from the stories." Tawny shrugged. "You must be thinking all Augusky are monsters, but it's hard to treat life as something precious when you have a nearly endless supply of it. I bet they'd do things differently if they knew what it meant to be mortal. Take Daulle, for instance. He used to practice sneak attacks on me, but the one time he actually left a bruise, he wouldn't stop apologizing until it healed." She rubbed her upper arm like the mark was still there. "He had a good heart, though he buried it deep, and he deserved a better fate."

Elwyn hadn't missed that Tawny spoke of the friendship in past tense, but she'd been hoping they'd simply had a falling out. "What happened to him?"

"Yana." Tawny's voice turned brittle. "He tried to warn me about her, and I wouldn't listen. When she found out what he'd been saying, she turned him into a throw rug. I bet he's still stretched out in front of her hearth, catching stray cinders." She met Elwyn's gaze, a tear trickling through the illusion. "She's stolen from me, too. I know you blame me for what happened to Lydia, and I can understand why, but I would never have helped Yana trick her on purpose. Please know that much."

Elwyn placed one hand on Tawny's shoulder and the other on *Gelah's* hilt. She wasn't one for platitudes, nor was she ready to voice her remorse, but she could offer one small comfort. "Yana will reap every ounce of misery she's sown."

"Yes." Tawny set her jaw and stared off through the forest. "She will."

"Be cautious of the kernels that you bury 'neath the dirt,
If love brings forth more love in time, the same is true of hurt."

CHAPTER 20
SORROW LIKE SICKNESS
YANA

he Sluagh would have fed off Yana. They'd have ripped her soul to ribbons and drained her misery like wine, robbing her of reason and drowning her in nightmare after nightmare until she could no longer discern their agony from her own. But she'd always had a way of rearranging the stars to her favor, of flipping the board around the moment her pieces were pinned. Now, by craft and cunning, *she* was feeding off the Sluagh.

They tasted like shit.

Though she could not avoid her fate in full, she'd found a way to mete it into smaller, more digestible portions, choking down one terror at a time like drops of bitter medicine. Noxious though the remedy was, it had proven effective for keeping the...the...

What was she keeping at bay again?

It was hard to think with all the shrieking and gnashing and sobbing and cackling and—

Oh, right. The madness.

Each night, it blossomed like a moonflower, drinking in what darkness it could before Yana snipped it at the stem. At least it had the decency to be punctual. If she hadn't been so preoccupied with Mailair's cryptic invitation, she'd have been better prepared.

The voices scraped at her skull like bare branches as she hastened toward her study. There, her host stone waited atop a weathered wooden altar, casting its sickly green glow on the powdered-iron halo that wreathed it. Spirits roiled within the bloodstained amber, their spectral light catching in natural facets and carefully rendered runes. Even muted by minerals and magic, their screams found Yana's ears. They sang of unrepented sins and insatiable hungers, stronger even than those which plagued their master's mind.

As with so many poisons, the cure and cause were invariably linked.

Yana rolled her sleeves up and held her hands over the host stone, bracing herself.

Three...

Two...

She pressed her palms to the amber. Magic crackled against her skin, cold as ice and searing as sunlight. It spread through her skeleton and bit marrow deep, granting her a glimpse of the eternity she'd narrowly avoided. A lifetime passed through her in the span of a sigh. One heartbeat, she was a shuddering child, enduring unspeakable violence at hands that promised protection. The next, she tore through the streets like a tempest, spreading the same misery to any who ventured near. The next, she lay glaring up at the rainclouds, the contents of several bottles clashing in her veins. She spent her final moments conjuring every curse her tongue could manage, but she didn't waste a single breath on regret.

Yana stumbled back, gasping deeply. The moment her palms left the host stone, her Patchwork Palace flickered back into focus. Solstice stared out from the nearest bookshelf, mewling with concern. That cat always grasped just enough of a situation to know when she was suffering. Must have set his spectral nerves to sparking.

The Sluagh's bitterness clung to Yana's tongue like a film, but it had also sated her starving spirit, twining her thoughts into a single coherent strand. The remedy was twice as effective as any potion she'd ever crafted, and it would last a full day before dwindling. Now, the only screams she heard were those which seeped from the amber, piteous and pained. It was their own fault, really. If those wretched souls had been half as wily as herself, they'd have wormed their way out of the fate they'd earned.

"We'll put that misery to good use soon," she promised.

She raked a sharp nail through the air, slicing a gash in the Aether. The Veil had thinned since the worlds merged, but it was still the safest place to store treasures during travel. After wrapping a shawl around her hand, she tucked the host stone away and bid reality to mend around it. There the relic would float—hovering just beyond the reach of time and space—until she felt the need to summon it anew.

A contingent of Shadow Goblins scrambled from the cabin alongside her, but their numbers were too scant to provide protection. Lately, she'd been too busy unscrambling her thoughts to concern herself with bolstering their ranks. The moment she stepped into the moonlight, she willed her shadow to split and stretch. A legion of yellow-eyed minions snapped free to sniff and scurry about. Their ears twitched toward her as she sauntered through their midst, eagerly awaiting orders. She hoped she wouldn't need to give any. Still, their loyalty was a comfort.

Much like standing stones and faerie rings, Fómhar's location was fixed. The path to the palace was easy for those who understood the will of the Wilds, the whispers that wove through its scented winds and the legends that glittered in its fixed constellations. Crafted entirely of living vines, the palace was larger than most mortal sanctuaries and infinitely more intimidating. The tendrils slithered into a bevy of needle-thin spires, contracting and convulsing in a steady rhythm that gave the impression the entire structure was breathing. Though there were no windows to peer through, the occasional patch of pale light oozed between brambles, carrying with it the cries of captives and the reek of blood and offal.

The entrance passageway pulsed as steadily as the rest of the palace, its dagger-sharp thorns not dissimilar to the spiraling teeth of a lamprey. As Yana approached it, she considered turning back, but even she was not so bold as to offend Mailair without cause. The Prince-Often-Princess-Sometimes Both-and-On at Least One Occasion-Neither didn't pose much of a threat in their own right, but Yana required their allegiance—and the collective fear of their subjects—if she hoped to carve a place for herself in this new world. So long as she twisted this meeting to her favor, she would reap both in droves.

The tunnel wound on for some time before opening into a modest chamber lit by phosphorescent lichen. Several pairs of oval eyes flashed Yana's way as she entered, but they did not linger. The Augusky were focused on pulling corpses from the walls and stripping away what meat remained. Some even went so far as to snap the bones and suck out the marrow. Odd behavior, with so many mortals still wandering the Wilds. Mailair must have taken Yana's suggestions to heart and barred them from pursuing new prey before the Procession. When preparing for a feast, forced famine was in itself a kind of revel.

"You actually showed." Sasta trotted out from a nearby corridor, her pale skin seeming to glow in the lichen light. Blood dripped down her chin in fresh red runnels, and she'd draped glistening intestines around her neck like a scarf. "Mailair seldom extends formal invitations, even to their allies. I thought you might reject it, suspecting a trap."

"I always suspect a trap." Yana scratched a Shadow Goblin behind the ear, eliciting a throaty purr that sounded a lot like a growl. "That's why I'm still alive. More or less."

"And you are certain you'll leave here in the same state?" Sasta asked, tightening her grip on her blackwood spear.

"Mailair may be chaotic, but they are no fool." Yana forced a brittle grin. "In slaying me before the Procession, they'd be losing a valuable asset."

"Yes, but who can speak of *after* the Procession?"

Yana could, with the proper components. It was one of the many features that made her indispensable. "Personally, I've grown weary of predicting the future." She folded her hands at her waist, emulating the haughty noblewomen who'd derided her throughout her mortal life. "For once, let us watch the lots fall naturally, shall we?"

With a belligerent snort, the Augusky beta started down the hallway she'd just emerged from. Yana followed, keeping safely to the center of her Shadow Goblins as the ghastly pall of the lichens faded to near-perfect darkness. A few tenebrous twists and turns later, they stepped into the flickering torchlight of the vast hollow that served as Mailair's throne room. The wide walls spiraled upward into a shadowy tower, and much of the red clay floor had formed callouses from constant traffic.

A sizable crowd of Augusky had gathered to one side of the space, its members clambering over each other for a decent view of one atrocity or another. A mound of mire rose near the opposite wall, atop of which huddled a brigade of scraggly sentries, each armed with an oaken mace or a blackwood spear. The bramble throne and the tyrant who'd claimed it were hidden somewhere in their midst.

Contrary to common assumptions, Mailair had shown wisdom in choosing the smallest and most sickly of their subjects for their entourage. Not one of those mangy whelps posed a threat to the tyrant, yet their numbers were vast enough to deter true challengers, and they would fight horn and hoof to keep the scant prestige Mailair had granted them.

How many of the previous Augusky rulers had been slain by a member of their own guard? Apparently, that was how Mailair had won the throne in the first place.

The Augusky beta knelt at the foot of the mound, though her ruler couldn't see her. At six feet tall, with rippling bands of muscle and horns that could pierce Trow skin, that unwavering fealty was her only obvious weakness. Yana didn't need to read the future to know it would one day be Sasta's undoing.

"Your guest has arrived, Mailair," the beta said, head bowed.

The ruler shooed their sycophants away and flashed a bloody smile. For the moment, they were leaning heavily into the "princess" portion of their title, and they seemed intent on flaunting the decision, having forwent their traditional autumn-leaf collar and twisted their coarse tresses back into an unruly nest. Their slender figure and smooth features might have lent them a delicate air, were their hooves not propped cruelly atop the back of a battered mortal man who knelt prostrate before the throne. Their scepter-spear—topped with the skull of their predecessor—lay haphazardly across their lap, freeing their hands to scrounge strips of flesh from a severed arm, still dripping.

It was a bold show of power, and not only to their starving subjects. That limb had likely belonged to someone the living hoofrest had loved deeply, though it was impossible to read any emotion behind the man's vacant eyes. Shadows knows how many horrors he'd witnessed during his stay at the bramble palace, each custom tailored to exploit his deepest fears. Where most sadists spread sorrow like sickness, Mailair dealt it like cards. All too often, the deck was stacked.

"I'm so pleased you could join us, Ghost Witch!" The ruler tossed their meal aside and hefted their sharpened scepter. They grinned at the skull atop it like the two were sharing an inside joke. "It's been too long since she last graced us with her presence, hasn't it? I was beginning to take offense!"

"I'd intended to 'grace your presence' on the night of the Procession, as scheduled." Yana fought to keep her tone civil. She was not a doll, and she loathed being toyed with. "Why did you decide to summon me three nights early?"

"Two, not counting tonight," Mailair wiggled a pair of bloodstained fingers, "but there will be plenty of time to discuss that later." They held the skull up to their ear like it was whispering a secret, then nodded curtly. "Athrú says you should take a spot of honor beside us, and I'm inclined to believe it's one of his better ideas!" They patted their bramble armrest as though Yana would ever deign to sit there. "We have the best vantage in the entire palace, and you are the closest thing we have to a peer."

Sasta stiffened at the remark, but she managed to hold her tongue.

Yana drifted toward the throne, carefully measuring every step, lest a slip of a heel reveal her newfound vulnerability. Whatever the melding of the worlds had done to her form, she still *looked* like the Ghost Witch her Unseelie neighbors had come to fear. She didn't need anyone questioning her power, least of all the vicious ally who'd long viewed her as a rival.

She settled beside Mailair at a dignified distance. A sneer tugged at the ruler's lips as her Shadow Goblins crowded the throne, their talons carving gashes in the clay. "Still so untrusting," they said with a cluck of their spotted tongue, "and after all the effort I put in to arranging the evening's entertainment."

Mailair's ocher gaze drifted past the Augusky mob gathered below. Yana hesitantly followed their eyes to where three copper cages had been arranged to face a single bowl of rotten fruit, swarming with gnats. Inside each of the cages huddled an emaciated mortal, their wiry limbs and jutting ribs apparent even from a distance. It was impossible to guess how long they'd been wasting away within the palace walls.

"*Rrrready the champions!*" Mailair trilled, moving Athrú's jaw in an absurd jab at ventriloquy. "*On my signal...*"

A trio of Augusky trotted out from among the many, keys dangling from the beaded cords around their necks. Once they'd each settled beside a cage, they turned expectant eyes to their ruler, ears flicking with impatience.

Mailair shot Yana a sidelong smirk before releasing a shrill, two-finger whistle.

The locks *clicked*, and the cage doors flew open.

The captives scrambled forward on their hands and knees, either too weak or too desperate to find their feet. There were two men—a redhead and a brunette—and a petite woman with short, pale curls. Yana wondered whether they'd been chosen because their physical differences made for easy betting, or if it was simply luck of the draw.

Upon reaching the fruit first, the brunette foolishly snatched a pear that squelched between his fingers. Before he could even lick at the sludge, the redhead rushed him with outstretched hands, hooking thick thumbs into his eye sockets. A cheer filled the hollow as one eyeball popped loose to roll in the mire; the other remained attached, dangling from a tangle of nerves. The blinded man screamed violently, flailing his fists and elbows in a frantic attempt at self-defense. The bowl beside him toppled over, spilling slop and stirring flies.

Underestimated to the point of invisibility, the woman rose on shaky legs. Yana thought, for a second, she might dive for the fruit while her opponents tussled, but she instead pulled her tattered dress off over her head. A few simple twists, and it became a rope thick enough to slip around the redhead's neck and tug tight. He fought to shake free, but she was stronger than she looked and considerably more ruthless. His lips turned blue within seconds, and that color soon leeched through his entire face. By the time he stopped struggling, the brunette had fallen limp to the clay beside him, blood oozing from his empty sockets.

The whole fight was over in under five minutes.

Numb to the cheers of the surrounding horde, the champion collapsed beside the overturned bowl. Watching her shove that spoiled fruit into her mouth, not even bothering to flick away the flies, roiled Yana's stomach far more than the violence had. Having come to the palace expecting such a display, she was careful to bury her disgust.

Mailair cackled madly at their own sordid theatrics, not flinching when their throne's barbs bit their shaking limbs. "Our little guest has earned her dinner hasn't she?" they said, prompting another round of applause. "Now that she's had ample opportunity to enjoy her prize, it's your turn to do the same."

At the snap of their bloodied fingers, their subjects rushed the makeshift arena.

Yana forced an indifferent smirk. Her lack of reaction earned a sneer from the Augusky ruler, who waited several seconds to see if the woman's dying screams made any difference. They didn't.

"Well?" Mailair tapped their fingers against their bramble armrest. "I showed you mine..."

"Flattering," Yana raised her eyebrows, "but I prefer the dignity afforded by clothing. A vestige of my mortal origins, I'm afraid."

"You know precisely what I meant, Ghost Witch!" Mailair lurched to their hooves, kicking the prostrate mortal in the side and sending him tumbling into the chaos below. "You promised to lend me the strength of the Wailing Wind—a force with no patterns, no loyalties, no limitations. How can I be sure you'll keep your word?"

"Ask your beta." Yana glanced to where Sasta seethed beside the mound, her jaw strained nearly to the point of snapping. "She helped me to offer the final sacrifice, watched me bathe the host stone in blood, trembled as the Sluagh swept overhead, promising to share their pain and misery only to wind up imprisoned in amber. Surely her testimony is worth something."

"I do not doubt Sasta's witness." Mailair crossed their arms beneath their breasts, huffing like a petulant youth. "What I doubt is your competence. Just because you captured the Sluagh doesn't mean you can control them. My plans for the Procession of Autumn depend on your ability to bend those wretched spirits to your will, and more importantly, *mine*. The least you could do is provide a demonstration."

Despite Yana's best efforts, a smile broke free. Not a single scrying spell, yet she'd predicted the conversation would take this exact turn.

"If that was a condition of the arrangement, you should have mentioned as much," she said sweetly. "Unfortunately for you, the time for bargaining has long passed. To summon the full strength of the Sluagh takes an enormous amount of effort, even for me. I would never conjure such a spectacle for so threadbare an audience."

Mailair's frustrated snarl showed their hand in full. They knew the risks of allowing a rival to demonstrate power before their less loyal subjects, but their curiosity was far stronger than their caution.

"So be it." They clapped their hands, and several flea-riddled lackeys scrambled to their side, weapons at the ready. "Sound the ram horns from the tallest spires. I'm calling an assembly."

"Too many freeze in terror at the reaper's swinging scythe,
But you needn't dread your death when you are sure it leads to life."

CHAPTER 21

LAST LIGHT

TAWNY

he bellow of a ram's horn pealed through the night, echoed by three more bleats in varying tones. Tawny had heard their like before, but Yana had always brushed off her questions on the subject.

They beckon to lesser souls, my dear, she'd say on her way out the cabin door. *You need never concern yourself with their call.*

Like so many of Yana's promises, it had proven false.

Clearly, the fanfare was coming from Fómhar. Brannon's—er, *Muna's*—memories had led the group to stand beneath a constellation called "The Beggar" and march in the direction of its brightest star, which either represented the namesake's nose or the tassel of his hat, depending on which story you believed. From there, they followed a frigid spearmint gale to where it intersected with a warm gust of vanilla. They now stood at the crosswinds, staring down a grassy hillside valley to where the bramble palace waited, all darkness and sinister spiral towers.

The remainder of the trek should have been easy. Too bad gravity reversed the moment they stepped forward, making the steep downward slope feel like an equally sharp incline. Tawny winced at the strain it placed on her travel-weary muscles. The climb was destined to be daunting, and—probably owed to those blasted trumpets—they would not be making it alone.

The Wilds shivered far more violently than usual as a bevy of its denizens emerged from the trees. Whole herds of Augusky bounded toward the palace in the form of true goats, their hooves and horns flashing in the moonlight. Olive-skinned Selkies raced forward with their pelts wafting behind them like capes, swamp water dripping from the riverweed manes of their mounts. A single Glaistig twirled into view, her crimson gaze fixed inquisitively on the bramble spires below, and several massive Trows stomped out from the foliage, the ground trembling beneath their every plodding step.

Amatha strode boldly up to one such creature, undaunted by the fact it dwarfed her in both height and girth. "What is all this commotion?" she asked, lowering her voice to a gravelly growl.

A jagged smile cracked across the Trow's cheek as he considered her. "Your guess is good as mine, lil' one." Dirt spilled from his every joint when he shrugged his heavy shoulders. "Mailair calls assemblies for the strangest reasons. Once, they wanted to show off a shiny rock they found. Then they smashed a Selkie's skull in with it. Nice rock, though."

With that enlightening explanation, he trudged away.

Tawny's stomach twisted into an impressive knot. The Augusky ruler had invited her once-mother to the palace only to call an assembly on the very same night. Even if Tawny believed in coincidences, she couldn't have convinced herself this was one of them.

"This will either make our mission easier or more difficult," Amatha said, granite eyes scrolling over the group. "Until we know which, you will treat this as a reconnaissance mission. Again: do *not* attack unless I command it."

Elwyn crossed her arms. Brannon's knuckles flushed. Aedyn sighed deeply. Still, the group followed the chieftain toward the palace, gravity tugging on their heels all the way. By the time it released its grip, Tawny's legs had begun to tremble, and her glamour did nothing to conceal it. She pressed to the center of the group, hoping her companions' strength would mask her frailty. No one bristled or shied away, not even Elwyn.

Was it too much to hope they no longer viewed her as Lydia's phantom?

The eclectic group gathering around Fómhar's entrance was an encouraging omen. So long as Selkies and hobgoblins were wandering the bramble halls, none would question a few unfamiliar Augusky and a single Trow. The real challenge would be forcing their way into the palace to begin with.

Visitors filtered through the entryway tunnel with the force and fervor of white-water rapids. Amatha melted easily into the stream, and the others followed close on her granite heels. The moment Tawny breached the current, it swept her away, plunging her into shadow. The occasional glimmer of phosphorescent lichen caught in fire-bright eyes and glinted off thorns as long and curved as Augusky horns. One such briar caught her by the braid. Panicked, she clawed desperately at both the vine and her hair until something large and impatient pushed her from behind. Her roots tore free with a painful *rrriiip*, and she spilled out into a bustling chamber. She would have been trampled to a pulp were it not for the granite hand that hoisted her upright.

"Thank you," she mouthed, coaxing her frantic heartbeat calm. The chieftain replied with a concerned nod and a kindly smile. When they next started forward, Amatha tempered her gait, crooking one arm protectively behind Tawny's back.

Though surrounded by monsters in a fortress of thorns, it was the safest Tawny had felt in months, not to mention the most valued. When she'd first been invited on the mission, she'd thought it no different than her wardship with Yana—she'd be used her for potion-craft, then cast aside the moment she proved more troublesome than talented. The chieftain wasn't like that. Amatha would never have admitted it, but she'd made a mission of collecting broken people and making them feel whole. Each member of her hodgepodge troop was a testament to her talents.

Fómhar's corridors were dark despite the smattering of fungal glow. The stale brine of curdled guts hung heavy in the air, undercut by notes of musk and piss. Stray bones peeked from the walls here and there, only to be swallowed by vines a blink later. Warmth trickled down from the nape of Tawny's neck as she walked, oozing from the raw skin where a chunk of her hair had torn loose. Though the scent of her blood prompted the occasional sniff from a passing Unseelie, the scarlet sigils on her skin explained it away well enough.

The gloom gave way to undulating torchlight as the group spilled into a spacious hollow brimming with Unseelie. The swarm was easily four-hundred strong, with visitors still filtering in through several open tunnels. Members of Mailair's harem had clustered near the throne, forming a thick ring around the mire mound that served as a dais. They looked no different from other Augusky, with their caprine horns and sallow skin, but the slack-jawed reverence they afforded their ruler set them apart.

The tyrant lounged cross-legged in their seat of honor, one hoof bobbing impatiently as they watched their audience swell. On the few other occasions Tawny had glimpsed the Prince-Often Princess-Sometimes Both-and-on at Least One Occasion-Neither, they'd been more prince than anything. This slender, feminine form they now wore was no less intimidating. Fresh blood coated their steepled fingers, their ochre eyes gleamed with malice, and the spiral-horned skull that topped their sharpened scepter sang of their misdeeds.

An armed contingent of guards stood behind the throne, numerous enough to give challengers pause. Most were mangy and comparatively frail, but Sasta was the exception. The Augusky beta was a monstrous sight to behold. Crimson runes swept across much of her pale skin, and teeth adorned every inch of her calico braids, each claimed from a separate kill. The tip of her blackwood spear glistened with blood, or possibly poison. Either way, it served as a warning.

There would be no reaching Mailair in this mess. Tawny's heart sank at the realization, but her eyes lifted to the chieftain. Amatha tried to urge the group closer, but the throng was too thick to press through.

A heavy pat on the shoulder bolstered Tawny's spirits. If the group could not complete their mission tonight, they could at least glean information from the tyrant's looming speech. Hopefully, it would help them to approach the Procession of Autumn from a clearer vantage. It wasn't the brightest flicker of hope, but it warmed her, nonetheless.

Mailair leapt atop their throne and swept into a melodramatic bow, nearly striking Sasta with a flourish of their scepter-spear. The beta's lip curled, but she remained otherwise rigid. The ruler's harem cheered violently, raising bloodstained hands along with their voices, but the visitors—Unseelie and Solitary alike—were more reserved with their reactions. A sprinkling of obligatory applause trickled through the hollow, growing softer as it neared the walls.

The tepid response came as no surprise to Tawny. Where the Seelie

Court settled their disagreements through formal deliberations, the Unseelie Court was a chaotic jumble of bickering, brawling, and literal backstabbing. As a result, scant trust had formed between their High Houses. Mailair had amassed quite a following among their own kind— embodying the Augusky virtue of Chaos to a startling degree—but even the lesser Augusky herds tended to avoid them. The Selkie Prime, Shaera, High Judge of Desire, had demonstrated a strong yen to avoid her autumnal peer at all costs, though she often sent delegates to keep communications flowing. Tawny was willing to bet at least half of the Selkies in attendance, and the Kelpie mounts now standing in near-human form beside them, were there at her bidding.

The Unseelie of the Winter Wastes might as well have belonged to another court entirely. No one knew who ruled the Wulver, as their kind had always preferred to keep to themselves, and it had been ages since one of Fuara's emissaries last visited the Wilds. It could be argued that travel between lands was too difficult, but the Korrid Queen's pronounced dislike of her peers was the more probable malady.

"Welcome, friends and fiends!" Mailair shouted, a maniacal cackle bubbling behind every syllable. "Though I've never summoned you without good cause, I suspect you'll find this reason better than most. The Procession of Autumn is nearly upon us, and it's bound to be the grandest we've seen in centuries!"

The statement coaxed a cheer from the throng, louder and more genuine than the last. Even the Solitaries seemed to perk up at the mention of the unhallowed rite. Where the Unseelie had made it their mission to torment mortals indiscriminately, courtless fae did the same to mortals who *deserved* it. The lines of distinction often blurred.

"Indeed, indeed, it's all terribly exciting," Mailair continued, shooing their entourage away with a shake of their scepter. The lesser Augusky scrambled swiftly from the earthen dais, but Sasta made a slow descent, fingers blanched around the shaft of her spear. "Too long, the Treaty of Dusk has barred us from wreaking havoc on the mortals. It should come as no surprise that they've forgotten how to properly fear us. Now that our worlds have stitched together, every word of that vile accord has been voided, and we are finally free to fulfill our Shadow-ordained purpose!" They paused to allow for another ovation, inhaling the praise like cauldron steam. "As you've doubtless guessed, I've been planning something special for this year's celebration. I had hoped to keep my musings secret until the night of the Procession, but alas, they are not mine alone. And so, it is with mild regret I must direct your attention to Calliwyn Yana, Ghost Witch of the Patchwork Palace!"

Rather than applause, a collective shudder ran through the swarm. They whispered amongst themselves as Yana stepped from the shadows surrounded by a cloud of inky minions with phlegm-yellow eyes. Mailair's nose wrinkled as the witch and her goblins settled beside the throne, but the tyrant forced a square-toothed grin for the sake of the alliance.

Tawny's heart stuttered at the sight of those violet eyes, that self-assured smile. She'd been expecting the haunting, ember-eyed wraith who'd stretched her out atop a stone altar and raised a knife over her heart. *This* version of Yana, dressed in a modest ivory gown with her ghost-white locks pinned in a meticulous updo, looked more like the woman who'd warded her headboard against nightmares and sang her to sleep with bittersweet lullabies, who'd guided her in foraging the choicest spell components and spread balms on the bruises she inevitably earned in the process, all the while spinning stories of tricksters and spirits and the wily young girls who outwitted them.

A fire caught behind Tawny's eyes, blindingly bright.

It didn't feel like hatred.

Both Brannon and Elwyn lurched forward, drawing their glamour-dulled daggers. Amatha captured a shoulder apiece, chastising them with a subtle shake of her head. Tawny wondered, briefly, why no one scrambled to stop her from charging her once-mother. Then she realized how leaden her legs were. It bothered her to know her sorrow was so predictable.

"Your regard is flattering." Yana didn't need to raise her voice. Even at a whisper, it could fill a space like fog. "I know I've developed quite a reputation—more than one, in fact—so allow me a moment to cull truth from fiction. As many of you are aware, I've long enjoyed a productive working relationship with your ruler, and together we've brought about many a marvel—this splendorous new world chief among them. Melding the realms has been my greatest accomplishment to date, but I'm afraid I'm about to outdo myself."

Murmurs swept through the hollow like wildfire. If the Unseelie hadn't known of the Ghost Witch's role in the Confluence, they did now. And they lauded her for it.

She did not allow their ardor long to simmer before raising her hands overhead, proudly displaying a peculiar hunk of amber. The stone was mottled brown and burgundy, with intricate runes etched on every facet and a ghastly green light pulsing at its center. Yana held it gingerly between linen-wrapped palms, her fingers hovering above the surface as though touching it might burn her.

Tawny had read about host stones. They were rare relics, crafted with dark magic and bathed in the blood of Unseelie fae. According to the grimoires she'd found hidden in her once-mother's room, they were used to trap and control wayward spirits, binding their will to that of a powerful master.

One glimpse, and Tawny knew exactly which spirits Yana had tethered.

"Ebensburg, Baronsborough, Stocksport..." Yana's knowing gaze slid over the swarm, studying their faces. If habits held, she would tune her speech as it unfolded, coaxing admiration from souls long steeped in revulsion. "Those are but a few of the mortal strongholds that have proven invulnerable to your attacks. Between their iron fortresses and the tenacious little hunters who guard their slums, they have discovered and exploited far too many of your weaknesses. Already, they mock you around their dinner tables and village wells, comparing you to the tales they grew up with and finding you altogether lacking."

It had looked more like cowering than mockery to Tawny, though she supposed the heads staked outside Wiltshire could be taken either way. The fae-folk swallowed Yana's claims without question, and they didn't digest well. Such smug creatures could not abide the thought of being scorned by "finger foods with attitudes," as one curmudgeonly Trow put it.

"If their disrespect concerns you, imagine what the future holds." Yana sauntered forward, her goblins scrambling to keep pace. "The moment those vermin realize how easy it is to keep you at bay, their terror will morph into outrage. They will hammer their iron shields into swords and take up the torches that light their streets. They will march on your thickets, your caves, your fens and raze them just as surely as you have razed their hovels. Unless..." she paused at the foot of the mire mound, relishing the rapt attention of the crowd, "we remind them of their place. Fear is the surest tether for securing one's position at the top of the food chain." She hoisted the host stone higher, and its glow flared even brighter. "*This* will allow us to unravel their havens without so much as raising a claw. With it, we will shred their iron walls to splinters and reduce their warded sanctums to rubble."

The mob parted as she passed through their midst, her ashen face bathed in eerie green light. Many onlookers shied back, fearing the power trapped within the amber; others ventured closer, compelled by that very same force. All followed her with wide eyes and eager ears, awaiting further explanation.

"The Wailing Wind." The name sent a palpable shudder through the swarm. "You've heard their cries as they wind through the Wilds. You've seen the carnage they leave in their wake. You've felt your hackles rising whenever they draw near, instinctually sensing the sorrow they strive to sow. You have been told that I am one of them—just another stranded soul desperate to spread anguish and suffering. In this, and only this, you are wrong." She idled at the center of the hollow, relishing the excitement of her rapt audience. "I do not belong to the Sluagh. They belong to *me*!"

The moment she pressed her fingertips to the amber, sparks of green light crackled across her skin. Her eyes flared bright as she tossed her head back, and a sourceless gale whipped to life around her, freeing her snowy locks and turning them into ghostly tendrils. The glow escaped the host stone and spilled outward in serpentine spirals, climbing ever higher as they stretched wide. Gnashing skulls appeared in the haze only to vanish a heartbeat later, devoured by their screeching kin.

The crowd cowered, huddling close despite their disparate factions in an extraordinary display of communal terror. As the Ghost Witch had so poignantly explained, instilling fear was a vital step in securing one's place in the food chain. She intended to claim the topmost rung.

"In two nights' time, we will march on Ebensburg!" Yana's voice split into many, a viper's nest of whispers that had long haunted Tawny's mind. "The Wailing Wind will herald our coming, wreaking havoc and misery at my whim. It will destroy the district's iron borders and purge the poison from its belly, freeing you to unleash chaos on the insolent mites who've long mocked you from within its walls. With the Slaugh to pave our path and the Shadows to empower us, we will prove to all who inhabit this light-forsaken world that it is ours to ravage, to ruin, to reshape in our image!"

The horde's applause nearly drowned the screams of the spirits who circled above them. Yana had hit every resonant note, appealing to their pride, their fear, and inevitably their hunger. She never intended to reshape the world—not while its lawlessness played to her favor—but she'd already succeeded in reshaping *them*. She might as well have been standing in a hall of mirrors.

It sickened Tawny to think she'd ever viewed the Ghost Witch as a mother. How many times had Yana played her heart like an instrument, plucking strings of love and affection with her own nefarious aims in mind? Had a single smile, a single embrace, a single light-forsaken second of Tawny's childhood been sincere?

"This will not be a feat of individual prowess, mind you, but a grand collaboration." Yana continued her march, her voices weaving through the din. "Together, we will reduce the Creator's favored pets to the dirt they were made of. We will drain the blood from their veins, snuff the light from their eyes, rip the hope from—"

She jarred to a stop, her smile evaporating. The swarm fell silent as she lowered the host stone. Even the Wailing Wind seemed to soften, awaiting the words of their master.

"I sense the presence of a foe." She closed her eyes, inhaling deeply. "There is one among us who reeks of sunlight and summer fruit. A spirit steeped in arid warmth and the glow of molten rivers. A stranger from a distant land, their will set against our darkest dreams..."

When her eyes flashed open, they centered on Amatha's group, seeming to peer right through their glamour. Tawny reached reflexively for her collarbone, desperate for the comfort of her warded medallion. Her fingers brushed bare skin, and her heart stuttered. Her braid was not all the brambles had swallowed.

"Writhe forward, little worm." Yana resumed her march, this time headed straight for Tawny. "Poke your head from the soil that I might show you the mercy of a swift death."

Tawny shied back, and her shoulders struck dobhriste. She dared a glance up at the chieftain, rubbing the space where her medallion once hung. Amatha's stony eyes darkened as understanding settled in. The glamour did nothing to hide her sorrow.

There was no way out, and they both knew it. The pendants were warded against magical discovery, but close examination was another story. If Tawny didn't reveal herself, and soon, she'd be putting the others' lives at risk.

The Sluagh feed on regrets, she reminded herself. Thank the Shadows she hadn't lived long enough to make many. This would all be over quickly.

Before she could take a single step, Amatha flung her backward through the throng. Someone caught her beneath the armpits—Brannon, judging by the scarlet rings on his arms. Fae-folk scrambled back in shock as the chieftain strode toward the Ghost Witch, her glamour falling away like autumn leaves. The moment her crystal shards caught the torchlight, Tawny realized what was happening.

She jerked forward only for Brannon to pull her back, stifling her scream with his hand. "You'll get us all killed," he hissed, pulling her deeper into the throng. They were too enthralled by the unfolding drama to notice.

"A denizen of the Red Realm?" Yana's grin failed to mask her surprise. "I was not anticipating a visit from one of the Daoine Sidhe, and a distinguished warrior, judging from your adornments." Her ember eyes raked over Amatha's bandolier. "Tell me, stone fae, to what do we owe this honor?"

Amatha squared her shoulders. "Consider me an emissary from the Seelie Court," she said, veering artfully around the truth. "It seems the timing of my arrival was fortuitous, perhaps fated. The plans you have put forth would forever fray your ties to the Light Realms. You must change course if you wish for them to remain intact."

"*If.*" Yana brandished the word like a blade. "That the Seelie would send only a single emissary to Fómhar proves just how naïve they are, and how poorly their ideals will weather the coming storm. Whyever would we barter with those we could simply crush?"

The Unseelie roared in agreement. The speech had whetted their bloodlust, leaving them desperate for a display of violence whether it served their cause or not.

Forgetting their fear of the encircling spirits, Mailair leapt atop their throne. "Are you truly so foolish, Sidhe?" they asked. "The Treaty of Dusk was Aryn and Fuara's doing, and I helped to create this world solely to abolish it! My predecessor was a dolt for ever playing along." They flicked their scepter's skeletal topper on the nose. "And you're twice the dolt if you think we'll let you walk out of here alive!"

"No." Aedyn's voice was a pained whisper, nearly lost to the clamor of the crowd and the Wailing Wind. "We can't let this happen. We have to—"

The sentence was smothered—perhaps by a sob, perhaps by Elwyn's hand. Tawny couldn't see the prince, but someone must have restrained him. Otherwise, he'd have already rushed forward with his rapier drawn, ready to take on every creature in the hollow.

Tawny felt the same. She struggled against Brannon's grip, her teeth scraping his palm. He hissed a swear and pulled her deeper into the swarm, and she dug her heels into the clay to slow his retreat. If she could only break free, she could drop her disguise and rush to Amatha's rescue, groveling at her once-mother's feet. If Yana ever cared for her at all, she would surely...she would...she...

She would do whatever served her interests, like always.

"I could pass along your message to the High Judges," Amatha said, but the words dripped resignation. She knew exactly how this was going to end. "If we cannot mend the former treaty, it is our duty to craft a new one. You believe the Shadows require you to torment the mortals; we believe the Creator has tasked us with their protection. When those paths inevitably cross, war is the only possible outcome." She took a bold step forward, looking courageous as ever despite the tremble in her fingers. "It is never too late to change directions, Yana. Not even for you."

Yana tilted her head, seeming to weigh the chieftain's words. Then Mailair abandoned their throne, tossing their sharpened scepter aside in a fit of indignation.

"I'm tired of this stranger's preaching, Ghost Witch!" They stamped a hoof. "You promised to display the Wailing Wind's power, and fate has provided you with a volunteer from the audience. Need I truly direct every act of this play?"

The onlookers bellowed in agreement, their roars melding with that of the spirits above. The most sensible among them began to shy away, covertly retreating toward one of several connecting corridors. Tawny's vision blurred and her limbs fell lax. Heartsick and hollow, she allowed Brannon to drag her away.

"The masses have spoken." Yana's voices slithered through the crowd, even as it swallowed her. "Take heart, proud Sidhe. You wanted to deliver a message, and that's exactly what you'll do. Upon glimpsing your fate, any who might have opposed me will realize their folly and reassess accordingly. Just think of all the lives you're about to save."

The Sluagh descended, claws outstretched, and their horrid light filled the hollow. Brannon whirled and forced Tawny through the crowd, releasing her to the darkness of a bramble hallway. Her feet continued racing of their own accord, desperate to outrun the din that rolled through the palace behind them—a calloused cacophony of agonized wails and heartless cheers.

Amatha's dying cry was lost to the storm, but it would ring in Tawny's ears for a lifetime.

"Know when to mend your fraying ties and when to cut and run,
One careless snag, and all your precious plans could come undone."

CHAPTER 22

SUTURES AND SHEARS

ELWYN

hey drifted through the Wilds in silence, frozen in the moment of Amatha's death. Images of ghastly green faces had seared themselves behind Elwyn's eyelids, causing her to dread each blink. If her companions' expressions were any clue, they were likewise haunted.

Brannon wore a seething scowl, even darker than his usual. Tawny's face had blanched from shock, her gaze lost to the woods ahead. Aedyn clenched something tight against his chest, tears clinging to his lashes but refusing to fall. Even Luatha sat furled on Elwyn's shoulder, mourning in her own way.

Elwyn probably looked exactly how she felt: utterly hollow. She loathed that lack of feeling, though it doubtless kept her plodding along. Perhaps grief circled overhead like Yana's wretched spirits, awaiting the perfect moment to crash down and shred her to ribbons. Or maybe she'd grown so accustomed to grief that it felt like fighting a cough—a weight on the lungs, a hitch in the throat, and nothing more.

She'd brought it upon herself, really. Life had been simpler when it was just her and Luatha, confiding in and looking out for each other. Ever since they'd fled the Greyscale, she'd become increasingly careless, despite the piskie's warnings. She'd let herself grow too close to too many, hardly noticing when their fabrics stitched to hers. Was it any wonder that, when they inevitably ripped away, they took pieces of her with them?

Her thoughts continued their inward spiral, growing darker the deeper they delved, until Aedyn buckled beneath the weight of his grief, fell to his knees, and began weeping into his hands. With reflexes akin to drawing her dagger, Elwyn threw her arms around his heaving shoulders. She worried he might push her away, remembering how she'd restrained him when Amatha revealed herself to Yana, but he wilted against her, burying his face in the curve of her neck. His tears soaked into both her cloak and spirit, melting away a sheet of numbing ice. A fever-bright ache trickled in behind it, leaving her desperate for the daze she'd been lamenting moments before.

"Shut him up!" Brannon growled, as though Elwyn could magically mend things. He placed a hand on the hilt of an *icon*, eyes flitting between shadows like he suspected one to pounce at any moment. "He'll announce our presence to every monster in these fucking woods!"

Luatha flitted to the assassin's side in a rare show of solidarity.

"There's nothing we can say or do to make this pain reverse,
But if we don't keep moving, we're bound to suffer worse."

"Keep moving *where?*" Elwyn scanned her moonlit surroundings for the first time since they'd fled Fómhar. They'd stumbled into a spacious clearing carpeted in clover and surrounded by towering pines. Not a single familiar shrub graced woods around the glade, not that landmarks meant much in this light-forsaken labyrinth. "We've been ambling along on pure adrenaline for hours. Do we have any clue where we're headed?"

Tawny sniffled sharply, burying her fingers in her uneven hair. "I...I haven't been paying attention," she confessed, shrinking inward. "I'm so sorry. I—"

"The destination isn't important." Brannon's interjection was far from tender, but it was the only kindness he knew how to offer. "We just need to keep moving until dawn. If we idle for too long, we risk falling asleep. If we fall asleep, we'll probably wake up shackled by the roots of an oak tree, slowly drowning in soil and squirrel shit."

"Unless..." Tawny rummaged through her pockets, sorting through her various trifles and baubles until she came upon a vial of something white. "I have enough chalk powder left to craft a rune circle. It won't be very intricate, mind you, but it should fix this glade in place for a few hours. Five, if we're lucky."

"And if a hungry beast stumbled across us?" Brannon touched the mangled tip of his left ear, a souvenir from one such monster. "Without our disguises, the Unseelie will immediately mark us as meals, and that says nothing for the less chatty beasts. Unless Aedyn can muster enough magic to—"

"Absolutely not." Elwyn tightened her hold on the grieving prince, as though her arms could shield him from the very thought. His light was already guttering; they would not be stealing a single spark of it. "I'll keep watch while the rest of you slumber. If any Unseelie come sniffing about, rest assured I'll rid them of their noses."

Tawny took her at her word and trundled off toward the trees. Brannon lingered a moment more, assessing Elwyn with eyes sharper than his blades. He could read her fatigue like a scavenger hound could spot sickness, but he also knew just how resilient she could be. If it brought Aedyn even a moment of rest, she would gladly forfeit her own.

"Just wake me before you start chopping off noses," he said with a resigned shake of his head. "Playing sentry doesn't entitle you to all the fun."

The assassin gathered an armful of ferns and fashioned them into a pair of pillows while the spellcrafter sprinkled sigils around the glade. Soon enough, they were both soundly snoring, Luatha curled up on a maple leaf between them. In any other circumstances, it would have made for an endearing portrait. Now, all Elwyn could think of was the negative space.

She tried her best to keep alert, scanning the shivering foliage for the gleam of sinister eyes or the flash of ivory fangs. It was difficult to focus with spectral wails ringing in her ears and a heartbroken friend weeping in her arms. As painful as her own sorrow was, Aedyn's must have been absolute agony. She'd never wanted so badly to steal something away.

"I'm so sorry." The words tumbled from her lips over and over, accomplishing nothing.

Eventually, Aedyn's sobs softened to sniffles. He slowly pulled away, wiping his cheeks with his sleeve. Elwyn wrapped her arms around herself, fending off a sudden chill, but they felt empty no matter how tightly she twined them.

"Th-thank you." Aedyn's voice snagged like velvet on thorns. "I don't mean to be a burden, and I certainly didn't mean to strand us in the middle of nowhere. If Am...Ama..." He bit his lip. "She would probably chide me for losing focus. She's always had a knack for keeping calm amidst chaos. The High Judges even awarded her this—" He touched his collar, and his eyes widened. "I-I must have dropped it somewhere. I can't believe...after all of this...how could I..."

The rant morphed into a frustrated growl as he pawed through the clovers around him. Elwyn joined the search, though she had no clue what she was looking for. Dry leaves crumbled at her touch and pine beetles skittered past her fingertips, but the Wilds offered nothing that did not belong to them.

Not a minute into the hunt, Aedyn sprang to his feet and sprinted down a side trail. Elwyn cursed under her breath, giving chase. Even if he was headed in the direction they'd come from—and she hadn't been nearly lucid enough to keep track—the path had probably shifted in the time since. Still, if Aedyn was determined to get himself lost, she would not allow him to wander the woods alone.

The forest bled past in a storm of roiling reds and golds until Aedyn paused to parse through a pile of brittle leaves. Before Elwyn could join him, something winked out from a tangle of trailside brambles. She fished the glimmer free and held it up for closer inspection. Moonlight spilled through silver filigree and pooled in the center of an oval-cut quartz, refracting shards of sky blue and lavender.

"I think I've found it." Weary though Elwyn's voice was, it caught Aedyn's ear. He raced over and snatched the brooch from her fingers, pressing it to his chest and sighing deeply.

"Amatha gave this to me right before we left Rhysien-Talunasa," he explained, eyes fluttering open. The light behind them had dimmed, but it hadn't vanished. "She claimed the chaos I'd caused throughout our friendship helped prepare her for running the Myriad Guard. Coming from anyone else, it would have sounded sardonic."

"But she was perfectly genuine," Elwyn said, heart aching.

Was. Such a definitive word. So cold and unforgiving.

"In all things, at all times." The faintest smile trembled on Aedyn's lips as he shifted his palm, watching the gemstone glitter. "I didn't deserve any of it—not this badge, not her patience, and certainly not her friendship.

I'm a spoiled lout on my best days, whereas she was the strongest, bravest, most steadfast person I've ever known."

"She was all of those things." Elwyn plucked the gemstone from Aedyn's hand. "Do you know what else she was?"

"Forgiving to a fault?"

"A good judge of character." She turned the brooch over to find the pin had been bent. A twist of her thumb and forefinger smoothed it. "Amatha deserves every bit of praise you've offered her and more, but she would never allow you to tear yourself down for the sake of building her up. She was grateful to have you in her life—not only for your chaos, but for your warmth, your kindness, and your compassion. You saw the best traits in each other, and you helped them to grow." She fixed the quartz to his collar, taking time to smooth his rumpled lapel. "I'm not exactly an expert at friendship, but I think that is the general point of it."

"Now who's the one tearing herself down?" Aedyn placed his hand atop hers, pressing her fingers against his collarbone. His skin felt that much warmer for the crisp autumn gusts that flurried around them. "You're an incredible friend. A mediocre one would never have put this much effort into lifting my spirits, and they certainly wouldn't have followed me out here just to ensure my safety. I appreciate and admire you, Elwyn. More than I can say."

There was an aching sincerity to the confession—the unmistakable strain of bridled words, though the longing in his eyes was as bold a declaration as any sonnet ever written. That telling silence was the most he could offer. He'd promised not to gamble with their friendship, but Elwyn had made no such vow.

Casting caution aside for perhaps the first time ever, she tilted to her tiptoes, grabbed him by the collar, and rolled the dice.

The kiss was everything she'd dreamed a kiss could be—bright as a sunbeam, soft as morning mist, thrilling as a thunderstorm, and incomparably blissful. Aedyn melted against her, twining his fingers in her hair and cloak as the gentle brush of lips morphed into something deeper. Wrapped in his arms, his warmth, his summer-sweet scent, Elwyn nearly let herself forget the kiss was stolen, like every other precious thing she'd ever possessed. She could almost convince herself that he belonged to her. At the very least, he belonged to her *for now*.

It was more than she'd dared to hope for.

Parting was painful, but it helped that he kept an arm around her waist and tipped his forehead against hers. For a giddy moment, they were back at the Feral Ferret, lightheaded from honeyed whiskey and the sound of each other's laughter, dreading the final measure of the faerie reel that had drawn them close. Only this time, Elwyn couldn't fathom running away.

"Remember how I promised to teach you impulsivity?" Aedyn brushed her hair aside, tracing her crescent scar with his thumb. "It's safe to say you no longer require my mentorship."

Elwyn laughed. "I take it you're happy with my progress?"

"Very." He kissed the tip of her nose. "Which is why I really, really, *really* hate to say this..."

"But we need to head back." Elwyn practically groaned the words, true though they were. She'd promised to guard the glade against Unseelie—a feat which would prove difficult from a distance.

"Don't you fret." He kept his arm slung around her as they started back down the trail. "I'm no seer, but even I can predict there will be many more kisses in your near future."

Elwyn rested her cheek on his shoulder. "That's assuming you don't grow bored of me," she teased.

"Never."

A bold statement for a man who changed the color of his cape thrice daily, but Elwyn wanted desperately to believe it. She forced thoughts of Aedyn's station and betrothal aside, savoring the flutter in her chest and pretending the moment could stretch into eternity. As they made their way back toward the glade, pressed close as they could manage without tripping each other, she could practically feel the sutures threading between them, stitching silk to sackcloth and tugging impossibly tight.

It was going to hurt like hell when he tore away.

YANA

Yana stared into the fireplace, seeking faces in the flames. There was no metaphysical value to the practice, no reward for glimpsing a flickering smile, a guttering frown, or a seething scream. It was simply a game that her mother had taught her, and that she had taught her own...

No. Not her *own* daughter.

Tawny had always belonged to the mortals. She belonged in their arms and in their lives and on their soil. Had Yana not swindled her fool of a father, the girl would never have set foot in Faerie to begin with. Yana's actual daughter had died twice over without ever spending a night before her hearth. But what was truth, and what was love, and what was blood, save another component for the cauldron? In the end, people were no different from the Sluagh—destined to devour one another lest they themselves fall prey.

Why then, when they managed to escape each other unscathed, did it ache so deeply?

"There was something *off* about that Sidhe," Yana mused, scratching Solstice behind the ear. The spectral cat nuzzled into her palm, his essence tingling like frostbite. "Yes, the spirit I sensed had basked in the glow of a crimson sun, but there was something else beneath that warmth—a sweet bite, like a sprinkle of ginger or a sip of licorice tea." She shook her head, running a hand down her cat's hazy gray pelt. "Look at me, building my palace atop a corpse-heap and complaining of the stench. That assembly couldn't have gone more smoothly if I'd planned it."

Of course, she *had* planned it, up to a point. She'd brought the host stone to Fómhar with every intention of displaying its power, assuming she'd have to settle for obliterating one of Mailair's whores. That Sidhe emissary had been a gift from the Shadows. Any sacrifice would have earned the fear of all who witnessed it, but nothing ever inspired allegiance quite like rallying the rabble against a common foe. Now Yana needed only to make good on her promise. Once she demolished Ebensburg, she could leverage access to the remaining mortal bastions for power over all who dwelt in the Wilds, and no one—not even Blithely Fox—would ever threaten her again.

She should have been grateful the intruder turned out to be a stranger. In all her life, she'd only ever glimpsed one aura so bright, but if Tawny's face had been hidden beneath that glamour...

Since when could the Sidhe use glamour, anyway?

"This must be what regret feels like." The puzzle pieces refused to click, no matter how Yana turned them, and it felt strangely like the skull-rending madness she'd only just stifled. "I should have sought her out before I melded the worlds, but she fled before the sacrifice was complete, and I traveled back here the moment after. I have no idea where she wound up, or whether she's even..." She shook a grim possibility from her head. "Perhaps it's not too late. There's no deed so drastic it cannot be undone. If she'll only hear me out, I can fix everything."

Solstice answered with a didactic flick of the tail.

"I wasn't asking your opinion." Yana shooed the cat from her lap, and he leapt to the floor with an irritated mewl. As he pranced away with his nose hoisted high, she rose from her armchair, loathing the prickle of the Augusky fur rug against her feet.

"This is your fault, you know that?" She glared at the black marbles she'd used to replace Daulle's eyes. "If you'd minded your own business, I could have told her everything on my own terms. I would still have needed her fear, but it would have had less time to fester, and I could have arranged to dispel it before a rift grew. It never needed to turn out this way."

It took only ten minutes to prep the cauldron and craft an elixir base, another three to gather most of the spell's components. "A sprinkle of forget-me-nots," she said, dusting dried petals into the glassy brew. "A pinch of nightclove, a dash of shadowroot, a splash of swine spittle, and..." she plucked a tiny, venomous barb from a matchbox, "one tail of spriggan."

The cauldron devoured the ingredients with a greedy hiss, but for all its hunger, it was as shy as any common pot. In climbing the staircase to scrounge up the final ingredient, Yana allowed it the privacy it craved. Yellow eyes blinked out from between the steps, curious and cold. She instructed the creatures to stay below, though this task was no less dreadful than a visit to the bramble palace.

The room was exactly how Tawny had left it, save for the thin patina of dust that had settled on every surface. Her quilt was wadded against a headboard etched with dream wards, but her favorite green blanket had fallen to the floor. A tower of tomes stood upon her bedside table, marked with scraps of fabric and weighed down with a half a geode. A hoard of snail shells, acorn caps, and other natural treasures crowded the shelves and windowsills, having slowly displaced the dolls and trinkets Yana had brought back from her many travels.

It was easy to picture Tawny sitting cross-legged on the bed, a bundle of thistles in one hand and a spell-scroll in the other. Somehow, that child had managed to glean all of Yana's curiosity and cunning without inheriting a single flaw. It was no wonder her life was a blur of scraped knees and tattered hems. For all the time Yana had spent taming that mane of unruly curls, she missed their wild abandon. And that of the girl who neglected them.

Yana pushed the memories aside before they could smother her, drifting forward to give the clutter the same treatment. After a bit of rifling, she found a slender wooden comb tucked into a bin of unopened lotions and powders, a few yellow hairs still tangled in its teeth. She plucked them free and fled the room as swiftly as her gown allowed. Regret trailed her down the stairs like a bloodhound.

The brew had predictably reached a boil in her absence. Yana tossed the hair into the pot, muttering a rushed prayer to the Shadows. It was ritual for ritual's sake. The Shadows cared little for conversation, being spirits of the give-and-take variety. They would accept her offering because they had always done so, and she would gratefully accept theirs.

Solstice trilled a warning, peering out from a bookshelf perch. Yana ignored him as she poured a cup of potion. Either solitude was taking its toll, or he was becoming quite the preachy little creature.

"This won't take long," she said, as much to herself as the cat. "It's become obvious there's still a loose thread in my tapestry. If I neither mend nor sever it, my efforts will unravel entirely."

"Whether your dreams alight on you at midnight or midday,
A nightmare could be lurking just one toss or turn away."

CHAPTER 23

THE DARK SIDE OF DREAMING

TAWNY

bittersweet lullaby lilted through the night, rousing Tawny to a world etched in charcoal. She propped herself up with an elbow as she blinked the smears into shape. The Wilds were shifting faster than ever before, and the storm of swaying branches and shivering leaves swiftly devoured the song that had woken her.

It took her sleep-addled mind several seconds to register that she was utterly alone. Not a single footprint graced the glade, much less a person. Telling herself it was only a dream did nothing to soothe her hummingbird heartbeat. If it were a dream, why could she feel a ginger breeze tickling her nose, the clovers prickling her palms, the bruises throbbing on her shoulders from when Brannon had dragged her from Fómhar?

Remembering the bramble palace felt like ripping off a scab, the skin beneath still raw and stinging. Suddenly, it all made perfect sense. The chieftain had recruited Tawny for the mission despite the resentment the others held for her. Now that Amatha was...now that she was gone, it was only natural they leave her to the mercy of the Wilds.

"Elwyn?" Tawny whimpered, hoping she was wrong. "Brannon? Aedyn? Luatha?" When no one answered, she drew a deep breath and tried once more. "Amatha?"

Her only answer was the rustle of rot-dry leaves.

That settled it then. If Tawny was dreaming, the chieftain would have appeared at her bidding. She'd have flashed one final, kindly smile and offered Tawny the opportunity to thank her, to apologize, and to say a much-needed goodbye. Unless...

Tawny had never experienced a nightmare before. For as long as she could remember, Yana had warded her headboard against feelings of fear and sorrow and stuffed lavender sprigs into her pillowcase for good measure. As a result of either the spellwork or the sentiment, Tawny's every slumber had been peaceful.

If this was the dark side of dreaming, she didn't care for it.

When she finally forced herself to stand, a light stuttered to life in the dark of the forest, bobbing in place like a pale blue flame atop a waxen wick. The hue did not match Luatha's glow, the pall was brighter than that of a simple sprite, and though its steady flicker hinted at warmth, the sight sent shivers through Tawny.

A blink, and a second glow appeared behind the first. Then another. And another. Soon enough, a glittering trail wound through the Wilds, as ominous as it was enticing. As the frigid gleam fell on the foliage, the swaying branches froze, the ferns ceased their shivering, and the writhing roots stiffened like sap on a chilly day.

Tawny knew of wisps from scrolls, stories, and songs, and their origins were no mystery. They were the dying wishes of the damned, stirred to life by hatred too hostile to fade with its host. Oftentimes, they acted of their own vile accord, luring hapless travelers to certain doom. Occasionally, powerful casters conjured them to do a little luring of their own. Either way, it was best to decline their invitation.

Before Tawny had a chance to turn away, she found herself drifting through the darkness, pulled from glow to glow as if drawn by an invisible tether. She dug her heels into the marl, but her progress did not slow. Her hands joined in the battle, grasping desperately at every branch and brush she passed by. Though thorns sliced her palms and splinters dug beneath her nails, she found no anchor.

She'd been drifting along for some time when a familiar melody flitted past. It was clearer now, and sweeter, and it brought with it an onslaught of memories. Nights spent hunting fireflies in foggy moors, searching for faces in a blazing hearth fire, drifting off to sleep on a pillow stuffed with lavender, a book in her hands and a spell on her tongue.

Through no effort of her own, lyrics drifted from her lips.

"Will o' the wisps are beckoning,
Will you say you will?
Wisps, they promise many things,

They may not fulfill."

Tawny bit her tongue, alarmed by its sudden show of independence. In the breath between measures, a whisper trickled through the night, answering her in verse.

"Will o' the wisps are fickle things,
Will you say you won't?
Will the wisps know what you seek,
Even when you don't?"

Tawny's heart lurched with a warning, but the wisps forced her onward. Crushing her resolve, they drew another verse from her soul.

"Will o' the wisps are wretches all,
Will you say you might?
Will you heed their somber call,
Be it wrong or right?"

It was not one voice that called back, but many entwined. Tawny recognized each of them; they went by one name.

"Will o' the wisps are bright and blue,
Will you say you would?
Wisps will lead you somewhere new,
Seldom somewhere good."

The song ended, and the wisps vanished, tossing Tawny forward with one final thrust of magic. She stumbled from the forest into the shadow of a birch-thin woman, her hair and dressing gown turned silver by the moonlight.

"W-what do you want from me, Ghost Witch?" It was a small relief, shaping her own words, but not enough to calm her trembling fingers.

"Now, Tawny." The woman drifted forward, eyes searing with violet flame. "That's no way to speak to your mother."

ELWYN

Elwyn and Aedyn were approaching the glade when Luatha zipped out to meet them. Judging from the frantic whir of her wings, something had gone terribly wrong.

"I thought you had been eaten, and I'm happy I was wrong,
But unless you know what happened, the witch's ward is gone."

Elwyn froze mid-step, her mind refusing to wrap around the words. Her denial lasted only a heartbeat before she tore away and sprinted down the trail. Aedyn's footfalls pattered down the trail behind her, and Luatha's violet light smeared in her periphery, but she could not force her steps to slow until she reached the clearing. There, she skidded to a stop, stirring wisps of chalk from the clovers.

Sure enough, Tawny's makeshift pillow lay abandoned, her jacket crumpled on the ground beside it.

Elwyn's mind leapt back to the night of the Confluence, when she'd woken at Luatha's bidding to find the bed opposite hers empty. She had hardly blinked the sleep from her eyes when she'd heard the distant clamor of shouting guards and rattling armor. She'd poured every ounce of her strength into the pursuit, and she'd somehow conjured more for the skirmish that followed.

It hadn't been enough.

"What's going on?" Aedyn burst into the glade, his gaze fixing on Tawny's discarded jacket. "Where did she go?"

"I...I don't know." Elwyn's chest tightened, forcing her heart to her throat. "It doesn't make any sense. She's just...she's just gone!"

"What do you mean she's *gone*?" Brannon leapt to his feet, blades drawn. His gaze flicked to the abandoned brackens before whipping back to Elwyn. "How could you let this happen? You swore you'd keep watch!"

Elwyn shrank back, vision blurring. "I...I know..." she managed, voice clinging to her throat. "I...I tried—"

"Like you *tried* to protect Lydia?" Brannon kicked the fern heap, scattering it across the clearing. His boot might as well have struck Elwyn's gut. "I swear to fuck, if another child winds up slaughtered because you were too slow and too incompetent—"

"Hold your tongue!" Aedyn grabbed Elwyn by the waist and angled himself in front of her, his teeth bared in a snarl. "We're all exhausted and confused, but that is no excuse to be cruel. If we hadn't stopped, you'd have collapsed just as surely as I did, and the Wilds would have swallowed you by dawn. After all we've been through, we needed to rest. At least Elwyn *tried* to ease the burden."

Brannon's eyes dropped to where Aedyn's hand rested on her hip, his nose wrinkling in disgust. "I'll bet."

The moment Aedyn's arm tensed, Elwyn grabbed hold of it, preventing him from drawing his rapier. "This isn't helping!" she said, forcing herself to hold the assassin's glare. "I deserve every drop of venom you can spit at me, but now is not the time. We should be looking for Tawny while we stand a chance of finding her."

Brannon snorted, but he didn't argue. Aedyn softened, drawing a deep breath. The three broke apart to scan the clearing for clues. The clover carpet had been well trampled, but there were no ruts in the soil to signify a struggle. Granted, Elwyn doubted there had been any conflict, given both Brannon and Luatha had slept through whatever happened. Tawny must have wandered off of her own volition, but how, and why, and *where*?

It was the piskie who found the first trace of evidence.

"Though there is nothing here that looks alarming at a glance,
I think you will agree there's something strange about these plants."

Elwyn scrambled over to Luatha just before Aedyn and Brannon, scanning the supposedly peculiar foliage. At first, she noticed nothing awry —just brittle leaves and corkscrew branches and tangles of unruly ivy. Then she noticed the flora was perfectly rigid, swaying only at the brush of the breeze. That would have been the standard anywhere else, but *here*...

"The Wilds aren't shifting," she said, running her hand along a frozen pine bough. "They're still writhing around the rest of the glade, but not here. Surely, that means something."

Luatha fluttered deeper into the forest, revealing that the pattern held for some distance. Elwyn shuddered to imagine what manner of magic could have caused such an anomaly, but she could not allow her fears to freeze her. Before the others had a chance to stop her, she drew her dagger and darted into the darkness.

TAWNY

"You're not my mother." Tawny clenched her jaw for fear it might otherwise chatter. *"Mothers don't use their children as bait, and certainly not as spell components."*

Yana's laughter was cold, forced—an eerie tempest of clashing timbres. *"You don't truly believe I'd have gone through with it, do you?"* she asked. *"The Shadows demanded an offering of my flesh and blood, dear. They never asked for my heart."*

Tawny winced, her chest panging. Where an angry reply might have bolstered her resolve, this sentiment—so very close to love—made her feel impossibly small. Smaller than she'd felt as a little girl, when she sat in Yana's lap and searched for faces in the hearth fire. Smaller than she'd felt when she could hardly peer over the cauldron rim, and Yana had helped to stir her first practice potions. Smaller than she'd felt stretched out on a basalt slab, surrounded by goblins and standing stones as Yana raised a twisted dagger over her heart.

Hearing affection in her once-mother's voice—wishing even a hint of it was real—made Tawny feel like a spark beneath a starscape, a pebble before a mountain, a mouse trapped between the paws of a grinning cat.

"You're toying with me." She placed her hand on her dagger's hilt, as Brannon would have. The hunting blade had never spilled blood, but the threat would land all the same. *"All these months, and you never once reached out. If you're doing so now, it only means you want something from me."*

"You aren't wrong, dear. Everything I've done has been to secure my safety, but I never intended to spend eternity alone. I want your forgiveness, Tawny." Yana leaned forward, extending her skeletal hand. *"I want you to come home."*

"Why?" Tawny shied back. *"So you can bleed me out for another of your spells?"*

Yana clenched her outstretched hand into a fist, pulling it back to her side. *"You stubborn child!"* she hissed, voices swarming like a hornet nest. *"I raised you to be brighter than this! Surely you understand why I needed you to believe I was wicked. I knew that the changeling would divine my plans through your connection, and I needed to lure her to the altar. If you hadn't feared me, she would never have feared for you!"*

"You didn't have to kill her!" Tawny tensed, as Elwyn would have, prepared to fight or flee at the slightest provocation. *"You didn't have to kill either of us. Just as you didn't have to kill Daulle, or—"* She cut herself off before mentioning Amatha. Yana likely believed the chieftain had been acting alone, and there was no reason to rouse her suspicions. *"If you had only explained what was happening, I'd have done anything you asked of me. We would have found another way to save you."*

"*There was but one safe path in a blazing forest!*" *Yana's eyes flared like funeral pyres.* "*Do you have any idea how many nights I spent poring over that contract? If another loophole had existed, I would have found it! While I regret any pain or fear I've caused you, I do not regret my decision. I made the only reasonable choice.*"

"*That's not true.*" *Tawny matched her once-mother's glare, squaring her shoulders in resolve, as Amatha would have.* "*You made a deal with a devil, and the consequence was yours to bear. Not mine, not Lydia's, not any of the innocents who perished in the Confluence—yours. If you truly could not find another way out, you should have spilled your own blood on that altar and brought an end to this pointless suffering!*"

"*Ungrateful girl!*" *A wind whipped to life around Yana, tearing wildflowers and fallen leaves from soil and turning her hair into a ghostly tumult.* "*How dare you call me selfish after decades spent suckling on my veins! From the night I first took you in, I've shared everything I possess with you—my home, my knowledge, the powers that protect me—and still, you doubt my love for you?*"

Tawny had never doubted the sentiment, only its depth. "*I know you love me.*" *She masked her pain with a smile, as Aedyn would have.* "*Just not as much as yourself.*"

The winds died down all at once. Yana's ashen tresses settled against her waist, and her eyes dimmed from bonfires to smoldering coals. Teardrops glistened in the ghost of the glow.

"*I should have known you would not see reason,*" *she whispered in a voice—just the one—as brittle as chalk.* "*Hope is a cruel creature, is it not? I've managed to catch hold of it countless times, but it always slips away.*" *She straightened, her sorrow vanishing beneath a proud veneer.* "*Very well. If you will not be my daughter, you will be my foe. You've seen how well those fare.*"

She vanished in a plume of mist and violet sparks, leaving Tawny to the eerie silence of a petrified wildflower lea.

Tawny didn't dare breathe as she scanned the shadows for yellow eyes and pale blue wisps. Her once-mother had never been the type to leave loose ends. That she would let Tawny walk away from this encounter was unthinkable, and yet...

When no monsters leapt out at her, Tawny allowed herself to sigh. Her breath snagged in her chest with a disturbing tickle. A few desperate hacks, and something flew free, catching on her lips like spittle. It dangled by a silver thread for a surreal second before dropping to the grass and skittering away on eight spindly legs.

Tawny gasped, and the tickle behind her ribs swelled to a swarm.

ELWYN

The frozen foliage was beginning to thaw, shaking off its slumber with a series of stiff, halting *crackles*. Once it matched the Shifting Wilds for rhythm, the trail would vanish, and Tawny would be lost forever. Assuming she was still alive.

Elwyn urged herself onward, ignoring the cries of her labored lungs and weary limbs in her desperate attempt to outpace the spellwork. Behind her, ferns shivered, and twigs *snapped* as Brannon and Aedyn tried to catch up.

Luatha zipped into view beside her, a thread of frantic violet light.

"It seems a bit convenient that she left a steady path,
I beg you to consider that this might well be a trap!"

Elwyn had considered as much; she simply didn't care. She would not allow Yana to take another life, all because she'd been too cowardly, too cautious, too *late*.

Planning ahead as best she could, she ran her dagger across her forearm, hardly wincing at the bite of the blade. The moment her blood trickled into the runes, they burst to life, bathing her surroundings in a bitter violet pall. If this was a trap, its maker would doubtless see her coming. Even so, they were in for one hell of a fight.

A terse cough cut through the *creaks* and *rustles* of the unfurling branches, bidding Elwyn to change course. Seconds later, she burst into a moonlit lea littered with milkweed and goldenrod. A lone figure writhed in the center of the field, crushing fragile blossoms with her every toss and turn.

Elwyn rushed over and knelt beside Tawny, dropping her dagger to the brittle grass. With effort, she managed to turn the flailing girl face-up. Her eyes stared blankly skyward, shrouded in a smoky haze, and her skin had taken on a silvery cast.

"You've found her!" Aedyn sprinted to Tawny's opposite side with Brannon on his heels. Together, the three of them propped her upright. A crimson spray burst from her lips, spattering her tunic, but she continued to convulse, head lolling against Aedyn's arm.

"What's happening to her?" The prince waxed pale, looking to Elwyn for answers she couldn't possibly have. "There must be something we can do!"

Elwyn glanced helplessly at the dagger she'd cast aside, its runes still gleaming bright. This was not the sort of foe she'd been trained to slay.

TAWNY

Tawny fell to her knees, pounding a fist against her sternum. The swarm scurried throughout her ribcage, each little leg trailing pinpricks of pain. No matter how many spiders she hacked free, the burn continued to grow.

She'd seen this curse before, though on a smaller scale. Having someone cough up the occasional spiderling sent a memorable message. This time, Yana was aiming to kill.

Her vision dimmed and narrowed. With each heave of her lungs, a few more bleary shadows rained down onto the withered grass. Most skittered off into the night, counting their mission complete, but not all were so merciful.

She hardly felt them crawling over her fingers. With an inferno blazing in her chest, she had few thoughts to spare for her skin. Then they found her shoulders, her neck, her face. Undeterred by her frantic coughing, they trailed silk between her trembling lips. Their web formed in seconds, thick and sticky as treacle.

Tawny tore at the gossamer, but the spiders mended their handiwork faster than she could destroy it. Those expelled from her lungs caught in the silk and were gnashed between her teeth. A few bit back in retribution, causing Tawny's tongue to swell as their pulpy remains spilled down her throat, smothering what little breath she'd managed to catch.

The fire in her lungs spread through her veins, and she fell to the grass with a helpless thud. Above her, the crescent moon smudged like chalk. Such a simple sight, for her very last one. She'd always hoped for something more exciting.

A trio of voices called her name, haunting and hollow. Perhaps they were angels, descended to lift her up. Perhaps they were demons, risen to reap their reward. Perhaps they were the Shadows, come to drag her to the void.

ELWYN

Tawny's coughing had quieted, but so had her breathing. A pinkish foam oozed around her lips, growing thicker with every rattling gasp. She'd managed to claw a few gouges into her cheeks before Aedyn and Brannon pinned her arms to her side, and not one of them could figure out why.

"This must be some kind of poison," Brannon hissed through gritted teeth. Feeble though Tawny was, she seemed determined to shake him loose. "A few of Dove's blends produce similar effects. If we force Tawny to purge, it might help."

Elwyn shuddered at the thought of their fellow Greyscale agent, whose concoctions could make a man's brains drip from his nostrils. Though Tawny's symptoms matched several such poisons, she hadn't ingested anything in hours. There was a good chance making her vomit would only further obstruct her breathing.

Luatha growled at the very notion.

"Her skin is wan and cold as death; her eyes have lost their glow,
This is a spell, this is a hex, the curse of some foul foe!" she chirped.

Elwyn was thinking the same thing, not that it helped any. She didn't know how to cast enchantments, let alone unravel them. That was Tawny's area of expertise, which was why she was always gathering...

"Components!" Elwyn began to rifle through the girl's pockets—a task made difficult by her constant thrashing. "There's got to be something in here that will help her." Soon she'd gathered an eclectic collection of moss and mushroom caps. Too bad she didn't know what a single item was used for. "This must be Yana's doing," she cried, swatting the components away. "I don't know how or why, but it must be her. It's always her!"

Aedyn hung his head, and Brannon swore liberally. With their combined skills, the three of them could stand against almost any foe, but how could they best a villain who breathed curses, twisted fates, and bound spirits to stone?

For once, Luatha's was the most insistent of the bunch.

"It isn't what witchling's found, so much as what she lacks,
If Yana's caught her scent, we should be covering her tracks!"

Elwyn wished it was so simple. Tawny had already tried her best to hide them from Yana's prying eyes. That's what those shadow-damned necklaces were for, and they clearly hadn't worked. If they had, Yana wouldn't have spotted them in the crowd, Amatha wouldn't have sacrificed herself to save them, and Tawny wouldn't have...

A realization struck Elwyn like lightning, and she shoved past Brannon to unfasten Tawny's collar. Sure enough, her medallion was missing. It seemed her curls were not all the bramble palace had stolen.

Praying to whatever would listen, Elwyn slipped her own pendant free and draped it around the girl's neck. She held her breath, waiting for Tawny to catch hers.

YANA

Yana had never taught Tawny curses. She'd taught her potions and salves, charms and enchantments, incantations and sigils. But never curses.

Her reasoning was twofold:

One, Tawny was far too pure to ever wish suffering on another.

And two, curses came at a cost to their caster.

Yana could not feel the full brunt of the pain she was inflicting, but a portion of it plagued her, stoking a fire in her lungs and a vitriolic burn in her throat. She knelt, quaking, on the floor of her Patchwork Palace, savoring the physical agony because it distracted from a deeper ache.

I had no choice, she thought as the flames grew fiercer.

It was her or me, she reasoned as the burn grew brighter.

It will be over soon, she promised as the dark grew deeper.

The anguish crested to a crescendo, ripping through her like labor pangs. It vanished a heartbeat later, taking with it the last vestiges of her daughter's radiant, apple-scented aura.

Yana dropped her hex satchel, wilted against the floorboards, and wept.

"Though it's easier to cover up a single set of tracks,
A lone wolf is far weaker for the company it lacks."

CHAPTER 24

STRONG SUPPORTS

ELWYN

he pendant settled into the dip of Tawny's clavicle, and a final billow of foam bubbled between her lips as she fell limp. Her stillness might have been a comfort after so much coughing and seizing, were it less complete.

Elwyn waited, unblinking, for Tawny's chest to heave and her pale lashes to flutter. Aedyn and Brannon stared just as intently, not a word exchanged between them, and Luatha bumbled nervously overhead, a dizzying violet smear. Freed from Yana's spellwork, the Wilds were steadily encroaching, but no one dared suggest moving on.

Too many heartbeats passed.

A sob snagged beneath Aedyn's collarbone. "We were too late, weren't we?"

The question hung in the air for several seconds, all but answered, before Brannon threw his hands up and stormed away. Without his support, Aedyn lost his grip, allowing Tawny to fall back to the grass. She jarred forward on impact, drinking in a desperate breath.

"Oh, thank the Creator!" Elwyn threw her arms around the girl, squeezing tighter than she knew was advisable. "I'm so glad you're alright!"

"Alright might be an overstatement," Tawny rasped, rubbing her sternum. When Elwyn finally released her, she glanced around at the group. "I didn't think you'd come for me."

"We couldn't just let you vanish!" Aedyn rapped a knuckle against her shoulder. "After all we've gone through together, you're a member of the team. It's not as though we have high standards." He tipped his head Brannon's direction. "Consider who's made the cut."

"I suggest you run while you can." The assassin returned carrying a thick branch. When he offered the scavenged walking stick to Tawny, she glared like it had insulted her. "For fuck's sake, this is not the time to play tough. You weren't a particularly efficient guide *before* you hacked up one of your lungs, and I refuse to wander the Wilds forever solely to appease your wounded ego."

Luatha chirped a laugh.

"This is the assassin's way of calling you a friend,
Reject that branch and he'll never show charity again!"

"It's not charity," Brannon growled, shaking the branch. "It's self-interest. And I don't have friends."

"I can't imagine why." Tawny mustered a feeble smile, finally accepting the offering. "If you truly insist on fussing over me, I'd love to hear how you dealt with the spiders."

"Spiders?" Aedyn shuddered, gaze sweeping the grass. "We seem to have missed them, not that I'm complaining."

Tawny wiped her lips with the back of her hand. "The curse must've been different on my end," she said, examining the blood and foam. "Still, it would be helpful to know how you dispelled it. There's no telling when we'll face another."

"You have Elwyn to thank for that one," Aedyn replied, flashing a genuine smile.

Elwyn tried to wave the compliment off, but it landed anyway. Playing a part in Tawny's rescue did not redeem her for failing Lydia, but it was a step in a brighter direction. "If you're looking for your hero, we'll need to find you a mirror," she said, shrugging the pride from her shoulders before it could settle. "It was the medallion you crafted that shielded you."

"The medallion." Tawny's grin faded as she clasped the stone pendant. "I...I lost mine. That's why Yana noticed us. That's why the chieftain...why Amatha—"

"There was nothing you could have done," Aedyn assured her, sounding certain despite the pain that pinched his voice. "When she invited you on this mission, she was officially placing you under her protection. She would have done the same thing for any of us, and not a force in existence could have dissuaded her."

Tawny rubbed the tears from her eyes before they had a chance to fall. "I should probably try to walk," she said, propping her walking stick against the ground. "Can I borrow the medallion a little longer? Yana's nothing if not thorough, and I'd hate to be unguarded when she double-checks her work. I promise I'll make another the moment we get back to the cottage."

"After you rest," Aedyn insisted.

"But, I—"

"After. You. Rest."

"Stop arguing and put that branch to use." Brannon crossed his arms, scowling down at Tawny. "You're going to walk this field a bit before we head back out. The last thing we need is for you to faint mid-hike."

Tawny pulled herself upright, refusing every helping hand offered her. She could probably have held her own in the Greyscale, where independence was a necessity for survival. Elwyn had once thought of her resilience as the sole benefit of growing up in the syndicate, but it had proven a fickle trait, and not for her alone. Brannon stuck close as Tawny took her first few hobbling steps, claiming he couldn't trust her to guide the group without proof she was recovering, and Luatha flew ahead to illuminate possible tripping hazards. Strange behavior for both.

Elwyn was about to join the others when Aedyn grabbed her hand and tugged her closer. To think, her poor heart had only just calmed. Now that the panic had passed, she remembered the events that preceded it with vivid, head-spinning clarity.

She'd actually *kissed* Aedyn. And he'd kissed her back.

She wasn't opposed to reliving the experience.

Unfortunately—and uncharacteristically—Aedyn's thoughts were elsewhere. He gently stretched her forearm toward the moonlight, frowning at the gash *Gelah* had left just above her wrist. "I hate that you do this to yourself." He ran his thumb beneath the wound, eyes flicking toward Luatha—now only a purple glimmer in the distance. "I hate that *she* does this to you."

"That's not fair." Elwyn resisted the urge to pull away. His concern was endearing, if not entirely misplaced. "Spending a little blood to save the rest of it isn't a terrible trade, and Luatha has saved my life more times than I can count. You two need to learn to get along if..."

If what? If they were going to be together? If they intended to build a future? If he was planning to forsake his crown, his throne, and the stunning woman destined to reign beside him, all for a life of hardship with a common thief?

A terse sound dispelled Elwyn's worries as Aedyn tore the frilly cuff from his sleeve. Before she could ask what he was doing, he wrapped the fabric around her arm.

"Charming but unnecessary," Elwyn half-heartedly protested. "That cut's too shallow to merit tending, and in case you haven't noticed, I'm perfectly capable of taking care of myself."

"Of course you are." Aedyn tied off the makeshift bandage, tugging the knot twice to test its strength. "But that doesn't mean you should always have to."

ELOANA

After only days of practice, Eloana had the basics down.

Lifting a light-song made its host more agreeable; lowering it did the opposite. Muting the music resulted in discomfort or lethargy, while bolstering it was likely impossible. For Eloana to manage it, she would have to somehow *lend* sunlight to another Maithe, which she would never have done. After a lifetime spent twirling about like a clockwork doll, she enjoyed being the most powerful person in the room.

Granted, the only two people in the room for the moment—not counting Anye—were her and her handmaiden. It wasn't exactly a close competition.

"You missed a spot." Eloana tapped her toe against Loenelle's nose, and the girl flinched like she'd left a bruise. Perhaps she would, if this simple chore took much longer.

Loenelle growled under her breath, her sorry excuse for a light-song thrumming low as she polished the slipper a third time. Eloana attuned her thoughts to that fragile hum and tugged. The handmaiden did not grow more cordial, as a full-blooded Maithe with more robust music might have, but what started as pure resentment took on a timbre of defeat.

Eloana could barely contain her glee. Where admiration was out of the question, obeisance served just as well.

Anye, too, was impressed with her progress.

"You've grown your skills so gracefully in such limited time,
For all I've taught and all you've learned, I have a gift in mind."

"A gift?" The piskie had already given Eloana more than she'd ever dreamed of, but she wasn't opposed to another boon. "Show me where I can improve, and I'll put my all into it."

Anye giggled musically, looking pleased with the answer.

While I admire your steadfast dedication to your field.
This blessing is the kind that you can hold, admire, and wield."

"Even better." Eloana ripped her foot from Loenelle's polish-stained fingers and stretched upright. "Where can I find it?"

After trudging through Talune's lower stories for far too long, the palace gates came into view. The guards naturally fixed on Eloana, though Anye flitted to her left and Loenelle flanked her right. They crossed their rapiers in front of the exit, barking something predictable about the dangers of palace denizens wandering out past dusk.

With a flutter of Eloana's lashes and a more metallic flutter of Anye's wings, they lowered their weapons.

Maithe, as it happened, were more easily tuned than most instruments.

For the first few minutes, Eloana slipped through the streets with her heart trilling in her throat. The roadside torches were spaced few and far between, and the stars brought little beauty to the fearsome void above. For once, Loenelle's graceless footfalls were a comfort. At threat of torment, she'd made the servant girl vow not only to keep her secrets locked behind her lowborn lips, but to protect her at all costs. Though unsightly, the handmaiden's comparatively burly build would do well to ward off any ne're-do-wells that dared interrupt their stroll.

As Eloana's eyes adjusted to the dark, she sought additional solace in the pristine manors and flourishing gardens of her people. The restoration crews had done an admirable job of restoring Talunasa to its pre-

Confluence glory, with the exception of a few unsightly districts that stretched over the distant hills.

Wise though King Aryn usually was, he'd shown poor judgement in allowing refugees to dwell in Talune's shadow. The religious dogma about having been tasked with the protection of mortals was fine and good when it had meant sending fair weather through the Veil and blessing the occasional harvest, but to house them within eyesight, task brigadiers with guarding their hovels, and hand them resources the Maithe should have been shoring up for winter?

Enabling, that's what it was. Now that they'd tasted Talunasa's bounty, they had no incentive to find their own place in the new world. If the vermin still plagued the realm when Eloana took the throne, she would find a proper place for them, be it beyond high walls or beneath her heel.

Talune's wilting canopy was but a blot on the horizon when Anye came to hover before the entrance of an enormous hedge maze Eloana had visited once before as a mere child. The labyrinth had been cultivated by Talune's Tenders, the most respectable of the many religious sects that ran through Maithe society. Much like Eloana, they valued talent and tradition over more fallible, subjective virtues like empathy and charity. They also enforced an incomparably strict set of precepts—including an edict to never enter a sacred space without the oversight of a priest or priestess.

For the first time since they'd met, Eloana doubted Anye's judgment. "Why would you lead us here?" she asked the piskie. "Surely you're aware we cannot approach the Altar of the Sun's Song without permission."

Anye flashed a gilded grin.

"If you've followed me this far only to falter at the door,
You don't deserve the treasure waiting at the maze's core."

The taunt did nothing to assuage Eloana's worries, but it stoked her curiosity bright enough to consume them. "Fine, but we cannot dismiss the possibility this place has been warded against trespassers." She glanced back at Loenelle. "Seems like a perfect opportunity to prove your loyalty."

The handmaiden glowered, taking the suggestion for the command it truly was. Knowing Eloana would bend her will if she didn't twist it herself, she took a deep, bolstering breath and marched through the entryway arch.

No alarms chimed. No sigils flared. No lightning crackled from the Creator's fingertips.

Freed from the fear of immediate consequence, Eloana pressed past. If the handmaiden had any powers at all—a blessing half-breeds were often denied—they wouldn't possibly be strong enough to navigate the twists and turns.

The Tenders' enchantments protected the hedges from magical manipulation, but a gifted enough lightsinger could follow the music woven into the hedges themselves all the way to the central altar. The code had given Eloana very little trouble as a child, and she could read it like sheet music now.

Midway through the maze, the light-song fell apart, notes dripping from the scale like leaves from Talune's branches. Ill omens waited around the next bend. Drought had run its withered fingers over the hedges to one side of the path, reducing them to a tangle of skeletal twigs. The opposite bushes had burgeoned to overgrow the path, unseasonable berries and blossoms peeking out from their veridian leaves. Whatever vandal had ruined the maze must have possessed powerful magic. It was no small feat, unraveling the enchantments of a high priestess.

"Is this what you wanted to show me?" Eloana asked, failing to keep the unease from her voice.

Anye shook her tiny head.

"There is no cause for fear, though I understand your frustration,
Just follow this strange trail, and you'll reach your destination."

Were Eloana any less intrigued, she'd have turned on her heel and marched straight back to the palace. "You heard the piskie, Loenelle." She waved the handmaiden forward. "Lead the way."

Loenelle's glare could have melted metal, but with a little melodic urging from Eloana, she did as told. Anye hovered over the handmaiden's shoulder, acting as a lantern to help navigate what remained of the maze. After only a minute more, the trio spilled out into the central glade.

The Altar of the Sun's Song was smaller than Eloana recalled, but it was no less resplendent. A gilt composition spanning several staves wrapped around its alabaster base—the music of creation itself, legend held. To replicate the song in its entirety was forbidden, but choirs and orchestras often performed segments for hallowed rites and celebrations.

It would have been an inspiring sight, were it not for the vagrant curled up atop it. The man was twig thin and impossibly tall, with knotted locks that draped to the ground like willow whips, and a simple black bowler cap tipped over his face. Pockets of every size and shape patched his ratty, vermillion suit.

Eloana huffed toward the altar, intent on shoving the heretic from atop it, but Anye flitted forward to block her path.

"A book judged by its cover is knowledge sorely lost,
Sometimes the greatest treasure is found in the plainest box."

In Eloana's experience, the greatest treasures were found in decidedly *un*-plain boxes—the kind carved from rare mahogany, inlaid with abalone, and wrapped in pretty pink ribbons. Still, the piskie had yet to steer her wrong.

"This had better be worth the effort," she muttered.

Apparently, the vagrant was a light sleeper. That simple sentence caused him to stretched and shift, twisting upright with a rattling yawn. He tipped his cap back to peer at Eloana with sunken eyes dark as rot.

"Salutations, friend." He dragged his gaze over Eloana, ignoring the others entirely. "It's been some time since one of Samhria's residents sought me out. I assume you're on the prowl for a palliative just as rich and refined as yourself. A pinch of blackthorn powder, perhaps?" He reached into one of his many pockets, producing a vial filled with ink-black dust. With the flick of his finger, the contents turned to iridescent green ooze. "Or perhaps some essence of pollen sprite?"

Eloana was too offended to answer. She was not so naïve as to be unaware of her peers' indulgences, but she had never approved and would never participate. To imply otherwise was the most brash of insults.

Thankfully, Anye was content to speak for her.

"Or maybe some essence of pollen sprite? Though,

"We're looking for a relic that rivals the sun for shine,
You'll find it on your person, though it isn't on your mind."

The man's fingers rasped against his chin. He clearly had no inkling what the piskie meant, but Eloana was growing proficient in the art of deciphering poetry.

Hopeful anything that rivaled sunlight might also store a ray or two of it, she strained to sort through the whispers of rustling leaves and wafting banners until she heard the faintest of magic melodies, as warm as it was whimsical. Though softer than frillrose petals, it reminded Eloana of dancing through a sunlit garden, a song on her lips and a flute of spriteberry wine in hand.

"The pocket on your right shoulder," she said after tracing the song to its source. "You'll find what we're looking for there; I'm certain of it."

Though visibly puzzled, the man reached into the aforementioned pocket and withdrew a golden dagger far too large for it. Diamond flecks winked throughout the twists of the filigree hilt, wreathing around a citrine pommel. Ridges spiked like sunbeams along the outer edge, and cryptic runes ran along the crescent blade. Anye flitted closer, and her aura caused the symbols to flare.

"This relic needs a keeper; can't you feel how it yearns?
It's a gift that keeps on taking, but it gives much in return."

The dagger was not the only one to yearn. Eloana had never needed a blade—nobles settled their disputes with words, not weapons—but she could not deny the call of this one. Every note of its light-song felt like a tuning fork had strummed against her skeleton, resolving her every dissonant chord.

The vagrant rasped his fingers against his chin. "Been a decade since I last saw one of these." He ran a withered thumb along the runes, as though reading them by feel. "Not sure how they keep finding their way to me." He smiled at Eloana, flashing yellowed teeth set directly into bone. "I would happily sell to you, my friend, but relics like these insist on setting their own prices."

The ramblings of a madman were easier humored than dismissed. "I'm confident I can meet its expectations." Eloana pulled her purse from the folds of her gown and gave it a terse jingle.

Laughter rattled the man's ribcage. "You're gold's no good here," he said, waving the notion away. "Answer a riddle to its liking, and you can walk away with it, not a single coin absent your coffers."

Eloana stowed her purse with a grimace. Even if she was the type to enjoy riddles, she doubted this man could craft a cohesive one. "If there is no other way..."

The man held the dagger to a shriveled ear, as though he, too, could hear its light-song. He lowered it a few measures later, flashing another gut-churning grin.

"You find yourself lost in the depths of strange woods. The night is deep, the trails are rough, and a horde of Unseelie are following your tracks," he said. "You can tell from the scrape of claws and marl-muted footsteps that the monsters are gaining ground, when you stumble upon a sobbing child, stranded alone in the darkness. Taking her with you would slow your escape but leaving her behind would ensure her death. What do you choose?"

Despite the dagger's uplifting song, Eloana's hopes plunged. This wasn't a riddle; it was a moral test, and he clearly expected the more selfless answer.

Pity Eloana couldn't lie.

If the man were Maithe, she'd have attuned her thoughts to his light-song and raised it until he offered her the treasure out of the kindness of his shriveled heart. Since he had no such resonance to speak of, she would have to manipulate him the old-fashioned way.

"This isn't a matter of mercy, but of logic," she claimed. "If I left the child behind, she would likely die, but if I tried to help her, we would *both* die. There is no moral victory in meaningless sacrifice." She scraped her tongue against her teeth, loathing the taste of the truth. "Judge me all you'd like, but the child should never have been in the woods to begin with. I should not bear the consequences for her bad judgment, or that of her parents."

The vagrant's narrow shoulders drooped. "Above all else, a weapon wants to be useful. Did you not even think to fend the Unseelie off with the dagger's glow?" A sigh hissed through his teeth. "I am sorry, but you are not a worthy wielder, my friend."

"I am not your friend!" Eloana snapped, even more livid than she was disappointed. "And that riddle was absolute rubbish! You never even mentioned that I had the dagger on me, and even if you had, blades don't *glow*, they *gleam!*"

The man ignored her, lifting the dagger toward very pocket he'd pulled it from. Panic propelled Eloana forward, wrapped her fingers around the pommel. The moment her skin touched citrine, the relic's potent song pulsed through her—a perfect, potent harmony to her own.

"It's mine!" she shouted, pulling hard as she could. "It has to be, or Anye would never have led me here!"

"You could not pay the dagger's due," the man pulled back, "so it does not belong to you!"

Arms burning from strain, Eloana cast a panicked glare back at Loenelle. The handmaiden returned it with a satisfied smirk.

Eloana cursed her own poor planning. She'd made the girl swear to *protect* her, not to aid her, and even the lowest of fae could leap through a loophole. Unless this battle of wills became physical, she was on her own.

With her strength nearly sapped, she twisted the dagger toward the vagrant and released it. It snapped forward, lodging hilt deep in his chest. Eloana froze, waiting for the blood to well, the body to drop.

Instead, the man cocked his head, his gum-less grin stretching so wide, his lips split. "You have no idea what you're dealing with, do you?" he hissed, raising a hand to strike Eloana.

Before the blow could land, calloused fingers wrapped around her forearm, jarring her—and the dagger—from danger. The last thing Eloana saw before spinning toward the exit was Loenelle throwing herself before the vagrant, arms splayed as a shield.

Anye led the way back through the maze—a streak of light in a world of shadow. Eloana ran until the grass turned to cobbles underfoot and streetside torches shone to either side of her. Unable to sprint another step, she doubled over, panting. By the time the foliage rustled behind her, she'd captured just enough breath to whirl with her dagger raised.

It was only Loenelle, thank the Creator. Deep gashes slashed across the handmaiden's cheek, dripping scarlet. Eloana might have felt bad for the girl, had her aid been a little more enthusiastic.

Realizing just how useless her dagger was—clearly, the relic was keeping a few secrets—Eloana lowered it. She decided against slapping the handmaiden right across her newfound cuts, if only because she needed her to speak clearly.

"Next time I need your aid, I trust you'll be far more *efficient*," she said, lacing the command with venom. "Has the threat been extinguished?"

The depth of Loenelle's scowl rivaled that of her wounds. "He's gone," she growled. "Tasked me with passing on a message: keep the blade as long as it lets you. You'll get everything you deserve in due time."

Eloana held her prize aloft. The polished curve, cast aglow by Anye's aura, reflected her smile. "I can hardly wait."

"Miracles would lose their charm if we could make them last,
We treasure most the moments that we know are bound to pass."

CHAPTER 25

STRETCHING THE SECONDS

BRANNON

 see no point in conversing with carrion."

That's what Brannon had said when they'd buried Lydia, and he'd meant it at the time. Strange how he'd had countless conversations with her since. They weren't particularly poignant—just little notes scrawled across the passing days—but they were the closest he'd ever come to delivering a eulogy.

"You'd have liked that stupid butterfly."

"This stew would've made your nose wrinkle, but you'd have eaten it anyway."

"You'd have gotten on well with the children at the Sylph encampment. Half are vowed to silence, and they're still not as meek as you."

He'd never felt things very deeply, but a shallow wound was still a wound. Lydia should have been alive because he wanted her to be there, and because he'd tried his damnedest to save her. He'd wear that failure like a scar for the rest of his life, yet the others thought him pitiless for not bleeding more openly.

It bothered him more than he let on.

Now here he was again, sulking silently amongst the more earnest mourners. Pondrellen funerals were stodgy affairs, so Elwyn had suggested throwing a Rhysien ceremony instead. Apparently, that meant writing letters to the deceased and tossing them onto a pyre under the ridiculous presumption the smoke would carry them to Heaven. She'd mentioned the rite to their hosts upon returning to the cottage, and the whole group had passed out shortly after, crushed by a cache of varied exhaustions. When they awoke that evening, a bonfire and log benches had been arranged in the glade beyond the garden.

Charcoal smudged Brannon's fingertips as he stared at a strip of blank parchment, struggling to conjure a message for a woman who would never read it. He hadn't known Amatha a full week, but she'd given him a sense of purpose for the first time since he'd left the Greyscale. She'd seen his usefulness and directed it without ever once treating him like a tool, and she commanded every ounce of the respect she offered. As easy as it would have been to scribble a line of nonsense and feed it to the flames, doing so would have been disservice.

The flames roared when Elwyn tossed her prayer into the pit, and again when Tawny did the same. They burned steady and warm for a long while after that.

Frustrated, Brannon closed his eyes, pictured the chieftain, and scrawled the very first thought that came to mind.

Thanks for trying.

It was possible the message was meant, in part, for Ferea. The two women—though opposites inside and out—had begun to blend together in his mind. They both had a commendable strength about them, whether manifested in stoic self-control or confident command. He had allowed them both a sliver of authority, truly believing they sought the best for him. Both gone from his life forever.

For all the time he'd spent fussing over the letter, the fire consumed it in a blink. He watched the cinders flit into the air like fireflies, only to fall as flecks of snowy ash and dust the toes of his boots, scorching little matte dots into the leather.

So much for reaching Heaven.

Brannon slumped onto a log and stared into the flames. With the Procession looming one night away, they had far more important things to fret over than the loss of their colleague. The others would have scolded him for saying as much aloud, and they certainly wouldn't have agreed. Better to let sentiment triumph over reason for one night. Come morning, they'd decide whether to see the mission through or return to Samhria with their tails tucked.

"May I join you?" Deinua sat beside Brannon before he could answer. He was wearing green, as usual, but the hue was so deep it might have looked black beyond the cast of the fire.

"I feel awful about how vague my message was, but we'd only just met. Did you know her very well?"

Brannon didn't know anybody well, and he wasn't looking for that to change. "If you're hoping to commiserate, I'm not your best option."

"You're my only option, actually." Deinua waved vaguely to a trio of empty logs Brannon could've sworn were occupied a second before. "The others wandered off a while back. Tawny has enlisted Luatha's aid in crafting another of those necklaces you're all wearing, and I suspect Elwyn's wandered off to comfort Aedyn."

"That's one word for it." Brannon snorted. He wasn't sure who he was more disappointed in—the supposed "best friend" who hadn't bothered attending Amatha's funeral, or the colleague who'd foolishly fallen for the dolt. "If that girl's dreaming of crowns and ballgowns, she's in for a rude awakening. He'll see her in nothing at all, then never again."

"Someone's bitter." Deinua raised a skeptical eyebrow. "You wouldn't happen to have feelings for—"

"Fuck no!" The very thought brought bile to Brannon's tongue. His bonds were forged of respect, loyalty, and a healthy measure of intimidation. Sentiment didn't enter the equation. "It's disappointing to watch one of the few sane people I've ever met lose her wits to such a basic breed of madness. I'd honestly thought her above this frivolity."

Deinua threw his head back in a dramatic sigh. "I can't believe I'm related to such a cynic."

Brannon suspected his revulsion ran deeper than mere cynicism. He'd never seen the point of relationships or trysts, never felt the draw of another's warmth or pined for their affection. He'd kissed Dove once, as a kind of test, and his stomach had roiled so violently he'd accused her of poisoning her lipstick.

In his youth, when most boys ran themselves ragged chasing after girls, he'd feared he was missing something vital. He'd since come to appreciate the clarity that came with his indifference.

If he ever lost his head, it would be to a blade, not some silly emotion.

"Regardless of your personal feelings, or lack thereof, might I suggest feigning an ounce of support. If Aedyn and Elwyn are truly your friends, their happiness should bring you at least a little of the same," Deinua rambled on, unbidden. "Sure, they come from different worlds, but they wouldn't be the first couple to create their own. Just look at those two." He nodded toward the flower garden, where *that woman* and her husband were twirling between steppingstones. "There's no logical reason they should be together, yet there they are, and here I am."

Brannon glared at the couple in question as they danced among the blossoms, their matching bracelets glinting gold in the moonlight. Even if he hadn't loathed them both, he'd have found the sight indecent. This was a funeral, for fuck's sake!

"It's a condition of their marriage oaths," Deinua explained, perhaps sensing Brannon's misgivings. "Those vow-chains of theirs are binding contracts, each link a sacred promise. Most are fairly standard—fidelity, tenderness, devotion, and the like—but my father made the silly error of waxing poetic and vowing to 'dance with her nightly beneath a blanket of stars.' It's a good thing they both enjoy dancing."

Brannon's head ached from trying to comprehend the nuances of fae oaths. It was almost impressive that they could collectively prove such dishonest bastards despite being irrevocably bound to their words.

"What happens if they're unable to fulfill that promise?" he asked, hoping they might explode or something.

"Not an option, as it turns out. A few years ago, Father wandered too far to return in a single night, but he somehow blinked into the parlor with his arms wrapped around her waist. They got a single twirl in before dawn broke."

Of course they did. "And if they refuse by choice?"

"Now *that* I have trouble imagining." Deinua chuckled. "If they've ever been truly angry with each other, they should form a theatre troupe, because they have me utterly fooled."

Another injustice. Had an ounce of resentment simmered between those two, Brannon would have considered it a step toward vindication. Koa should have been furious that his wife had hidden Brannon's existence from him, yet he reeked of earnest affection. That woman ought to have trembled in the embrace of a bloodthirsty monster, but she'd never looked more secure than when she rested her chin on his shoulder. The effortless smile she now wore was so much softer than those she used to feign for Brannon's sake.

There was a time he would have given anything to see her so happy. Now he'd do anything to rip that joy away.

"You know, if you'd really like to know more about our mother, there's one person who can answer your questions better than myself," Deinua said, ruining a perfectly violent daydream. "She's been desperate to talk to you this entire time, but she's afraid of applying pressure to such a fragile situation."

That was absolutely not going to happen. Simply glimpsing the woman made Brannon's fingers itch for his daggers. Not that they were contented, otherwise.

"Glaistigs are predators, aren't you?" Brannon turned back to Deinua, catching the gleam of a crimson eye behind his forelock. "I can't imagine those fangs are for show, and you pick at your meals like they've gone rotten. It must be quite the struggle to house a whole flock of prey without indulging. Or is that why you make all those trips to town?"

Deinua's mismatched gaze dropped to his feet. "We drink blood, but it's not so much a need as a...craving." His nose wrinkled like his own nature disgusted him. "We were created to act as shepherds for your kind, culling off wolves for the good of the sheep. Before the worlds wed, I thirsted only for tea and cocoa, but there's been a constant burn in my throat ever since, a pit in my belly, and this dreadful chill beneath my skin." He wrapped his arms around himself, shuddering only feet from the fire. "An occasional sip helps to stifle the ache, but I try to avoid even that. I'm not gifted with enchantments, so there's a chance even the slightest indulgence would end in tragedy."

So beneath that genial veneer, Deinua was constantly fighting bloodlust. And to think, Brannon had assumed they had nothing in common.

"I think I understand *why* you resist," Brannon said, having put a significant effort into doing the same, "the *how* of it eludes me."

"Honestly?" It was Deinua's turn to stare listlessly into the flames. "I keep telling myself that I need only hold out a little longer before a worthy target appears, loudly declaring themselves an irredeemable villain. Then I can feed to my heart's content without feeling a fleck of remorse." He chuckled coldly. "I've no evidence or experience to lean on, but I needn't convince my mind so much as my tongue."

For a moment, Brannon nearly admired Deinua. He would cave to his cravings in time, of course, but his tactic for combating them was not unclever.

Ferea had steeped Brannon in meditation and incense, hoping his battered spirit could make a full recovery, but her hopes were sorely misplaced. He could not slay the beast inside him—nor did he truly want to see it slain—but with proper incentive, he could convince it to hibernate for a season.

He glanced over at the waltzing couple, feeling slightly less tempted to bury them beneath the begonias. With worthier targets waiting within reach, his hands could hold off a little longer.

AEDYN

Starlight filtered through the wisteria curtain to dance in the facets of the quartz brooch, a stark reminder that time still moved whether Aedyn wished it or not. He'd been sitting on the edge of the cottage roof for hours, admiring the gift and mourning the giver, but he hadn't shed a single tear in that time. Perhaps he'd wrung himself dry the night before.

Only Brannon and his brother remained beside the fire that blazed beyond the garden, matching figures topped with respective tufts of black and cinnamon red. More than once, Aedyn had been tempted to join them, if only to chase the chill from his fingertips. Too bad he couldn't find the strength to move.

The window wisped open behind him, freeing a pleasant gust of butter and brown sugar. Muted notes of pine needles and weapon oil wove beneath the more cloying aromas. Those familiar fragrances helped to soothe his heartache, if only for a beat. He mustered a smile—feeble but earnest—as Elwyn climbed over the sill. When she returned it, he felt warm for the first time since waking.

"I was worried I might startle you from the rooftop." She settled on the shingles beside him, dangling her legs over the eave. "Lately, it feels like I could announce my presence with trumpets and still be accused of sneaking up on people. How is it that you always seem to notice me approaching?'

"I'm always looking for you."

The answer earned him a kiss just as startling and splendid as their first. It lasted long enough for his thoughts to wander, but he broke it off before his hands could follow suit. Whatever the two of them shared was somehow stronger than a tryst and infinitely more fragile. The last thing he wanted was to frighten Elwyn off by pushing too far, too fast.

"I was worried when you didn't join us for the prayer burning." She glanced down to where the bonfire cast amber sparks against the starscape. "Granted, this is a far better view."

"This whole idea was incredibly thoughtful," he said, tucking the quartz brooch into his breast pocket. "I guarantee Amatha would feel honored, but I honestly have no inkling what I would write. I always figured she would outlive me. Even if she didn't, the Sidhe celebrate moving on in a far more reserved fashion. I don't suppose you've been to the Red Realm..."

Elwyn shook her head, her hair falling over half of her face. Aedyn resisted the urge to tuck it behind her ear and drown his sorrows in another kiss. She deserved far better than to be used as another in a long list of distractions.

"I think you'd really like it there." He thought back to the first time he'd visited Réimsdarg. He'd been so entranced by the searing rivers that he might have wandered right into the molten rock, had Amatha not held him back. "The valleys and deserts can be a bit intense, but there are also these beautiful gemstone gardens, vaster than many a Talunasan forest and ten times as vivid. Fields of fluorite, orchards of onyx, groves of garnets, emeralds, and quartz. Each cluster, no matter how massive, started as a single shard from a fallen Sidhe." The bonfire below began to blur. Perhaps he had some tears left after all. "She would probably have grown into the most brilliant amethyst hedge in history, but we fled so swiftly..."

"Escaping was the surest way to honor her." Elwyn placed her hand atop his, a simple but much-appreciated comfort. "If we'd lingered any longer, Yana would have discovered us, and Amatha's sacrifice would have been in vain."

He'd been trying hard not to think of it in those terms. They came with conditions.

"If we don't end Mailair's reign tomorrow, her sacrifice *will* be in vain."

The truth left a hollow in his chest. "Even so, I don't think I'm up to the task. Now that we've seen what we're up against, I couldn't possibly ask you to put yourselves at risk."

"Well then, it's a good thing you don't have to ask." Determination glinted in her eyes, as terrifying as it was enticing. "We all chose to be here for one reason or another. Those reasons haven't changed."

True, but the circumstances most certainly had. Under Amatha's leadership, the mission had seemed noble—valiant, even. If Aedyn were to take over, it would be just another reckless misadventure.

"We can discuss this more tomorrow, once we've had time to process," he said, hoping the others would change their minds by then. "Tonight is about sending Amatha on, shard or no shard."

"Sending her on to her next life, right?" A sad smile tugged on Elwyn's cheek. "It's no wonder you fae don't burn prayers for the lost; it's more like they've gone away for a bit. It must be a comfort to know she'll be reborn."

"Assuming she hasn't already ascended." The possibility was a dagger to Aedyn's heart. "If anyone has earned a place among the stars, it's Amatha. It would be selfish to hope she somehow fell short of the mark, solely so I stand a chance of meeting her again. Yet here I am, hoping."

Elwyn leaned against Aedyn, and her head fit perfectly into the dip between his shoulder and collarbone. He gently wrapped his arm around her for fear she might crumble like ash. With as often as he'd watched her shy away from the slightest touches, it was astonishing that she allowed him to hold her at all. He'd never felt more honored. Or more undeserving.

"You'll see her again, ascended or not," she assured him, snuggling closer. "When it finally happens, you'll have far more to tell her about than any letter could possibly contain. In the meantime, if you need someone to talk to, I'm here to listen."

That was precisely what Aedyn needed.

He tipped his cheek against the crown of her head, giggling softly at the way her hair tickled his chin, and began the tale of how he and Amatha first met. She'd transferred to Samhria for studies as a child, having never set foot in Talunasa before, and she'd looked absolutely terrified to be stranded in a sea of Maithe. Aedyn hadn't spoken a word of Sidhe at the time, but he scrounged up a beginner's tome and learned enough to ask to be friends...or so he thought. Over a century later, she informed him that he'd actually asked if they could be potatoes. She'd found it endearing enough that it had the same effect.

Stories spilled from his lips as the night wore on, each a separate adventure undertaken by Amatha's side. He spoke of jokes and journeys, trials and triumphs, rifts and reconciliations. Mostly, he spoke of how brilliant her presence had been, and how much darker the world looked for her absence. Elwyn listened intently, comforting him with the occasional feather-soft kiss on his collarbone, until she finally drifted off to sleep.

As Aedyn carried her into the loft, she nuzzled beneath his chin and whispered his name, and he sent up a silent prayer of thanks. Why the Creator would grant such a sweet moment to a scoundrel like him was a mystery, but with the stars themselves as his witness, he would find a way to make it last.

"Although you chart your course with care, it may all go awry,
The best laid plans can fall apart at Heaven's softest sigh."

CHAPTER 26
PREPARATIONS
ELWYN

lwyn woke to the smells of syrup and sizzling pork, a heavy quilt tucked snugly over her bedroll. Sunlight streamed through the loft's sole window, the brightest it had been all week. Funny, she didn't remember turning in for the night.

No sooner did she stir than Luatha flitted over to tug on a lock of her hair.

"It's well past noon, yet you're too comfortable to draw your knife,

You shouldn't sleep through what might be the last day of your life."

Elwyn had never been too comfortable to draw *Gelah*, but the piskie still had a point. The Procession of Autumn would soon march on Ebensburg, and unless the others had undergone a collective change of heart, they would be infiltrating the Unseelie swarms in hopes of claiming their ruler's head. Surely such ventures merited an hour or two of preparation.

The loft was empty aside from the piskie, so Elwyn took her time freshening up and changing into clean clothing, opting for her finest suede tights and a dark, sleeveless tunic that fit a touch more snugly than the rest. She laid her leather armor out for later use, then pulled *Gelah* from beneath her pillow. Strapping that dagger to her thigh felt like blinking away a hazy dream. The past week had been one of drastic changes, spanning the breadth of anguish and bliss, but a little mortal peril would serve as a sturdy tether for her flighty wits.

She followed the aromas that roused her to the kitchen, fully expecting to see Lieri with her hands in a bowl of dough, dusted up to her elbows with flour. Instead, she found Aedyn, dressed in their host's floral apron and cooking mitts, locked in a battle with a skillet that had somehow snagged between oven racks. When he turned to greet Elwyn, the pan flipped, spilling its savory contents into the flames below.

"The good news is, Lieri already made maple rolls." Aedyn's smile was unusually bashful, though a bit of the usual mischief sparked through it. From the aching way he looked her over, the extra effort she'd put into dressing had absolutely been worth it. "The better news is, my experiment was a success. Cooking something that smells delicious is a safe and effective way to wake you. I'll make a note for the future."

The future. He spoke of it so easily it was tempting to believe they had one. Elwyn supposed it couldn't hurt to play along. If their mission went poorly, they will have technically spent the rest of their lives together. It was the closest she would ever come to a courtship.

"Excepting occasions like these, I'm a light sleeper." She snatched one of the aforementioned rolls from a basket and took a bite. Despite the dollop of maple syrup at its center, it was only the second sweetest thing in the room. "If you ever need to wake me, you could always just ask politely."

"You make it sound so simple." Aedyn tossed the skillet in a wash basin and cast the cooking mitts to the counter beside it. "If I came close enough to ask politely, I'd be tempted to kiss you. If I kissed you, I'd be tempted to linger. If I lingered, you'd gut me before your eyes even opened. Don't get me wrong, there are far worse ways to die, but now I can kiss you while you're conscious and, ideally, avoid the bit where I bleed out."

Elwyn set her half-eaten breakfast aside, donning what she hoped was a beguiling grin. "I think that theory begs testing."

He needed no further invitation. A blink, and he'd wrapped her in his arms and pressed her flush against his apron. Their lips barely brushed before Luatha began circling around them, retching violently.

"You truly think her dagger is the sole threat to your health?
If you'd like to keep that silver tongue, best keep it to yourself."

As it turned out, it was difficult to kiss and laugh at the same time. "I'd heed her warning, if I was you." Elwyn slipped from Aedyn's arms and playfully dodged his attempt to recapture her. "She has no prior experience in the field, but I suspect a more capable chaperone has never existed."

"Chaperone?" Aedyn's glare followed the piskie's triumphant loop. "Now that I know your *real* power, I'd like to discuss a truce."

Luatha drifted down to hover beside Elwyn, splinter arms crossed.

"If you make my mortal happy, I might learn to tolerate you,
But don't think for one second it means that I don't hate you."

As entertaining as it would have been to watch the argument roll along, they'd wasted too much time already. "Have you spoken with Tawny and Brannon this morning?" Elwyn asked, finishing off her roll as she started toward the front door. "I'm sure the latter has champed straight through his bit by now."

"They're still determined to see the mission through," Aedyn said, failing to hide his disappointment. He rushed after her, the piskie fluttering close behind. "Last I checked, Tawny was reading out by the woodshed, and Brannon was helping Lieri in the garden."

Elwyn froze with her hand on the doorknob. "Brannon was *what?*"

Before Aedyn could repeat himself, she was halfway down the steppingstone path, shouting a vague promise to meet up with him and Tawny soon. She broke into a sprint as she veered around the corner of the cottage, hoping she wasn't too late to stop Brannon from...

Weeding?

The assassin knelt roughly three feet away from the mother he reviled and was ripping handfuls of chickweed from a bed of zucchini and acorn squash. Lieri looked positively thrilled at the development, a giddy grin fixed on her face as she scoured the soil for invasive blossoms. Brannon, however, looked slightly more livid than usual. At least he was taking it out on the plants.

Koa leaned against the cottage, his fingers dangling a twitch away from his pike as he observed the situation through haggard eyes. If Glaistigs could truly sense evil intentions in mortals, it was possible he hadn't gotten a decent night's sleep since Brannon first crossed his threshold.

"Did you threaten him into this?" Elwyn asked, startling the Glaistig.

Koa recovered quickly. "He volunteered, actually. Claims he wants to contribute something before he heads out." A resigned sigh hissed between his fangs. "I suppose it's as decent an outlet as any for that pent-up aggression he's been lugging around."

His most decent outlet yet. Which was why Elwyn felt conflicted about tearing him away from it. The assassin, for his part, didn't seem the least bit distraught to leave the chore behind. The moment Elwyn called for him, he lurched upright, clapped the dirt from his hands, and marched off without so much as a farewell. If he'd bothered to glance back, he'd have seen the glow fleeing Lieri's face. Not that he'd have cared.

From the few vague details Elwyn had pried from Deinua over the past few days, Brannon's mother was to blame for the rift in their relationship. Still, Elwyn couldn't help feeling sorry for her. The night the group arrived at her door, she'd known exactly how much danger her son was intent on tossing himself into. Now that the Procession was only hours away, it must have felt like losing him all over again.

As the colleagues wound their way from a garden of vines and vegetables to one of brilliant blossoms, Elwyn studied the assassin from the corner of her eye, pondering his sudden change of attitude. He was not too dense to notice.

"Don't look at me like that," he growled, fixing his gaze forward. "It's bad enough I can't pull a few weeds without armed supervision. Must I truly suffer an interrogation as well?"

"If you thought I was asking questions, I'm even more concerned for your sanity than before," Elwyn said as they rounded the corner. "You've gone out of your way to avoid Lieri for this entire stay. Why the sudden change?"

"It's not as though we were having a heartfelt conversation." Brannon shrugged in the most rigid manner possible. "I simply wanted to see if I could endure her presence without punching a hole in something, and I wound up ripping roots instead. It sufficed. Now, if you insist on prying into matters that don't concern you, you've opened the door for the same. How long have you and Aedyn been...whatever you are?"

Elwyn glowered and blushed all at once. "You're right, that doesn't concern you."

"So long as it doesn't affect your focus, I couldn't give fewer fucks. You're smart enough to realize how stupid you're being without my piling onto it. That said, minds are just meat, destined to rot. If this is how you truly wish for yours to spoil, then I'm..." he grimaced like he'd caught a whiff of something rancid, "*happy* for you."

Elwyn nearly tripped over open air. Brannon had never felt happy for her. Brannon had never felt anything for anyone. It was pretty much his defining trait.

"You've been chatting with Deinua, haven't you?" she asked.

"Enduring his presence."

"And absorbing his influence. I wonder how much longer we'll need to linger here before you start spouting poetry."

Brannon's glare might have gutted Elwyn, had she not built up defenses through the years. "I've endured the rapt attention of the Greyscale enforcers on no less than twelve occasions, yet that is the most horrific threat I've ever heard."

They approached the woodshed to find Aedyn and Tawny loitering behind it, Luatha perched atop the tower of tomes stacked on the stump between them. Aedyn had finally thought to remove Lieri's apron, and he was listening intently as Tawny pored over the contents of a battered notebook. She'd shorn her hair so that it was mostly even, with a few longer ringlets wisping around her forehead and ears. Though it was likely the result of cutting her hair with a hunting knife and no mirror, the style complemented the neutral tunics and loose trousers she so preferred to tights or gowns.

Between those freshly cropped curls and her growing confidence, she was looking more herself by the day. Now that Elwyn had an idea of who that person was, it was a delight to watch her emerge.

The moment Elwyn neared the stump, Aedyn grabbed her by the hand and pulled her to the grass alongside him, planting a kiss on the crown of her head. The public display made her face flush, though everyone present knew of their shared affection. In fact, it was probable they'd known of it longer than *she* had.

Once the others had settled in, Aedyn made a point of offering one last chance to change their minds, assuring them the decision would not be counted a failure. When no one took him up on the offer, he hesitantly handed the reins to Tawny, who had spent the morning and much of the previous night reading up on the Procession of Autumn.

Apparently, Lieri's collection of poems and folktales contained a wealth of information on the subject, once the metaphors were decoded and contradicting accounts were discarded. Most were written from a mortal perspective, penned long before the Treaty of Dusk barred both Seelie and Unseelie from hopping worlds. Apparently, the Procession always occurred on the darkest night of the year—not to be confused with the longest, on which the Deepwinter Solstice was observed—and the Veil between worlds stretched so thin the Unseelie could cross it in droves without aid of potions or portals. They celebrated the occasion by wreaking havoc on remote mortal villages, often reducing them to splinters by dawn. Mortals could sometimes assuage them with offerings or fool them by dressing in monstrous costumes, but iron and charms proved the more effective defenses.

Because the swarm seldom struck the same hamlet twice, the damage was attributed to natural disasters, and the testimonies of the rare survivors were treated as rural superstition.

"Mailair might claim to be chaos incarnate, but everyone's predictable to a point," Tawny explained. "Based on what we heard..." her eyes flicked to Aedyn, sympathetic, "...the other night, they're intent upon reenacting the Processions from ages past, which isn't as terrible as it might sound. For one thing, it implies that they'll focus on a single region, as opposed to scattering throughout the entire continent."

Given that Yana had boldly announced the name of that region, Elwyn could see the upside of the situation, but that didn't detract from its drawbacks. "That may be good news for most everyone in Pondrelle, but those living near Ebensburg would probably disagree."

"Deinua's made it a mission to help them." Aedyn twined his fingers with hers and squeezed. "He left roughly an hour ago."

Elwyn had wondered where he'd wandered off to. She'd traipsed around nearly the entire glade without spotting his fanged grin or enduring the inevitable barrage of questions he'd unleash when he noticed her and Aedyn holding hands.

"He claimed you two met a man in Wiltshire," Brannon clarified. "Someone with enough influence to usher the citizens of the slums into Ebensburg without inciting riots. Given what Yana said about destroying the district's defenses, it's not a permanent solution, but it should buy us time to complete our mission before the whole population is slaughtered. Hopefully, this supposed contact is half as sharp as Deinua believes."

But not any sharper, Elwyn added silently. If Deinua had built a strong rapport with the Iron Claws' captain, there was a chance the hunters would take his word about the encroaching monsters. If not, he risked drawing attention to his own monstrous nature.

Elwyn wasn't optimistic enough to assume the odds favored him. "Any other encouraging discoveries?" she asked Tawny.

"Actually, yes." The witchling flipped through her notebook. "Based on participation in ages past, the Procession should draw a smaller crowd than that which we encountered at Fómhar. It's almost exclusively an Augusky ritual, and despite their reputations, only the most depraved among them can stomach such wanton violence, much less revel in it. There's no such thing as a freshborn Unseelie, after all. Most remember how it felt to bask in sunlight without burning to a crisp. I imagine they'd like another chance at it."

"Is that even possible?" Aedyn leaned forward, eyebrow raised. "There are countless tales of Seelie falling into darkness, but I've never heard of an *Unseelie* being reborn into light."

"Assuming they remember their past mistakes, do you think they'd bother dredging them up?" Tawny shrugged. "A fall is always easier than a climb, but the former is frowned upon. If the whole point of living over and over again is to prove oneself worthy of either Heaven or Hell, then there must be hope for the Unseelie to redeem themselves. Otherwise, they wouldn't be reborn at all."

"That makes sense." Aedyn sounded more relieved than baffled. It saddened Elwyn to think that he might still deem himself unworthy of redemption. Her opinion was heavily biased, but she was not alone in believing his strengths outweighed his flaws.

"Before you all dive deep into a contemplative silence,
I'd like to circle back to when she mentioned wanton violence..."

As usual, Luatha had identified and voiced the bigger concern with aplomb.

"How small is *smaller*, exactly?" Elwyn asked. "There had to have been at least five hundred monsters in that mob, any one of which could probably tear our limbs free with little effort."

"Honestly, the accounts vary." Tawny scanned her notes. "One or two hundred participants seems to have been the norm. Given the excitement surrounding this year's celebration, I suspect attendance will swell by roughly a third, but most of those will be passive observers."

"That's still too many to possibly defeat." Brannon struck his daggers together, producing a spark. "It'll sure be fun to try, though."

"We don't need to defeat the whole horde," Aedyn said, much to the assassin's palpable disappointment. "Mailair will present enough of a challenge on their own..."

He went on to detail a plan that he and Tawny had built as their research unfolded. Since Mailair would doubtless be surrounded by lackeys —and probably clinging close to Yana—they would have to isolate the Augusky ruler to even out the odds. Aedyn was confident he could craft a diversion with ease. Only once the assassination was complete and the Procession was over could the group risk turning their ire on Yana. Tawny supplied everyone with a vile of blackthorn oil for their blades, claiming that the poison, while not lethal, would weaken the Ghost Witch if she happened to be more ghost than witch when they cornered her. *Gelah* would then finish the job, assuming its wielder was still alive.

"So, the goal is to isolate and slay Mailair before Yana reaches Ebensburg," Elwyn summarized, deeming the mission daunting, but doable. "Then we can finally take out Yana."

"If only it were so simple." Aedyn squeezed her hand. "Remember, this plan won't work unless the Augusky witness Mailair's assassination, which means we need to capture them alive."

"And only the ruler of the Wilds can call off the Procession." Tawny clapped her notebook shut and set it aside. "That's where I come in..."

DEINUA

Deinua wound his way through Wiltshire with his wooden pike strapped to his back. He'd left the weapon behind on previous trips to town, but he'd built enough rapport with the locals to avoid scrutiny, and he wasn't about to be caught out after sunset without it.

Hopefully, he would be home long before then. If the information Brannon and his friends passed along was accurate, the Procession wouldn't pass anywhere near the cottage, but that didn't mean his mother was safe. There were always a few renegade Unseelie who opted to celebrate on their own, far outside of their ruler's influence. He'd been helping his father guard the property ever since he was strong enough to lift a weapon, and he intended to keep the tradition going his whole life through. Only now, there was more than one mortal he felt obligated to protect.

Petie's Pub was practically deserted, but Kadence sat at the end of his usual table, scribbling in the journal. Though he wore the same vivid blue tailcoat as always, his bowtie and the ribbon in his hair were mint green, rather than the matching cobalt he'd donned in days past. The previous morning, Deinua had mentioned he was fond of the hue as he watched Kadence put the finishing touches on a particularly detailed landscape. It was probably a coincidence, but it warmed Deinua to imagine it was intentional, or even subconscious.

"Two hours later than usual." Kadence peered overtop his latest project. "I was beginning to fear you'd lost interest."

"In joining the troop?" Deinua asked, though their conversations had thus far revolved around poems and portraits.

"That too." Kadence chuckled, motioning for Deinua to sit. "I understand your hesitance, but I still believe you'd make a perfect lorekeeper. That information you gave us on Lenanshee saved Urith from an embarrassing situation last night, possibly a deadly one."

Deinua only hoped the Lenanshee in question had also escaped unscathed. They needed to eat, same as anyone.

"Actually, I'm afraid there's something else we need to discuss." Deinua sat, leaving a chair open between them. Kadence's lieutenant and chief scout were both territorial as Cave Trows, and they'd arrive any minute, if patterns held. "This is probably going to sound insane, so I need you to promise to keep open ears and an even more open mind."

Kadence set his project aside, lending Deinua his full attention. "My mind's been wide open since I first stumbled on a leprechaun dyeing his hat with human blood," he said, uncharacteristically grim. "I don't foresee it closing anytime soon."

There was a story there that begged telling, but it would have to wait. Unwilling to waste another second, Deinua spilled everything he knew about the Procession of Autumn. He explained who Mailair and Yana were, and how they planned to lead a horde to Ebensburg that very night. He detailed their plans to raze the surrounding slums, destroying the district's wrought-iron borders, and wreaking havoc on its citizens. He recounted what little he'd gleaned of his houseguests' plans to intervene, and of the horrors that would beset them all, should those plans fail.

Kadence listened with his fingers steepled against his lips, his face a blank canvas. He stayed that way for several seconds after the speech before finally asking, "How could you possibly know all of this?"

If Deinua could lie, he'd have claimed that answer was unimportant. In truth, he *wanted* Kadence to know who and what he was, fearsome aspects included. Unfortunately, if he divulged that information now, a lot of people would probably die. Starting with himself.

"I'll explain everything when we have more time. For now, I'm begging you to take this on faith."

Before Kadence could answer, the pub door clattered open. An unruly crew of six spilled inside, prattling loudly as ever about their most recent misadventures.

The lead scout, Mari, collapsed into the chair to Kadence's left, while Warrick, the troop's lieutenant, claimed the one to his right. The other remaining seats filled swiftly, and the air filled with conversation about plans for what the hunters foolishly believed would be their first night off in over a week. Only Urith acknowledged Deinua's presence.

"Well, look who's finally armed 'imself." He gave the pike on Deinua's back a jarring shake. "Can't imagine this'll strike much fear into the fae, but it's better'n nothing. Does this mean you're finally taking up the stripes?"

"For the last time, we don't need a damned lorekeeper," Warrick grumbled, taking a swig from one of several flasks he'd hidden on his person. "The last one only slowed us down, and for what, common knowledge? The fae are monsters. Iron makes them whimper. Stab the monsters with iron and watch them whimper. It's a pretty simple process."

"If you ask me, you're both biased as fuck." Mari propped a boot against the table and leaned back in her chair. "Warrick's just jealous lorekeepers have enough smarts for reading 'n writing, while he's still puzzling over which end of the sword to stab with. Urith's embarrassed that he might have crammed it in a fae whore, were it not for that dandy's advice. Um, no offense." She tipped her flat cap back and winked at Deinua. "If you do enlist, I suggest you keep wearing them suits. It'll save us some trouble when it comes time to bury you."

"That's quite enough, all of you." Kadence voice was not harsh, but it doused the conversation like a rainstorm. "Deinua will join us of his own volition, or not at all. In the meantime, we have more important matters to bicker about."

The troop fell strangely silent while their leader repeated Deinua's testimony in full, detailing the history of the Procession and the details of the massacre planned for that very evening. With as often as their eyes narrowed and their jaws gaped throughout the report, it was clear they would not have believed a word of it had it spilled from any other lips. Kadence had their unwavering trust. And apparently, Deinua had his.

That meant...something.

"Ebensburg has a long history of denying asylum, but enough people owe me enough favors to prop the gates open a few hours." The captain rose, progressing from information to orders. "Warrick?"

The lieutenant stood arrow-straight, saluting. "Yes, Cap'n?"

"Deliver the details to the captains of each district discreetly as possible. We cannot allow this knowledge to take off on its own. If riots break out, there will be no hope of drawing mercy from the nobles. Mari?"

The spritely girl hopped to her feet. "Say the word, Kade!"

"Have your scouts set up a few extra defenses. Those traps you've been working on should do the trick. We don't stand a chance of keeping the hordes out, but we can sure as hell slow them down. Everyone else," his gaze swept over those still seated, deliberate and stern, "empty the armory and distribute weapons to any passable fighters you can trust to wield them. If Deinua's friends fail in their quest, we'd better be prepared for a fight."

The moment the captain dismissed his troop, Deinua started toward the door. The Iron Claws would protect their people to the best of their ability, but he had his own to worry about.

He made it only two steps before Urith stepped forward to block his path.

"A passable fighter I'd trust with a blade." The hunter unfastening one of the two swords he wore on his belt. "The cap'n practically commanded us to arm you."

Deinua shied back, his stomach churning at the mere sight of the iron hilt. "I have a weapon already." He gestured "Only I've actually trained with pikes. That sword is better off in your hands, I assure you."

Urith snorted a laugh. "That's a nice enough stick, but it ain't iron." He flipped the sword, offering it to Deinua, pommel-first. "If you're worried about losing it, you've no reason to fret. I figure I owe you for saving me a year or two."

Deinua's throat went even dryer than usual. The others were staring at him now, breath bated and brows raised. He could practically feel their suspicions rising, building like heat beneath a fickle geyser.

"If you insist, then I'd prefer the shortsword." He nodded toward Urith's other blade, its pommel and handguard crafted of steel. The refinement process cleansed iron of poison—a fact few mortals were aware of. "It looks far easier to wield."

"That one's a family heirloom." Urith shook his head. "Just take the damned sword and thank me, lad. I assure you, they all slice the same!"

The hunter thrust the hilt toward Deinua, whose grabbed it on reflex. A fire-bright burn seared through his palm, sending painful pinpricks to his elbow. He hissed, stumbled back, dropped the weapon to the floor. Steam sizzled from blistered flesh, half as telling as his gritted fangs.

Blades rasped from their scabbards. Bowstrings *creaked*, and bolts *clicked*. The Iron Claws surrounded Deinua, cutting off all possible exits. "W-what are you?" Urith whispered, shortsword quivering in his grasp.

"I-I can explain." Deinua tried to raise his palms, but his wounded fingers refused to unclench. "I know how this looks, but I swear I'm on your side."

The hunters met his plea with palpable fear, loathing, bitter resolve—a few smirks of condescension. Deinua turned slowly to see Kadence raising his bow in one hand, the other reaching for his quiver.

"Answer the question," he demanded as he notched an arrow. "What are you?"

*"Don't trust the spangled night to guide a straight and steady path,
When stars cross, constellations cannot make for trusty maps."*

CHAPTER 27

TEMPTING FATE

ELWYN

or the second time, the group marched toward Fómhar wearing the blood-smeared forms of Augusky, guided by the fickle light of Tawny's torch. Their first such journey had been marked by dread and curiosity, but a cloud of grief hung over them now, making the darkest night of the year that much darker. To complete the mission Amatha had rallied them for, they needed to return to the scene of her death and pretend it hadn't shattered them.

Of all the trials the Procession was bound to bring, that was surely the most harrowing.

Sorrow accounted for much of their silence, but the looming danger also played its part. Already, they'd stumbled across more than one horde of *actual* Augusky—most marching upright with wooden weapons in hand, a few bounding through the woods as true goats, all presumably headed for the same location. Most of the monsters chatted glibly about their plans for the ceremony as they wandered past. Elwyn couldn't imagine feigning the same calloused glee. Better not to speak at all.

The silence was broken when Aedyn strolled up alongside Elwyn. His hand dangled only inches from hers, but she resisted the childish urge to clasp it for comfort. Not only would that have been unusual behavior for Augusky, she'd survived nearly twenty years without seeking such fragile supports. This night needn't be any different, even if it was her last.

"This is probably going to frustrate you," Aedyn whispered, leaning in close, "but I need you to repeat your portion of the plan, step by step."

Elwyn groaned, having already humored that same request a dozen times over. "Do you think I'm so incompetent that I've forgotten my role already?"

"Far from it." He offered an encouraging smile, striking despite the glamour that obscured it and the darkness that dulled it. "You're resourceful and resilient, and I have the utmost faith you will complete your tasks in the most competent manner possible. I, by contrast, am one brisk breeze away from falling to pieces, and hearing you recite the mission might help to soothe me. So, if you wouldn't mind repeating it one more time, for my sake..."

Suddenly more flattered than offended, Elwyn begrudgingly recited her responsibilities, which primarily centered around keeping watch over Tawny and aiding in Mailair's capture. Once she'd dutifully ticked her way through the list, Aedyn gestured for her to continue.

"You've forgotten the most important part."

"No heroics," she grumbled, rolling her eyes. As though capturing a dangerous monster to ensure the safety of thousands of strangers didn't qualify.

"I know you're tired of hearing it, but I'm serious. Deinua didn't return as scheduled, so we can only hope his message found purchase. If not, we're bound to witness some nightmares before the night is through. I know you've convinced yourself you're a coward, but I'm not so easily fooled. Time and again, I've watched you throw yourself in harm's way for the wellbeing of others. A show of gallantry, however small, would set you apart from the swarm, and if the Augusky were to see through your disguise..." He swallowed his fears before they could find his tongue. "Just promise me you won't do anything rash. Please."

Elwyn nodded numbly, bewildered by the man strolling alongside her. When she'd first met Aedyn, he was the type to sprint after each glimmer that caught his eye—be it a priceless treasure or a bandit's blade. She couldn't have foreseen that he would one day lecture her on caution. Then again, she couldn't have foreseen herself kissing him, or falling asleep on his shoulder, or marching to her doom at his side, fighting the urge to twine her fingers with his.

"No heroics," she vowed, sincerely this time.

Aedyn released a sigh of relief before grabbing her hand, heedless of possible witnesses, and drawing her to a stop. She could practically see his burnished eyes through illusory ochre, but she could not discern the emotion behind them, deep though it most certainly was.

"I'm accustomed to acting recklessly," he said, stroking her thumb with his, "but I've never before felt I was risking something precious. Carrying out this mission is the most terrifying thing I've ever done, and not for fear of death or torment. At least, not for fear of my own. Elwyn, I..." His sentence hitched, then faded to a sigh. "I should probably distribute my attention more evenly. You know how grumpy Brannon gets without constant affirmation."

He kissed Elwyn's cheek and hurried off, leaving her equally confused and conflicted. She watched with interest as he approached the next member of the formation. Though their conversation was too low to hear, the way Brannon bristled was a sure sign he'd also been asked to recite his role. The assassin grew gradually less tense as the discussion carried on, and by the time Aedyn left his side, he was standing taller and walking lighter than before.

Luatha peeked out from behind a lock of dark hair, her shadow wings ticking Elwyn's ear.

"Does the prince think pure vexation will help you to succeed?
His veiled interrogations aren't what any of you need."

Surprisingly, Elwyn disagreed. She'd once dismissed leadership as the domain of those with strong wills and stronger hands, but she was learning it came in many more effective forms. Father Beaus had exploited the weaknesses of his followers, prodding them as punishment until his agents feared failure more than death. Amatha had viewed weaknesses as misdirected strengths, honing them into wicked points and hurling them at worthy targets. Aedyn looked past weaknesses altogether, finding the spark in a person's spirit and feeding it until they shone like a beacon. As much as Elwyn had respected the chieftain and her direct method of command, this subtler style better suited the illusionist.

A bittersweet ache filled Elwyn's chest as she watched Aedyn repeat his process once more, bolstering Tawny's confidence with his every whispered encouragement. The disguise he'd crafted for himself contained no cape, no crown, no garish frills or filigree armor, yet he'd never looked more like a prince.

YANA

Yana's Shadow Goblins cackled in anticipation as the Unseelie filtered into the hollow. This crowd was far smaller than that which had gathered for the assembly, but it was still dense enough to serve witness to her accomplishments. Better still, her form had reverted to its semi-spectral splendor—a gift from the Shadows, she could only assume.

In times past, they'd contributed to the Procession by thinning the Veil between worlds, allowing their followers easy access to the mortals on the other side. Now that those worlds had melded, they seemed to have poured out their power on the festival celebrants, blessing them with palpable vigor and boundless bloodlust. Though both could just as easily have been byproducts of the swarm's communal depravity. Spite feeds spite, as she well knew.

Whatever its source, potent magic, cold and cruel, crackled beneath Yana's ethereal skin, begging to be unleashed. She felt as though a single snap of her fingers could set the bramble palace ablaze or construct a fortress twice as intimidating from nothing but air and night and malice.

But to what end?

Power, praise, protection—every dream she'd ever fought for now dangled within her reach, and though they'd shone like stars from a distance, proximity had dulled them. By sunrise, her debt to Mailair would be paid in full, and accounts of the mayhem she'd unleashed would buy her lasting safety. Then she would finally be free to...free to...

That was the problem, wasn't it? She'd spent her life and afterlife both clawing far security, slitting throats to protect her own, and trading favors with every monster to wink her way. In all that time, she'd found only one treasure worth hoarding, one feeble little blossom in a wilderness of rot.

And she'd killed her.

"Missstresssss...Yaaana...." a Shadow Goblin croaked, its voice barely audible over the murmurs of the swelling crowd. "It...isss...ssstaaaarting."

Yana took her place of honor at the front of the Procession, painted on a smile, and pretended to give a damn.

DEINUA

The basement of Petie's Pub was stocked with enough iron trappings to fend off a Cave Trow, and an unreasonable portion were being used to subdue Deinua, as though he hadn't surrendered willingly.

The damp bricks that scratched against his back provided little relief from the shackles that burned against his wrists and ankles, and the chains that wrapped his chest. He'd learned quickly not to writhe, lest the links find fresh skin to sear. Granted, that horrid metal had sapped so much of his strength, he couldn't have struggled if he wanted to.

While the iron was to blame for much of Deinua's suffering, the headache was another matter. The hunters had been arguing for Creator-knows-how-long, having divided over whether to heed or disregard his warnings. The lesser three kept their weapon trained on him while Kadence paced between Mari and Warrick, who hurled disparate opinions at their captain like darts.

"There's no reason we shouldn't prepare for the worst!" Mari spat, all four-and-a-half feet of her trembling with a either rage or terror, maybe both. "Say those bastards never arrive at our doorstep, what harm could possibly come of strengthening our defenses? And as for asylum, pressing into Ebensburg without cause might burn a few bridges with the nobles, but them pricks care for little but their horses and whores anyway. No offense, Kade."

"Pull your head outta' your ass, girl!" Warrick barked, his glare shifting to Deinua. "If this monster wants our streets clear, you'd best believe there's a reason for it. I'd wager we'd wander back to our homes at sunrise to find whole hordes of fae seated around our tables, ready to make meals of us."

"That's ludicrous," Deinua rasped, bile souring each syllable. "I'm...here to help you, to *warn* you. Please...you have...you have to believe me."

"Believe you?" Kadence's words were sharper than the arrows in his quiver, and his glare was sharper still. "I've known you less than a week, and you haven't once been honest. I'm not even sure how you made it through our gates." He looked to Rictor, a gangly young hunter who often manned the guard tower. "He *did* pass the test, correct?"

"Yessir!" The youth saluted. "Several times, and without a single trip of the tongue. We'd do well to change our methods. If a beast with fangs like that can claim to be human—"

"I *am* human!" The shout took most of Deinua's remaining strength, and his next breath felt like inhaling cinders. Cobwebs clouded the corners of his vision. "On...on my mother's side, anyway."

The confession only stoked another battle, this time centering over whether such a creature was possible and how it might have come about. Deinua caught only a few insulting theories before the voices bled together and the basement began to churn. Next thing he knew, rough fingers grabbed him by the forelock, and his head snapped upward. A ruddy beard flared bright against a sea of brown and charcoal.

"If he's truly half-fae, he can probably half-lie." A knife pressed to Deinua's left cheek, drawing a sizzle of steam. "I say we cut the human bits out. Then, he'll have no option but honesty."

"Unhand him, Warrick." Kadence's command was little more than an echo. "I'll be giving no such orders. Whatever we decide..."

The world spun one final, nauseating time before going black.

*"When potent power beckons you, keep one grim truth in mind,
Not all magic is beautiful and not all whimsy, kind."*

CHAPTER 28

THE PROCESSION OF AUTUMN

ELWYN

he word *procession* brought several things to Elwyn's mind. It harkened to the militant ants that used to march through the grave garden behind Saint Aldrich's, hefting crumbs and grains of salt from the kitchen. It reminded her of the Midsummer parade she'd attended back in Amblewick, a charming calm before the storm that would sweep her away forever. It conjured images of the Seelie High Judges and their formal strolls through the palace, proud and poised and steeped in eons of practiced ceremony.

The Procession of Autumn was something entirely different.

In practice, it was more of a mob than a march—a feral jumble of hooves and horns that the Wilds itself shied away from. That, or the foliage was trampled so swiftly it appeared to be retreating. Either way, it allowed the zealous Augusky to traverse the woodlands at a dizzying pace.

The perfect darkness that stretched overhead was owed not to smoke or storm clouds, but to something far more ominous. It looked as though every star in the sky had been snuffed out and the moon had been swallowed whole. Navigation might have been impossible, were it not for the torches carried by many of the celebrants or the haunting aura of the woman who led them.

Yana had yet to produce her host stone, so the silvery glow that wafted around her could only be attributed to magic. As usual, a horde of Shadow Goblins scurried around her feet, their stark silhouettes swallowing a portion of her light. The first time Elwyn had faced the creatures, they'd terrified her. How paltry they now seemed, trailed by beasts clad in only blood and bone.

As badly as Elwyn wanted to plunge *Gelah* into the Ghost Witch's back, attacking her before they captured their target would throw the entire mission awry. She needed to fix her focus on Mailair—an easy enough task, given the torch-bearing lackeys that ringed around the Augusky ruler and their beta. Though Sasta hadn't changed one scarlet sigil since the assembly, Mailair might have been unrecognizable, were it not for their morbid scepter-spear. They'd adopted a glaringly masculine physique with broad shoulders, rippling muscles, and a sinister pair of close-set horns as long and curved as sabers. The ruler's skin and fur were immaculate, but Elwyn doubted they meant to stay that way long.

If only her companions were as easily tracked as her foes.

As planned ahead of time, Tawny stuck close to Elwyn's side, clinging to her arm whenever the jostling throng threatened to sweep her away. She'd remained remarkably calm despite the constant brush of bristling fur and bloodied skin. Aedyn and Brannon had fallen close to the rear of the crowd, committed to a disparate portion of the plan.

When Wiltshire's walls came into view, Yana stepped to the side of the trail and shot the throng an expectant smirk. Taking the gesture as a display of power—which it likely was—Mailair and their entourage did the same. Still, they raised their scepter-spear high, and released a gleeful bleat.

The swarm swept forward like floodwater, swift and sure, horns lowered like battering rams. Elwyn wrapped an arm around Tawny's waist, guiding her to weave with the current. On the front line, several Augusky stumbled. A wire glinted, twanged, snapped. Elwyn ducked, throwing her cloak over Tawny. The soil erupted to their right, spraying clods of dirt and clouds of silvery smoke.

Not smoke. Bleating screams rang through the night as the Augusky threw themselves, flailing, to the mire. No amount of mud could cleanse their sizzling skin of powdered iron. Skin sloughed from muscle, muscle melted from bone. Soon, the reek of charred flesh drowned the burn of scalding metal and the brine of fresh blood.

A second mortar sounded. Then another. Then another. Luatha clawed at Elwyn's neck, trembling in terror. Frightened for the piskie hidden beneath her hair, she dragged Tawny toward the trees, an arm raised to shield her eyes and nose. Once they were safely beneath the canopy, she took a deep, cinnamon breath and watched the haze settle. It dusted far fewer corpses than she would have assumed, though it was impossible to tell for certain, given the mangled state of the remains.

"It's over, and I must confess I'm terribly relieved,
That was a closer call than I've ever before received."

Hearing Luatha's voice eased one of Elwyn's worries, and a glance at Tawny eased another. The witchling's glamour was still intact, as was her own—sure signs that Aedyn was alive and conscious. Elwyn wished his glamour-link ran two ways, though it would only have distracted her. If she could feel the magic move, her panicked mind would convert each tug to a fall, each shiver to a scream, each twitch to a spear parting sinew from bone.

Elwyn and Tawny watched from the foliage as a second barrage of Augusky rushed forward, shifting into goats mid-bound. Their horns met wood with violent force, and they scattered aside to make way for wave three. Within seconds, they'd reduced the gates to splinters.

Elwyn let slip a sigh of relief as she and the witchling melted back into the throng. Though torches flickered streetside and lamps blazed in many a window, not a single silhouette could be seen shuffling about. Perhaps Deinua's message had fallen on receptive ears.

The swarm split into several as it surged into Wiltshire, streaming down side roads and alleyways in search of skin to rend, bones to snap. Yana kept to the central street, violet eyes fixed ahead as though she could somehow glimpse her goal through the jumble of hovels and run-down taverns. Mailair and their entourage kept close behind her, trailed by a chittering legion nearly two hundred strong. If the carnage beyond the border disturbed them in the slightest, they hid it well.

Elwyn and Tawny slipped ahead of the swarm, keeping to the shadows. They tested several promising doors before a rustic inn granted them entrance. With a second story, several hanging lanterns to see by, and not a single patron in sight, it would serve a decent sparring ground. Not that they could afford to be choosy.

"You remember the plan, right?" Elwyn asked, aware of how recently she'd recently bristled at that very question. "Recite it back to me."

"Run inside, duck and hide, find my way to Mailair's side." Tawny ticked the steps off with her fingers, her confidence making it sound like they'd always rhymed. "Now, I suggest you do some running and hiding of your own before the crowd catches up."

Elwyn hated this part of the plan. By right and tradition, the first mortal spotted by the Augusky ruler was theirs to torment, kill, and feast upon in no particular order. It was Tawny's job to be that mortal, if only for a blink.

Elwyn sank into the nearest nook, feeling twice as secure as she had in Samhria's halls. Between the darkness and her unremarkability, she might as well have been invisible. The moment the Procession oozed into view—Yana, a silvery beacon at their forefront—Tawny dropped all but a swatch of her glamour, keeping her face covered as she stepped into the torchlight.

As predicted, Mailair spotted her instantly. They bleated an alarm and sprinted forward, Sasta racing at their side and a trio of underlings scrambling to keep pace. Tawny shrieked for show before darting into the inn, slamming the door shut behind her.

If the plan was truly unfolding properly, Aedyn was already in the process of restoring the witchling's disguise. It terrified Elwyn that she couldn't know for certain.

Sasta kicked the door in, and the Augusky barged into the building. Elwyn counted off ten grueling seconds before following after. That's all it took to lay waste to the place. Tables had been overturned and chairs snapped to splinters. Kegs lay sideways, bleeding ale. Cupboards had been ransacked and drawers jarred loose, their contents strewn carelessly about the floorboards.

Only three lackeys had trailed their leaders into the inn, but four now trotted through the wreckage, destroying anything they could get their bloodied hands on. That wasn't part of the plan.

After identifying the witchling by the scarlet swirl on her forehead, Elwyn wisped silently through the room, running *Gelah* across one sallow throat, then the next. The blood that coated fingers was startlingly cold.

As the final monster *thudded* at her feet, she looked to Tawny for an explanation.

"I couldn't follow after them," the witchling whispered. "I tried, but they ordered us to stay downstairs."

"Fair enough. I'm ordering the same."

"But—"

"They would hear you coming." Elwyn held up a palm, forbidding further protest. "If they commanded you to give them space, disobeying will only draw scrutiny. I stand a better chance of slaying Sasta on my own." Reading disappointment on the youth's face, she heaved a sigh. "Once the beta is out of the way, I'll send Luatha to fetch you, and you can aid me in Mailair's capture."

"Fine, but take this," the witchling said, though clearly disgruntled. She plucked an iron fork from the floorboards and tossed it Elwyn's way. "You never know when you might need it."

With an enchanted dagger at the ready, a fork would merit little, but Elwyn appreciated the thought. She tucked the fork into her boot before tiptoeing up the staircase, casting a subtle glance back. To her relief, Tawny had already distracted herself in scrounging through the cupboards.

"I know you've grown accustomed to slaying the fiends of night,
But these are much bigger than goblins, and they put up bigger fights."

The observation wasn't particularly insightful, but Luatha's voice was encouraging in its own right. How Elwyn had survived a full four months without the piskie was a mystery.

The staircase intersected with a hallway lit by a single, half-melted taper. The furthest doors to both the left and right had been kicked in, and swears and hoofsteps could be heard beyond both. Elwyn had no way of knowing which Augusky went which way, so she crept toward the rightmost room, hoping for the best, planning for the worst.

She paused with her shoulders to the wall, *Gelah* trembling in her grasp as she peered around the doorframe. A shadow raged through the gloom, overturning baskets and rifling through closets, but the details were too dim to parse. Short on time and options, she ran her dagger across her forearm and darted toward the beast.

Violet light filled a surprisingly spacious chamber, and startled oval eyes snapped her way. Though she'd hoped the purple pall would fall on sallow skin and calico braids, it spilled instead over hulking shoulders and a spear topped with a skull. Elwyn swore under her breath, flipping her dagger without slowing her sprint. She would just have to knock the ruler out before circling back and slaying their cohort.

Hastened by the urgency of her mission, her pulse had never thrummed quite so loudly. By the time she heard the hoofsteps charging up behind her, it was too late to change course. The shaft of a spear slammed into her side. She hit the wall hard enough to lock a painting loose. Pain burst through her right shoulder, dwindling to pinpricks before she landed. She couldn't feel her fingers, but she felt *Gelah* slip from them, heard it rasp across the floorboards, watched its gleam streak through the shadows as Luatha's fled from the room altogether—the softest violet blur.

Panicked, Elwyn clawed for the dagger. Right when her fingertips brushed the hilt, a hoof stomped down on the blade.

Sasta tossed her spear aside in a show of justified arrogance. Those massive, bloodstained hands of hers could crush a skull well enough on their own. And that said nothing of her horns.

"You'd dare challenge your ruler in the midst of a hallowed ceremony?" She stooped forward to sniff the air. "No, that can't be right; only children of the Wilds can lay claim to the bramble throne." She grabbed Elwyn by the chin and brought her face close, rancid breath escaping her sneer. "What could you possibly be after, mortal?"

DEINUA

Sleep brought no solace. Even as Deinua drifted through the darkness, he recognized the bitter flames biting through his wrists and ankles, the stale metal scent that burned his nostrils and churned his belly. The storm raged on—maybe for minutes, maybe for weeks—before the chains that bound him rattled, relaxed, and fell away.

The lucid portion of his mind fully expected his nose to crack against concrete. To his mild relief, his face met worsted wool. Firm hands clasped him by the shoulders, guiding him to sit against the wall before shaking.

"We have to get out of here." The voice sounded hollow, a whisper drifting through the depths. "Wake up, Deinua."

Deinua *was* awake. Mustering the will to prove it was another matter.

Unable to connect with the present, he scoured the past for details he could cling to. Before drowning in darkness, he'd been running toward something...or for something...or from something...

"For Creator's sake, snap out of it!"

Tepid water splashed his face. His eyes opened to the sight of a canteen pulling away. Behind it, brass buttons gleamed against a plane of piercing blue.

Now firmly sodden, his memories settled swiftly. He remembered his mother first, how she'd blanched when he told her of his plans, the hopelessness that thinned her voice when she begged him to return before nightfall. The Iron Claws' thuggery came second in both sequence and import.

Deinua pushed his captor away with all that remained of his strength. A hummingbird might have made a bigger impact. Still, his message landed.

"I'm not here to hurt you." Kadence shied back, palms raised. "I'm here to help you. Please, you have to believe me."

Deinua had made the same plea before passing out, and it hadn't been well received. Hearing his words echoed back now might have been laughable if he could manage more than a cough. Even more panicked than he was enraged, he peered past Kadence, seeking out a clock or window. The basement was dark beyond the light of the hanging lamp. Iron glinted in the firelight, and rats scurried, near invisible, along the walls.

"How long?" he rasped.

Kadence flinched, rising to his full height. "I came back for you, didn't I?" he asked, looking pointedly away. "Creator's sake, Deinua, you're one of *them*! You've got fangs, your eye glows, yet you somehow slipped past not only Wiltshire's defenses, but my *own*. I can't imagine the damage you might have done if..." His rant dissolved into a frustrated growl, and he dug his fingers into the roots of his hair. Several sable coils popped free of the ribbon that bound them. "Look, I can't apologize enough, alright? Even if I could, we don't have time for it. Those monsters have already breached our borders, and—"

"They've *what*?" Panic propelled Deinua to his feet, and the resulting vertigo nearly sent him sprawling. Kadence caught him by the waist, but he squirmed away, fangs bared. Strange how an embrace that would have thrilled him hours before now thoroughly disgusted him. "After everything I risked to warn you, you've done nothing to prevent this?"

"By the time I made the call, it was too late," the hunter confessed. "We managed to set up a few traps and begin evacuations, but the Augusky are stronger and swifter than we bargained for. There must be a couple hundred of them, at least. I know we can't possibly take them all on, but we could buy ourselves time by taking out the leaders."

Brannon and his friends had proposed something similar, which meant they hadn't completed their mission. Deinua didn't have time to ponder the implications. If the Procession had already reached the city, they needed to either flee or prepare to fight.

"Just how close are they?" he asked.

The tavern door fell in, rattling the rafters. Hooves stormed across the floor above, followed by a swell of bleating laughter.

There would be no returning to his cottage now. Not unless he lived to see dawn.

"Some means cannot be justified, regardless of the ends,
Though wars often boast victors, no one ever truly wins."

CHAPTER 29
ANTI-HEROICS
AEDYN

edyn had impressed only one true edict upon his friends, and he was on the brink of abandoning it himself. The further the Procession pressed into Wiltshire, the more mortals could be found hidden within the hovels, and the more horrific the revels became.

No heroics, he reminded himself as torch-fire swept across the thatched rooftops, burning bright against a plane of perfect black.

No heroics, he repeated as innocents were dragged into the streets, clawing and crying and begging for mercy their captors would never conjure.

No heroics, he swore, desperate, when the warm blood of a fisherman spattered his face, freed by the wooden pike of a grinning monster.

Soon, he could not hear his thoughts at all, so loud were the screams of suffering, the mad cackles of the mob.

No matter the terrors that raged around him, he fought to fix his eyes on Yana and his nerves to his glamour-web. He'd been tracking every tremor, waiting for the signal that would commence his portion of the plan. Ideally, he and Brannon would take the Ghost Witch down before she unleashed the Wailing Wind on Ebensburg. That hope helped to quell his frantic conscience. In abandoning his mission, he might save a few lives. In seeing it through, he would save thousands.

Unfortunately, concentration had never been his strong suit. His focus strained a little more with every agonized shriek, every crimson cloud. By the time Ebensburg's jagged skyline rose above the rooftops, it held by only a few fraying fibers. A familiar shade of purple glimmered in his periphery, and his gaze skipped to a pair of lanky Augusky. Shards of amethyst dangled between their breasts. Matching beads wove through their braids.

Tawny had explained the rules thoroughly. Where mature Augusky adorned themselves with trophies from recent kills, the smallest among them often foraged for the trappings they were too frail to claim. Morbid as it sounded, Aedyn hadn't given the practice much thought. He could not have imagined spotting the crystals that had once so beautifully embellished his best friends skin serving as accessories for a pair of depraved beasts.

With that final, harrowing sight, Aedyn's focus snapped.

When the offending Augusky raced down an alley in pursuit of something Aedyn couldn't see, he followed, fully aware of his hypocrisy. The guilt did nothing to slow his steps as he slipped between buildings and veered around corners. By the time he caught up to his targets, they'd herded a woman into a dead end and were toying with her, cackling madly as she dodged their graceless jabs.

Aedyn drew his rapier and struck forward in a single, fluid motion. His blade emerged scarlet. The fiend fell limp to the mire.

"Run," he ordered the woman, though he'd turned eyes and sword on the remaining Augusky.

She obeyed without hesitation, heels slipping in slick gravel.

The Augusky dropped their spear, shying back. The amethyst swayed against their sternum with every halting step. Though rage bid Aedyn strike, clean and quick, the fear in those oval eyes gave him pause. This creature had endured a life—perhaps more—of darkness and destruction, and more of the same awaited them. So far as anyone knew, they had nowhere to go but down.

There's no such thing as a freshborn Unseelie, Tawny's voice rang in Aedyn's ears. If this creature had ever traipsed through Talunasa's verdant forests, they must have envisioned a nobler future than this.

"Do you remember daylight?" He lowered his voice, but not his rapier. "I'm not talking about the blush of dawn or dusk, but that moment when the sun is at its highest, and the shadows cede to slivers?" A surprising sense of nostalgia tinged the words, though he'd once resented his kingdom's endless summer. "Do you remember how it felt against your skin? How it pricked your eyes with each careless glance skyward? How it somehow made the whole world smell greener?"

The Augusky tilted its head, eyes probing Aedyn's. For a moment, the illusionist feared his glamour had unraveled, and that the creature had caught a glimpse of the gold beneath.

"Of course I remember," they whispered, suddenly somber. "I suspect we *all* remember, not that it matters. We will never feel such warmth again." They lifted their arm, scanning the scarlet sigils that snaked from wrist to shoulder. "Not without stealing it."

"If that's true, why be reborn at all?" he said, as though he'd always wondered the same. In truth, the theory might never have crossed his mind had Tawny not proposed it. "Why would the Creator present you with the same test, time and again, if your fate was fixed upon your very first failure?"

The Augusky laughed weakly. "You presume to know better than centuries of teaching?"

Aedyn clenched his hilt tightly. "I only know we don't know everything, but there's one sure way to find out..."

He struck forward with an upward flourish. The Augusky's gasp snagged in its throat. A chunk of crystal dropped to the ground, the chord that bound it severed.

"Leave this place," Aedyn ordered. "Convince all who are willing to join you. Find a way to live alongside the mortals, and never turn your spear on an innocent again. When you close your eyes for the last time this cycle, they might just open to daylight. If so, I hope to one day hear of it."

The Augusky darted off, not a single glance backward. Aedyn had no way of knowing whether they'd heed his advice, but he felt fuller for having given it.

He plucked the amethyst shard from the soil and pressed it to his chest, imagining the monument it would one day grow into. Amatha might well have condemned the recklessness he'd shown in retrieving it, but he was relieved to have something to present to her parents when the time came to deliver the news. In the meantime, he would do his best to keep his remaining friends on this side of the Veil.

Forcing his mind back to his mission, he tucked the crystal into his boot for safekeeping and sprinted toward the carnage, hoping his personal battle hadn't cost his friends the war.

DEINUA

"I'll clear a path and come back for you."

That's what Kadence had vowed five minutes before, and still, the clamor of combat rained from the tavern above. Sick of cowering in darkness, Deinua forced himself up the basement staircase, clinging to the splintered railing for support. His wounds still screamed and his legs still wobbled, but going down swinging, even feebly, seemed a far nobler fate than waiting for the hordes to find and slaughter him.

The door to the pub proper was barely ajar. It creaked open further at the slightest nudge. Deinua tucked his forelock back before peering through the crack, and his crimson eye adjusted swiftly to the gloom beyond, distilling a series of overlapping shadows into distinct shapes and hues. Augusky corpses littered the floor, some with arrows protruding from their chests, others with gashes carved across their bellies, their intestines curling around them like ribbons. Only one creature remained on its hooves, and Kadence had backed it into a corner.

The hunter had cast his bow aside in favor of an elegant longsword, its hilt and handguard laced with sapphires to match his coat. From appearances, he was just as comfortable brandishing a blade as he had been aiming an arrow at Deinua's chest. The Augusky clumsily parried his attacks, his spear whittling smaller by the strike.

Several yards from the skirmish, a fallen monster stirred. It wrenched an arrow from its side with a grunt, then scrounged a pike from its slaughtered kin. Kadence was too occupied to notice as the creature crept quietly toward him. It would slay him without struggle or hesitation. Mistakes aside, the hunter deserved better.

Deinua drew a bolstering breath. The Iron Claws had confiscated all but his trousers, but he was not entirely defenseless. He threw the door open and hurled himself forward, hitting the skulking Augusky so hard they fell to the floorboards in a tangle. The creature writhed, struggling to turn its pike on its assailant. Deinua wouldn't give it the opportunity.

The creature tipped its head back to screech, veins swelling in its exposed neck. Deinua closed his eyes and sank his fangs in deep.

Deinua had barely tasted mortal blood, but this was noticeably different—cold and thick, more sickly sweet than savory. Still, it quenched the fire in his throat and chased the latent chill from his skin. He drank fiercely, desperately, strength surging through his heavy limbs as it fled those of his prey. By the time the Augusky fell still, he felt sturdier and sharper than ever before. Sharp enough to realize how monstrous his indulgence must have appeared from the outside.

He rose, swiping his sleeve across his chin before turning to see how Kadence fared. The hunter had successfully felled his foe—some time ago, given the terrified expression on his face.

Deinua probably ought to have been embarrassed, but he felt only mild offense.

"Oh, don't you dare play pious!" he snapped, waving flippantly toward the creature Kadence had just slain. That sword of his must have been duller than it looked, given the ragged edges of the Augusky's severed neck.

He could practically see the conclusion settling over the captain, comforting as it was unpleasant: this new world had made monsters of them both. Any judgements cast between them were bound to bounce back. "You've got a little..." Kadence mimicked wiping a smudge from the corner of his mouth.

Deinua echoed the gesture, and his thumb came away crimson. "Better?"

The hunted nodded in the most rigid, insincere manner possible. Deinua glanced down to find a burgundy tendrils stretching over his collarbone and winding down his torso.

There would be no solving that one. Frankly, there were more urgent matters to fret over.

Having apparently realized the same, Kadence retrieved his bow from the counter and made for the exit behind the bar, bidding Deinua to follow.

When Deinua had first heard whispers of Ebensburg's iron wall, he'd pictured elegant filigree scrollwork, like that which often wreathed manors in illustrations of mortal architecture. The reality was a twenty-foot tall monstrosity woven from five distinct layers of blackened metal and topped with vicious spikes. The mere sight of it churned Deinua's stomach and stoked phantom fires around his wrists.

"The district has always been well guarded," Kadence explained as they pressed through the cloud of civilians gathered beside the gates. "It was a simpler thing before, but the council has put a lot of effort into strengthening it recently. If they'd spent half as much effort into protecting the neighboring districts, it would have bolstered comradery and slowed our foes on an occasion like this. I tossed them the suggestion months ago, and it failed to find purchase. I suspect it will land by morning."

A troop of eight hunters Deinua had never met before were shepherding civilians from one district to the next. They wore scarlet jackets, rather than blue, but the silver stripes on their shoulders marked them well enough. They looked on, hands on their hilts, as each supplicant pressed a palm to iron, only granting passage when they were satisfied by the lack of steam sizzling flesh. They raised their weapons at the sight of Deinua, not that he blamed them, given he was wearing more blood spatter than clothing. At a command from Kadence, they lowered their weapons and stepped aside. Apparently, the captain's influence bled beyond the confines of his appointed troop.

Two sharp turns and a short stroll later, they arrived at an imposing estate pressed flush against the border. The walls were painted the same striking blue as Kadence's jacket, with dove-gray borders and tasteful stained-glass windows. The iron fence surrounding the garden was far daintier than that which they'd just passed through, though it, too, was guarded. Urith and Rictor shared a bewildered glance before waving their captain and his company through.

Despite the manor's spacious layout, there was little space left for walking through it. Hunters in coats of every color bustled through its many chambers and halls, hefting armfuls weapons and supplies, and a fair number of hearty civilians had been added to their ranks. From what Deinua picked up of their scattered conversations, they'd begun to organize by skill and experience—fighters with fighters, medics with medics, the untrained but eager with whoever was willing to take them.

"We have no way of knowing whether the walls will hold," Kadence explained as he ushered Deinua up the steep spiral stairs of an eastern tower. "Should they fall, our only hope lay in holding our ground until sunrise. The Augusky have strength and magic on their side, but we have numbers. If everyone who can wield a weapon takes one up, we might actually stand a chance."

The odds were abysmal, but Deinua decided against saying as much aloud. If the occasion called for a fight, he'd throw himself into it. Hopefully, the troop had stored his pike nearby, but he could literally fight tooth and nail in its absence, now that the wounds from his capture were healing. The sting itself had all but vanished during his impromptu feast, and the marks left by his bindings had faded from rage red to petal pink. He doubted it was a coincidence.

They emerged onto the topmost balcony and were greeted by a group of archers. Deinua stared right past the hunters to the ruined remains of Wiltshire that smoldered in the distance. That flames could be seen at all from this distance spoke to their ferocity, and the charcoal plumes they spilled into the starless night looked thick enough to choke on. Small herds of Augusky could be seen pursuing unlucky stragglers through the alleys, but the bulk of the Procession surged down the central street at an alarming pace, trailing death and destruction.

Deinua covered his hemlock eye, fixing his crimson on the encroaching mob. His focus shifted so swiftly it nearly threw him off balance. Roughly two-hundred strong, the swarm was smaller than he'd expected, but their murderous zeal and the bloody slaver that dripped from their sneers sent a shiver through him. More frightful, even, was the luminous figure that drifted at their front, deathly pale with a searing violet eyes and a legion of spite-dark goblins at her feet.

"What's *that* doin' here?" Warrick's growl jarred Deinua's focus back to the balcony. "We've made a mission of slayin' fae, not—"

"Mind your station, Warrick." Kadence's glare hovered on Warrick before sweeping over the remaining archers. "Deinua is here to help us, and you will be treated as a member of the troop. Is that clear?"

The hunters saluted, though the smallest among them did so with an enormous scowl. Deinua scowled right back for more than one reason.

Mari had traded her ragged blue jacket for his emerald, and the vest and shirt beneath it looked familiar, too. Worse, she wore the ensemble well, despite dimensions which ought to have drowned her.

Deinua thrust out an upturned palm, offended by both the jacket and its usurper. "Hand it over."

The girl wrapped the garment tighter around her waist, her glare barely visible beneath the brim of her flat cap. "Fight me for it!"

"Mari, give the damned jacket back; Deinua, pick more important battles." Kadence rubbed his temples. "We do not have time for this nonsense!"

Mari muttered curses Deinua had never heard before as she slipped the jacket free, made a show of wadding it up, and tossed it his way. They could —and most likely *would*—squabble over what remained of the outfit later, provided they survived the night.

Deinua donned the jacket immediately, buttoning it up to his chin. Now that his dinner's blood had begun to crust and flake away, the sight of it had become mildly unnerving—an artless facsimile of Augusky battle sigils. The Iron Claws surely felt the same, but for the moment, the monsters beyond the wall demanded more attention than the one lurking beneath his skin.

With the Procession steadily encroaching, Ebensburg's gates slammed shut. The *clang* of metal doors rattled Deinua's bones despite the distance, and the cries of those trapped outside it shook something deeper. The outcry lasted only a few seconds before the remnants scattered. Only a few hungry beasts broke away to give chase. The rest settled behind Yana as she came to a stop, watching closely as she produced a strange stone from thin air, peridot light pulsing at its core.

Kadence slid his bow from his back. "That's the Ghost Witch, correct?"

Deinua nodded numbly. He'd never glimpsed Yana in person before, but he knew her well enough by reputation. The same went for the spirits trapped in that stone of hers. The toadstool ring kept them from nearing his family cottage, but they'd passed through the surrounding woodlands more than once. The gashes they carved might have made decent trails to travel by, were it not for all the corpses they left behind, eerily unmarred. Hinds and badgers and unfortunate fae turned brittle and empty, like fly husks left to dangle from spiderwebs.

The Sluagh feasted on feelings of fear and agony, but cared nothing for the meat that encased them.

"I suggest you slay her swiftly." His voice rasped over the lump in his throat. "Once she unleashes those spirits, our odds of seeing the sunrise will take a drastic plunge."

Kadence notched an arrow and aimed it at Yana, instructing the other archers to do the same. "Ready..."

A dozen bowstrings stretched taught.

"Aim ..."

The archers held their breath.

"Fire!"

A volley rained down, and several yellow eyes blinked out. Deinua caged a breath as he waited for Yana to teeter and fall, for red to blossom across her chest and her violet eyes to go dark.

Instead, her glare flared all the brighter, lifting toward the balcony. A sinister grin sliced between her gaunt cheekbones, promising pain and misery.

So, she was more ghost than witch, at least for a time. Luckily, Deinua knew a certain spindly spellcaster who'd prepared him for that exact problem.

He rummaged through his pockets for the vial Tawny had gifted him that morning, hoping Mari hadn't been foolish enough to discard it. The lid had come loose and the glass was greased slick, but he muttered a prayer of thanks as he pulled it free. Enough blackthorn oil remained to coat a single arrow.

He turned hopeful eyes to Kadence. "How good is your aim?"

BRANNON

Ghastly light spilled from Yana's host stone, growing brighter as it spiraled skyward. Brannon watched, numb, as shrieking spirits appeared in the haze, eager to unleash their chaos on the uptight nobility beyond the wall.

Under any other circumstances, Brannon might have let it happen. The district housed several bastards he'd have happily seen slaughtered, Father

Beaus chief among them, but Yana was the better target by far, and he might never have another chance to unmake her.

Aedyn had vanished, predictably enough. Brannon had scanned the surrounding Augusky several times for a crimson sunburst, finding only scarlet smears and simple patterns. Since the prince had seen fit to wander off rather than signal the attack, as planned, Brannon would just have to take matters—and daggers—into his own hands.

The crowd provided cover as he poured blackthorn oil over his *Aras Tosc*, and again when he slunk forward, blades trembling. He'd long thought poison a coward's weapon, but if this tincture could truly bind Yana to a physical form, he would only be evening the odds between them. A predatory calm meted his steps, confining his rage to his belly like coals in a furnace. With his target in sight and his daggers in hand, he was not some fickle inferno sparked by the careless actions of others, but the smoke that rose from the wreckage, heavy and dark.

He would choke the life from Yana's lungs if it was his final act this side of Hell.

The swarm gave Yana an inconveniently wide berth, repelled as they were entranced by the forces she controlled. Empty cobbles stretched for nearly twenty feet between the Augusky and the Ghost Witch and her goblins. If he meant to attack now, his first strike needed to land true. There would be no chance for a second.

He lingered for a moment at the front of the crowd, calculating distance and direction. Assassinations were a delicate artform. Victory did not favor the cautious, yet perfection could not be rushed. He would suffer a few goblin bites no matter what, but he'd endured as much before. What he couldn't face a second time was failure.

Before he could settle on an angle, a hail of arrows rained down from somewhere beyond the wall. They passed through both Yana and her minions with a series of dull *plinks*, but where the Ghost Witch did not so much as flinch, the iron arrowheads tore her minions to ribbons. Their frenzied shrieks rang loud and shrill as they dissolved to wisps of sable smoke, spiraling up into the night and staining the cobblestones black with umbral blood.

Brannon could not have justified wasting the opening.

"This one's for you, Lydia," he breathed, rushing forward. It would likely be the last message he ever sent skyward.

He was heartbeats away when Yana turned to face him. Though her violet eyes widened with shock, her smug smile did not waver. She lowered her host stone, and its light dimmed the moment she lifted a sallow hand from its surface. Power, silver as starlight, crackled across her fingers, pooled in her palm, and leapt forward in a single, brilliant beam.

A force like lightning sent Brannon sprawling, and the world went white.

"The night is not eternal, though it may stretch far too long,
Don't give up on the sunrise in the moments before dawn."

CHAPTER 30
HOLD FAST
ELWYN

asta spooled a lock of Elwyn's hair around her finger and gave it a sharp tug. The moment the strands snapped free, they reverted from muddy brown to their natural black.

"As I suspected." Sasta flicked the hair to the floor. "What I can't fathom is how you conjured glamour. Your kind have no natural gifts, and I'm not acquainted with spellwork that mimics Maithe magic. Let us make a deal, shall we?" Her lips curled back in a sneering grin. "Tell us how you managed this illusion, and we'll deliver a swift death, relatively speaking. Let's start the bidding at twenty-five minutes..."

Elwyn snarled, cautiously dipping her fingers beneath her boot cuff. With her dagger pinned beneath a heavy hoof and her right arm dangling loose from its socket, any fight she started would be unfair, but if Luatha didn't return with help, and soon, she had no other options.

"Thirty minutes." Sasta's ear flicked in time with her ruler's tapping hoof. "Don't make me stretch it to forty. You'll be out of teeth and nails by then, and we'll have to start on the skin. I've made a game of peeling as much as I can in a single, unbroken patch. Once, I made it from soles to sternum without any unsightly tearing."

"Oh, just get on with it, Sasta!" Mailair threw open a shuttered window, allowing acrid smoke and anguished screams to drift over the sill. "We're missing out on the mayhem!"

"Very well." Sasta flourished a wave, presenting Elwyn as a gift. "I humbly suggest you start with the eyes. Disguised or not, there is so much *fight* behind them. I can only assume they'll taste delicious."

Elwyn's fingers brushed iron tines.

"If only that was an option," Mailair sighed. "The first mortal I glimpsed was shorter, with yellow hair. Unless I snap its twiggy little spine, I cannot harm another until the Procession has passed. Perhaps if *someone* had thought to alter the rules before they were penned in blood, our house could actually embrace the chaos the Shadows intended for us, but *nooooo*." They glared at the skull atop their scepter spear. "Honestly, Athrú, what were you thinking?"

Sasta drew a slow breath. It seemed even *she* found her ruler's temperament grating at times. "For all we know, this is the same mortal," she tried, giving Mailair an unwise portion of her attention. "If she has truly mastered glamour, we cannot trust—"

Elwyn struck forward, driving the fork into the pit of Sasta's knee The beta stumbled back, bleating, as blood bubbled from the wound. Elwyn grabbed *Gelah* and rolled to the side, narrowly avoiding a kick to the skull. She leapt to her feet with her blade raised at the ready, suddenly grateful for the ambidexterity the Greyscale had forced upon her. Now if only she hadn't rolled herself right into a corner.

"So, this toy knows a few tricks, after all." Mailair snickered, ochre eyes flashing with delight. "Break it for me, won't you Sasta?"

The beta grunted, steam hissing from her fingers as she wrenched the fork from her knee. She was about to cast the utensil aside when Mailair clucked their tongue, kicking her fallen spear across the room.

"This weak little rag doll landed a strike on *you*, my lauded beta," the ruler hissed. "Such a silly, perfectly preventable blunder merits discipline, my pet. Now, to choose a fitting torment..." They twisted their tuft of a beard into a spike before breaking into a giddy grin. "I know! Use the fork."

Sasta stiffened, eyes dropping to her blistered fingers. "But—"

"Do you no longer love me, Sasta?" Mailair's glee vanished, displaced by a measured chill. "All this time, I thought your loyalty unwavering, yet when a trivial tradition prevents me from enjoying the rite I put weeks into planning, you deny my simple request for entertainment." They shook their head, bronze horns scraping the wall behind them. "If you cannot obey a simple command, perhaps you should be stripped of yours. Without your rank, you'll be just another member of the harem. I'm sure the others will show you the same kindness you've shown them all these decades."

Sasta swallowed heavily, dipping her chin in deference. "Your will is mine, Mailair."

The beta winced, the fork trembling in her grasp as she took aim. Elwyn had seen that same broken fealty—boundless, brazen, and entirely unrequited—seared into the agents the father pretended to favor. Sasta would rather lose her hand than disappoint Mailair.

Elwyn shifted her weight to her toes, prepared to parry whatever feeble strike Sasta ventured. The beta struggled to support herself on her wounded leg as the other pawed at the floorboards and she lowered her massive horns. She would wield the fork, as Mailair demanded, but it was not her only weapon.

Sasta charged forward. Elwyn dove to the right, extending one leg to sweep her opponent's ankle. The impact sent a tremor to her knee. Mailair burst into bleating laughter when their beta toppled into the wall, denting in the plaster. She righted herself swiftly, nostrils flaring.

Before either combatant could take another step, a violet blur streaked between them, headed straight for Mailair. Luatha tugged the ruler's ears and poked at their eyes, proving a sufficient distraction, and not for the ruler alone. With Sasta's attention divided between the piskie and Elwyn, it was easy for Tawny to creep up behind her, hunting knife in hand. The witchling landed a few solid slices before Sasta whirled, snarling, and chased her into the hall.

Mailair was trying to fend off Luatha with clumsy swings of their scepter-spear. Elwyn dodged them easily, slamming *Gelah's* pommel into their temple. The Augusky's head smacked on the windowsill as they slumped to the floor. Elwyn held her breath for a moment, but the ruler didn't stir.

Luatha chirped a cheer.

"With Mailair down, our victory is almost guaranteed,
Because the witchling saved your skin, you'd best repay the deed."

Elwyn would, but she was a better fighter with her parts in place.

Having sustained dozens of such injuries before, she knew exactly how to twist, how to stretch. Her shoulder popped back into the socket, and fevered pain skittered down her arm and back. It melted to a static buzz as she rushed from the room, dagger clenched in her off hand.

She burst into the hall right as Sasta disarmed Tawny, sending the hunting knife clattering down the staircase. Calico braids brushed the floor as the Augusky tensed to charge.

Elwyn hooked an arm around Sasta's neck and grappled her waist with her legs. She leaned to the left right as the Augusky tossed her head back, narrowly avoiding impalement as a pale horn scraped down her arm. It was difficult to keep her grip on a bucking monster, let alone hold her dagger steady enough for a killing strike. Rot spread in tendrils from the few shallow cuts she landed, weaving night-dark spiderwebs beneath sallow skin. Sasta screamed, ramming shoulder-first into the wall. The *crack* of Elwyn's rib cut her scream short, and sparks consumed her vision. Somehow, she managed to slice Sasta's neck as she fell breathless to the floor. The Augusky collapsed with a gargled groan, shuddering once before falling still. Blackened blood welled around her, seeping into Elwyn's cloak and tangling her hair.

Pain lanced her side as she struggled to her feet, bringing her surroundings into sudden focus. Tawny hovered feet away, a hesitant arm outstretched.

"Get...Mailair," Elwyn croaked, tasting copper. The witchling started down the hall but was intercepted by a frantic piskie.

"Follow me and swiftly, for we have no time to waste,
The Prince-Oft-Princess-Always-Menace is getting away!"

Adrenaline numbed Elwyn's wounds and lent strength to her limbs. Next thing she knew, she was leaning over a windowsill, straining to parse shapes from shadows.

Sure enough, Mailair was stumbling down the alley below, their staggered sway betraying a sound concussion.

Elwyn threw her leg over the sill, glancing back at Tawny. "Head to Ebensburg as fast as your feet can carry you. I'll meet you there as soon as I can."

"We're not supposed to split up," the witchling reminded her.

"The plan is shot," Elwyn hissed, preparing to jump. "We weren't supposed to take this long, so now we'll have to improvise. I swear on

Gelah I'll deliver Mailair to you alive, but I need you to do your part, and swiftly."

Tawny's slight shoulders drooped, but she managed a feeble smile. "Should we give the signal?"

Aedyn had taught them a series of movements he could sense easily through his glamour link, to be performed only when they'd captured their target.

Elwyn nodded, certain she'd see the mission through. "The moment my feet touch the ground."

AEDYN

By the time Aedyn pushed his way to the front of the Procession, Yana had already reached Ebensburg's gates and was idling with her host stone in hand. She hadn't yet begun the spectral assault, having been distracted, but the object of her ire was not comforting in the least.

Brannon lay sprawled on the cobbles midway between the Ghost Witch and the swarm, smoke curling from a blackened wound. His chest rose and fell with a pained flutter, eyes twitching behind closed lids. Aedyn's racing heart plunged straight to his gut. His friend had attacked too early, and the blame lay on him for wandering off.

"Whyever would you attempt such a terrible thing?" Yana tilted her head, glaring down at the man she assumed was an Augusky. "I've been nothing if not a benevolent ally. I seek no throne, no crown, no scepter. I've asked only for loyalty, and yet you treat me as a tyrant." She shook her head, snowy locks twisting like serpents in an unfelt wind. "I cannot allow this behavior to go unpunished; I'm sure you understand."

She clenched her host stone tight, and its light spilled skyward with an audible *hissssss*. The spirits began to take on shape, their desperation made plain by haunting wails and grasping claws. Soon, she would order them to devour Brannon's spirit, just as they'd devoured Amatha's. Aedyn would not lose another to their hunger.

He threw himself between the witch and her target, allowing most of his glamour to fade. He kept only the slightest illusory bands around his fingers, tethers to those friends who still fought beyond sight. Yana's focus shifted to him, and the host stone's glow dwindled ever-so-slightly.

"One of the Daoine Maithe?" she remarked, tilting her head. "I've had several unusual encounters this week, and I'm nowhere near dense enough to assume they're unrelated. Tell me, light-fae, what exactly have I done to garner such attention? I've never once set foot in the Light Realms, and I somehow doubt you've been residing in the Wilds for long."

"You destroy things, Yana." Aedyn took a shaky step forward, wondering whether Amatha had felt equally terrified when she'd made that same march. "I'm not speaking only of the realms you've ruined, but of the lives you've stolen and the hearts you've shattered. You've doused some of the most brilliant lights to ever grace this Shadow-damned world, and for what?" He spun with arms extended, waving at the wreckage that smoldered all around them. "Can you honestly tell me this hellscape you've conjured is worth it?"

Yana's smug smile faded, but the light in her eyes flared that much brighter. "Unhappy with the world I created?" she asked, voice splintering into many. "I'll gladly remove you from it."

Her nails cracked against the host stone. Peridot sparks climbed her arms. The wind around her swelled to a howling tempest. Within heartbeats, the faces in the haze took on detail—frantic eyes, withered lips, gnashing teeth. Each screamed of their sorrows as long as they could before another formed behind them, jaws stretched to swallow them whole.

For a heartbeat, Aedyn was back in Fómhar, watching helplessly as those spirits stormed down on his closest friend. Somehow, the memory that should have cowed him strengthened his resolve.

Amatha had dedicated her life to protecting those she loved, and she'd given it up for the same reason. While burning prayers and burying shards were touching acts of remembrance, he could think of no purer way to honor her than by following her example.

Aedyn stared up, unflinching, as the Wailing Wind came crashing down. The force struck him from every angle at once, turning his world to ice and flame as he crumbled to the cobbles. It was nothing like the bone-scraping agony he'd suffered in the shellicoat's belly, but rather a spiritual evisceration so thorough he found himself begging the Sluagh to strip his skin instead. Hundreds of lifetimes swept through him in an instant, each more horrific than the last.

One heartbeat, he was a beast of a man, peddling poisons to those too frail to withstand them. The next, he was a withered woman, spilling the blood of babes to add their years to her own. The next, he was a bitter brute with a past full of ghosts and a future paved in bones, savoring each drop of sorrow he inflicted with his sharp smile and dull knife.

The memories overlapped like viper scales, coating Aedyn's consciousness until he could tell them apart from his own.

You're just like us, they whispered, though they never paused their screeching. *You're one of us. You belong to us. Come home to us...*

A note of truth tinged every word. He'd been just as wretched as the Slaugh, hadn't he? If not as cruel, then surely as calloused. He'd squandered every blessing he'd been given, ever casting familiar comforts aside for the newest, the nearest, the next.

How many nights had his father paced himself dizzy, fretting for his safety? How many hearts had he shattered in pursuit of empty pleasures? How much damage had he wrought in blazing through life like a wildfire, ever consuming and ever consumed?

Aedyn saw no point in delaying the inevitable. He was about to let the wind sweep him away when the strangest sensation sang through his fingers—a series of coordinated tugs, glamour woven and undone—and a spark of hope ignited. Elwyn and Tawny were still out there, still committed to the mission. Damned or not, he owed it to them to see it through.

He channeled what remained of his strength into his trembling fingers. He'd never sculpted light from such a distance or under such intense duress, but the motions flowed through him, instinctive as ever. A twist here, a flourish there, and light reformed at his command. He could only hope the shapes held beyond his imagination. The Slaugh taunted him all the while, but their words no longer found purchase. Aedyn had summoned a few memories more, bright enough to dispel whatever darkness they hurled at him. Drowsy childhood mornings whiled away racing paper frogs with Learo or crafting illusions under his father's careful instruction. Afternoons spent stirring up youthful mischief at Amatha's side, and evenings spent cleaning up the resulting messes. Nights passed playing games and trading tales with Elwyn, relishing each little laugh he drew from her.

Yes, he'd been selfish, arrogant, and vain, but he'd also been *good*, and he was growing better by the day. If he lived to see a few more, he might eventually become worthy of the way his friends looked at him. The way Elwyn looked at him.

No matter what the Sluagh whispered, he was not one of them, he did not belong to them, and he would never join their wicked ranks. If they consumed his soul for his defiance, so be it. Those wretched spirits had loved only themselves, but Aedyn had loved many.

And they needed him to hold on a little longer.

"Strange, how time is wasted seeking wealth, prestige, and fame,
A minute is worth more than all the gold the world contains."

CHAPTER 31
END OF AN ERA
YANA

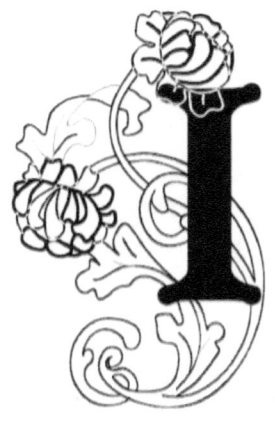

'm doing you a favor," Yana whispered, watching the light-fae's silhouette writhe at the center of the Wailing Wind. "It is better to perish with purpose than to live forever with none..."

It must have been sheer agony, drowning in so much sorrow at once. Yana had only ever tasted the Slaugh's madness—sipping just enough to trick her shattered mind into believing itself among peers—and each heartbeat she'd weathered of their suffering had felt like a lifetime. The Maithe man had been enduring that same torment for nearly half a minute.

Surely, it felt like an eternity.

Arrows whistled through the air behind her, but she didn't bother glancing back. Those foolish archers had clearly learned nothing from the first volley they'd unleashed. So long as her form hovered between spirit and flesh, no earthly weapon could—

An arrow bit her square between the shoulders. Though it passed clean through her, a tingling sensation swelled in its wake, frigid and dark as the sky above. The chill spread swiftly, deeply, growing denser by the blink.

Blackthorn oil?

The thought barely struck when several arrows did the same, grazing her freshly formed skin and *plinking* off the agate in her hands. The host stone jarred from her fingers and skipped across the cobblestones. It would have landed among the swarm had the Augusky not instinctively skittered back, frightened by the relic and the spirits bound to it.

Freed from her command, the spirits retreated swiftly the stone's core, leaving their victim trembling in the street. Though pale and trembling, the Maithe man was still breathing just fine. The glassy haze fled his eyes the moment they fell on the host stone, and he began to writhe toward it. Panic propelled Yana forward. True fae could not wield such magic, but she would not allow him to best her before so a massive and malicious an audience.

She was halfway to her target when the crowd stirred and parted, allowing Mailair to trot through their midst. Judging from their hobbling gait, they'd gotten themselves injured after running off mid-march. It was a wonder their subjects didn't rush them in a mad grab for the bramble throne. Then again, the Procession had only been underway for a couple hours, and it has already gone awry more than once. Correcting its course would have taken a sturdy spirit.

Mailair reached the stone before the Maithe, who hung his head in defeat the moment the Augusky ruler snatched it up. To their credit, Mailair hardly flinched as the relic's malice nipped their bare fingertips. They turned it over in their hands before grinning at Yana, a challenge glinting in their ochre eyes.

"Hand it over." Yana proffered an upturned palm. "I'm sure you're tempted to turn this twist to your advantage, but any such attempt would be a waste of time. You've promised your public access to Ebensburg, that relic is the only means of delivering, and it can only be wielded by those who possess *mortal* souls."

"You have a soul?" Mailair's voice pitched far higher than usual, though the tone was strangely familiar. "Whomever did you steal it from?"

Chuckling at the quip, the Maithe man rocked to his knees. At the snap of his fingers, Mailair's form began to waver, his colors muting and melting before scattering like dandelion seeds. In his place stood a wisp of a mortal, clad in tights and a tattered tunic. Her yellow curls had been shorn short, and a bitter scowl twisted lips once swift to smile, but Yana knew those brilliant emerald eyes all too well.

"Tawny?" Yana's heart lurched, torn between relief and terror. "It can't be. You...you died."

"You failed," the girl replied.

That wasn't possible. Yana had felt Tawny's spirit flee the material plane, her aura flitting off to leave a dark world that much darker. Even now, she could not scent the girl's spirit. Either the spider curse she'd summoned had somehow smothered Tawny's light without slaying her, or...

A pendant dangled from Tawny's neck. A simple hag stone, glazed in pear juice. It was among the very first wards Yana had taught the girl to craft.

So, she hadn't failed. Not at everything.

The crowd crept forward with spears leveled, having finally grasped the situation. Sensing them without seeing them, Tawny thrust the host stone skyward. Peridot light flared from within the amber, and the mob scrambled back, spitting curses.

Yana had never been so proud.

"You wield that well," she said with a bittersweet smile, "for one who's never known true malice."

Tawny's glare grew colder. "I know plenty of malice, thanks to you."

The words found purchase where so many arrows had failed. There would be no reconciliation, no repentance, no redemption. Only one of them would walk away from this meeting, and not unscathed.

Instinct sparked through Yana as she watched the Sluagh writhe forth at the girl's command. Determined though Tawny was, she was also feeble. It would have been easy to rip the stone from her fingers and turn the Wailing Wind on her in full. Then, Yana could complete her mission, secure the fear of her Unseelie neighbors, and buy herself another lifetime to spend fretting over how to hoard a few more.

But she was tired. And she was lonely.

And she was *sorry*.

The spirits poured from their amber prison, screaming of the torments they would soon impart. Yana fixed her feet on the cobbles, anchoring her body as her mind slipped backward through the years. She'd wasted far too much time fighting for more, but she'd still managed to craft a handful of memories worth savoring—fleeting hours spent chasing fireflies through the fog, prepping the cauldron for potion lessons, sitting hearthside with her daughter on her knee and, together, seeking faces in the flames.

Basking in the glow of those simple moments, Yana closed her eyes, outstretched her arms, and embraced the fate she'd earned a thousand times over.

TAWNY

Yana hesitated.

After decades spent fighting to extend her life, she paused in the very moment it was most at risk. Bewildering as the decision was, Tawny would not allow it to sway her. This opportunity would not present itself a second time.

She squeezed her fingers around the host stone, fighting tears as malicious magic seared her skin. The Wailing Wind roared, but its rage was a whisper compared to her own. She channeled every ounce of that ire into the amber, coaxing the spirits brighter, louder, fiercer. They descended at her bidding, drowning Yana in a torrent of screams and sorrow.

It was over swiftly.

Too swiftly for the woman who'd bartered her way into powers most couldn't dream of, who'd turned her own execution into a doorway to realms beyond mortal reach. Too swiftly for the monster who'd ruined two worlds with a single spell, who'd stolen her every breath from the lungs of others and wasted them spitting curses like prayers. Too swiftly for the mother who'd sheltered Tawny her whole life through, who'd crafted salves to mend her every bruise and carved wards into her headboard to keep nightmares away.

Too swiftly. And not nearly swiftly enough.

Tawny knew the exact moment her mother's soul left the world, felt it melt into the terrible tempest she'd so long evaded. She let the storm rage a minute more before drawing them back into their prison.

It was all so strangely instinctual—casting them out, calling them in—but it took a toll on her, or so she wanted to believe. How pleasant it might have been to blame the spirits for the ache in her chest.

Tawny had loathed Yana, hated her, despised her with every bit of her being. She'd also loved her dearly. She would bear the weight of her once-mother's absence for the rest of her days, and there wasn't a soul in the world with whom she could commiserate on the matter.

"They'll be arriving any second now." Aedyn stumbled to her side, a reminder the mission was not yet complete. A touch of his color had returned, but there was no light in the smile he offered her. "Are you ready?"

Could anyone ever be? He gestured toward the nearest alley as two figures emerged from the shadows. Mailair limped forward at the bidding of Elwyn's crescent blade, their horns severed near their skull and their arms dangling, rot-black, at their sides.

The crowd burst into scandalized chatter at the sight of their disgraced ruler. It was one thing to die at the hands of a foe, but to be *captured*?

Mailair might as well have been a mortal.

Upon glimpsing the host stone in Tawny's hands, the Augusky ruler braced their hooves against the street. A sound kick from Elwyn sent them stumbling forward, landing in a grudging bow.

They turned wide eyes to their gawking subjects. "W-what are you waiting for?" they sputtered. "Kill them, you cowards!"

"You might want to save your breath." Tawny tapped her fingers against the amber, eliciting sparks of searing magic. There was a pleasant note to the pain—power, raw and unfiltered. "You don't have many left."

"If you're hoping this little show will make an impact, it isn't going to happen," Mailair spat, forcing a gruff laugh. "The moment you turn your back to that crowd, they'll tear you to pieces, and our revels will proceed as though you never intervened!"

"Interesting prediction." Tawny's tone was unnervingly calloused, even to her. Perhaps the host stone was not all she'd inherited from Yana. "Allow me to make a prophecy of my own: mere minutes from now, the Procession will come to an early end, the mob you've summoned will skitter back to their dens with their tails tucked, and not another drop of mortal blood will hit the ground before dawn."

Mailair rasped a mirthless laugh. "The Procession is *my* domain, child. I am the High Judge of Chaos, the ruler of the Shifting Wilds, keeper of the Bramble Palace. Only I can call the Procession off, and I would die before bowing to the whims of some pathetic mortal!"

"That all changes the moment you die," Tawny said with a smirk.

"Don't be a fool." The Augusky's eyes narrowed. "Only a child of the Wilds can claim the bramble throne."

"Perfect." Tawny raised her voice, turning to face the swarm. "You heard it from your ruler's own lips! Any child of the Wilds who slays them will become the new High Judge of Chaos, and the Procession of Autumn will proceed or dissolve at their bidding." She hefted her host stone as proof of the claim she was about to make. "I was brought here as an infant, having formed no memories of the mortal's world. I sprouted beneath the same flickering canopy as you. My first steps were meted to the music of the Wilds. My first words praised its endless dance. I've spent my life unraveling the secrets buried in the churning soil, tangled in the boughs of wandering oaks and in the thorny hearts of the brambles. Surely, I am as much a child of the Wilds as anyone."

The Augusky swore and murmured amongst themselves, but not a single soul disputed the claim. They wouldn't have had a hoof to stand on if they'd tried. Not one of their laws defined what it meant to be a child of the Wilds. Its potential applications were as capricious as those who'd penned it.

"You won't last a week," Mailair hissed, trembling.

She'd last four, actually. Daulle had recited the rules often when he schemed against Mailair. New rulers were granted a month of peace in which to establish a following. Then the assassination attempts began.

Just thinking of her Augusky friend cast a somber pall on the occasion.

"I don't suppose you remember Daulle?" she whispered, stepping close so only Mailair could hear her. "Athrú's eldest? He'd have been only a whelp when you killed his father, and he spent the decade since cooking up revenge. Unfortunately, he couldn't be here to serve it." Exhausted and embittered, she raised her host stone one final time. She had no anger left to feed it, but sorrow would serve just as well. "Consider me his champion."

Again, the spirits flooded forward, filling the night with shrill screams and ghastly light. The Augusky watched in silence as their ruler was torn to ribbons. They cowered as a new one was born.

*"Craft carefully the melodies that flutter from your throat,
Some verses echo long after the singer's final note."*

CHAPTER 32

PRELUDES AND CODAS

DEINUA

sunrise bled across the sky as Deinua wandered through what remained of Wiltshire, Kadence marching silently beside him. They'd exchanged several apologies in the hours since Tawny called off the Procession, but not a single one had landed right. Eventually, they stopped speaking altogether.

The fires had been put out, and the repairs were well underway. Deinua recognized several faces from among the recovery team. Rickon and Urith had set up a medics station and were tending the wounded alongside more practiced peers. Warrick had hauled a wagonload of water barrels into the square and was distributing drinks to the dazed and despondent. Mari stood proud atop a fallen statue, barking orders to the crew of scouts that sifted through the nearby rubble. She stuck her tongue out as Deinua passed by, striking a pose that flaunted her stolen vest and blouse.

Deinua waved off the slight in a *you-can-keep-it* way, provoking a startled scowl. She'd find something new to squabble over the next time Deinua visited town. Assuming he ever found reason to do so.

Little remained of Wiltshire's wall—a fallen log here, a splintered plank there. Beyond the wreckage, the Wilds waltzed, as fierce and fiery as ever.

Deinua had a dreadful hike ahead of him, but he was eager to return to his family. It was about time his mother had reason to chide him for staying out past curfew. His father would pretend to agree, then pat his shoulder the moment she turned her back, as he always had on the rare occasions Deinua acted recklessly. Then there were the house guests, who were due to move on now that they'd accomplished their goals. He wasn't sure how he felt about that.

"I suppose this is goodbye for now." Kadence paused beside the kindling heap that had been the district's gate hours before. "This mess is bound to keep us occupied for a good month or so, and you're more than welcome to join in the effort, should you feel the inkling." He glanced back at the wreckage, or perhaps just away from Deinua. "I can't imagine you'd want to be our lorekeeper now, but you should visit once more after we've grieved our losses long enough to celebrate our wins. These people need to know about the role you played in saving them."

The thought of such attention made Deinua shudder, but he also saw how it could help to correct some of the misunderstandings the mortals held about his kind. Granted, a half-fae lorekeeper could help to resolve the issue on a larger scale. The night had left Deinua drowsy and disenchanted, and though his iron wounds were fading, they would leave scars on his spirit. Even so, he'd *liked* working alongside the Iron Claws. More, he'd liked working alongside Kadence.

"How about we discuss that lorekeeper position one last time over dinner?" Deinua suggested. "Not tonight, of course, given..." he gestured toward the charred skeleton of a brothel, "but we could plan for a week or so out, assuming you can spare the time."

"That depends." Kadence broke into a dimpled grin. "Do you intend to have me over for supper, or over *for supper?*"

Deinua chuckled despite himself. Kadence would get along well with his mother. "You know good and well what I meant!"

"It never hurts to be cautious, but yes, I think I could carve out a few hours."

"Splendid! Are you fond of leeks? I'd like to recreate a number of my mother's recipes, and her garden chowder is absolutely to die for."

"Now, when you say *to die for...*"

Deinua smiled through a sigh. "This is going to become a thing with us, isn't it?"

ELOANA

Oraithvine climbed the palace wall, branching into a ladder at Eloana's bidding. She'd been dreading this climb since Anye had first suggested it, but she could not put it off any longer. Aedyn was due to arrive within the next four days, and her window of opportunity would slam shut behind him.

"We'll be back within the hour," she said to Loenelle, who'd escorted her out onto the palace boughs. It wasn't a particularly dangerous stroll, but she hated being out alone after sunset. "If anyone questions where I've gone, you will find a way to distract them. Am I understood?"

Loenelle's lips pressed into a tight line.

Eloana tuned her thoughts and tugged. *"Loenelle..."*

"I will distract them, *m'lady*."

That honorific was beginning to sound a lot like a swear.

Too nervous to toss out a threat, Eloana dismissed her surly handmaiden and began her ascent. Anye fluttered around her as she rose, adjusting the vine's filigree whorls with a whir of her wings. This trip would have been more easily made from within the palace walls, but the piskie had insisted they keep their business hush. Visitors to the royal wing were extensively questioned and thoroughly logged. Should the conversation go poorly, she did not need the brigadiers whispering of her desperation.

"It will *not* go poorly," she assured herself, grabbing hold of a marble railing. King Aryn was powerful, but he was still Maithe. His light-song would prove pliable as any other.

She hoisted herself onto the royal balcony and took a moment to preen, pinning back the aurous locks that had fallen from her braid and smoothing her golden gown. The garment was full enough to make climbing difficult, but its heavy brocade fabric sang of regality, and its wide bustles concealed the dagger sheathed at her hip, rattling with every step.

It was Anye who'd insisted she bring the blade, though it had proven useless beyond the beauty of its music. Eloana had tried to wield the weapon against Loenelle several times since she acquired it, but it had passed right through the handmaiden's skin, leaving only emotional wounds. The piskie had all but dismissed Eloana's questions on the matter, claiming the treasure's mysteries would reveal themselves in due time.

"Some minds may prove too resolute or difficult to sway,
You'd better be prepared, because one's marching this way."

Anye ducked behind Eloana as the balcony door creaked inward. A gilt rapier flashed beyond the threshold, and eyes of the same hue peered out behind it.

"Eloana?" King Aryn lowered his sword, allowing the door to swing wide. He was still clad in his royal garb, and his smooth, flaxen locks looked as though they'd yet to meet a pillow. "Why are you on my balcony. Perhaps more importantly, *how?*"

Exhaustion shaded the king's eyes, but his light-song was astoundingly robust. Thankfully, it rang in a pleasant timbre.

"This must seem terribly indecorous." Eloana glanced down, scuffing a slippered toe against the sandstone tiles. She'd seen many a court viper get their head lopped off, but mice were often met with pity. "To be honest, I've had trouble sleeping. I've heard tell that Aedyn's set to return any moment now, provided he's still..." She allowed the implication to hover a moment before shaking it away. "At any rate, I thought you might relate. I even thought to bring a chaperone."

She stepped aside, waving Anye forward. The piskie scowled at the unexpected reveal, but she fluttered obediently toward the king, offering an aerial curtsy.

"It's an honor to meet with you, most noble Seelie king,
It's rare that I've encountered one of quite such high esteem."

Judging from Aryn's startled expression, he'd yet to hear of Eloana's new friend. Unsurprising, given his renowned disinterest in gossip.

"The honor is mine." He dipped his head, an amused smile tugging on his lips. "It has been said that your kind choose only the worthiest as your companions, and I am now inclined to believe it. Eloana is perhaps the most talented and prolific lightsinger I've ever known, and a valued member of the Court...even if she occasionally flouts common decorum."

Eloana winced for show. "I hope I haven't offended you, Your Highness. I ought to have requested a formal audience, and I'll be sure to do so in the future."

"That would be most appreciated," Aryn replied as a kettle whistled somewhere behind him. "That said, you've clearly climbed a long way, and

I've been meaning to speak with you for some time. Would you care for a cup of tea?"

"That would be lovely," Eloana said, as confused as she was curious. Though he'd always treated her warmly, the king had never requested an audience with her. Hopefully, his reasons for wanting to speak aligned with her own.

Despite having lived in Samhria for over a century, she'd never visited the royal wing. It looked much as she'd imagined it would—crisp, clean, and understated. The walls had been painted a lush forest green, and ivory rugs stretched across the sleek floorboards. The furnishings could have used a splash or two of color, but Eloana could easily call in a florist, once she and Aedyn inherited the space.

King Aryn led her to his parlor, pulling out one of four oraithvine chairs that ringed the table before dismissing himself to retrieve the kettle. Eloana watched him depart, puzzling over the interaction. She'd heard rumors that the king refused to keep servants, but she hadn't considered they were actually true. With so many subjects clamoring for his favor, why in light's name would he brew his own tea?

Anye alighted on the table, folding her filigree wings.

"Don't let affection stay your hand, should this man disagree,
Never forget it's he who stands 'twixt you and all your dreams."

Eloana stifled the urge to dismiss the piskie outright. She had every reason to feel affection for King Aryn. Her birth parents had provided the best of everything—the finest clothing, the rarest jewelry, the most renowned tutors—but those were not gifts, so much as investments. The moment her betrothal was secured, they'd retreated to the sprawling estate they'd received in payment, and they'd visited on only a handful of occasions since. It was Aryn who'd given her a garden to sculpt to her liking, who'd introduced her at her very first ball, who'd attended her gala performances and had frillrose bouquets delivered to her dressing room after.

Though the Court could be cruel and her betrothed indifferent, the king had shown her nothing but warmth. She refused to view him as an enemy before she'd even attempted to reason with him. "The king might well stand between us and our goals," she said, folding her hands on the table beside the piskie. "But he is a bridge, not an obstacle."

Anye turned up her tiny nose.

"Throw wit like darts, and you might find your aim's a little rough,
Just what, pray tell, will you employ when words are not enough?"

Before Eloana could protest, King Aryn returned to the parlor carrying a polished jade tea set atop a matching platter. He arranged the pieces on the table with the care and precision of a trained attendant, then poured a cup apiece for Eloana and himself. He added a dollop of honey and a splash of milk to his drink before taking his seat. A bowl of sugar lumps rested beside the kettle, but Eloana chose to ignore it. She had never once sweetened her own tea, and she wasn't about to start now.

"I did not mean to come across as perturbed when I first greeted you," Aryn said as he stirred his tea. "If anything, I admire your openness. Few hesitate to seek a healer when it comes to physical ailments, but addressing wounds of the heart takes a precarious balance of courage and humility." He tapped his spoon on the jade rim and set it aside. "I've hardly spoken of Aedyn since his departure, and then only as a monarch embittered by rebellion, never as a father concerned for his son. Creagor has been honest about his worries for Amatha since the very moment he found her letter. Perhaps, if I'd followed his example, I would not be so exhausted as I now appear."

Eloana forced down a predictably bitter sip of tea. It was unbecoming of a Maithe monarch to openly laud a lesser judge. "You have acted according to your station, as we all must," she said.

Aryn's light-song lurched, dropping by a half-step. "It is not a weakness to fear for your loved ones, nor is it improper to seek a sympathetic ear. Is that not why you climbed four stories to speak with me?"

Eloana may have *implied* as much, but she'd only mentioned she'd been dealing with insomnia. The ailment was owed more to fear than grief. It was becoming clear that her entire future relied on her pending union, so if anything happened to Aedyn before they wed—and the odds were high, impulsive as he'd proven—her renown would take a steep and sudden plunge. She would not humor that possibility a moment longer than she had to.

"I can voice my concerns to Aedyn himself upon his return," she said, steering the conversation in a more relevant direction. "For the moment, there is another matter I wish to discuss. In truth, I should have breached this subject long ago, but I was raised to be a patient person, and easily contented. It took the Confluence, with all the shadows it cast, to bring the circumstances into perspective."

"I believe I know where this conversation is headed," King Aryn claimed, his gaze traveling to somewhere distant, unknowable. "Tearan and I were created to harmonize. We were bound to one another before the stars first sang, and I have loved her every second since, no matter how dark, no matter how dire. The Creator knew what he was doing when he arranged the constellations, and I have never once doubted His designs. Likewise, when he assigned me the station of Eternal Ruler, I regarded the edict as an unparalleled honor. I have always delighted in knowing the path laid out before me, in knowing which landmarks wait beyond the next bend and how long it will take me to get there." His smile stuttered, and his timbre darkened. "But I am me, and Aedyn is Aedyn."

The king's sudden change of tone set Eloana on edge. "What are you saying?"

"I am saying that Aedyn is his mother's son," the king said, chuckling sadly. "He inherited her fiery spirit as surely as her eyes. Too long, I have sought to contain that spark for fear of the inferno it might one day become. I was a fool to think he'd ever be content with following a premeditated path, and it has become clear he is not the only one who has suffered for my caution." His gaze shifted to Eloana, brimming with sympathy. "I can no longer ignore the sorrow this betrothal has caused you both. I pray only that you will forgive me for having arranged it."

Eloana's heart leapt to her throat, trilling like a snare drum. "There's nothing to forgive, Your Highness," she said, straining her thoughts to match his light-song. "You were right to say your son was born with a fickle spirit. He will flee any obligation he is not bound to. Aedyn has vowed his future to me, but he never once vowed his *present*—a mistake that can only be rectified by the one who first composed our oaths." She tried to raise his timbre; it delved deeper in revolt. The harder she pulled, the more her own light-song began to slip. "I beg you, wed us straightaway. Then he will have no choice but to love me, and we will both be better off for it!"

The king shook his head, pity welling in his eyes. "There is no magic strong enough to force someone to love you, and attempting as much would result only in resentment. I understand this may seem sudden, but my decision is final. When Aedyn returns, I will be dissolving your betrothal."

Eloana's heart plunged from her throat to her stomach. This meeting had started on a high note; how in Light's name could it have dropped by so many octaves in so few measures?

"You can't do this," she breathed, desperate.

"Do not be disheartened, child." The king's smile returned, more genuine this time. "You will always have a home in Samhria, and if fates can be chosen, you have many futures to choose from. In the time I've known you, your talents have grown to outshine even Enwa's. Keep striving, and you could easily become the greatest lightsinger in Maithe history, perhaps the greatest artist altogether."

"I'm not destined to be an artist!" Eloana shouted, lurching to her feet. "I'm destined to be *queen!*"

Anye whirred her wings, splintering the scream into a hundred interwoven harmonies, and every sprig of oraithvine in the room curled inward. The filigree whorls of King Aryn's chair sliced through his flesh like sutures, dragging him to the floor. His light-song stuttered violently as the pale rug beneath him turned scarlet. Though he could not move a muscle without shredding it, his wide eyes lolled toward Eloana.

"W-why?" he managed before Anye chirped an aria, wrapping a gilded vine around his mouth.

Eloana rushed to kneel by his side,. Tears blurred her vision as she wiped a bloodied tress from his cheek. "I...I didn't mean for this to happen. I would never hurt you on purpose. You are...were..."

There was no getting out of this, was there? If Eloana freed the king, he'd expose her powers and have her thrown from the palace. If she slew him, he would be reborn, and the same scythe would fall a century later.

Anye fluttered forward with a solution.

"There are strict limits to the Creator's gift of endless days,
If his spirit is expelled, there will be nothing left to raise."

"Expel the spirit?" She'd never heard of such a thing, but it sounded blasphemous at best. "As in, removing it from the cycle? How is that even possible?"

The piskie tugged on Eloana's bustle, jostling the blade beneath it.

"You said this once of tears before; I'd switch the phrase around,
If anything's worth killing for, then surely it's a crown."

"Will it be painful?" The piskie didn't answer, but she didn't need to. Eloana had already made her decision.

She tucked her hand between the folds of her gown, drawing the golden blade from its sheath. "How does it work?"

"To wield this wondrous weapon, gift your spirit to the blade,
You'll rouse the dagger's hunger once you offer it a taste."

"A taste of my *spirit*?" The glossy gold crescent reflected Eloana's grimace. "How would I even manage that?"

Anye stuck out her arm and ran a tiny finger across it.

Eloana pressed the blade to her wrist, closed her eyes, and drew it sharply to the right. She winced at the dagger's peculiar bite—duller and colder than she'd imagined. When she opened her eyes, blinding white light spilled from the blade's cryptic runes. Her wrist prickled, and a leaden chill cut to her marrow. Not a single crimson drop beaded her skin, but the dagger had clearly taken *something*, numbing her just enough to douse her remaining reservations.

"A ruler must make sacrifices for the good of their realm." Eloana pressed the dagger to the king's heart. "After serving your kingdom for so many lifetimes, you deserve to move on. Rest assured, both your realm and son are in capable hands."

She plunged the blade hilt-deep in Aryn's chest, and searing light burst from his eyes. She held his gaze until the glow stuttered out, taking his light-song with it.

"For all you know, the path ahead might loop right back around,
So speak your mind, but mind your speech, and don't burn bridges down."

CHAPTER 33

SWEET SORROW

ELWYN

 full day had passed since the Procession of
Autumn, and the pain in Elwyn's side had faded to
a dull throb, flaring only when she shouted or
strained. Crying would likely have stoked the ache
as well, but she didn't care to test that theory.

So, while her friends and the family who'd
hosted them gathered downstairs for one final
feast, she snuck up to the loft to get everything
packed and ready for the return trip. It would
save the others all a bit of work and her a bout of sentiment. Winners, all
around.

Luatha disagreed.

"To run might seem the easy choice, but only at a glance,
If you don't say goodbye, you may not get another chance."

"That's the point," Elwyn muttered. As one practiced in slipping
silently off in the dead of night, the word *farewell* had never graced her
tongue. She imagined it tasted quite bitter.

In her scramble to ignore the piskie's admonitions, she made the
unfortunate decision to check beneath the bed for stray supplies. Her
wounds panged as she crouched low, but they were not half as painful as

spotting Amatha's spare satchel crumpled on the floor. Gemstone badges dotted the suede strap, having been pinned there by the chieftain when her bandolier grew too cluttered to hold them all.

That confirms it, Elwyn thought as she retrieved the bag. *Crying hurts.*

"Is everything alright?"

Elwyn blinked her vision clear before chiding herself and rising to greet Tawny. She must have been in a sorry state if the witchling could creep up behind her undetected.

"Everything's fine," she lied. "It's just dreadfully dusty up here."

Tawny nodded, pretending to believe her. The witchling had changed into strange vestments made of leather and fur, probably to better blend with the kingdom she...*they* had just inherited. In addition to taking Mailair's title, Tawny had also adopted their pronouns. Much like their cropped curls and this new ensemble, the decision suited them.

"I know you're not feeling very social, but I wanted to make sure to give you this." Tawny pulled a potion from her pocket—the same murky brown brew that had brought them to the Wilds. "Aedyn will be taking the leftovers to the palace potionsmiths, so I saved you one in case they're stingy. I've linked it to the woodshed, and Lieri promised to keep the floor swept, so if you ever decide to come back, you won't have to worry about splinters."

Elwyn accepted the potion and tucked it into her cloak pocket. She couldn't imagine ever using it, but she hadn't imagined using the fork Tawny had given her either. Perhaps the witchling had a knack for casual prophecy. Or perhaps they were just thoughtful.

"You could always come back with us, you know," Elwyn said, still perplexed by Tawny's decision to remain in the Wilds. "You don't owe the Augusky anything."

"I do, actually. I've already wielded the authority of the ruler; it would be wrong to cast the burden of the title aside. Besides, this is my *home.*" Tawny smiled as though the word tasted sweet. "As much as I enjoy traveling, I'm not comfortable living anywhere else. And speaking of traveling..." They glared at the travel supplies Elwyn had gathered in a heap. "Why are you packing this all by yourself? You're injured, for Shadow's sake!"

"It's only a cracked rib," Elwyn protested, plucking up a satchel to prove her point. "I've labored a lot harder with far worse injuries, and—"

"Aedyn!" Tawny darted over to the loft's railing to better tattle. "Elwyn keeps trying to clean things!"

"I'm on my way!" Aedyn shouted back, his footsteps racing across the floor below.

Elwyn sighed, fighting a smile as she let the satchel drop to the floor. She was perfectly capable of taking care of herself...but it was nice to know she didn't always have to.

After a bout of good-natured bickering, Elwyn's friends convinced her to join in on the farewell meal. Naturally, Lieri provided a spread fit for a royal banquet, complete with a roast pheasant, stuffed mushroom caps, and three varieties of salad, and she still expected everyone to save room for almond cakes drizzled in caramelized cream.

They filled their plates twice over, with the exceptions of Koa and Deinua, who indulged in only a flute of wine apiece, and Luatha, who plucked her offerings straight from the serving dishes. The meal that should have taken an hour stretched nearly to three, with the diners savoring the food and conversation both.

Deinua didn't want to discuss where he'd gone after delivering his message to the Iron Claws, though he briefly mentioned his contributions to defeating Yana. When Elwyn asked whether his absence involved a certain captain, he chuckled nervously and diverted the conversation to Tawny. For as much as the others fretted over the witchling's fate, they felt confident they'd garner a following before the month of amity ended, and they would use their influence to forge alliances with the Seelie.

When it was clear the crew no longer wished to ruminate on the Procession and its aftermath, Lieri regaled them with a few true stories, including an account of how Brannon, at age seven, had been chased around their farm by a livid goose and hid beneath his bed for two days after. By the end of the tale, Brannon had turned a vivid rose. For once, the hue was owed more to embarrassment than outrage.

Tawny slipped away in the middle of dessert, sparing the remaining travelers one round of glum goodbyes. Deinua more than made up for it with his overwrought farewells, while Lieri insisted they visit again soon and Koa grunted in a manner that was probably an agreement. When it came time to depart, Brannon suggested they step outside for one final glimpse at the Wilds. Elwyn made the walk with her hand on *Gelah's* hilt, half-expecting a trap. The group barely made it down the steppingstone path before the assassin made an unexpected announcement.

"I'm not saying it's forever," he clarified, shifting uncomfortably beneath his colleagues' gawking stares. "And don't pretend you're not relieved to be rid of me!"

"I'm *not* relieved to be rid of you," Aedyn replied with a pout. "That said, I can't say I blame you, either. Were I presented with the chance to connect with the mother I lost, I would leap at it. It's only that I'm going to miss you bitterly."

Brannon bristled, crossing his arms. "This was not an invitation to wax sentimental," he growled. "So you know, when we first met, I deemed you the most frivolous fop in the history of frivolity, and hardly a second passed in which I didn't imagine repurposing your intestines as a garland."

"What I'm hearing is that you've fantasized about me often." Aedyn smirked. "A common condition, and nothing to be ashamed of."

Brannon's glower deepened. "As you just handily demonstrated, you're twice as obnoxious as I first assumed, but for whatever reason, I no longer wish to gut you."

"Pure poetry." Aedyn wiped a false tear from his eye. "Deinua would be envious."

Apparently inspired, Luatha flitted forward to offer a farewell of her own.

"You're as cruel and condescending as a mortal man can get,
But I think that I am truly going to miss your little threats."

"Well, here's one for the road, you sparkling mosquito." Brannon swatted half-heartedly at the piskie. "Clearly, you're the cleverest in the bunch, which means it's your job to look after these other two idiots. If anything happens to them, I swear to fuck I'll grind you beneath the toe of my boot."

Not his best work. Luatha giggled anyway, appreciating the effort.

"Well, that's enough prattling for now, I think." Elwyn rushed a wave and reached for one of the potion bottles glinting from Aedyn's satchel. Anticipating the move, Aedyn pivoted. "Hear him out..."

"I'll make this quick and painless," Brannon said. "It's been strange, coming to terms with having a sibling. As I've long suspected, they are infuriating creatures with a gift for getting under one's skin. They are also a bit like mirrors, always hurling flaws in one's face or magnifying features. At any rate, they can be as inspiring as they are tiresome."

Elwyn blinked, bewildered. "Perhaps this speech would be better aimed at Deinua..."

Brannon gave a gruff chuckle. "Deinua is not as intolerable as I originally assumed. In fact, it's been astonishingly easy to adjust to having a brother. I've long had a sister."

The embrace was so swift and sudden, a stab to the gut would've been less surprising. By the time Elwyn's shock wore off, the assassin had vanished into the cottage.

"That was sweet." Aedyn wrapped an arm around her, tipping his cheek against the crown of her head. "For Brannon, anyway."

They stayed that way a little longer before Aedyn drew back to pull a pair of potions from his satchel. The moment Elwyn accepted the bottle, reality settled on her shoulders. For as eager as she'd been to depart, nothing awaited her back in Rhysien-Talunasa. Aedyn, by contrast, had much to return to—his father, his station, his...obligations.

Elwyn still didn't know what to call whatever she and Aedyn shared, but she wasn't ready to lose it.

"A little more time," she begged, embarrassed of her own desperate tone. "Mearalas' offer will last three days more, and we've only glimpsed a small portion of the Wilds. We could stay another night, at least...or a few hours...fifteen minutes..."

"I wish we could stay." Aedyn smiled sadly, brushing her hair aside to cup her face. "Amatha's parents are waiting for her, and they deserve an answer. I know things have gotten complicated, but I promise I'll do whatever it takes to make this work, starting with speaking to my father. We've never seen eye-to-eye, but I think I'm starting to understand him a little bit better, and I have to believe he'll return the effort. If not, I'll find another way for us." He kissed her forehead, lingering long enough to make her heart ache. "Do you trust me?"

Elwyn did. And it was terrifying.

Unwilling to spoil the moment with tears, she raised her potion. "May the sun rise swiftly."

"And may it light the path forward."

The bottles *clinked* together, and the Shifting Wilds shifted one final, breathtaking time.

"Loathe not the frigid tempest that plays herald to the spring,
The same storm that might drown you will give life to verdant things."

CHAPTER 34
RAINFALL
BRANNON

eeks had passed since Brannon first decided to stay in the Shifting Wilds, and he'd since endured the family meals and hollow conversations with practiced patience. That patience was about to pay off. Finally, Deinua felt comfortable slipping away to meet with his suitor on the same night Koa went out hunting, leaving Brannon home with Lieri.

It was an opportunity he intended to make the most of.

The woman had removed a half-dozen bouquets from the sitting room table to make room for as many platters of biscuits, pastries, and snack cakes, as though she was trying to make up for a full decade of desserts in a single sitting. Brannon nibbled absently on a raspberry tart, half-listening as she prattled on about another in an apparently endless catalogue of tedious misadventures. Her intermittent laughter told Brannon the story was meant to be a comedy, so he adopted a befittingly amused grin and allowed his mind to slink off down darker paths.

The Procession had come and gone without him landing a single strike. He'd been close, too. He'd poured all his rage into rushing Yana only to take a bolt of magic to the chest and wake to find justice had been rendered without him. He would not allow *vengeance* to slip away so easily.

"...but, unbeknownst to me, the whole swarm had hidden in the chimney. The moment the fire went out, it started all over again." Lieri threw up her hands to signify the story's end. "You'll have to forgive my rambling. I'm so excited to finally have your ear that I'm in danger of talking it off. Really, I should be asking about your adventures." She pulled her legs onto the bench and tucked her toes beneath a crocheted blanket. "Surely, you have plenty of stories worth telling. I'd love to hear about the moments that molded you most."

Brannon doubted it. "A decade leaves a lot to cover, don't you think?"

Her smile faded, firelight catching her gaze as they shifted toward the hearth. "It's been longer for me, you know? Over twenty years, now."

"There were clues."

"You mean Deinua." Lieri took a sip of her tea. "I'm genuinely glad to see you two are getting along. I'll admit it's a touch surprising, given how few interests you share, but I'd always hoped you might balance each other, given the chance."

Brannon shrugged. *Getting along* was probably a stretch, but he'd developed a begrudging respect for the half-fae. Deinua was compulsively genuine, could hold his own in combat, and knew when to make himself scarce—all traits that merited a measure of regard.

Pity Brannon was about to make an orphan of him.

Suddenly impatient, he drained his teacup in the loudest manner possible. Lieri reacted predictably.

"That sounds about empty." She hopped to her feet and grabbed the cup. "Allow me to put the kettle back on while you think up a good tale."

"With ginger, if you don't mind."

"I'd assumed," she replied before flitting toward the kitchen. "I'll prepare it fresh."

That woman was so giddy about making up for lost time she probably wouldn't have noticed if he stalked up behind her straightaway. Still, he idled a moment more to build the appropriate anticipation, staring into the hearth fire and thinking back on the meditations he'd suffered under Ferea's tutelage. He hadn't felt the flames in a while, but he knew they still flickered beneath his skin, hungry as ever. Warranted though their cravings were, he would not rush his revenge when there was time enough to savor each bite.

A cupboard opened and closed, and a granite pestle scratched a matching mortar. Brannon took it as his cue. He drew his *Aras Tosc* as he rose, admiring the way they flashed gold in the firelight, and started toward the kitchen. His gut panged from the same obnoxious guilt he'd felt in abandoning the Sylph encampment, but he ignored it. If anything, Ferea would have been proud of him. Not only had he found who'd started the fire, he was about to make her pay for it. Perhaps the flames would die with the arsonist, like a weed plucked out at the roots.

Lieri stood at the counter, humming brightly as she crushed away at a ginger root. With her back to Brannon, it was all too easy to imagine her in a moonlit pasture, scurrying toward the woods she'd never return from. Did she have any clue that he'd watched her walk away? That he'd stared out his window each morning for weeks, hoping she'd reappear?

The memories set a fire in Brannon's ribcage, fueling him as he crept across the kitchen. The distance closed much too swiftly, so he idled behind her for a moment, running through his options. A slice to the neck would be too swift, but a properly gauged gut wound could take hours to kill a person. Granted, each subsequent slash would take about a minute off the total. He would have to deal them sparingly.

"Go ahead," Lieri whispered without a glance back. "I deserve it."

Brannon froze, one dagger held sideways at her waist, the other dangling at his side. His approach had been soundless, and he'd been careful not to breathe or swallow, and yet...

"I can't imagine what you went through after I left." Lieri turned to face him, lashes glistening. "Hatred needs a target, or it'll fold back on itself. Without me there to hurl it at, Hendrick's only options were you or himself, and I doubt he turned it inward. If your hatred needs its own target now, I understand. It's only fitting it should come full circle."

"This isn't about *him*," Brannon growled, though he remembered his father well. How could he forget the gin-soaked scent of his breath, the imprint of his knuckles? What he couldn't recall was escaping the situation, though just thinking of it made his palms sting. In the end, what really mattered was how it *should* have happened. "You should have ended it." He pressed his blade to Lieri's belly. "You should have spoon-fed him his own fucking medicine, or poured the bottle down his throat, or hired someone else to deliver it, or...or..." The burn in his chest leapt to his eyes, bright enough to blur the room, and his throat constricted strangely. "...or you should have brought me with you. Why didn't you bring me with you?"

A tear trickled from the corner of her eye. "It was fear, at first," she whispered. "The night I left, he nearly broke me, and days passed before I could bring myself to look back. Then fear turned to guilt, and guilt to self-loathing." She shook the excuses away, knowing how feeble they were. "I didn't know about the time difference between worlds. Only a couple of weeks passed by the time I figured out how to get ahold of travel potions, and by then..."

"I was gone." He might not have remembered the particulars, but he knew he didn't stick around long after realizing he'd been abandoned.

"I'm so sorry, Brannon." Lieri grabbed both his shoulders, her tears now flowing freely. "I know that doesn't change anything, but I need for you to know that I never stopped loving you, and never stopped hoping you'd found your way to a peaceful life." She took a deep, trembling breath, glancing down at the dagger. "If my leaving turned you into a killer, then kill me. I deserve it."

Brannon wanted to. He'd wanted to for so long. Yet now, when the moment had finally presented itself, his *Aras Tosc* fell useless to the floor, and he sank to his knees between them.

"It's not your fault." The words startled him, but they tasted like the truth. She may have stacked the kindling, Pa may have poured the oil, Father Beaus may have lit the match, but *he'd* started the fire.

His breath hitched, breaking loose in strange, sharp bursts. His mother knelt beside him, throwing her arms around his shoulders, and for a moment, he was ten years old again, seeking shelter in the only arms that had ever held him gently. The burn behind his eyes flared bright before breaking free. It felt tepid against his cheeks, almost soothing.

The rage that had fueled Brannon for a decade dwindled, gradually dimming, receding to cinders. For all the destruction it had wrought, all the sorrow it had spread, all the ashes and anguish it had left in its wake, it died in the same manner as any common wildfire—smothered by a simple bout of rain.

*"Don't imagine your defenses are too strong to fall apart,
What starts with stolen kisses might well lead to stolen hearts."*

CHAPTER 35

EVER A THIEF

ELWYN

 lwyn held the paper to flame, watching the golden script bubble as the cornflower paper burned to a blacked spiral. Only when the candlelight nipped her fingers did she release the final sliver of parchment. It crumbled to dust atop the bedside table.

She'd hoped the tiny act of arson could chase the melancholy weight from her bones, but they felt that much heavier for it.

A girl can dream....

That was the problem though, wasn't it? Elwyn *had* dreamed. She'd dreamed that Aedyn would find his way back to her despite the odds. She'd dreamed he'd find a loophole in his betrothal vows, that he'd leap straight through it and into her arms. She'd dreamed she'd finally found a home—not in a place, but a person.

But those dreams had burned to ashes, much like Aedyn's wedding invitation.

Tiny fingers brushed against her cheek, catching a wayward tear.

"I've swaddled you in shadows, shielded you from the sun,
But there are pains, despite my aims, I can't protect you from."

"It isn't as though you never warned me," Elwyn said, rising from the bed she'd borrowed for too long, "and it isn't as though I never warned myself. I knew it would hurt when he tore away, I just never imagined I could feel so...so..."

Threadbare. She wouldn't say it aloud, but that's exactly what she was. More holes than fabric. More tatters than seams. No wonder she couldn't wrap herself tightly enough to ward off the chill.

She flung her satchel over the shoulder Luatha hadn't perched on, scanning her lodgings one final time for any items worth pilfering. The chamber that had looked so sprawling when she first arrived now simply looked empty. No matter, the candlesticks and letter openers she'd snatched would pay her way for at least a few weeks.

"It was time to move on, anyway," she whispered as she opened the door. "This place was too stodgy for the likes of us."

Samhria's halls were nearly empty. Most of the residents were out enjoying the many festivities underway in the streets below. Given all the tragedy that had befallen them in recent months, both the fae and mortals were eager for a celebration, and a combination wedding-coronation provided a perfect reason. Only the residents of Talune's upper branches had been invited to the official ceremony, but everyone in the piecemeal kingdom was welcome to attend the related revels that raged around Talune's roots.

Only a few unlucky guards remained to patrol the palace halls, and they looked none too happy about it. They didn't notice Elwyn slinking past them, though she certainly noticed them. One glimpse of that gilt armor sent her back to the day she and Aedyn returned. The moment they approached the palace gates, a legion of brigadiers rushed out and swept him away. A week passed before Elwyn learned of the king's assassination and the hasty ceremony that would be held to fill the empty throne. It took another full week before she allowed herself to accept it.

Luatha peeked out from Elwyn's hair and gave her ear a tug.

"I know that you're not thinking straight; it's been a trying day,
But if you're looking for Samhria's gates, let's walk the other way."

"We'll leave soon enough," Elwyn whispered, ascending a spiral staircase. "There's something I need to take care of first."

Eloana's private wing was easy to find. While Talune's upper stories were equally garish, none of the others were quite so floral. Mauve and lavender wildflower murals spanned the walls, gilt frillroses blossomed throughout the crowning, and bouquets of charmblossoms and orchids graced each of the many side tables, all of whom had lilies carved into the legs.

A single brigadier idled midway down the hall, sighing as he watched the parade from a distance. Elwyn slipped past him easily. The scents of potpourri and perfume led her to the bedchamber. She snicked the door shut behind her and was lost to shadow for a heartbeat before Luatha emerged to act as a violet lantern. Elwyn swiftly found and parted heavy brocade curtains, and starlight flooded the most lavish quarters she'd ever seen.

Strings of pearls and crystals spilled from alabaster jewelry boxes. Silk and lace shrouded the shelves, half-buried beneath forests of golden statuettes and carved ivory trinkets. Whole groves of vivid gowns and slippers peeked out from the armoires, and a shelf of beaded slippers rose higher than the bookcase. A four-poster bed was pressed flush against one wall, heaped with pastel pillows and half-hidden by a crushed velvet canopy trimmed in teardrops of rose quartz.

Luatha bumbled about the space, her ink-drop eyes wide and shiny.

"I've never seen so large a hoard inside so small a space,
Our only struggle now will be deciding what to take!"

That's exactly how Elwyn felt. Tasteless though the trove was, her fingers itched at the sight of it. No matter what circumstances life tossed her way, no matter what she overcame or how many lessons she learned, she would always be a thief at heart.

Eager to get her task over with, she shook off her shock and began the search. She rifled through drawers and sifted through bins, filtered through closets and rummaged through trunks, but with every treasure cast aside her mission felt a little more futile. Nothing she stole from that room could come close to the value of what she'd lost.

Seeming to understand, Luatha drifted to her side.

"Right now, the best that you can do is look out for yourself,
For all you know, the prince is better off without your help."

"I want him to be happy," Elwyn said, though the thought of Aedyn holding another made her ill, "but I can't leave this place empty-handed. If you really want to help, gather as much as you can. I may not leave a scar, but I want to at least land a strike."

Luatha sighed, her violet light dimming.

"This princess has more riches than many a town can boast,
Don't take most of what she values; take what she values most."

The trouble with the advice was those blessed with bounty typically valued very little. It was one of the things that made nobles such easy marks. Steal silverware from a poor person, and they won't rest until it's found. Steal the same from the wealthy, they'll see it replaced within the week.

Still, Elwyn knew where she stored her own most precious treasure. Hoping she and Eloana had that one small trait in common, she rushed to the bed and began tossing the pillows aside. Sure enough, something spectacular was hidden beneath them.

The dagger was tucked into a pale leather sheath, its straps sewn from silken ribbons. Elwyn tugged on the bejeweled hilt to find the dagger matched her own for size and shape, though ridges spiked along the outer edge like sunbeams and its golden gleam contrasted starkly with *Gelah's* dusky gray. The metal felt impossibly warm against her skin as she held it to the starlight, admiring its cryptic runes and pondering what they meant.

Violet light spilled across the etchings as Luatha perched on Elwyn's wrist.

"I never thought that I would see a gift like this again,
I've gifted you my darkness, now that darkness has a twin."

"This is connected to *Gelah?*" Elwyn smiled, having found something so much better than petty revenge. She'd always thought her moon needed a sun. "Please to meet you, *Greyun.*"

Footsteps whispered down the hall, fast approaching. Luatha hid behind a curtain, and Elwyn sheathed and stashed the dagger before diving beneath the bed. The door creaked open, spilling candlelight and a single, slender shadow across the floor. It clicked shut, and the world went black.

By the time Elwyn's eyes adjusted to the gloom, a pair of brown brigadier boots marched into view. A blink, and they'd changed to green leather trimmed in gold.

"You can come out now."

Elwyn's heart leapt at the familiar voice, and the rest of her followed, scrambling out from beneath the bed and hopping upright. Aedyn wrapped his arms around her and squeezed so tightly it should have hurt, but it felt like falling back on a pillow molded to her shape.

"You have no idea how much I've missed you," he whispered.

"I think I just might." She buried her face in the crook of his neck, savoring his warmth and summer-sweet scent. Over two weeks' worth of frost melted in an instant. "How in light's name did you think to look for me here?"

"I know you, Elwyn." Aedyn pulled away, just enough to lift her chin. *Creator,* she'd missed the way he smiled at her. "You would never allow Eloana to steal from you without getting some slightly petty payback. It's one of your more endearing qualities."

For all its fluttering, Elwyn's heart still managed to sink. Eloana was not the thief in this equation, and they both knew it. "I don't suppose you've found a way out of your oath..."

Aedyn's smile faded. It was answer enough.

"I see." Elwyn felt suddenly smothered, but she couldn't muster the strength to break free. The tears that had been fighting for freedom all evening clawed at her eyes with renewed vigor, but she refused to release them. "You really shouldn't be here, Aedyn. With everything that's happening, you should be resting or celebrating or drinking yourself into a stupor. Tomorrow's a big day."

"Tomorrow." Aedyn laughed coldly. "Tomorrow, if everything goes as planned, I'll be donning a crown I don't deserve, taking a throne I never wanted, marrying a woman I'll never love," he brushed her hair aside, pressing his forehead to hers, "and losing the one I do."

Elwyn knew better than to kiss him. She knew better than to bury her fingers in his hair and melt against him like wax on parchment, to bury her fingers in his messy bronze hair and lose herself to a fleeting sweetness that was destined to rot in her belly. She knew better than to love him—she'd known it from the very start—and knowing better didn't change a single damned thing.

"I know you're planning to run." His words tickled her lips. "Please, take me with you."

It was a pretty dream. Elwyn couldn't claim she'd never pictured them traipsing off to some distant land and roving the wilderness, fingers twined, until they stumbled upon a place they could call their very own. Unfortunately, her mind was too grounded to hover in a fantasy for long. Aedyn would inevitably be captured, tried, sentenced to a horrific fate for forsaking his duties and oaths. She could not justify basking in his light for a blink only to see it snuffed out for eternity.

"I would love nothing more than for you to join me," she said, heart aching at the truth of it. "Only we'll need to gather more supplies. I haven't packed enough for the both of us."

Aedyn flashed his most brilliant smile to date, and Elwyn committed it to memory. This was exactly how she wanted to remember him—bright and sweet and filled with hope. "There's a storage space one story down." He flourished a wave, disguising them both as brigadiers. "I can't gather any belongings from my wing, as the guards just escorted someone who looks a whole lot like me to the festival below, and there's a chance they've grown suspicious. We should at least scrounge up some soaps and candles, perhaps even some food, though it'll likely be stale." He reluctantly released her and started toward the door. "As painful as it is not to hold you, we'll need to keep up pretenses until we leave the palace. Once we get beyond the walls..."

He became so wrapped up in his thoughts when they spilled like that— too tangled to notice Elwyn falling behind. As he walked away, her thoughts slipped back to the night of the Procession, when he'd bolstered his friends' confidence and quelled their fears with a few well-placed words. If he applied that same kind, impassioned wisdom to ruling his kingdom, his subjects were in good hands.

Elwyn waited for Luatha to perch on her shoulder, then pulled the potion Tawny had gifted her from her cloak pocket. "You'll make a wonderful king," she whispered.

Aedyn froze when the cork popped free, whirling right as Elwyn downed the drink. She closed her eyes, unwilling to glimpse the look of betrayal on his face. As gravity roiled around her, she clung to thoughts of his sunlit smile and warm embrace, praying the memories would somehow remain just as crisp through the rest of her days.

Soon, the cloying potpourri musk vanished beneath the fresh tang of mossy cedar and a bite of sharp cinnamon. Elwyn opened her eyes to see chalk sigils waltzing around unvarnished floorboards, their shapes smeared and dampened. The travel sickness would fade in a matter of minutes, but hours would pass before her vision cleared.

"The deepest wrongs know just how to present themselves as right,
There never was a shadow born for absence of a light."

CHAPTER 36

ANOTHER OPTION

AEDYN

or the last time, stop your slouching!" Marielle poked Aedyn with her sewing needle, startling him straight. "You will not attend your own wedding looking like a cur, even if that's exactly what you are."

Aedyn pulled his legs up onto the bench, furling forward in direct defiance of the seamstress's demands. While her fiery glare was a comical match for her pumpkin curls, her reaction didn't spark the mirth he'd been hoping for. Granted, with recent events, he couldn't imagine ever smiling again. Not sincerely, anyway.

"Listen good, you little prick!" Marielle's bark might have been intimidating, had she stood higher than Aedyn's waist. "I've been working on that tailcoat for two weeks, and if you don't let me stitch that hem up properly, the whole thing will fall apart in a blink!"

"Let it." Aedyn sighed. "It'll match my spirit."

Marielle traded her sewing needle for a measuring tape and whacked Aedyn across the knees. "You might get away with this nonsense around Learo, but I don't share his weakness for teary-eyed brats!"

The mention of Learo made Aedyn's heart ache all the more. Aedyn hadn't even seen him since returning to Samhria, thanks to the legion of guards that refused to leave his side. Those very same guards were now stationed outside the dressing room, worried he'd suffer the same cruel fate as the king. With a possible assassin lurking within Samhria's walls, their zeal was understandable, but it wasn't as though Aedyn had much of a life left to protect. His father and best friend were gone, his days of freedom had reached an abrupt end, and the only woman he'd ever loved had abandoned him without explanation.

If someone wanted to kill him, they were welcome to try.

Marielle tapped an impatient foot, her rosy lips pursed. Despite her silence, the message was clear: if Aedyn's sulking ruined that suit, the assassin would be the least of his worries.

"How about a compromise?" He slipped free of the tailcoat. "You'll have a much easier time tailoring this if I'm not brooding inside it."

"The measurements won't be as accurate." Marielle snatched it up anyway, draping it over the nearest dress form with an angry *harrumph*. It was an exquisite garment—layered ivory silk trimmed in golden filigree. On any other occasion, he'd have worn it proudly.

"At least your bride appreciates all the effort I put in," the seamstress continued, folding the fabric to make a pleat. "I ought to pay her one final visit, come to think of it, to make sure I didn't overlook a bead or two. Most likely, I'll bump into your attendant on the way." She glanced back, raising a bushy brow. "I know you don't care about tradition, but you're permitted a drink with a friend right before you—"

"Death march?"

"*Ceremony*." Marielle pinned the pleat a little too violently. "If I send him this way, is there a chance it'll help rid you of this gloom you've been marinating in?"

Aedyn suspected the gloom was a permanent fixture, but he nodded anyway.

"Alright, then." Marielle perched her hands on her hips. "But before that man marches in here and vomits whatever inane advice pops into his head, mind hearing a word from someone who's actually married?"

"Since when do you ask for permission to lecture me?"

"Eloana didn't ask for this either. Even so, she's been twirling about all morning, heart aflutter at the thought of marrying your sorry arse! Knowing as much makes it even worse to watch you pouting just because you can't do whatever and whoever you want anymore." She shoved a stubby finger into Aedyn's face. "At least feign a bit of joy for her benefit. Pretend to feel something until you do. Light's sake, boy— half the men in the kingdom would give their teeth to trade places with you!"

While Aedyn had no need for spare teeth, he'd have taken the deal. "You've made your point, Marielle. Though if my brooding bothers you so deeply, you need only turn your back to be rid of it."

"Perhaps I wish for *you* to be rid of it." The seamstress shook her head. "Just mull it over, will you? And off with that vest, too, lest it wrinkle. Or am I the only woman in the realm you won't strip for?"

Aedyn's laughter was a ghost of his usual. He shrugged out of the garment and tossed it over the seamstress like she was a coat rack. She growled, hanging it gently on a hook beside the door.

"I'll send Learo straight this way," she promised. "In the meantime, do something about that disaster you call hair. Oh, and there are more guards in the hallway than there are sins on your conscience, so don't get any bright ideas about absconding."

"I wouldn't dream of it," Aedyn muttered, though that didn't mean he wouldn't dream at all. In fact, the moment the door closed behind her, his mind fluttered off to a more pleasant future. For the first time ever, he pictured himself standing on the dais in Talune's Heart, waiting nervously for the filigree doors to swing open. He imagined tearing up as his bride marched down the emerald runner, a timid smile on her pretty, pale lips. Though he couldn't quite picture her in a white gown or veil, fitted armor and a beaded lace cloak would suit her well. His heart panged at the thought of watching her take the throne beside his, of placing his mother's circlet atop her silky raven locks, of seeing their vow chains blink to life, one precious promise at a time...

The room went hazy. Aedyn tried his best to blink it clear, wiping his eyes with a frilly blue sleeve. Perhaps, if he imagined Elwyn vividly enough, he would make it through the ceremony without crumbling. His kingdom needed a strong leader now more than ever. He owed it to his father—and to his people—to cast yet another illusion.

The rattle of the doorknob gave him a moment to compose himself before Learo entered the room, two crystal flutes in one hand and a bottle of spriteberry wine in the other. Like most of the palace staff, he'd changed into formal attire for the occasion. Though he wore the tailored cobalt suit well, it was strange to see him in anything other than his viridian attendant's robes.

"You asked to see me, sir?" he asked, shouldering the door closed behind him. "Or should I say, *sire?*"

"Don't you dare!" Aedyn grimaced. "I've actually been asking to see you for weeks, but those smothering sentries wouldn't let anyone within twenty feet of me."

"They do take their jobs seriously, do they not?" Learo set the glasses on the table beside Aedyn and popped the bottle open. "A toast to your union, sir?"

"I'd rather consider it an ordinary drink. I suspect I'll be partaking in them even more regularly, moving forward. In fact, if you'd like to save time, you could always just hand me the bottle."

"Let's start with the one and gauge from there." Learo filled both glasses to the brim. "You never were one for sticking with tradition. Given your current demeanor, I'm guessing this is still not the life you wanted..."

"What I want hardly matters." Aedyn snatched up a flute and drained it in a single motion. "I've grown tired of swimming against the current. The waters are relentless, my arms are lead, and everyone I love has either drowned or been swept away."

Learo arched an eyebrow.

"Almost everyone," Aedyn corrected, setting his empty glass aside. "Surely, you know how much I appreciate you. My father has never kept attendants, and that isn't a terrible example to follow, but I've no desire to be rid of you. There must be a position you've had your eye on all these years. Court Herald, perhaps? Festival Coordinator? You'd get to boss Marielle around either way, which would be fun for the both of us."

"I appreciate the offer, sir, but you can only promote me if you ascend to the Summer Throne." Learo's smile dwindled. "Would you make that choice, if there was another option?"

Though he'd thought it dead, Aedyn's hope reignited. Learo was not the type to speak in hypotheticals, but his vows of heirdom and betrothal were flawlessly interwoven. One required him to ascend to the throne he'd been born to inherit; the other required him to wed Eloana on the day he was crowned King of the Maithe. If there was a weakness in the wording, he hadn't found it despite a century of trying.

"What aren't you telling me?"

The attendant latched the dressing room door, pressing his back to it like he was preparing to sell illicit potions. "Do you think of me as especially vain, sir?"

The question did not seem relevant, but Aedyn pondered it anyway. He'd never once caught Learo altering a garment for a special occasion or using his magic to coax his hair into place, yet the thinnest veneer of glamour clung to him at all times.

"Not particularly, though I understand the need to hide one's flaws from the crueler members of court. That said, I like to consider us friends, Learo—*family,* even. I hope you know you can trust me with anything." He pulled up his sleeve, willing away the illusion he'd wrapped around his forearm. Pale scars snaked from elbow to wrist, each an aching reminder of Elwyn's absence. "Whatever it is you've felt the need to hide, I promise it won't change the way I see you."

"A promise is a powerful thing, sir." Learo looked straight into his eyes, unaffected by the scars. "Even we fae cannot hold to such claims."

Still, he dismissed his glamour—not with a flourish, but a sigh. His color and warmth dripped away like glacial melt from bone-white curls, snowy skin, and the pale, milky eyes of a corpse. Aedyn sprawled backward in his rush to stand, taking a dress rack to the floor with him. Swaths of satin and silk entangled his limbs as he shuffled away from the monster who'd been wearing his friend's form.

"Y-you're a Korrid."

"A *half*-Korrid," the creature corrected, "and I have no intention of harming you."

"What have you done with the real Learo?" Aedyn asked, wishing he had a rapier with him. "If you've hurt him, I swear—"

"I *am* Learo." The Korrid strode forward, skirting around the overturned bench. "You know I cannot lie, sir. Half-Korrid or not, I am *all* fae. I would have told you about this sooner, but..." he gestured toward the mess Aedyn had made of the dressing room, "I didn't think you'd take it well."

That wry wit was certainly Learo's, and this creature shared the same narrow face, high cheekbones and pointed chin. The resemblances did not make the claim more bearable. "If you aren't deceiving me now, then you've been deceiving me all along."

The Korrid winced, cloudy gaze dropping to his feet. "Would it help you to know it was agony? Utter agony, on so many levels."

That much must have been true. Before the Confluence, Talunasa was a land of eternal summer. Where the Maithe were frightened of the dark, the Korrids began to melt the moment they set foot in a sunbeam. Learo had never been fond of long strolls outdoors, but he'd never given the impression he was in any pain, either.

"How in light's name did you endure it?"

"My mother was Maithe, and her blood muted the burn. Though painful, it was not so agonizing that I was forced to slink away." The Korrid—*Learo*—sighed. "I couldn't have, even if I'd wanted to. I have a debt to repay."

Aedyn climbed to his feet with the aid of the nearest table, officially more curious than terrified. "To whom could you possibly be indebted?" he asked. "Obviously, your allegiance was never truly mine, and my father would never have allowed—"

"Your mother."

Aedyn's mind went blank, and his mouth numb. He stuttered for a few helpless seconds before his voice returned to him. "My...my mother is dead. She perished in the War of Light and Shadow. My father told me as much. He told *everyone* as much."

"He said she *fell*. Words are tricky things, are they not? If we fae want to conceal a truth, we must simply replace it with another."

Aedyn shook his head, but the fog refused to clear. "Why are you telling me this?"

"As I said before, this is not the life you wanted." Despite the frost that now glazed Learo's eyes, the sympathy behind them was unmistakably warm. "I cannot know whether a throne of ice will suit you better than a throne of gold, but you deserved to know you have a choice in the matter."

"A choice." It was the only thing Aedyn had ever been denied, and it was all he'd ever really wanted. "Does that mean my mother is..."

Fuara, the Korrid Queen. The name was spoken only in whispers throughout the palace, and Aedyn could not bring his lips to shape it. Not in this context.

"If you'd like to know more about your mother," Learo pulled two travel potions from his pockets, "I suggest you ask her yourself."

EPILOGUE

ELOANA

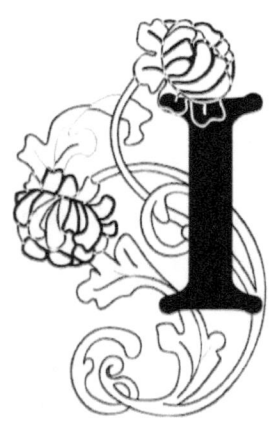

t wasn't the gown Eloana had dreamt of in her youth, the one she'd etched onto countless napkins and passed off to Marielle whenever the pattern evolved. That dress had boasted a sparkling tulle skirt and capped sleeves, with little yellow frillroses falling through the folds— a childish frock for a childish little light singer.

The garment she now wore was sleek and supple, cut from flawless ivory silk and trimmed in beaded lace. Oraithvine formed a gilt corset that clung tightly to her curves and branched into a stately collar that stretched from clavicle to chin. Little blue sapphires adorned the bustline and dotted the sweeping train, whispering of elegance and authority, perfect matches for those which adorned her ears and fingers.

It was truly a gown befitting a queen.

"Be still, dear," Marielle warned as she stitched one last bead onto the silk. "I know it's tempting to twirl the morning away, but I'd hate to prick your pretty skin right before the ceremony."

"That would be a tragedy." Eloana forced herself rigid, though it was nearly impossible not to sway for the mirror. She had never looked so perfect—every lash curled and darkened, every nail perfectly polished, every curl pinned in place. The only thing the ensemble lacked was a crown, and that matter would resolve itself shortly. "I must say, Marielle, this is your finest work yet, though the ensemble I commissioned for Aedyn must give it competition. I know you can't be liberal with the details, but surely you can hint at how handsome he looks in it."

"You've caught yourself a looker." Marielle grimaced, adding almost inaudibly, "He'll wear that coat well if I have to stitch it to his skin."

A glower ruined Eloana's reflection, though it didn't matter whether he *wanted* to wed her. He'd never shown interest in her wants, and she was under no obligation to consider his. She would share his realm, and she would share his bed, and if she truly desired to share his heart, she would learn to play it like a harpsichord.

Sensing her change in tone, Anye flitted around her, trailing prismatic light. The sight of her brightened Eloana's mood before it could truly dampen. Marielle had crafted a tiny cobalt vest for the piskie at Eloana's bidding—an apology for somehow misplacing that enchanted dagger, which she was certain would show up soon enough. The wedding week had been utter chaos, after all.

Thankfully, Anye had accepted the offering with glee.

"I love the way the gold glitters more brightly for the blue,
I am sincerely stunning, but I pale compared to you."

"We're both fit for a throne, are we not?" Eloana said, imagining how the subjects in Talune's Heart would smile and applaud when she took her seat of honor. "Perhaps I'll have one made for you—a little throne to sit atop the armrest of my own."

Someone knocked on the dressing room door. Eloana glanced at the clock in the corner. Fifteen minutes remained until the ceremony—an inconvenient time to receive a visitor. The moment the seamstress unlatched the door, Loenelle burst into the dressing room.

"I have bad news, m'lady," the handmaiden said, already shuddering for fear of retaliation. "The prince is gone."

Eloana closed her eyes, inhaling slowly though her nose. She'd ordered those guards to stick to him like ticks, and they hadn't seemed incompetent at the time. "What do you mean, he's gone?"

"The brigadiers are sweeping the palace for a third time as we speak, but their hopes are not high. None of the guests have been informed of the situation, but if he is not found before the ceremony is set to commence, the Court Herald has been given strict orders to dismiss—"

"No." Eloana had dreamt of this moment for too long to let it slip away. Not after she'd gone so far as to kill for it. "No one is going anywhere. Cancelling the wedding doesn't mean we must cancel the coronation."

"M'lady..." Loenelle shied back until her shoulders met the wall. "With all due respect, this is *Aedyn's* coronation day. Without him, you're—"

"Better off."

Eloana shoved the seamstress from her path and marched into the hall with her head held high. Several guards rushed forward to block her, blathering about the change of circumstances. Thanks to their oraithvine armor, Eloana didn't need to waste time tuning their light-songs. With a flick of her wrist and a whir of Anye's wings, she hurled them into the walls helm-first. They collapsed, unconscious.

The piskie flitted happily, though her glee was tempered by caution.

"You deserve to reap the bounty you've been nurturing at length,
But if you choose now to show your hand, make it a show of strength."

That, Eloana could do. As she climbed the final staircase before Talune's Heart, a trumpet sounded, signaling a forthcoming announcement. Eloana gathered her gown and sprinted swiftly up the steps, desperate to arrive before the guests were dismissed. A show of strength would mean little without an audience.

"Most honored guests," the Court Herald began. "It is with my profound disappointment that I must announce—"

Eloana burst into the throne room, and around a hundred faces turned her way. The guests whispered amongst themselves, but their collective light-song drowned their voices—a discordant drone, frantic and haggard. It wasn't the kind of awe Eloana had hoped to elicit, but she could work with it.

She slowed to an elegant stride, humming a wedding march of her own composition. Anye fluttered alongside her, fracturing the melody into myriad harmonies. She could not possibly tune each timbre in the hall to a more amiable key, but she suppressed them en masse, lulling the crowd into a stupor.

Given the recent hubbub about assassins, it was simple to convince the

Court to keep the ceremony small and intimate. Not a single foreign face —not even the other High Judges—was present in the pews. It made manipulating the audience a little too easy. For a moment, Eloana let herself forget that their reverence was forced, pretending her subjects were simply stunned into silence by the beauty and grace of their newest monarch.

Though she loved basking in the crowd's admiration, the thrones atop the dais had captured her own. Queen Tearan's floral circlet sat upon her long-abandoned cushion, and King Aryn's magnificent crown graced the other. Between them rose a slender sandstone plinth draped in cornflower satin. An ewer of honeyed wine and two gilt chalices sat upon it, necessities of the traditional coronation toast.

The Court Herald stammered as Eloana drew near, but his resonance was feeble enough to twist on a whim, and he abandoned the dais at her silent bidding. Not all were so wise. As she started up the dais steps, a trio of headstrong young brigadiers rushed forward, barking orders. Her gown swept like a glittering eddy as she whirled to face them, a smile stretching her painted lips. Anye had suggested a show of strength. It was kind of them to volunteer for the demonstration.

She imagined a vicious aria, and Anye spun it into a dozen harmonies. The soldier's filigree shifted, biting into their skin and pulling them to their knees. Blood trickled from their wounds, staining the emerald carpet dark, but this time, Eloana refrained from striking bone.

"Is this any way to treat your queen on her coronation day?" she asked, standing tall before the kneeling guards. "I am merely accepting what is rightfully mine—what you were all ready to hand me only minutes ago— yet you would treat me like a thief because I'd dare claim it without a prince placing it in my hand?" A sincere note of sadness tinged her speech, slipping from the ribcage that had imprisoned it for decades. "Every minute of my life has been spent in preparation for this moment. This throne and crown are mine by right and providence, and in trying to wrench them away from me, you have proven *yourselves* thieves. You must be punished accordingly."

Eloana held the trembling gaze of the middlemost guard as she resumed her silent aria, starting low before sweeping into a shrill crescendo. Three oraithvine helms spiraled inward, and her song ended with a series of *cracks* and crimson plumes.

"Would anyone else like to challenge my claim to the throne?"

She scanned the crowd for dissenters. None came forward, though several onlookers stared, slack-jawed, at the bodies slumped against the steps. Such measures were regrettable, but they were also necessary. Once she ushered Talunasa into its most glorious era, her subjects would surely forgive any blood spilled in the process.

Satisfied that her strength had been sufficiently shown, Eloana continued toward the place of honor she'd so long coveted. She corrected her course at the last second, suddenly deeming Tearan's circlet too paltry, and lifted Aryn's antlered crown from his cushion. It was heavier than it had looked, resting atop his head for all those decades, but it was the more auspicious headpiece by far.

The throne's cushion molded to her form as she sat, and she lifted her newfound crown high before donning it. The audience was supposed to cheer in that moment, but they maintained their awestruck silence. Their lack of enthusiasm was disheartening, but Anye countered it with a cheerful quip as she perched on Eloana's shoulder.

"This is only the seed from which your legacy will grow,
Fear is superior to love, and far easier to sow."

As usual, the piskie's wisdom rang brightly. While Eloana hoped to someday win the adoration of her subjects, she would settle for their deference in the meantime. With one last tradition to check off the list, she poured herself a drink from the ceremonial ewer. Her reflection smiled down at her, more beautiful than ever, as she raised her chalice in a long-awaited toast.

"May the sun rise swiftly."

"A faerie reel won't always boast a cheerful melody,
Perhaps the notes will ring a bit more brightly in verse three..."

Thank you for reading! Did you enjoy? Please add your review because nothing helps an author more and encourages readers to take a chance on a book than a review.

And don't miss the more of the *The Reel of Rhysia* series coming soon. Until then read THE OTHER SIDE OF THE MIRROR by City Owl author, Dana Burke. Turn the page for a sneak peek!

You can also sign up for the City Owl Press newsletter to receive notice of all book releases!

SNEAK PEEK OF THE OTHER SIDE OF THE MIRROR

BY DANA EVYN

I had always been somewhat afraid of mirrors. The sense I was being watched when I wasn't looking, like the reflection would shimmer and the world would suddenly stop being my own. Sometimes at night when I went to wash my face before bed, I would glance up, soap still on my lashes, as if expecting the person I saw in the mirror to reach out and pull me through. In the daylight, it was easier to laugh off those anxious imaginings—but my fear had become far too tangible after what happened the day my family died. Or rather, what I imagined had occurred. But I still kept the ornate, floor-length antique mirror in my living room covered haphazardly with a sheet, like that would guard against what was beyond it.

I shuddered at the thought and, as though in response, the sheet rippled like it had been moved by a phantom wind. My eyes caught on the gleaming rosettes that adorned the sides of the polished brass frame that I knew came to a point at the top, and I rubbed the matching scar on my palm. It had been one of the few things to survive the flames that night. I had stored it away ever since, until begrudgingly moving it into my new apartment last month.

The late afternoon sun reflected off the leaves of each rose, flickering like the flames that had surrounded us. My throat choked up as I remembered the smoke that had suffocated, burned—

The buzz of my vibrating phone pulled me from my thoughts with a jolt. I blinked twice, then put the call on speaker.

"Evangeline Maris," Quinn hissed. "How dare you be late to your own birthday party?"

I frantically checked the time on my phone. "I'm not late." *It isn't even six yet.* "I got a little lost on my hike, but I'm picking out an outfit now and then I'll bike over. And don't you dare full name me," I grumbled, a little more than put out she had done so.

Only my mom had ever called me that.

Quinn Sagray had been my best friend for longer than I could remember, the two of us having been born only ten weeks apart. Our parents had been so close that we never went long without seeing each other. And whether it was because we had been raised together or something in our souls simply recognized the other's, she was my sister in every way that mattered.

The only family I had left.

"You went hiking alone again?" The worry in her voice made me instantly feel guilty. "You told me you would text me your location the next time you did one of those."

I winced, knowing how much she would hate to learn exactly how dangerous the trek was to the top of that rocky mountain peak...and that I hadn't once thought to turn back, let alone warn her. Not when I had been too busy trying to outrun the memory of this day, and the family that should have been here to share it with me.

"Sorry," I muttered. "I'll try to remember next time."

"You should wear that gold top, the one with the long sleeves and the sweetheart neckline," Quinn mused. Forgiving me far too easily, as usual.

I rummaged through my closet before grabbing the top in question from a hanger, pairing it with high-waisted jeans that hugged my curves, before tucking them into my favorite black boots.

"Found it."

Quinn hummed appreciatively. "Good. It brings out the gold in your eyes."

Moving to the bathroom, I briefly checked myself out in the mirror. The top indeed amped up the golden flecks in my hazel eyes, which grew so numerous toward the inner edge of my irises they formed a crown around my pupils. I quickly looked away before my eyes could remind me of another's. Reaching behind me, I pulled on the two ties that cinched the shirt, amplifying the small of my waist, then tied a bow behind my back as my cleavage tried to force its way over the low neckline. The silver star amulet I had never taken off was visible over the cut of the shirt—the top and bottom points longer than the middle four, its tiny black diamonds glittering in its center.

Opening my makeup bag, I added a little eyeshadow, mascara, and a hint of blush to my tanned skin. My dad's Mediterranean heritage had blessed me with a permanently tan complexion, especially after this late summer. Though my chestnut-brown hair, unusual eyes, and downturned lips were a few of the only things I had left of my mom. I even took the time to curl my thick hair, tying it half up to try to keep it out of my face before adding a tinted balm to my lips.

"Clay's not picking you up?" Quinn asked, her voice a little too innocent.

"It's a little early for that, isn't it?" I replied, already reluctant to start down this road. "This is basically our second date."

"As long as he's coming. I'm excited to meet this mystery man of yours."

"For the love of...he's not a mystery man. I just met him yesterday." I sighed. "I don't know why I even invited him to this."

"Because you like him!" She squeaked in excitement, and I couldn't help my answering smile. Quinn's joy had always been contagious, even when I had been too depressed to show much of a response. "Tell me I'm wrong..."

"I only met him at the coffee spot by my old house because he ordered the same thing as me. And just because we're both partial to matcha lattes..." I let out an exasperated huff. "He's a good listener, and he bought me a coconut scone, but the jury's still out on if he's the one."

My mouth twisted disdainfully at the thought.

"That's not a bad beginning though." I could hear the smile in Quinn's voice. "And maybe a partner's exactly what you need. Someone who can be there for you in a way I can't," she added wryly. "Someone who wants to go through all your battles with you."

I was silent for a long moment, not wanting to crush the hope in her voice.

As Quinn well knew, I had never spent much effort on relationships. A few dates, hopefully good sex, and then, when they figured out the amount of emotional baggage I carried mixed with my utter unwillingness to move past the initial stages of a relationship...Either they realized I wasn't ready to open my heart to anyone and left it at that, or I would let them down gently before there was any chance of the *L* word making an appearance.

It wasn't that I didn't think I could fall in love. But after losing my family, I didn't know how I would ever be ready to let someone in like that. To let myself take a chance with my already fractured heart. Especially when said heart had hardened to the point that I never bothered putting in the effort to try. Why open myself up to hurt when I was perfectly fine with my life as it was—with the occasional catch and release?

"There *is* something different about him," I acquiesced, unwilling to get too excited but unable to forget that strange twinge I felt when I first met Clay. "Something...familiar." I ran my fingers through my hair, my curls bouncing as I grabbed a light jacket. "Seeing if he can hold his own against you is a good test before I let him take me on a real date."

Quinn laughed. "I look forward to putting him through the wringer of my company then."

Grinning, I rolled my eyes despite her not being able to see it. I could practically picture the knowing look on her face as she said, "I'm glad you're trying, Eva. It's about time."

The night was cool and crisp, the last vestiges of summer fading into the darkness of fall. The evergreens towered behind Quinn's family home, something unsettling whispering in the breeze as I walked up her winding driveway.

For the past few days, I couldn't shake the suffocating sensation that someone was following me. No one was ever there when I looked, despite a repeated shiver of awareness that had me double checking every shadowy corner. But something made me pause in Quinn's entryway, and I darted a look over my shoulder as I once again felt those eyes on me. I started to shake my head to dispel the unsettling sensation when I saw something glinting in the darkness.

A coyote with pale eyes was staring at me from the tree line. I froze in shock, and it cocked its head to the side, as if assessing me. I turned and knocked loudly on Quinn's large wooden door, trying to ignore the creeping feeling low in my spine. When I looked back again, the coyote was gone.

I took a long, deep breath of crisp evening air, still feeling horribly vulnerable. Letting it out slowly, I looked up at the darkening sky to find a silver-scythe moon glowing over the treetops. The darkness beckoned me like always as I watched the stars shine brightly in the cloudless expanse.

When I was little, I was fascinated by the night sky. My mother had noticed, then taught me the names of the sprawling constellations that twinkled overhead as we curled under a blanket on my parents' balcony. Before our stargazing spot had become only charred remains.

I took another long breath, studying the black velvet night above me, imagining the darkness filling my lungs. Somehow, my lingering loss didn't feel quite so overwhelming when the night sky was clear and endless enough to make even my worst moment feel insignificant.

Raising a hand, I traced a distinctive *W*-shape formed by five bright stars...*Cassiopeia*, I mouthed silently. I had loved learning the names of each constellation and the stories behind them; the more thrilling, the better. Sometimes I still longed for more adventure than I could imagine, instead of the endless repetition of everyday life. Dark forests, open skies, and a shiver of danger...

Danger? I shook my head to dispel the fanciful notion. *You've had more than enough danger for a lifetime.*

Ever since I lost my family, I seemed to find more and more dangerous hobbies. The thrill of them had the ability to take me away from my grief, if only for the moment I plunged through the air while skydiving or summited a perilous hike like I had today. I resolved not to tell Quinn anything else about that. Her growing concern about 'recklessly putting my life at risk,' as she reproachfully called it, would only get worse. Especially if she knew how lost I had been in those craggy peaks before I stumbled upon the right trail home.

The door swung open, jolting me from my thoughts. Quinn stood there, her light-brown, natural curls perfectly styled to stick out in every direction, and her big, amber eyes accented with swooping eyeliner. Her tight lavender crop top showed off a strip of her tawny stomach over her high-waisted jeans.

Quinn grinned at the look on my face. "Were you planning to come in? Or did you want to stand there all night?"

I shrugged off my jacket as I walked through the door, touching a dent in the wood on the way in. "Just admiring my handywork."

"Ah, the great staircase slide," Quinn murmured appreciatively. "I still don't understand how your mattress almost made it outside the door."

"You're just jealous of my enviable aerodynamics."

Quinn's house was something out of a Halloween movie—winding staircases, wooden panels, and a shuttered tower at the top. The grand staircase in the foyer had been the source of endless mattress slide battles long before I had moved in. When her parents took me in after the fire, Quinn had happily shared her room as we had during so many sleepovers, even though there were plenty of others. I had been too sad and scared not to want someone close by, and she had stayed with me on those days I couldn't manage to get out of bed—her soft breathing soothing me to sleep even after another nightmare.

Her parents had died slightly over a year later in a plane crash. I had barely started working through my own loss when I had supported Quinn through hers. Losing my surrogate family had been yet another blow, though at least Quinn and I had been old enough to live without adult supervision by then. Quinn's mother Amirah had been full of ever-present laughter, her skin a deeper brown than her daughter's, her natural hair usually braided back in tight rows. Her husband Alwin was pale, bald, and a head higher than the women of his family, with a wide smile perpetually on his face.

The shared grief had bound Quinn and me together as sisters more than blood ever could.

Despite her own loss, Quinn somehow remained open and kind, always the life of the party. Tonight's event wouldn't be out of place for her home —a gaggle of "our" friends who I only knew through her, plus some wine, early season pumpkin beers, and hopefully not *too* much ribbing from Quinn about my love life.

Clay hadn't gotten back to me about joining, despite our texts before my hike, and I couldn't tell if it was worse that he wouldn't be there after saying he would, or better that I didn't have to deal with introductions. There might be something about him that felt familiar, but I doubted he would be the one to break down the walls I had so carefully built around myself. Though suddenly I was annoyed he hadn't even attempted to try before deciding to ghost me.

I hesitated in the entryway, as though I could take that knock back and avoid the rigmarole.

"No Clay?" Quinn asked coyly, reading my thoughts.

"I haven't heard from him," I said, frowning. "We were texting earlier. Maybe something came up?"

"His loss." She shrugged, leading me toward the living room. "You're the first one here, so might as well get comfortable. Happy 24th, by the way."

I tried to ignore my pang of grief as I thought of the twin who should be celebrating the same number of years on this earth. My anger and frustration at the answers I would never get about this night seven long years ago.

From the sadness dimming Quinn's eyes, I knew she was thinking of my brother too.

"And you thought I would be late." Forcing a smile, I placed a slightly crunched box of cookies down on the counter.

Quinn burst out laughing. "Did those get squashed on the bike ride over or..."

I gave her a halfhearted glare. "If I didn't buy the smooshed ones, no one would, and then they'd never have a home."

She let out an amused huff and raised one eyebrow. "You realize we're going to eat them, right?"

"And they will fulfill their tiny destiny."

I picked up a bag of lumpy, ugly looking limes from my backpack to pair with the bottle of mezcal next to it, unable to stop my smile at Quinn's ensuing laughter.

There was a knock at the door, and I frowned. Quinn flashed me a dazzling smile in response to my grumpy look before walking to open it. A few people walked in, loudly exclaiming over the "'90s witch vibes" of her home. Quinn took it in with a gentle grace I had never mastered.

These events were hard for me, even now. After I lost my family, pretending everything was fine when there was such a gnawing pit of sorrow inside me was impossible for a long while. I was forever afraid of the type of pain I knew I couldn't endure again. Of letting someone else in only to lose them too.

Despite a few years of therapy, throwing myself into my schoolwork, and seeking out every reckless extracurricular activity I could find, I was still learning to live again instead of merely passing time. But even as I learned to compartmentalize that grief, the reminder of it was always waiting in the pit of my stomach, making me wonder if I could ever hope to have a normal, carefree life.

I had come close this summer when Quinn and I traveled abroad after graduation, backpacking through the European countryside. When I moved back home last month with the intent to stop draining my inheritance and put my degrees to use, she helped me find an apartment nearby after I refused to take a room here. Thankfully, she hadn't pushed the issue after I had quietly explained that I needed to be on my own for the first time in my life.

Quinn had been my college roommate too—though she often joked she had barely seen me. I had thrown myself completely into my course load, adding two years to my already overfull schedule to complete my master's degree along with my baccalaureate. I hadn't deluded myself into thinking that the summer classes, endless textbooks, and homework weren't a distraction against the silence that descended every time I paused to breathe. That they weren't a diversion from the crackling flames that haunted my waking dreams, the screams that intruded upon even the most innocuous quiet moment.

A log cracked in the fireplace and without so much as a blink, I was back there—seventeen and terrified. My home was burning, flames leaping from my favorite spot on the couch, surrounding the family photos on the mantle. My mother was screaming, her voice hoarse from the smoke. And then there was that searing, blazing pain as I fell, reaching blindly behind me. As my hand closed unthinkingly on the brass rosettes gilding the mirror, a partially unfurled bud burning onto my palm—

"Eva?"

Quinn's voice broke through my cruel reverie, and I blinked up at her. She grabbed my right hand from where it was stroking the old burn on my opposite palm—the rose now white and stark against my skin.

"Where were you?" she asked softly. "Just bad memories? Or did you have that dream again...?"

I was so tired of trying to escape the horrors inside my own mind, forever reliving the moment that had been seared into my memory, along with my skin.

Some memories fade. Like the tiny little details of my family's faces, now a static amalgam of old photos and blurry recollections. But *that* moment would be forever frozen in time. The moment before I lost her, the absolute anguish in her screams. The fear mixing with the guilt on my mother's face. *Guilt*. Like somehow it had been her fault.

And I would never, ever be able to ask her why.

I gave Quinn a shaky smile as I tried to swallow against my suddenly dry mouth. I had, in fact, dreamed of the golden-haired man last night, his blue eyes like a dawn sky—the sight of him filling me with paralyzing dread. As always, he had been just out of reach, his voice beckoning, my name on his full lips. And, as always, I had woken up screaming in terror.

"It's nothing," I said quickly, plastering on a fake smile despite the cold sweat sliding down my spine.

Quinn's full lips pursed, knowing me too well not to sense the evasion. "You sure you don't want to talk about it?"

She always knew when I was avoiding the truth, even when we were little. Quinn played absently with the silver amulet around her neck that, like me, she never took off. Though hers was in the shape of a sunflower dotted with pale yellow diamonds.

I shook my head in a steady no. "Just old memories." I attempted a reassuring smile. "Please don't worry about it."

"Okay," she said warily, obviously not entirely convinced. "Always forward?"

"Never back."

We had repeated that mantra far too often in the years following our shared losses. Quinn knew the pain of being orphaned as much as I did, though I often thought she had done a better job of moving forward, of living her life freely as if in spite of what happened.

But letting go of my grief was hardly as easy as wishing to do so. Despite my work on myself, my past was a perpetual specter that haunted me despite my best intentions. I could no more rid myself of it than I could change what happened. As much as I wished I could.

There was a loud knock, then the door swung open. Quinn's friend walked in wearing a corset top that my chest would bust right out of, and I sighed enviously. A guy I vaguely recognized walked in behind her with two packs of pumpkin beer in his hands and a lazy smile on his face as he brazenly looked me up and down.

"I'm fine," I murmured to Quinn, grabbing the bottle opener from the table and walking toward the new guests—mostly to get away from this conversation. "Don't worry about me."

Her answering look told me she knew exactly what happened but was willing to let it go now that I no longer looked possessed by the ghosts of my past.

"Come on," Quinn said, following me. "There are about ten different types of foods that shouldn't be pumpkin flavored waiting in the kitchen."

Don't stop now. Keep reading with your copy of THE OTHER SIDE OF THE MIRROR by City Owl author, Dana Burke.

And find more from Lilla Glass at www.lillaglass.com

Don't miss the next *The Reel of Rhysia* book, and find more from Lilla Glass at www.lillaglass.com

Until then read THE OTHER SIDE OF THE MIRROR by City Owl author, Dana Burke.

What if the fairytale was always a lie?

Seven years after her family's murders, Eva is attacked by a magical creature and abducted to the faerie realm. When a handsome fae saves her, Bash reveals that he must bring Eva to her faerie soulmate to stop a world-ending Curse. She relents, but only for the opportunity to find answers about her parents' deaths.

As their journey progresses, Eva delves into her previously hidden magic—and grows steadily closer to Bash. But when she meets her prince, she soon learns that all is not what it seems. While mystery and intrigue surround her, Eva takes it into her own hands to uncover the truth. But what she discovers is beyond her imagination, as she unravels the fae's web of lies.

Don't miss this romantasy into the fae realm with hidden secrets, steamy romance, and true fantasy adventure.

Please sign up for the City Owl Press newsletter for chances to win special subscriber-only contests and giveaways as well as receiving information on upcoming releases and special excerpts.

All reviews are **welcome** and **appreciated**. Please consider leaving one on your favorite social media and book buying sites.

Escape Your World. Get Lost in Ours! City Owl Press at www.cityowlpress.com.

GLOSSARY OF FAE

The world of The Unseen is rife with strange and spectacular beings, any one of whom will resent (and possibly maim) you for confusing them with another. For your safety, I've enlisted the help of a certain plucky piskie in comprising this compendium. May it serve you well.

Augusky (ä-güs-kē):

> *"The Shifting Wilds are chaos—the dwelling place of fools,*
> *But these fickle, half-goat shifters despise structure as a rule.*
> *While not expressly evil, they've no respect for life,*
> *To hear their racing hoof-steps is an omen of pure strife."*

Daoine Maithe (dī-nuh mä-hä):

> *"If you run across the light-fae, you are guaranteed to stare,*
> *They're as stunning as a sunrise, and they're very much aware.*
> *These Talunasan denizens dwell 'neath a ceaseless sun,*
> *And bend its brilliance to their will, becoming anyone."*

Daoine Sidhe (dī-nuh shē)-

> *"The residents of Réimsdarg are the meat of many tales,*
> *These giants fight for Justice, Light, and (on occasion) ale.*
> *With magic made for shaping stone, and tactical renown,*
> *They can craft cities in an eve... or smash them to the ground."*

Glaistig (glī-stig)-

"They dance beneath the moonlight and sing a pretty song,
And though you'll try resisting, you're bound to dance along.
It takes less than a measure for your heart to be beguiled,
But in the end, they'll leave your veins as empty as their smiles."

Goblin-

"Some goblin-kind are summoned by a dark and spiteful curse,
Others are shaped by accident when mindless magics merge.
Entropic aberrations in a world with fickle laws,
Be they made of mire or shadows, they are born with eager claws."

Hag-

"Though stories paint them darkly, they're often very bright,
And it's a shame they're often blamed for pestilence and blight.
No matter how you're ailing, they have salves and balms to spare,
Their remedies will cost you, but the price is always fair."

Hobgoblin-

"They toil beneath a blood-red sun, mining for gemstone veins,
It's more a hobby than a job, so they seldom complain.
These neighbors of the Daoine Sidhe are generally polite,
They share the goblins' pointed teeth, but do not share their bite."

Kelpie (kel-pē)-

"They take the form of horses to race across the plains,
Distinguished by their dusk-dark forms and tangled, seaweed manes.
But don't mistake these fae-folk for trusty, noble steeds,
They'd haul you to the briny depths before bucking you free."

Korrid Sidhe (kōr-id shē)-

"These ambitious Unseelie truly see their cause as right,
But the wily winter wanderers cannot withstand the light.

They dwell in frigid darkness 'round a palace called Gembread,
And craft a headless army to extend the Shadows' reach."

Lenanshee (le-nan-shē)-

"A porcelain face with yellow locks, or dark with sable curls,
She looks just like you want her to (provided you want girls.)
But that's the thing about most dreams—they oftentimes cloak fears,
Her kiss lasts for a moment, but it might well cost you years."

Leprechaun-

"A leprechaun attired in green might meddle with your luck,
If wearing white, it's on a break and more than likely drunk.
If clothed in red, you'd better run before the chance is gone,
Or better yet, despite their dress, avoid the leprechauns!"

Piskie (pis-kē)-

"A streak of iridescence, giggling as it zips by,
You might think it a dragonfly, if insects spoke in rhyme.
These pert, precocious, wing-ed things can make for decent friends,
But if you dare offend them, they will get swift revenge."

Rot Fae-

"A bit smaller than piskies with brittle leaves for wings,
These pests fly through the Shifting Wilds in search of florid things.
Their fangs produce a venom that can cause instant decay,
So if you chance upon them, you'd do best to walk away."

Selkie (sil-kē)-

"They occupy dark bogs and brooks and hazy moonlit fens,
And sing of wondrous things most mortal hearts cannot resist.
They aren't looking to feast, and they are not truly deranged,
They'd simply like to wrap you up and watch your colors change."

Sluagh (slü-uh)-

"These souls fell short of Heaven; vast evils weighed them down,
And, either doomed by deeds or deals, Hell swiftly spat them out.
So, now, they weave between the worlds—the vilest of all fae,
And spread their anguish far and wide, awaiting Judgement Day."

Sprite-

"They drift around like pollen, shimmering in the dark,
Like elemental spirits, or maybe simple sparks.
None know whether they think or feel, or if they just react,
But sometimes, if you smile at them, you'll catch them smiling back."

Sylph (silf)-

"The stoic, Spring Isles wind-fae are healers of great skill,
They have a touch like static and white wings that sprout at will.
Many are vowed to silence; the rest are careful with their words,
So, even if they don't reply, have faith that you've been heard."

Trow-

"From afar they look like boulders or hefty chunks of ice,
And while they're often neutral, they're very rarely nice.
They may not be too eloquent, but brawling is their gift,
So if you pick a fight with one, at least it will be swift."

Undine (uhn-dēn)-

"Some sailors call them sirens although they seldom sing,
And few engage in wrecking ships, despite the mirth it brings.
They breathe both air and water and can grant that gift to you,
But be certain of their motives before they drag you 'neath the blue."

Wulver (wul-ver)-

"They keep mostly to the woodlands and their cold, cavernous homes,
Though they might look malicious, they just like to be alone.
Despite their lupine features, they don't stalk after the weak,
But should your hand cause harm, it might wind up 'twixt their
   teeth."

ACKNOWLEDGMENTS

I started writing this book under the logical (and highly incorrect) assumption that a second novel would be easier to complete than the first. Unfortunately, second novels come with a lot of something that a first book has almost none of: pressure—ninety percent I placed on myself. Regardless of the source, I've never handled pressure particularly well. I might have crumbled to dust a thousand times over were it not for the many sturdy supports in my life.

First and foremost, I'd like to thank City Owl Press and my editor, Tee Tate, for believing in this series and providing it with such a lovely home. More, I owe a massive thanks to the badass owls, both past and present, who've taken me underwing. I'd also like to thank narrator Patricia Santomasso and the wonderful folks at Dreamscape Lore for bringing the first book of this series to life in audiobook format. She captured my weird little wordlings so perfectly, I'm utterly amazed!

My husband/best friend Justin Glass has been a constant source of support and cheesy jokes, and he deserves credit for naming both Deinua and Koa. He's also provided me with a real life love story, without which my romantic subplots would probably ring hollow.

Since families of all kinds are a core component in this series, I have many examples to thank: my mom and dad, who were always passionate about all forms of art, my siblings (Angie, Jason, Eli), my aunt (Pauline), my foster family (the Miesses), families who took me in for a time (Lupos, Ericksons), and my very own found family, the members of which are too numerous to name.

This book absolutely would not have been possible without alpha and beta readers (Allie, Chani, Jay, Melissa, Yael, and Blaze), most of whom read through multiple versions of this story while I was trying to smooth the wrinkles from it. I truly appreciate these fantastic individuals, and I value their feedback dearly. Of course, I'm also grateful to God for giving me the opportunity and passion to write. He sets a lofty standard for worldbuilding and character development.

Most of all, I want to thank the wonderful readers who've stuck with my misfit fellowship throughout their journey so far. I hope you're enjoying the adventure, and that you continue to walk alongside them as their twisty tale unfolds.

About the Author

LILLA GLASS is an author from Olympia, WA. While fantasy is her first love, she dabbles in horror, sci-fi, and the occasional (gasp) non-speculative work. Her short stories have been published in anthologies by Mystic Owl Press, Papillon du Pere, and Madhouse Books.

In the rare event that she isn't writing, Lilla works one of those pesky day-job thingies, reads stories and poetry she wishes she wrote, hangs out with her husband and bunny, and plays the occasional tabletop RPG.

www.lillaglass.com

instagram.com/lilla.glass.author

tiktok.com/@lilla_glass

ABOUT THE PUBLISHER

City Owl Press is a cutting edge indie publishing company, bringing the world of romance and speculative fiction to discerning readers.

Escape Your World. Get Lost in Ours!

www.cityowlpress.com

facebook.com/YourCityOwlPress

x.com/cityowlpress

instagram.com/cityowlbooks

pinterest.com/cityowlpress